THE DEVIL'S TRIALS

THE DEVIL'S TRIALS

JESSI ELLIOTT

INIMITABLE
BOOKS
UNFORGETTABLE STORIES

Published by Inimitable Books, LLC
www.inimitablebooksllc.com

THE DEVIL'S TRIALS. Copyright © 2025 by Jessi Elliott.
All rights reserved. Printed in the United States of America.

Library of Congress Cataloguing-in-Publication Data is available.

No part of this book may be reproduced in any form or by any electronic or mechanical means, including information storage and retrieval systems, without written permission from the author, except for the use of brief quotations in a book review.

First edition, 2025
Cover design by Keylin Rivers

ISBN 978-1-958607-25-1 (hardcover)
10 9 8 7 6 5 4 3 2 1

Praise for
The Devil's Waltz,
Love in Hell, Book 1

"An addictive and unputdownable debut."
—#1 *New York Times* bestselling author Sasha Alsberg

"Prince of Hell vs ex-demon hunter? Sign me up! An action filled romp reminiscent of *Buffy the Vampire Slayer*!"
—*New York Times* bestselling author Maria V. Snyder

"*The Devil's Waltz* was just what I needed! A villainous love interest and reluctant heroine who has to rise to meet her potential. Love!"
—*New York Times* bestselling author Wendy Higgins

Also by Jessi Elliott

The Devil's Waltz
Taken by the Fae
These Wicked Delights

Trigger Warning

Portrayal of PTSD and panic attacks; implied memory of sexual assault, reference to past grooming and repeated sexual assault of a minor; implied and on-page portrayal of torture and murder.

To anyone fighting a battle they don't talk about.

When is a monster not a monster? Oh, when you love it.
— Caitlyn Siehl

One
Xander

Pain lights up my body like a billboard in Times Square.

I can't hear anything over the blood rushing through my ears as fire fills my veins. The sensation is so intense, so *real*, that I expect to find my skin blistering and melting off my bones. But it isn't. Despite the stench being so harsh it singes the hair in my nostrils, my skin is blemish free.

Sharp pain ignites between my ribs, something akin to heartburn—only a hundred degrees worse. It somehow has the power to slow time and go on forever.

After an eternity, the sounds of Lucia's throne room filter back in and the pain in my chest lessens, morphing into a pang of emptiness instead of the agony that moments ago threatened to bring me to my knees—like the demons before me are now. Their heads are bowed in respect or fear. I can't quite decipher which, as my heart pounds and a chill fills the air despite the ornate chandeliers hung from the vaulted ceiling.

The demons are bowing to me. Their new ruler—their king.

My gaze sweeps the room, the deep red walls and black curtains, the marble floor now stained crimson and black, littered with demon ashes.

And then my eyes meet hers.

Camille doesn't move.

Her eyes are dark, like freshly watered soil, and filled with confusion. Fear ripples off her in dark, smoky tendrils, her chest rising and falling shallowly, as if she's struggling to keep her composure.

In an instant, Noah appears behind Camille and snakes an arm around her waist, hauling her toward the doors. Away from me. It ignites a fiery rage that has me visualizing how easy it would be to shred the hunter to ribbons. But I don't move.

Camille's gaze holds me in place like an anchor even as she's pulled further away.

JESSI ELLIOTT

She doesn't fight Noah's grip or make a sound as her eyes stay locked on me until she disappears into the hallway, along with Harper and the hunters, whose names don't matter.

I take a step forward, and my foot slides through the pile of black ash in front of me. What's left of the queen. *My mother.* Perhaps I should feel something over that, but even as I search for an emotion, nothing comes.

Blake rises from where he'd bowed with the other demons, coming to my side and clapping me on the shoulder. "You trust me?"

When there's no one left to trust, not even myself, I still trust Blake. My protector and confidant.

I incline my head just enough to answer.

"Good. Let's go."

We're moving a beat later, Blake shoving me toward the front of the room to avoid the crowd of demons slowly getting to their feet. We slip through the heavy black curtains and walk down a short hallway leading to the kitchen.

"Blake—"

"Not yet," he cuts me off sharply. The focus in his nearly black gaze has the question of what we're doing dying on my lips. I let him lead me through the building, our shoes pounding the marble floor as we move at a dizzying speed that isn't doing any favors to the thoughts racing around my head.

The cool mid-October air hits me in the face when Blake opens a door, and I realize we made it to the back entrance. The breeze is a small reprieve from the sheen of sweat covering my skin, but I don't have more than a moment to appreciate it before we're getting into my Camaro. It goes without saying that I'm not in the headspace to operate a vehicle as Blake slides behind the wheel and I drop into the passenger seat, grimacing at the flare of pain that charges through my limbs, cutting through the fog in my head.

Blake's emerald eyes slide to me as he starts the car, and the concern in them is unmistakable.

"Where are we going?" I ask as he shoves the gearshift into drive and presses hard on the gas.

"Somewhere safe," he mutters, keeping his gaze focused on the winding stone drive, putting distance between us and Lucia's compound. His face is pale, his jaw sharp as he grinds his molars.

THE DEVIL'S TRIALS

"Blake—"

He curses. "I don't think you fully understand the magnitude of what just happened, mate."

"I do," I say automatically, tipping my head back against the seat as I struggle to fill my lungs. The weight on my chest keeps me from breathing without significant effort, which only proves to worsen the spinning sensation behind my eyes. I squeeze them shut, gritting my teeth against this feeling of not having control over myself. It slips through my fingers like water, and I grip the seat on either side of me until my knuckles turn white.

A muscle feathers along his jaw when I look at him again. "Please warn me if you're going to vomit so I can attempt to pull over." Blake's voice sounds far away, as if he's speaking to me from the bottom of a well.

I press my fists against my eyes and force out, "I'm fine."

"Liar." He sighs. "Just hang on. I'm taking you back to Seattle. I have a place there no one knows about. We'll go there and come up with a plan to figure this shit out."

Figure this shit out.

"I killed the queen, Blake," I say in a detached voice, swallowing the bile burning my throat.

He nods. "I was there."

"We both know what that means. What comes next."

He drums his fingers against the steering wheel. "Maybe not."

"There's no running from this. Unless I want to face treason for killing my own mother, I don't have a choice."

His only response is a quiet sigh as the dark sky outside opens to a steady rain. Thunder claps through the air in between flashes of lightning, and Blake puts on music as we get closer to Seattle, quiet enough that we can still speak, though neither of us do.

Instead, I replay the last moments of my mother's life. I should feel sad or guilty over being the one to end her life. But the only emotion that registers is regret, and it has less to do with killing her and more to do with the consequences of it.

I've been heir to the throne for as long as I've been alive, but if I'm honest, I never truly considered the day I would come into the position. Lucia wasn't going to vacate it for at least a century, and by that time, I would've come up with a plan to get out of taking her place.

"What's going through your head?" Blake's voice brings me out of the haze, and I blink a few times before clearing my throat.

"I'm trying to process...everything."

He glances sideways at me for a moment before returning his attention to the road, where he speeds up to change lanes. "Talk to me."

Scratching the stubble along my jaw, I admit, "I don't know where to start."

Blake nods, pausing before he asks, "Were you planning to kill Lucia all along?"

Part of me bristles at that, but another, newly stronger part nearly purrs at the idea. It calls to me, promising to quiet the unpleasant emotions warring in my chest.

"No." Dragging a hand through my hair, I exhale a heavy breath. "When I saw her hand wrapped around Camille's throat, something in me broke. I've never felt fear like that. I lost control of myself and acted on instinct. I couldn't let Camille die, and I was prepared to do anything to ensure her safety."

Blake adjusts his grip on the wheel before his words pierce the space between us. "Including sacrificing your own soul."

I nod without a word.

Killing my mother to save Camille...it shattered my soul.

"You notice the change, don't you? You're a full demon now."

Another nod.

"What's it feel like?"

Wetting my lips, I tell him, "A space in my chest where I know something used to be but isn't anymore. It doesn't exactly hurt, but it's new and uncomfortable. And considering I've never heard of a demon getting their soul back, I'd say it's pretty much a done deal, so I need to get used to it."

"And you're okay with that?"

I shrug, grimacing at the flare of discomfort in my chest. "I made the choice. I have to face the consequences."

"I'm fucking sorry, mate. I really thought we had a fighting chance."

"Yeah," I say, "so did I." My chest tightens, restlessness making my knee bounce as I stare forward and swallow against the tingling sensation in my throat. The uneven tick of my pulse tells me I should feel something, like uncertainty or fear—and perhaps there are subtle hints of both weaving through my rib cage—but those emotions seem to be ebbing away.

I stare out at the traffic in front of us as the wipers clear the rain falling on the windshield.

The drive back to Seattle offers too much time to think. To come up with scenarios of what's going to happen next. What Camille is going to do.

My chest constricts at the thought of her. Of the last look we shared. She's likely questioning everything about what happened at the compound, trying to figure out why things went down the way they did.

What is she thinking right now?

Will she believe I didn't plan to kill Lucia?

It doesn't matter.

Whatever path my life was on with Camille just became a dead end. The best—the *only*—option now is to leave it behind. Leave *her* behind.

I shouldn't feel the tug of discomfort in my gut at that, and yet there's something urging me to feel *something*. It's as if my emotions are locked behind a door I no longer have the key to. They exist somewhere, but I can't access them.

That makes it far easier to move closer to complacency with the darkness that lingers closer to the surface than ever. It would be so simple to let go and give myself over to it. To be honest, I'm not entirely sure what keeps me from doing just that. I suppose there's a shred of humanity left in me, after all. Maybe that will fade in time, too, or perhaps not having a soul doesn't mean a complete absence of human emotions like I once feared.

"Hey," Blake says, and my gaze cuts toward him. "There's a lot happening at the moment, but you're not alone. I've got you, mate."

All I can do is nod.

"Were you thinking about Camille?" he asks, cutting into my spiraling thoughts.

My temples throb until I realize I'm clenching my jaw so tightly I'm sure to crack a molar if I don't relax. I blow out a breath. "You're going to tell me to forget about her." It's not a question. Hell, she'd be far better off without me in her life, especially now. And yet, I'm not confident I have the power to walk away from her.

"Do you want to forget about her?"

"I want *her*," I say without hesitation. My desire for Camille didn't vanish with my soul, but it feels darker. More carnal, possessive. Like I'll destroy anyone that tries to keep us apart.

She. Is. Mine.

Nothing and no one will keep me from her.

Two
Camille

Memories play on a loop in my head like the flashes of lightning striking across the dark sky as we speed toward Seattle.

The cold throne room with crimson walls and marble floors.

My best friend, bloodied and bruised.

Lucia's hand around my throat.

Xander shoving an obsidian dagger through her heart.

Flames burn between my ribs, and I wince at the sensation of heartburn that blossomed in my chest when the queen of hell turned to ash. It was slowly fading...until my thoughts tumbled back to the scene we left in Portland.

By the time we arrive at headquarters nearly three hours later, news of Lucia's demise has swept through the organization. I don't know if it was one of the demon hunters who'd fought with us—the twins, Rylee, or Sophia—who filled them in. It doesn't matter. Everyone knows Xander is...That he...

"Cami." Harper's voice pulls me back from the edge of a downward spiral, and I blink until I can focus on her face. "Come on," she murmurs.

We follow Noah from the parking garage into the building, and I frown when Harper nudges me to get in the elevator.

This is the last place I want to be. I'd like nothing more than to go home, crawl under the blankets in my bed, and pretend today didn't happen. The urge to curl in on myself, to hide from reality, is strong. My stomach is queasy, and I briefly consider the chances of throwing up as I grit my teeth against the bile rising in my throat.

I stand in the corner, gripping the handrail so tightly the cool metal digs into my palms as we ascend to the office level in silence. The buzz of multiple voices slams into me as the elevator door slides open, and I immediately press against the wall, unable to draw in a full breath.

Noah steps off first, casting a look over his shoulder. His tired blue-gray eyes connect with mine, and I clench my jaw as I struggle not to cry. He shakes his head and offers in a gruff voice, "You can't fall apart yet."

I bite the inside of my cheek, willing the burning in my eyes to recede as Harper wraps her arm around my shoulders, squeezing gently until I start moving.

My steps are heavy, as if I'm trudging through ankle-deep mud as we pass a row of meeting rooms filled with a sea of all-black uniforms. Hunters are shouting to be heard over others, while the rest sit and stand around the rooms with grave expressions.

When we reach my mom's office, Noah knocks once before opening the door. The three of us file in, and Rachel stands from the chair behind her desk. She's on the phone but waves us over, a grim look darkening her features when her eyes land on me. A stomach-knotting mix of anger and worry fills them, making my throat go dry, as if I'm expecting her to reprimand me. Maybe I am. Old habits and all.

"I have to go," she says quickly. "I'll call you back when I have more information, Senator."

Harper and I sit in the stiff chairs in front of her desk while Noah stands behind us.

Rachel sets her phone down and looks at each of us before exhaling a frustrated breath. "I'm not sure where to start."

Noah clears his throat, and the minute he begins explaining what happened at Lucia's compound, reality starts slipping from my grasp. It's just as well—I don't want to exist here right now.

My gaze wanders over my mom's pristine desk, stopping on the incredibly ugly mug I made years ago sitting next to her laptop. I can't believe she kept it, or that she uses it. It's a small thing, something most likely wouldn't notice, but I can't stop staring at it. The purple polka dots are faded, and the handle is close to breaking off. It looks wildly out of place in this office where everything is lacking personality.

I tear my eyes away from the ceramic monstrosity and shift in my seat, wincing inwardly at the flare of heartburn that seems to be back with a vengeance. I clench my jaw against the fiery sensation as it travels upward through my chest.

Dropping my gaze to my lap, I close my eyes and inhale slowly, trying to breathe through the pain I can't figure out. Originating deep in my chest, I've never felt anything like it. It ebbs in and out, reminiscent of an oncoming anxiety attack. My pulse hasn't been normal for hours and it's taking a toll, filling my head with fog and my limbs with exhaustion. The day we lost my sister Danielle was the worst of my life, but today comes in just below that.

"Are you okay?" Harper whispers next to me.

"I'm fine," I force out despite it being the furthest thing from the truth. I suddenly wish I hadn't closed my eyes, because all I can see is the carnage we left in Portland. Demons and hunters alike, dead. Bodies and piles of ash.

It wasn't supposed to happen that way.

Xander wasn't supposed to kill his mother.

Or take her place on the throne.

"For as long as you want me, I'll be by your side. The gates of hell couldn't keep me away from you."

The memory of his words hit me like a brutal punch to the gut.

Did he know how things would go down?

Did he plan to kill Lucia?

"—Camille."

I blink back into focus at the sound of my name, but I'm not sure who said it. I glance over at Harper, but her gaze is on my mom. Her face is white as a sheet and her knee is bouncing, though I don't think she notices she's doing it. I frown at the tightness in her jaw, her rigid posture. She's in shock as much as I am. Finding out Xander is her half-brother...I can't imagine what's going through her head right now.

"Sorry," I say, my voice hoarse. I swallow and try again. "What was that?" I ask my mom.

Her brows knit. "Perhaps you and Harper should get cleaned up while I speak with Noah?"

"Okay," I say automatically, reaching for Harper's hand and gripping it tightly in mine as we stand and cross the room to the private bathroom attached to Mom's office. It's equipped with everything, including a shower and shelves with towels, extra training gear, and clothes.

As soon as the door shuts, I pull her into my arms. "I'm so sorry."

She hugs me back just as fiercely. "You have nothing to apologize for." Her voice is thick with unshed tears and her chest rises and falls unevenly against mine. "None of this is your fault."

JESSI ELLIOTT

When we pull back, my chest tightens at the glassy sheen in her eyes. "I don't know what to say about Xander being your—"

"Don't," she rushes to cut me off. "Please. I can't. I need to keep a level head right now, and if we talk—If I think about..." Harper shakes her head, swallowing hard. "I can't," she repeats.

"Okay." I grab a face towel and get it wet with warm water before directing Harper to sit on the closed toilet seat. She doesn't argue as I get to work cleaning the blood and smudges of makeup off her face, but she winces a few times even as I try my best to be gentle. I have to rinse the cloth a few times to get rid of all the blood, then grab the first aid kit from under the sink. I find the alcohol and get to work disinfecting the cuts on her lip and brow. Her jaw locks as she grits her teeth, keeping her gaze trained forward.

"Sorry," I murmur, "I know it stings."

"It's fine," she says through her teeth.

I smear antibiotic ointment over the cuts once they're clean. "I don't think they're deep enough for stitches, so that's good."

She nods without a word.

I toss the used gauze into the trash and the towel into the hamper across the room. Exhaling softly, I say, "Harper?"

She turns her head to look at me.

"What do you think is going to happen now?" My bottom lip tremors, and I press my mouth shut as my throat clogs with emotion.

"I have no idea," she admits. "What happened today is unprecedented. Lucia has been the reigning monarch for over a century. No one expected Xander to take the throne from her." She stands, placing her hand on my shoulder reassuringly. "That said, you don't need to rejoin the organization. As much as I would love to train with you again, being a demon hunter has never been what you pictured for your life. Don't let this shit storm force you into something you don't want."

I try but fail to smile through the bursts of pain with every beat of my heart. "I need the training. If for no other reason than to protect myself." I look away.

Maybe if I'd been capable of fighting, Xander wouldn't have been in a position where he needed to save me from his mother. Maybe we would've sent her back to hell like we'd planned and my heart wouldn't feel like it's being shredded to ribbons inside my chest.

THE DEVIL'S TRIALS

Harper nods. "I understand, and I think that's a smart move. None of us knows what to expect now."

Her words trigger the pressure in my chest to intensify, and I pull in a shaky breath, trying to calm the storm. The more I think about training again, the deeper fear's claws embed themselves in me. I've never had the blissful ignorance of the demon world that most do, but returning to the organization is accepting that my life will constantly be in danger for the sake of protecting those who are unaware of the supernatural. Call me selfish, but that is absolutely terrifying.

Harper drops her hand and crosses the room to grab a fresh set of clothes, quickly changing into them as I turn to the sink and splash my face with cool water. Catching my reflection in the mirror, I pull in a sharp breath at the bruises blossoming across my throat. Startling evidence of just how close I came to death at the hands of the devil.

"They'll heal," Harper says in a soft voice, coming to stand behind me and patting my back. "Do you want to change?"

I glance down at my clothes. Honestly, I'd love a long, hot shower, but we don't have time for that right now. "I'm okay," I tell her.

We walk back out to Mom's office, where she's on the phone again, while Noah perches on the corner of her desk.

Dad's voice comes through on speaker, and my chin quivers. Fuck, I could use one of his squeeze-the-life-out-of-you hugs right now. "I can get on a flight first thing tomorrow morning."

Noah and Mom glance over when Harper and I approach, and my mom says, "I don't think that's necessary, Scott. You need to be there to keep things calm at Ballard and the surrounding facilities."

There's a stretch of silence before Dad sighs. "I suppose. Please have Cami give me call as soon as—"

"Hey, Dad," I chime in. "I'm here."

His voice softens immediately. "Camille, I'm so glad you're okay."

Okay is relative, but I'm alive and figure that's all I can ask for at this point so I don't correct him.

"Me too."

"I'll let you speak with your mother, and we'll talk soon. Sound good?"

"Sure," I say, feeling weird having this back and forth with an audience. "I'll call you later."

"Okay, kiddo. I love you."

"Love you, Dad."

Mom ends the call without adding anything, then glances from Noah to where I'm standing next to Harper. "I'd like to speak with my daughter alone for a moment, please."

"Of course," Harper says before she gives my arm a quick squeeze and follows Noah out of the office.

I drop back into the chair on the other side of her desk, pressing a hand to my stomach as if that'll ease the nausea there. It's ebbing away, but still bad enough it has me worried I'm going to vomit. "I know I'm in a lot of trouble."

My mom frowns, exhaling through her nose. "Camille, I could sit here and list all the organization's rules you broke with your off-the-books mission. However, that isn't going to change what happened. I'm deeply disappointed with everyone involved, but we need to move forward. There are far more pressing matters that need to be dealt with."

I nod, the tiny flicker of relief easing a fraction of the tension in my chest. At least I don't have to endure a lecture from my mother on top of everything else today. "What happens now?"

She leans back in her chair. "The organization-wide hunt for Xander Kane is still active. We suspect he'll be keeping a low profile with this change in power."

"Right." The word is hollow, much like the feeling in my chest.

I'm so unbelievably stupid.

To think we'd come out of a fight with the ruler of demons unscathed. To believe Xander and I...That we could ever have a chance of making things work between us.

Mom's expression softens ever so slightly, making me blink at her in surprise after she says, "I'm sure you were in distress when we spoke on the phone earlier. When you asked to train again. Are you ready to talk about that?"

"Not really." I sigh, wringing my hands in my lap. "It doesn't feel like there's time to wait for me to be ready, so we probably should. I'm going to re-enroll in training. I don't know what that looks like, but I figure you already have a plan."

She regards me thoughtfully. "I know what happened today has been incredibly shocking and difficult to process, but that doesn't mean you need to re-enroll. The organization is taking care of things. You will be

THE DEVIL'S TRIALS

protected, Camille. I'm not—" Her voice cracks, and she clears her throat. "I'm not going to let you get hurt again."

I press my lips together as my eyes burn, threatening tears. I'm not entirely sure how to express to my mom how I feel responsible for what happened. I asked the hunters to help and keep the plan to send Lucia back to hell from the organization. Our group had my back. Elias lost his life, and for what?

"Camille?"

"I have to do this," I say in a low voice, struggling to meet her gaze.

"Why?"

That one little word grips me as tightly as Lucia's hand around my throat, constricting the air in my lungs.

"There's a good chance this will sound insane, but it's the only thing I feel like I can control, and I need that. Everything else has swiftly spiraled so far out of my control, it feels like the world is closing in on me. I can't fucking breathe." By the time I finish speaking, my shoulders are shaking and wetness tracks down my cheeks. There's a dull ringing in my ears and a pressure in my chest that makes it impossible to take a proper breath. I can feel the tendrils of anxiety pounding at the door of my mind, demanding entrance and threatening to consume me the second my guard slips.

"Okay," she says gently. "I understand."

I swipe at the tears that escaped, clearing my throat. "Thank you."

"I will grant your request through the official channels in the coming days. That said, your lack of experience is going to put you behind the rest of the trainees."

"I'll do whatever I need to catch up," I say without missing a beat. "I'll defer my semester at school and dedicate my time to training."

She nods. "You'll need extra training."

"Of course," I agree. "Whatever it takes."

There's a knock at the door before Noah slips back into the office. My mom glances up and smiles.

"You have good timing, Noah."

What the fuck for? I want to say, but bite my tongue against the quip.

"Oh? Your assistant wanted me to check in and see if you were going to join the meeting in a few minutes."

"I am, but we need to discuss Camille's training."

His gaze shifts to me as his brows lift.

"You will need to work closely with Noah," she tells me. "He will help you get caught up to where you need to be."

I'm shaking my head without a thought, my pulse spiking at the idea of training with Noah. It threatens to send me into a spiral of panic, especially as I recall the weird jealous vibes I picked up from him during the meeting we had before the epic failure of a mission. From there, I can't stop my thoughts from drifting to the memory of our shared time in New York. How oddly normal it felt to spend time with him—fun even. Not to mention the ridiculously stupid crush I had on him years ago. Part of me is worried all of that will affect my training.

Another part is scared at the prospect of getting close to him. There's also a shallow inkling of concern that I'll embarrass myself by how unskilled I am. I shouldn't care what Noah thinks of me—I *don't*, I try to convince myself, but the uptick in my pulse works to make a liar out of me. Of course I care. Despite my mixed feelings about Noah, there's just something about him that I find myself...I don't know, seeking his approval? It's ridiculous, and I definitely don't have the time or emotional stability to explore the reasoning behind it.

"I'd like to train with someone else," I force a level tone in hopes it comes across professional enough for her to at least consider it.

She purses her lips, her eyes flitting toward Noah for a moment before returning to me. "Why?"

"I fear his arrogance will impede my learning."

So much for professionalism.

Noah chuckles, and I jump when the sound is much closer than I expect it to be. He grips the back of my chair, leaning down until his lips are next to my ear. "I'm the best this organization has, Cam. You'd be lucky to have me train you." There's a film of annoyance clinging to his tone, even as he uses the nickname no one else does. "If it makes you feel better, I get the feeling this assignment is a punishment for *me* and not you."

Mom sighs. "You're lucky unpaid mentor hours are all we're giving you, Noah. You could very well be tossed out of the organization for participating in that mission."

Would they really do that? I can't picture Noah doing anything outside of demon hunting, and the organization doesn't seem to be in a place where they can lose anyone. His response leads me to think he doesn't see it as an empty threat, though.

THE DEVIL'S TRIALS

His jaw works, and he nods tightly. "I understand."

Fuck. He did just help me and defy the hunters' rules in doing so, and I'm basically throwing it back in his face by requesting another trainer.

Whatever. He's still a jerk.

Mom's sharp attention returns to me. "I don't need to remind you of Noah's experience."

Please don't.

I bite my tongue. Her tone is warning enough. There is no room for argument. I want to so badly, but the longer I'm here, the closer I get to bursting into tears. So I resign myself to sit in silent acceptance of this hand I've been dealt. I don't have the strength to fight. Not now. Not with the pit in my stomach and the indescribable emptiness in my chest. It's akin to grief, though sharper somehow.

As the seconds tick by on the wall clock across the room, my pulse speeds up and my palms dampen. The hair on the back of my neck tingles, and that awful, familiar sense of dread pours in. My thoughts are short-circuiting, and I swallow against the dryness in my throat.

I'm shooting to my feet before I fully realize it, the room swaying around me.

"Camille—" Concern laces Mom's tone at my abrupt movement.

"I'll do whatever you want," I say, desperation creeping into my voice as the walls feel as if they're moving suffocatingly close. I just need this meeting to be done. I need to get out of here.

I don't look at Noah as I flee the room. Don't stop moving until I'm standing outside headquarters, pulling in slow, deep breaths of cool air until my pulse returns to a relatively normal pace. Anxiety still coils tight in my chest, and when I catch sight of Noah coming toward me, I have half a mind to make a break for it in the opposite direction. He's the last person I want to witness me having a panic attack. And I sure as hell don't want to talk about the mess of things going through my head. I just agreed to return to the life I was desperate to leave behind.

No, I *asked* for it.

Memories of hours spent studying the history of hunters and demons, the stark, constant fear of losing everyone I love to the monsters I was learning to stalk and kill...And now I'm right back there. It makes my skin crawl, sending a shiver down my spine at the same time.

I step back when Noah gets close, and he sighs.

"Just wait, Cam."

"For what?" I snap. "Are you going to recite your mile-long list of reasons you're the best hunter in the organization? Or boast about why I should be absolutely star-struck by the prospect of learning from you? Hard fucking pass."

His gaze holds mine, and his voice is devastatingly gentle when he says, "You're allowed to be scared."

My stomach drops. I shake my head. I resent the burning in my eyes. *Don't cry, don't cry, don't cry.*

Not in front of *him*.

I stay silent. I won't give him the opportunity to call out my lie of denying the razor-sharp fear building a home inside me. Instead, I spin on my heel and hurry away from him, refusing to look back. My heart is pounding in my throat as blood rushes through my ears, and feeling so utterly unstable is making it very difficult not to burst into tears in the middle of the sidewalk.

Once I'm far enough away to know Noah isn't following me, I stop to catch my breath and pull my phone out to text Harper.

> Sorry I left without you. I couldn't be there a second longer. I'll meet you at home.

I slip my phone away and press a hand to my chest, closing my eyes as I try to center my breathing. My head is still spinning with a million questions I'm almost certain I'm not prepared to get answers for. Of course, most of them are about Xander.

Was his intention all along to execute his mother and take her throne?

He hated her for the pain she put him through, but the idea that he would be capable of not only killing his own mother but having the foresight to plan it has nausea rolling through me in vicious waves once more.

And if he *did* plan it, did he know what would happen?

When I consider that, it only begs more questions.

Is he still at the compound? What's his next move? Is he going to continue with his mother's plan to destroy the hunters? Something tells me no, especially after the conversation we had about how important it was to stop Lucia from doing that very thing.

That said, I feel as if I can't trust anything I think I know anymore. And that has anger searing my skin just as fiercely as the fear wrapping its dark, thorn-filled tendrils around my heart.

THE DEVIL'S TRIALS

I keep walking, and with each step, I home in on the anger. Because in the world of demons, anger is safer than fear. And if I'm going to survive this, I need to focus everything I have on that feeling, training as hard as I can, and pray to any higher power listening that it's enough to save my sanity.

Three
Xander

It takes a mere twenty-four hours for word to spread, for demons and hunters alike know what happened to the late queen of hell.

While demons feed on fear, I have half a mind to believe they could survive on gossip alone with the number of rumors surrounding my involvement and subsequent plan to take the throne.

I haven't left the safe house since we arrived two days ago, and being cooped up is driving me mad. It's a small bungalow with two bedrooms, a bathroom, a kitchen with a dining table, and a living room with just enough space for the black leather couch, oak coffee table, and one armchair in the corner.

I've been pacing for half an hour, tuning in and out of the flat screen TV mounted on the wall in front of the couch, when Blake comes through the front door into the living room. He's carrying a takeout tray in one hand and a paper bag between his teeth as he pulls the key out of the lock and kicks the door shut, disrupting the curtains across the front window. They've been closed since we got here, even though there aren't many houses around us.

Blake walks to the kitchen, sets everything on the table, then turns to me, bowing at the waist with a faint smirk. "Good morning, Your Majesty."

"Fuck off with that shit," I grumble in a low voice, claiming the to-go cup with my Americano.

"You abuse my loyalty so flippantly," he comments, feigning disappointment as he grabs his iced matcha and stabs a straw into the cup.

I shoot him a dark look.

"Too soon?" He cocks his head to the side.

Instead of answering, I swipe the paper bag off the counter and go to the couch. Blake follows, dropping down beside me and kicking his legs up on the coffee table.

THE DEVIL'S TRIALS

We eat in silence for a few minutes before he glances toward me and asks, "How are you feeling?"

I swallow a mouthful that tastes like nothing. "The pain I felt from Portland back to Seattle is mostly gone, besides a dull ache in my chest. Otherwise, I'm not sure I feel much of anything. Everything is...subdued."

"Is that intentional?"

I arch a brow at him in response.

"Are you choosing not to feel?"

I consider that. "Perhaps."

That door hiding my emotions—could I open it with force? There's a twinge of sensation, a mild pressure in my chest that says yes, but that begs the question, *Why the hell would I want to?*

Blake nods. "Why do you think that is?"

"I wasn't aware that 'therapist' was in your job description," I remark dryly, taking a drink of my Americano. "I can't let emotions distract me right now."

"You're concerned they'll cloud your judgment?"

"That was made clear when I killed our queen to save a human."

His forehead creases. "I don't believe you would've done that for just any human, mate."

"I suppose not." I resent the way my lungs constrict at the thought of Camille. She should be at my side, and knowing she likely left the compound and went right to the hunter organization's headquarters with her friends makes me want to go after her.

"Not to add salt to the wound, but the royal guard contacted me. They're pissed about us going into hiding. I'm essentially flipping them the bird by refusing to disclose where you are, but I wanted to give you a day to adjust before you answer to them."

"I appreciate your consideration."

The royal guard has existed forever. They're mostly ornamental, rarely getting involved in the day-to-day lives of demons, royal or otherwise. But when there's something as significant as the death of a monarch and a transfer of power, they're the ones who dictate the process and ensure things happen in accordance with the succession plan created a millennia ago.

"Have you given much thought to the ascension trials?" Blake asks, referring to what's standing between me and the throne. Truth be told,

I haven't considered them as I didn't plan to face them, but now, I can't deny the pull, the deep-rooted desire to take my rightful place in power.

I shake my head. "I figure you haven't stopped thinking about them since we left Portland."

Blake nods, inhaling the rest of his breakfast sandwich. "We'll talk about them in detail after we meet with the guard later today. You know, before they send an army to eviscerate me for helping you avoid them for days."

My back straightens at his words. "They're not going to touch you," I assure him firmly, earning a cheeky grin.

"Ooh, possessive. I like it." He shoves my shoulder. "Have you decided who you want on your council?"

"Besides you?" I offer, shaking my head. "Not really." I take another bite of my breakfast sandwich, chewing slowly. I'm not sure if my body requires human sustenance anymore, but the pang of hunger seems to fade. Demons who didn't once have a human side don't have to consume food to survive, though some, like Blake, enjoy it nonetheless.

His lips twitch before his expression turns serious again. "With the explosive news of you making a move for the throne, I've been keeping my ear to the ground."

I swallow a mouthful of egg and cheese. "Oh?"

He leans against the cushions, extending his arm along the back of the couch. "There have been whispers of doubt surrounding your reign, provided you complete the trials."

I laugh humorlessly. "Do tell."

Blake appears less than pleased when he says, "Some believe you're too human to rule."

After crumpling the empty parchment from my sandwich and tossing it onto the coffee table, I angle myself toward him. "Perhaps I was," I say, "but not now. That throne is mine, and I'm going to take it."

He crosses one leg over the other, drumming his thumb against his thigh. "Hang on to that. I think you'll find you need to embrace your deepest demonic nature to make it through these next couple of months."

"Right," I offer mildly.

"Easy peasy," Blake adds, slapping his knees before standing. "Now, let's get you ready. This—" he gestures at my casual attire, "isn't going to cut it."

THE DEVIL'S TRIALS

The royal guard is comprised of four high-level demons that have been around for millennia. If they ever had an ounce of humanity between them, it burned out centuries ago. Lucia Kane was a golden retriever compared to these demons.

Blake keeps a few paces behind me as we climb the cracked front steps to a large wooden door that has seen better days, with chipped white paint and a dull, once-gold handle. The door creaks as I push it open, announcing our entrance to the rundown foyer, and the gloomy sky outside adds to the eerie atmosphere.

"It's a foreclosure property that was abandoned decades ago," Blake explains as he closes the door behind us, the sound echoing through the empty space. We walk further inside, and I look around at the wallpaper peeling away and the sconces barely hanging on by thin electrical wires. Any windows are either smashed or covered in a thick layer of dust, making the air stale and warm.

I swipe at the sweat dotting my brow as we pass the grand staircase in the middle of the space leading to the upper level. An unlit antique chandelier hangs from the second floor, hinting at the opulence that this house once had.

"Are you ready?" Blake asks under his breath as we walk to the back of the house, down a dim hallway toward a set of closed mahogany doors.

"As I can be."

A meeting with the royal guard isn't something I had on my bingo card, but here we are. While I never expected to be in this position, to have any desire to sit on the throne, losing my soul to stop my mother from taking Camille's life has changed things.

The only way I can describe it is like waking up after being in a deep sleep for the last twenty-five years. I'm stronger, my path is clearer. I know what I have to do.

Blake opens both doors with a flourish, and I almost chuckle before remembering why we're here. I inhale deeply through my nose, then exhale and step into what appears to be a formal dining room. My eyes immediately land on the four demons dressed in crimson robes, sitting at the dark wood table facing us. Behind them, a dozen more stand against the wall, wearing all-black attire and blank expressions.

I focus on the ones we're here to see, meeting their gazes one by one. Dominic, Rupert, Malachi, and the only female in the windowless room,

Lorraine. The royal guard is nothing if not behind the times. They should be thrilled for the return of a *king*.

"Xander Kane," Rupert says first. "I can't say I truly expected this day to come."

I simply nod, and Blake stays silent beside me.

Dominic clears his throat, and I shift my attention to the demon with shoulder-length black hair and olive-green eyes. His expression is mild, as if he's bored with this meeting already. His hands are folded on the table in front of him, and he taps his thumb absently as he stares at me.

No, *through* me. It's rather unsettling.

"You killed your queen," he finally says. "Your mother."

I swallow, my eyes narrowing slightly. "I did."

Dominic cocks his head to the side. "Why?"

My mind goes blank. Any response I could've crafted vanishes, replaced by a heavy, barbed pit in my stomach. I knew as soon as it happened that killing Lucia would have consequences. It would come with questions, and Dominic just asked the most obvious.

I could lie, tell them I was sick of waiting for the throne and decided to take it by force, but my confidence in successfully selling that is abysmal. The real reason won't go over well with my present company. I can't stand before them and explain that I was terrified to lose the human woman I'd fallen in love with and acted on instinct to save her life.

So, I don't say anything.

The royal guard can't know about Camille. Who she is, that she even exists. If any demon discovers her, they'll believe they found something to use against me.

Things would be a lot easier if I could simply stop caring about her. But even as I stand here having decided to leave her in my past, there's a stone-cold certainty that some part of me still somehow *does* care. My connection to Camille is so deeply ingrained in me that the thought of losing it—

I nearly stumble back a step as realization hits me like a vicious blow and my pulse careens into dangerous territory.

No.

No, no, no.

I felt that connection shift in my chest. I felt it *break*. It shattered along with my soul when I killed Lucia and lost my humanity.

THE DEVIL'S TRIALS

But that feeling was more than heartbreak.
More than fear for what came next.
I didn't know it then, but now, there isn't a doubt in my mind...
Camille was my soulmate.

It's a ridiculous notion, and yet, it's the only thing I know to the marrow of my bones to be true. I haven't a clue how I'm certain, but I've never been more certain of anything. If I'm honest with myself, I think I knew the moment before Lucia was going to end Camille's life. There was too much happening from then until now that I didn't fully consider it. I couldn't.

Soulmate. Soulmate. Soulmate.

"Xander," Blake says in a near-whisper, his tone deep with worry.

I shake my head and swallow the bile in my throat, standing straighter. I have to keep it together. They can't see me stumble.

Malachi sighs, scratching the dark stubble along his jaw. "It doesn't matter why he did it, Dominic. What's done is done."

Dominic holds up a hand as if to disagree. "Had it been any other demon than the queen's son and heir, they would be facing punishment for treason."

"The trials will be punishment enough," Lorraine chimes in with a subtle twist of her lips. The delight shining in her piercing blue eyes tells me the idea of my torment is of great amusement to her.

"Perhaps we should discuss the trials," Blake offers.

"Hmm," Rupert hums, seemingly in agreement. "The ascension trials were created to ensure the strength of the one meant to sit on the throne." His eyes meet mine. "You will be tested physically and mentally. You must complete the trials before the next solstice or you will be deemed unfit to rule and banished to your birthplace, where you'll exist as a lowly guard patrolling the pits of hell."

I hold the demon's dark gaze, and while I've never felt quite so out of my element, I force a level tone and say, "I understand."

"Have you selected your council?" Lorraine asks.

My eyes flit toward the female demon. "Not yet."

She scrutinizes me with an unwarranted level of disdain. "You have one week to put it together. The trials will commence shortly thereafter, when and where we decide. There will be no warning, so I suggest you prepare yourself now."

"Not a problem," Blake says, and I have to stop myself from shooting him a look. His breezy response offers the illusion it'll be easy to gather a group of demons I can trust and who will want to stand with me. His confidence in that is much stronger than mine. There are bound to be demons who judge me for killing Lucia. She had a vast collection of devoted followers. Those who are certain to see me as a monster. Someone unfit to rule. And perhaps I am. Maybe killing Lucia is proof that I'm no better than she was.

"Very well," Rupert says, and I don't miss the flicker of suspicion in his eyes. "You are dismissed."

I turn to leave with Blake at my side. My heart thumps against my ribs with each step through the empty house, and I don't stop moving until we get to the car. Blake says nothing until we're far away from the property.

"Care to tell me what revelation you had back there, mate? You froze the second Dominic asked you why you killed Lucia and then you got this look like you'd seen her fucking ghost."

I shake my head, my chest constricting as my lungs struggle to fill with air. "Camille," I force out.

"Is fine," he says, glancing toward me. "She—"

"Camille was my soulmate."

In seconds, Blake pulls off the road and slams the gearshift into park. "I'm going to need you to say that again because there's no shot I heard you correctly."

I sigh. "You did."

He blinks, the utter shock on his face nearly laughable if the situation wasn't what it is. "Fucking hell, Xander."

"But you—"

"I know."

"This can't—"

"*I know*," I all but growl at him.

He blows out a breath, turning his attention forward again. "Do you think she knows?"

My stomach drops at the thought. "I don't think so. Even if she felt what I did when everything happened, she wouldn't think that. Why would she?"

Blake presses his lips into a thin line for a moment. "Right." He glances sideways at me. "Where do we go from here?"

THE DEVIL'S TRIALS

I rake my fingers through my hair. "Wherever we can find a group of demons just crazy enough to agree to be on my council, I guess."

He exhales a short, hollow laugh that lacks any real humor. "We'll figure it out, mate."

I nod, drumming my fingers on my thighs as I stare out the windshield.

"What's that look?"

I cut a sideways glance at him. "What look?"

His eyes narrow. "You're going to do something stupid, aren't you?"

I offer a short laugh. "Probably."

"Xander—"

"I want to see her."

Blake blinks at me. "No good can come of that. Not to mention getting anywhere near her, especially right now, is reckless as shit."

"You're right."

His brows knit, and he mutters, "Bloody hell." Sighing deeply, he gets back on the road, shaking his head. "We need to figure out the safest way to pull this off that doesn't end with either of us on the sharp end of a dagger."

I nod, adjusting my seat to lean back a bit. "Still sure you want to stick by my side?"

Blake rolls his eyes, keeping his attention on the road. "Prick. You know I'm not going anywhere."

I may not always deserve the loyalty Blake has shown me since we met, but there's no question that I'm glad for it. And something tells me that'll be especially true in the coming weeks.

Four
Camille

Sleep continues to evade me since the night we got back from Portland. I spend hours staring at my ceiling or shifting from my back to my side, desperate to find a position comfortable enough to fall asleep. Nothing works. Nothing eases the foreign sensation in my chest that I can't quite explain. It's almost like a nagging ache that I'm forgetting something important. I know it's missing, but I can't put my finger on what exactly *it* is.

It's shortly after ten on the third night of barely any sleep when I give up tossing and turning and switch on my bedside lamp to grab my phone. Dad's always been a night owl, so I'm not worried about waking him when I hit the call button.

He answers on the first ring, his voice laced with concern. "Camille, what's wrong?"

"Nothing," I say quickly to put him at ease. "I just couldn't sleep and figured you were up."

"I understand," he says in a less panicked tone. "I'm about to head home from the office."

I lean back against the mountain of pillows at my headboard, tucking my knees to my chest. "Sounds like a long day."

"One of many to come, I'm afraid."

"Right." I stop my train of thought before it can speed away and exacerbate the anxiety making my lungs feel too heavy to take a deep breath.

"Do you have something specific you want to talk about, kiddo?"

"Not really," I admit, plucking at a loose thread on my comforter.

He hums softly. "I spoke with your mom after you left her office. There were some logistics to work through regarding you coming back to the organization."

"Oh, um, yeah. Thanks for figuring all that out." *I'm certainly in no headspace to do it.*

THE DEVIL'S TRIALS

"We still have some things to coordinate. I wanted to talk to you about your training with Noah."

I groan. "Do we have to?"

"He agreed to accept a temporary transfer to Seattle to work with you, but I think a change of scenery might be beneficial. What do you think about coming to stay in New York for a while? You could train with Noah at Ballard."

I sit up, my heart beating faster as I hug a pillow to my chest. "You want me to move there?" The fluttering in my stomach can't decide if the idea is more exciting or terrifying. I adore New York, and being close to my dad would be great, but the thought of leaving Seattle is equal parts enticing and heartbreaking. As if packing my bags and boarding a plane will be accepting that I lost the love I thought Xander and I had.

"I'd like you to consider it, yes," Dad says. "You're welcome to stay with me, but if you want your own space, we can arrange an apartment rental. I'm not sure how long you'll be here, and I want to make sure you're comfortable."

I take a deep breath, exhaling slowly. *Distance will be good for you*, I tell myself as pressure lingers in my rib cage at the logistics that'll need to be worked out. "Okay...I'll come."

Dad makes an audible sound of relief. "I'm glad to hear it, kiddo."

"I told Mom I'd defer my semester at UW to focus on hunter stuff considering how far behind I am in training and how much work I'll need to do to catch up."

"How do you feel about that?"

Like I've already lost so much. I bite my tongue at the sudden burn of tears in my eyes. "I'm—" My voice cracks, and I clear my throat. "Honestly, I'm really overwhelmed, Dad. I'm doing my best to stay clear-headed, but I feel my control slipping and I don't know what to do. Now I have to book a flight and pack and pull out of classes and—"

"Camille," Dad interrupts gently. "Take a breath."

"Sorry," I force out, my voice thick with tears as I try to blink them away, licking the dryness from my lips.

"You're not in this alone," he assures me. "Let me book your flight and contact the admissions office at your school, okay?"

"Dad, you don't have time for all that. I can do it." *I just need to cry about it first.*

JESSI ELLIOTT

"I know you can, but you don't need to. Let your old man deal with these things. Let me take care of my little girl."

His words pull at my chest, and I sniffle, my vision still blurred with tears. "Okay," I finally say.

"Whenever you're ready to leave Seattle, I'll get you on the next flight to JFK. Sound good?"

"Sure. I'll start packing some things and let you know. Thanks, Dad. I love you."

"I love you, kiddo. See you soon."

We end the call, and I set my phone down as the building pressure in my chest gets too strong to swallow. I inhale a strangled breath and immediately choke on a sob that clogs my throat.

The weight of the world presses down on me and heat flushes through me as my limbs tingle. I squeeze my eyes shut, willing the bile churning in my stomach and burning a path up my throat to recede. My thoughts race, and I rock against the pillows, white-knuckling the one in my hands.

I resent the tears that roll down my cheeks as my shoulders shake, but letting them flow seems to ease the weight in my lungs. The sensation of dread still coils around me like an unwanted embrace, making me lightheaded as I climb out of bed and pace my room. I need to move—I can't sit still right now.

I swipe at the tears still rolling down my cheeks and try my hardest to focus on my surroundings in an attempt to ground myself and diffuse the panic attack. It feels as though it takes forever, like time slows to force me to endure the anxiety, but finally, the tears stop. Or maybe I've cried myself dry. I sniffle, wiping my nose with the back of my hand. My eyes are tired and puffy, and exhaustion clings to every muscle in my body.

Crawling back into bed, I'm desperately grateful when sleep finally pulls me under.

After sleeping in for the first day in too long, I spend the next afternoon going through my things to decide what I'm taking to New York and what Harper gets to keep for herself or donate. It feels oddly therapeutic, as if I'm starting fresh, parting with things I no longer need.

It's also helped to keep busy. The less free time I give myself, the fewer chances I have to relive almost dying at the hands of the devil and spiraling into a panic attack. It simmers just beneath the surface, waiting for me to let my guard slip so it can flood in with the power of a tsunami.

I pause my closet clean-out to have lunch with Adrianna and break the news that I'm leaving Seattle. We haven't been as close since Phoebe and Grayson died, but I've done my best to keep in touch.

After a misty-eyed goodbye, I return to my apartment and spend the afternoon stress baking cookies, muffins, and several loaves of banana bread. I blast music and drink wine until I have a decent buzz, making my list of problems seem not so scary. It's too bad the reprieve from one emotion gives way to a profound sense of emptiness the minute I slow down.

Collapsing onto the couch, I press a hand to my chest over my heart. I close my eyes, counting beats that feel hollow and untethered. My most vital organ is utterly broken, beating only for the sake of mocking me and my stupidity for getting into this mess in the first place.

Except, this feels deeper than heartbreak. It's as if something in me has been severed, leaving jagged edges behind, and there's nothing I can do to repair them. I've never disagreed with time being a powerful healer as vehemently as I do now.

It's a day short of one week since Xander killed Lucia. I haven't seen or heard from him, not that I expected to, but I haven't stopped thinking about him. What happened to him after Harper and Noah dragged me out of the room of demons? I have no idea what follows the death of the monarch in the demon world, just that it's caused turmoil in the hunter organization. Harper has been out of the apartment most days, and Noah flew back to New York almost immediately.

I resign myself to finish going through my clothes the rest of the day. After wrestling another sweater off its hanger and folding it to fit in my suitcase, I glance at my phone to check for any messages from Harper. It's nearly midnight, and she's been gone since lunchtime, either on patrol or in training sessions to expedite her hunter graduation. If I had to bet, part of her is keeping busy so she doesn't think about Xander either. She's not ready to address being related to him, and I don't fault her for that.

The front door shuts as I zip my suitcase closed and exhale a soft sigh. I rub my eyes and yawn, walking out to see how Harper's day went, in hopes she picked up food on her way home.

JESSI ELLIOTT

"Hey," I call out as I open my bedroom door. "I went through my jackets and left you the—" My voice vanishes, and I freeze the instant I find Xander standing in my apartment, barely ten feet away.

He's dressed casually in dark jeans, a black shirt, and combat boots. His hair is messily tousled like usual, and his jaw is shadowed with stubble. I'm not sure what to think about him not shaving in over a week. Was it intentional to make himself appear older? Or does he not care about keeping up with it? The flare of concern that invites makes my jaw clench, because as much as I wish I could switch off caring about Xander, that's not something I can do—and I hate how weak it makes me feel.

Xander slides his hands into the pockets of his leather jacket. "Hi."

I blink hard, waiting for him to disappear, but he doesn't.

He's really here.

When he steps closer, I move back, keeping distance between us.

He frowns briefly as his gaze sweeps over my face. "Camille—"

"Why are you here?" I'm surprised at how even my voice comes out while my heart beats like the wings of a hummingbird in my chest. "You shouldn't—You can't be here."

"I know," he offers, but makes no move to leave.

I find myself stepping closer, my pulse in my throat as I repeat, "Why are you here?"

His chest rises and falls with a sigh. "We need to talk."

I nod. I have so many questions, yet the only thing that leaves my lips is, "Thank you." I have to get it out before he says what he came here for. I anticipate the look of shock on his face and continue, "For saving my life. I can't imagine how difficult it was—"

"It wasn't," he cuts in, stealing more of the space between us. He's close enough now I could reach out and touch him, but I keep my hands glued to my sides.

"Choosing between Lucia and you was the easiest decision I've ever made. Everything that's come since, however..." He trails off, pulling his hands from his pockets and flexing them.

"Taking the throne," I offer.

Xander purses his lips, a conflicted expression passing over his features. He looks tired now that I'm seeing him up close, his eyes shadowed by the dark circles beneath them. "I haven't taken anything," he says. "I have to earn it. Prove myself worthy of it through the ascension trials."

THE DEVIL'S TRIALS

My brows lift. I'm not sure why I didn't think there'd be more to it than killing the queen to take her place. "Is that why you're here? Is this part of your trials?"

He shakes his head. "I had to see you before it all starts."

I stare at him as understanding washes over me. "Because once it does…" I trail off. The 'we can't be together' goes without saying.

"Once it does," he echoes in agreement, nodding. "I don't know who—*what* I'll become, just that I won't be good for you."

I stare at him, resenting the burn in my eyes. The carpet continues to be pulled out from under me again and again. "You've gone ahead and decided this for me, have you?"

"Camille—"

"No," I interrupt harshly. "You did this. You fucked up, Xander." I bite the inside of my cheek, willing the burning in my eyes to recede. I can't lose it right now. I will *not* cry in front of him. "If you had just stuck to the plan, none of this would be happening, and we could—"

"We could what?" His brows tug closer, and he shakes his head. "Live happily ever after? You're not naive enough to believe that."

Xander's words are as sharp and painful as a slap to the face. I swallow past the lump in my throat, praying my voice doesn't crack. "Get out."

His expression softens just enough I notice the subtle shift. "I didn't come here to fight with you."

"No, evidently you came here to break up with me—even though we aren't together." Despite my words, the feeling of my chest caving in threatens to steal my breath as I cross my arms.

He still doesn't move. "I'm sorry."

His words ignite fire in my gut, making my cheeks flush with warmth. "I don't believe you."

"I know," he says in a low voice.

I exhale a heavy breath. "Just…Get out. Now."

The glimmer of darkness in his eyes makes me think he's going to refuse. That there's more he needs to say. But after staring at me a moment longer, he turns and walks to the door, leaving without another word.

I rush to the door, shoving the lock over as the burning in my eyes becomes impossible to fight back.

Tears spill down my cheeks, and I fall against the door, choking on the lump in my throat. My chest tightens until I'm desperately trying to pull air into my lungs, and I slide to the floor as my shoulders shake with silent sobs.

I let myself cry until I can't stand sitting on the floor any longer. Only then do I force myself up and go to my room, where I push the clothes I'd been sorting earlier off my bed and crawl under the covers.

Tossing and turning, I struggle to find a halfway comfortable position, cozy enough for the thralls of sleep to come.

When I open my eyes, my blood runs cold.

No, no, no.

I'm back in that place, that room. Lucia sits upon her throne, looking every bit as chillingly regal as she did that day.

I try to move, but I can't. I'm stuck in place against the wall, watching the horror unfold exactly as it did the first time. And when Lucia appears in front of me, fingers wrapped around my throat, my lips part in a silent scream. Not for fear of my own life. But for what I know is coming. I'm powerless to stop it, forced to watch Xander take his mother's life again.

It's not real.

It's not real.

IT'S NOT REAL.

But when my eyes meet Xander's pitch-black gaze, I almost forget. The air gets stuck in my lungs, and I choke on a gasp. I swear it's happening in real time, as if Xander's experiencing the nightmare with me. Something shifts in his expression, but it's gone too quickly for me to decipher before the entire scene fades, giving way to endless darkness.

My bedroom materializes as I wake with a gasp, my chest heaving with each breath and my skin coated with sweat despite the shivers wracking my body. I press a trembling hand over my heart where it pounds so loud it drowns everything else out. Slumped against the headboard, my eyes burn with tears, my mind racing as I desperately claw for answers.

What the hell was that?

Five
Xander

Everything comes in flashes of violence and pain. I'm powerless—I can't change the course. I'm forced to endure this fucked-up out-of-body experience where I kill my queen, my *mother*, again.

My eyes meet Camille's as the demons left standing sink to their knees before me. The confusion in her eyes and pure terror radiating from her in dark waves steals my breath. I can't pull air into my lungs as I stand frozen in that moment. It suffocates me. My chest burns, lungs demanding oxygen they're not getting.

And then everything goes dark.

I shoot upright, blinking quickly as the newly familiar bedroom of the safe house comes into focus around me.

Fucking hell.

It was a dream—a brutally vivid nightmare—but it felt so damn *real*, as if Camille was there with me, reliving the single worst moment of my twenty-five years.

Going to see Camille at her apartment last night is a very close second. She didn't deserve the pain I caused her, ending things so coldly. The sound of her crying on the other side of the door stuck with me the entire drive back to the safe house. But I had no other choice, and what I said about not being good for her is the simple truth. Because even if she could get past what I did to save her, what I'll become to take my place on the throne, she'll never be safe in my world.

Unless once I'm king I make it clear that Camille is off limits...No. It wouldn't work. Demons would deem me weak for assigning importance to a human life, especially over them. They'd target her, use her against me, and I won't allow that to happen.

With an aggravated sigh, I snatch my phone off the table next to the bed and squint at the backlit screen to see it's a few minutes before six. I toss my phone aside and scrub a hand down my face. Exhaustion clings to me like a heavy film, nagging at me to feed. It's not something I'll be able to neglect as much in my position now, and the idea of feeding more frequently sparks a twisted sense of excitement in my chest.

That's new.

Before I can sit with it for any length of time, I get up and shuffle out of the bedroom. Blake meets me in the hall, bare-chested and hair tousled from sleep. He grumbles a quiet, "Morning," around a yawn as he makes his way past me and to the coffee machine in the kitchen.

I follow him, lured by the promise of caffeine. Once I have a steaming mug cradled in my hands, I lean against the counter and close my eyes, allowing myself a sliver of peace as the coffee warms a path to my stomach.

"You look like shit, mate," Blake comments, his British accent is thicker when he first rolls out of bed. He's looking at me when I pry my eyes open and narrow them at him. "In all seriousness," he adds, "you good?"

Offering a tight-lipped smile, I lift my shoulders in a shrug. "The universe has a delightful sense of humor."

He cocks a brow. "Sarcasm noted."

"I woke up from a nightmare this morning."

Blake chuckles. *Prick.* "Oh, that's unfortunate. Do you want to, like, talk about it?"

I take a drink of my coffee. "Not particularly."

He hesitates before asking, "Was it Lucia? Or Camille?"

So much for not talking about it.

"Both," I say, raking a hand through my hair and scratching the back of my head. "I relived the last moments of Lucia's miserable life and woke up after I drove the dagger into her chest."

Blake nods, his eyes searching my face. "Why do I get the sense there's more?" He keeps his gaze on me over his mug as he takes a drink of his coffee.

I shake my head, trying to work out a clear way to explain it. "When I saw Camille, it was jarring. Like she was actually there."

"There...as in, she was in your dream?"

I nod. "It was over before I could tell anything for sure, but I had the distinct sense that she was experiencing it with me."

"Huh. Maybe she was." Blake shrugs before walking to the fridge and pulling out a carton of eggs. "Or, another viable explanation, you're fucking exhausted and messed up over what happened, and reliving the attack is how you punish yourself for how it went down."

I bite back an irritated growl and mutter, "Forget it."

He frowns at me briefly. "You want breakfast?"

My gut is way too unsettled to eat, so I shake my head.

Blake blows out a breath and returns the egg carton to the fridge before leaning against the counter and pinning me with a serious look. "Okay, then let's chat about your options."

No sooner are the words out of his mouth does someone bang on the front door. My eyes narrow, immediately sensing the person on the other side is a demon.

No one is supposed to know where I am.

"Unclench, mate," Blake says as he strides toward the door. "I told her to come."

"What the f—"

He opens the door before the words are out of my mouth, and Francesca glides inside, barely acknowledging him as her vibrant emerald gaze finds mine. She looks the same as the last time I saw her, though it's been years. Her tawny skin and auburn hair that falls past her breasts, which are on full display in a black bodysuit hugging her figure like a second skin.

Paired with dark navy jeans and a worn black leather jacket, I'm reminded of how confident she's always been with her sense of style. It's no wonder she and Blake get along so well.

I walk into the living room to meet them, and my posture doesn't relax as Francesca approaches, stopping a few feet from me. "Francesca," I say in a low voice. "What are you doing here?"

Her dark red lips curve into a slow smile, and she lowers her lashes as she dips her head in what I could easily mistake as a bow. "If you'd like to be formal about it, I'm here to swear my loyalty to you, my king."

Blake snorts, and she shoots him a glare, to which he responds by pressing a fist to his mouth to stifle his laughter as he flops onto the couch.

"Francesca," I say her name again, and she looks up at me. I'm at least a foot taller than her despite her knee-high heeled boots. "While I appreciate the sentiment, I'm not—"

Blake clears his throat, interrupting me, and I slowly turn to look at him. He lifts his brows at me, as if he's silently—though certainly not subtly—reminding me of the time crunch I'm on to build my council before the trials start.

I'm not surprised Blake brought Francesca into the fold but I'm also not entirely thrilled about it. She wanted a royal title at one point. How can I be certain that isn't why she's here now?

I turn back to the demon my mother would've seen me marry for no reason other than power. "What did Blake tell you?"

Her eyes glimmer. "Nothing. He didn't have to, because I understand the politics of our world, Xander. You're going to be in charge once you pass the trials and ascend the throne, and I want a spot on your council in whatever position you see fit."

"Give us a minute," I say to Blake, not taking my eyes off Francesca.

"Already gone," he mumbles as he pops up from the couch and moves at preternatural speed out of the room.

"Do you want to sit?" I offer.

Francesca nods, and we relocate to the couch.

"I'm not sure what you've heard about what happened," I say in a level tone, choosing my words carefully. "But now is a pivotal time to choose who you align yourself with."

She cocks her head to the side, her gaze never leaving mine. "What makes you think that matters to me?"

My brows lift. For as long as I've known Francesca, she's been concerned with one thing—obtaining power by whatever means necessary. At one point it was by marrying me—which was ultimately never going to happen—and now it appears to be by swearing her loyalty, whatever she believes that to mean.

"Compared to many others that will attempt to sway you and garner your favor, I'm a good bet. Even Blake agrees, otherwise we both know I wouldn't be here right now."

I consider that and really have no argument. Still, she continues.

"We've known each other a long time. We grew up together. I'm more trustworthy than a lot of the demons we know."

She's not wrong.

"Hmm," I hum, scratching the stubble darkening my jaw. I haven't shaved in a week, and when I went for the razor, Blake suggested I leave it, that it made me appear older.

I didn't care much, but I listened to him, nonetheless.

THE DEVIL'S TRIALS

"I've shouldered your rejection in the past," she says. "You would be foolish to send me away now." Her tone isn't sharp exactly, but it's not warm either. She has an air about her. There's power in her presence. I can feel it brush against my own power, but she continues to regard me with respect.

"Noted."

She exhales a heavy sigh. "Come on, Xander. You know me. Better than most, to be completely honest. Let me do this—*be* this for you."

I arch a brow at her. "What exactly do you want to be for me, Francesca?" I don't miss the subtle tinge of color in her cheeks.

"Whatever you need," she offers in a velvet-smooth voice that makes my cock stiffen. Francesca is skilled in many ways. She'd be the perfect distraction from thinking about the impending trials. But as physically attracted as I am to her, the haze of arousal is tainted by a wave of nausea at the idea of letting her touch me. I chalk it up to needing time to figure out my life without a human connection. Considering that also means adjusting to living without a soul—and my soulmate—it doesn't seem entirely far-fetched.

Leaning toward Francesca, I lower my voice to shift the conversation. "What do you expect Marrick to say about this choice of yours?"

Francesca's father was on Lucia's council. He was one of the demons who fled after the compound attack and has essentially gone MIA. While he hasn't expressed opposition to my new position, he also hasn't granted his support—and he won't. He's always hated me almost as much as he was obsessed with Lucia. If I had to bet, he's off somewhere pathetically trying to figure out how to make a play for the throne. *My throne.*

She shrugs. "I'm not sure how you'd like me to answer that. I don't talk to him. I heard he relocated somewhere on the west coast."

I put that information away to share with Blake in the unlikely event he isn't listening in. It's something we need to keep an eye on—what's left of Lucia's inner circle, even the ones who have decided to stand with me. I have no illusions of trust in any of them until they prove themselves to me. Even then, I'll be incredibly selective about what I share.

That said, I *do* take Francesca at her word, not sensing any hint she could be lying. She'd be rather stupid to try at this point.

"Just so you know, we will be keeping tabs on him and what's left of Lucia's council," I tell her.

Her brows lift. "'We'? So I'm in?"

I inhale slowly. "If you're sure this is what you want."

"I am," she says in a level tone. "Who else will you ask to stand with you? Besides Blake, of course."

The aforementioned demon chooses that moment to return to the living room, sitting with his legs draped over the arm of the chair in the corner. "I was getting bored pretending not to listen. Plus, I should be part of this conversation."

I glance over at him. "Do you think Stephen and Will would accept positions on my council?"

Blake purses his lips. "I agree they'd be good additions, but you remember what they said when we asked them to help with Lucia. They prefer living their quiet life. I don't think they'd be down for the risk involved in sitting on the council."

I can't fault them for that, especially after the failure that was sending Lucia back to hell. "That's fair. The others I'd consider at this point are Greer and Jude." They were part of Lucia's inner circle and fought with us at the compound. I've known them since I was a kid. Greer's always had a soft spot for me—unconventional for a demon but incredibly useful in getting her to betray her queen for us. And I earned Jude's loyalty when I saved her from a hunter attack shortly after we came topside a decade ago.

"Where are they, then?" Francesca asks.

"I'll get in contact with them," Blake says, flicking a piece of lint off his shirt, "while you think of who else you'd like to join us."

I don't miss a beat. "I'm content with a small council. Four trusted members are far better than a dozen whose loyalty I'd likely doubt."

Blake grins at me. "Look at you. You're thinking like a king already."

I merely roll my eyes, but the warmth of satisfaction proves just how much I like the sound of that.

He gets up, glancing between me and Francesca. "You kids behave while I'm gone. Maybe put on a movie or something."

"Gee, thanks, *Dad*," Francesca mutters.

"I'd much prefer you call me 'Daddy,' Fran," he says with a wink in her direction, and she flips him off as he leaves the house.

"I won't blame you for changing your mind and hightailing it out of here," I offer once we're alone again.

THE DEVIL'S TRIALS

She turns her attention to me, chuckling. "It'll take a lot more than Blake being a pervert to make me bail." Swallowing, she adds, "I'm here. I'm in this."

The sincerity in her tone is the reassurance I need to exhale until the tension releases from my shoulders.

Francesca tucks her hair behind her ear. "What's your plan now that mommy dearest is out of the way?"

"Considering it wasn't my intention to take the throne until now, I'm still figuring out the logistics."

She nods. "Well, at least you're not so unpopular that you have to face the trials alone, so really, things could be worse."

A short laugh escapes my lips. "Thanks for your optimism."

No more than an hour later, Jude and Greer walk into the house after Blake, along with Jude's brother Roman and a male I don't recognize. The twitch of concern in my gut eases as I remind myself that Blake wouldn't bring anyone here we couldn't trust.

I stand from the couch as Jude rushes over to me, her heels clicking against the hardwood. She throws her arms around my neck in a blur of movement. "King Xander," she says in my ear, a smile clear in her pride-filled tone. "That certainly has a nice ring to it."

I chuckle as she steps back, patting my chest as our eyes connect. Hers match the cobalt collared shirt she's wearing, paired with subtle makeup and dark brown curls. She's nearly a decade older than me, but we've always been civil. It wasn't until I saved her from the lethal end of a hunter's dagger that we became friendly.

Roman steps up beside his sister. "You didn't formally request my expertise on your council, but you should know by now that Jude and I are a package deal."

The corner of my mouth tugs up, and I offer Roman my hand. "I'm glad to have you."

He shakes my hand, then moves aside for Greer and her partner to step forward.

My eyes shift from the petite demon to the muscular male next to her. He appears to be around her age, perhaps slightly older—I'd guess mid-forties—and dressed impeccably in black dress pants and shoes and a dark blue button up.

"Xander," Greer murmurs in greeting. "This is Declan."

Declan bows his head, his mop of black hair falling forward. When he straightens, his light blue eyes meet my gaze. "I've heard a lot about you," he says in a deep voice.

I cut a look to Greer, who smiles faintly, tucking her long, copper curls behind her ear.

"Don't believe a word she said," I warn Declan in a light tone.

He chuckles. "Oh? So, you're not an intelligent and sharp young man with immense leadership potential?"

My eyes narrow as I school my features to mask my surprise. Greer has loved giving me a hard time for as long as I can remember, though it's always felt like it came from a place of fondness. "Hmm."

Greer steps up beside Declan. "I know the invite to your council probably didn't include a plus one, but I figured you could use another show of support."

I survey the demons filling the small living room. The determination in their faces, the steady beat of their hearts. While I'm hesitant to trust anyone I've just met, my gut tells me I'm better off giving the new additions a chance.

Clearing my throat, I say, "I want to be clear that choosing to align yourself with me will pose challenges. There are demons who will oppose me. So long as you're prepared to face whatever lies ahead during the ascension trials, I welcome you to my council."

Blake pulls a pocketknife out, flicking it open. "Last chance to walk away," he says, slicing into his palm as I hold my hand out to him to do the same.

The blood oath has been completed by every royal council since the very beginning of time. Each member of the council must offer up their own blood, mixing it with mine and connecting us.

I barely feel the blade when Blake slices into my skin before pressing his palm to mine. The moment our blood mixes, a surge of adrenaline spills into my veins like electricity. My lips part in a silent gasp at the power that surges through me as my heart thumps wildly.

It feels fucking incredible.

Blake grins at me, his own chest rising and falling faster at the shared sensations. "We're blood brothers now, mate."

I roll my eyes, pulling my hand free from his and holding it palm-up to keep the blood from spilling onto the floor at my feet.

THE DEVIL'S TRIALS

Blake waves the bloodstained blade at the others. "Who's next?"

One by one, each demon gives their blood, connecting themselves to me and securing their place on my council. After the last one, my veins are singing with power, leaving me feeling ready to take on anything.

The seven of us sit around the living room as Blake makes a production of popping open a bottle of champagne and handing us each a flute.

"To the new king of hell," he says, lifting his glass, and everyone else follows suit while I opt for taking a drink instead.

"Have you thought about your trials?" Jude asks.

"No. I was more concerned with securing my council. Now that I have, I can focus on the trials."

She nods. "They've always been tailored to the demon facing them, meaning they'll be specific to you and not the same as what your mother would have experienced."

I shrug. "That's just as well. She never spoke of them to me."

"Each trial will force you to face a potential weakness. Something you're likely to deal with as the reigning monarch so the royal guard can see how you'd handle yourself."

"So they're going to be observing the trials as they happen?"

"Not necessarily," Greer chimes in. When I arch a questioning brow at her, she continues, "They'll be able to tap into your subconscious while you're asleep and *see* the trial once you've completed it. From there, they will determine if you are successful."

"Seems kinda lazy of them," Francesca comments, picking at a hangnail on her thumb.

Blake snorts. "Bingo. Alas, we have to play by their rules." His gaze finds mine across the coffee table separating us. "Your council's main job is to support you. We can't participate in the trials, but we can help you prepare outside of them."

"And celebrate when you pass them," Jude offers with a smile.

I return the smile briefly. "So, how exactly do I prepare when the trials can happen any time and place at the royal guard's whim?"

Greer leans back into the couch cushions, snagging my attention. "I recall your mother's trials. She did little to prepare, aside from maintaining her strength by feeding regularly and training with members of her council. You'll need to tap into your demonic nature and allow it to guide you from here on out. I understand that's new for you, having been plagued by that pesky humanity for two and a half decades, but it's for your own good. For your survival, really."

I nod curtly. She doesn't say anything I disagree with.

"Are you prepared to leave your human girlfriend in the past?" Francesca asks.

My eyes narrow at her. "I have."

"Really?" she pushes.

"Watch it," I warn, shifting at the flare of possessiveness heating my gut. I know she's pressing intentionally.

It's no secret that the demons around me are wary of Camille jeopardizing my ability to ascend the throne. But I don't see the need to explain the shattered soulmate connection—it's gone, making it a nonissue where my council is concerned.

I'm not sure how known the history of soulmate bonds is in our world—among a human and a demon at that—and I won't let myself explore it further. It doesn't matter. The bond is gone.

"Okay," Blake cuts into my trailing thoughts, turning his gaze to me. "I think we should plan for you to feed daily. Keep you at your strongest."

"Fine," I offer mildly, despite the prickle of excitement along the back of my neck.

The power that comes from feeding on human fear can feel like a drug hit. I never used to feed for pleasure, just necessity, but now…the thought of it makes me nearly salivate.

"I can train with you," Francesca offers. "I've taken up pilates and boxing over the last few years. I'm probably your best option."

Declan laughs. "Cocky much?"

She shrugs. "Think you can do better? I'd be more than happy to show you my skills if having your ass handed to you sounds like fun."

"I'd pay to see that," Roman adds with a grin.

Declan holds his hands up in surrender, shaking his head. "All yours."

"Excellent," Francesca says, turning her attention to me. "I'm ready to start whenever you are, Your Majesty."

"That stops now," I tell her, glancing around the room. "That goes for all of you. Whatever happens in the next six weeks before the winter solstice—"

"You're already our king," Jude interjects gently, and the others nod in agreement, bowing their heads in respect.

THE DEVIL'S TRIALS

"Very well, but you are my council." I meet each of their gazes one by one. "You do not bow before me, you stand beside me."

Blake shoots me a wink. "Long live the king."

Six
Camille

A few days later, with two nearly bursting suitcases in tow, my mom and Harper dropped me off at the departure doors, and I boarded an early-morning flight to JFK.

Had it been up to me, I would have fled Seattle the moment Dad suggested going to New York, but that would mean explaining why. Telling my parents—or at the very least Harper—that I saw Xander isn't a door I want to open.

I never pictured myself living in New York City, but putting some distance between me and Seattle will be good. I have no delusions that the move will solve anything, but I hope it's a step in the right direction.

There's also the added bonus of having my housing expenses covered, though it would be a much sweeter deal if it hadn't included the stipulation of moving into Noah's building *for my protection*. I guess I should just be grateful they didn't make me move into his apartment.

Living in the same building makes it far too easy for him to show up at my door before sunrise, and I curse him out for the ungodly hour as I flip the lock and let him in the second morning I've woken up in my new place. At least he wasn't waiting for me when I arrived with my suitcases. He gave me a couple days to settle in.

Today is my first training session. Noah texted me last night and offered to drive me to Ballard Academy this morning. I accepted for the sole reason that if I didn't go with him, there's a very good chance I would succumb to the anxiety swirling in my gut and bail.

"You could at least fake being happy to see me," he says with a smirk as he closes the door behind him, leaning against it.

I squint at him, sleep still clinging to my muscles as I stifle a yawn. "I have never been and will never be a morning person. You're lucky you have me vertical right now. My bed was extra cozy this morning."

THE DEVIL'S TRIALS

He pushes away from the door, coming closer. "If I wasn't such a gentleman, I'd make a joke about getting you horizontal."

Heat blossoms in my cheeks as I stare at him.

Did he seriously just say that?

Noah chuckles. "Relax, Cam. I'm only messing with you." He lowers his voice. "You make it so easy."

I shift back a step, rolling my eyes and grumbling, "It's too early for this." Not that any time is ideal for Noah's blatant arrogance and generally annoying personality.

He gives me a once-over. "Is that what you're wearing?"

Glancing down at my dark gray hoodie and black joggers, I shrug. "Something wrong?"

"I guess it's fine."

I shoot him a look. "What is it, Noah?"

He rubs his jaw, still looking at me. "You should wear something more form-fitting."

I scowl at him, but before I can tell him to fuck off, he holds up his hands in surrender, imploring me not to snap at him like I so desperately want to.

"I'm not trying to be an ass. Honest. It's purely a professional suggestion. Do you have a pair of leggings and a sports bra? Mobility is incredibly important."

I swallow my annoyance at his 'professional suggestion' and nod. "Give me five minutes."

He nods. "Tie your hair back as well. Preferably in a style that's difficult to grab."

"If you want to braid my hair, you should just say so." The words are out of my mouth before I can clamp it shut.

"Don't be cute," he mutters, though I catch the quick twitch of his lips. "Hurry up. I want to beat morning traffic."

When I come out of my room wearing a matching olive-green workout set with my hoodie tied around my waist and my hair French braided with the tail pinned underneath, I find Noah standing at the window.

"Ready," I say, grabbing my water bottle off the counter in the kitchen. The whole apartment is basically one room, besides the bathroom and bedroom, which are separated from the main space with frosted glass doors. It's much smaller than the apartment I shared with Harper in Seattle, but that's what I get for moving to Manhattan. I remind myself for the hundredth time since I arrived that this isn't permanent. Harper has been nothing but supportive, and leaving her at the departures entrance before my flight was one of the hardest things I've ever done.

Arriving at Ballard Academy half an hour later, I find my gut twisted with nervous energy. I've never been here, only heard of the high-level training facilities. Most of the organization's top hunters come from this place, including Noah, who drums his fingers along the steering wheel as we pull off the main road onto one made of dirt.

After a few minutes on a winding drive, we reach a wrought iron gate with a small security shelter. Someone pokes their head out and gives Noah a wave before the gate ahead beeps, then slides open. Noah smiles at the male guard as we pass and continue on.

The main building looms beyond a large parking lot. It stretches wide and at least five stories tall, its exterior a sleek blend of glass and steel that reflects the pink and orange hues of the sunrise. The walkway leading to the entrance is lined with manicured shrubs, adding a touch of green to the industrial look of the facility.

I clench and unclench my hands in my lap as we pull into a paved parking lot, and Noah parks his SUV at the end of a row of matching vehicles. When he cuts the engine and unbuckles his belt, I can't force myself to follow suit. I just sit and stare at the sign we parked in front of, because *of course* Noah has his own parking spot.

Noah was recruited by the organization back when they scouted institutions for smart, athletic candidates who, once they passed all of the background checks and tests, were invited to interview for an upper-level government position. At least, that's how they framed it. Once the candidate passed enough of their cognitive and physical tests, they found out what job they were really being recruited for. At that point, it was up to them to decide if they wanted to join the organization. Noah was the perfect candidate. He's a clear success story of the organization, which has to be why they love him so damn much.

"This is the part where we get out of the car." His tone is teasing, but it does nothing to ease the heavy pit in my stomach.

"Yeah. I just...need a minute."

He sighs. "Class starts in—"

"I need a fucking minute, Noah," I snap.

THE DEVIL'S TRIALS

He turns to me. "What is it?"

I shake my head, not sure I'll be able to put words to what I'm feeling. Not in a way he'll understand, anyway.

"You need to trust me if this is going to work, Cam."

I swallow hard and nod, hesitating for as long as I can before the words I hate the most fall from my lips, "I'm scared." I can't force my gaze from my lap.

There's a beat of silence before Noah says, "Look at me."

I can't do this. I can't do this. I can't—

"Camille." His tone isn't harsh, but the use of my full name snares my attention and gets me to look over at him. "What are you so afraid of?"

I let out a humorless laugh that says, *You're kidding, right?*

Noah presses his lips together, turning in his seat so he's angled toward me. "It's just you and me today."

My brows lift. "What about class? Don't you have a bunch of trainees to teach?"

He grabs his phone off the dash and taps on the screen for a few seconds. "There. Class covered. We can take one of the private rooms."

I blink at him and offer a hesitant, "Okay."

"I know you're going through a lot, and this—training again—is overwhelming. I also know you'd much rather have someone else for a mentor, but your mom was right, even if you don't want to admit it. I'm your best shot."

I stay silent, mostly because I *don't* want to admit it, but also because I'm not sure what else to say.

Noah chuckles. "Are you ready to dive in?"

I nod, grabbing my water bottle from the cup holder as we get out of the car. Following Noah away from Ballard's main entrance, my brows knit as we walk to a smaller, nondescript door around the side of the building. Noah pulls a key fob out of his jacket pocket and taps it against a black panel beside the metal door. There's a small *beep* before he pushes it open and gestures for me to walk ahead.

I take a deep breath and step through the doorway as Noah flicks on the lights. Taking in the room that can't be much bigger than my apartment, I walk around the outside of it. I let my fingers skim over the cardio machines and weight lifting equipment as I make my way back to where Noah stands, having closed the door behind us.

JESSI ELLIOTT

This place doesn't look much different than the gym in my old apartment building that Harper dragged me to on a handful of occasions before giving up. Except this one has massive windows on either side of the door we came in through, but they must be one-way, because I didn't see inside as we approached the building. The ceiling height is insane, and exposed pipes give the room an industrial feel, paired with dark blue painted walls. Where normal gyms would have mirrors covering at least one wall, I'm relieved this one doesn't. I don't need to see myself getting knocked on my ass. And I have an awful feeling it's going to happen more than once.

Noah crosses the room, shrugging off his jacket and setting it on a small table before connecting his phone to a sound system that starts playing music with a catchy beat. He turns back to me and points to the row of cardio machines, including a treadmill, an elliptical, and a spin bike. "Warm up with a light, ten-minute jog on the treadmill, no incline."

"Right," I say, walking over to the treadmill and setting my water bottle in the cup holder as I step onto the belt. I push a few buttons to get the treadmill moving, then glance sideways to find Noah leaning against the wall on his phone. My cheeks flush hotly when he looks over to find me watching him, and I nearly scowl at the way his mouth ticks up at the corner. He leaves his phone and approaches as I turn my attention to the treadmill screen, untying my hoodie from around my waist and hanging it over the machine out of the way.

"You need to build your endurance," he says in a level tone. Gone is the arrogant, sarcastic Noah I'm used to. In his place is the demon hunter extraordinaire the organization worships.

"Okay, so—"

"We'll start and end every session here. Ten minutes to warm up and a ten-minute walk to cool down after we train."

Instead of trying to speak again, I only nod. My heart is beating a bit harder, a physical reminder of just how much I've neglected fitness over the years.

"Meet me on the mats when you're finished here." He walks away without waiting for a response.

After my ten minutes are up, I take a few gulps of water as I cross the room to where Noah is waiting for me.

"What do you remember from your training?"

THE DEVIL'S TRIALS

I press my lips together, considering it. I didn't get past the in-class lectures five years ago, but I'm afraid if I remind Noah that, he'll realize just how much his work is cut out for him and bail on me. "I think we need to start with the basics here."

He arches a brow. "I figured. But you didn't answer my question."

My eyes narrow, and I exhale through my nose before I say, "I really only remember the textbook stuff. Demons feed on fear and are able to create it in humans in the form of nightmares and hallucinations. They aren't completely immortal but are as close as it gets, so long as they feed regularly. Their weakness is obsidian, which is why our weapons are crafted from it."

Noah nods when I finish listing off what I remember. "What else?"

I shrug. "They're fast and strong."

He exhales a breathy laugh. "Wow. They should have you teaching Demons 101."

I flip him off.

"That's not very nice," he comments, tutting his tongue.

I prop my hands on my hips. "Are you done quizzing me?"

"For now." He stands back and looks me over. Not in a creepy, leering way, but it still makes the tops of my ears burn. I have his complete attention and it's definitely not helping with the nerves. If anything, it's making my pulse tick faster. His scrutiny makes me want to look away, but I know that'll only give him more power, so I force myself to keep my eyes on him.

"See something you like?" I retort.

"No," he says plainly, and heat spreads through my cheeks. "You need to build muscle. I could knock you over with no effort at all."

I scowl but say nothing to refute that, because he's right, and we both know it. I let my arms fall back to my sides. "Fine. I need to start lifting weights. Got it."

He nods. "And I checked your fridge while you were changing this morning. You and I are going grocery shopping later."

I gape at him for being so blasé about going through my stuff, then quickly come up with, "I'm not giving up carbs. You'll have to pry them from my cold, dead hands."

"Did I say that?"

"Just so we're clear," I mutter, shifting back and forth on my feet.

He exhales through his nose. "Can we focus on your training now, or do you want to keep running your mouth at me?"

I give him a look, which he ignores.

"I need to see what you can do so I know where to start. If I was a demon and you didn't have a dagger, what would you do?"

"Run?" I offer weakly, knowing full well that is pretty much the worst course of action. Demons love the chase.

"Want to try that again?"

I blow out a breath. "I don't know. Try to call for backup and keep myself alive long enough for them to show up?"

He nods. "How would you do that?"

"Charm them with my dazzling personality?"

Noah stares at me.

"Okay, okay." I roll my bottom lip between my teeth for a few seconds. "Uh—"

"And you're dead."

I scowl. "Tell me what to do, then."

My tone is snippy and irritation prickles along the back of my neck, tempting me to shout at him and his incessant need to make me feel like a complete dumbass.

You're doing a stellar job of that yourself, an annoying voice at the back of my mind taunts.

Noah rakes a hand through his stupidly perfect hair—seriously, I'd kill to know how long he spent in front of the mirror this morning, tousling it with just enough gel to make it look like that—before regarding me. "Plant your feet shoulder-width apart. You want a sturdy stance. One that'll give you solid grounding when someone comes at you."

I follow his instruction, shuffling my feet a bit on the mat until my stance feels good. "Like this?" I glance up from the new pair of shoes Mom sent me to find him watching closely, utterly focused on me.

"Hmm," he hums in approval, stepping close enough his breath skates across my cheek. "You should enjoy this next part." There's a glint of something I could easily mistake as amusement in his gaze. "Hit me."

I can't help the grin that twists my lips. "Care to provide any more direction than that?"

He shakes his head. "I need to see your instincts in action before I can correct them."

THE DEVIL'S TRIALS

My eyes narrow, my dominant hand twitching at my side. "What makes you think they'll need correcting?"

Noah shrugs. "By all means, show me I'm wrong."

I curl my hand into a fist and let it fly toward him without hesitation. He blocks it easily, effortlessly catching my fist in his hand. I suck in a breath at the impact, gritting my teeth as he makes no move to release me.

"Sloppy," he chastises. "And you lost your stance the second you started swinging." He uses his grip on my fist to push me back, proving his point as I stumble a few steps.

I correct my footing, refusing to give him the satisfaction of seeing me flustered. I didn't expect this to be easy, but it's dawning on me more by the second how wildly out of my element I am. It's going to take more than a few extra sessions to get up to par with my training.

"Try again," he directs.

I rear back as if to throw another punch at him.

"Stop." When I freeze, he comes around me and stands at my back, gripping my hips and making my next breath halt halfway up my throat. "You need to fix your footing," he says, using his foot to nudge my stance back into place. "You're off balance."

"That's kind of the understatement of my year," I mumble as his fingers warm my skin through my leggings.

He doesn't laugh. "So channel that. Use it to fuel your determination instead of allowing it to be what holds you back."

"When did you add 'motivational speaker' to your resume?"

That earns me a short chuckle as his grip on my hips tightens. "Focus. You need to be more in touch with your body. Besides an obsidian dagger, it's going to be your best weapon."

His words elicit a shiver in me, and I swallow past the dryness in my throat before speaking next. "How do you suggest I do that?"

"Close your eyes." When I start twisting toward him, he holds firm and adds, "Trust me."

It takes me a few seconds to accept that and follow his direction, letting my eyes fall shut. "Now what?"

"Tell me what you feel."

Talk about a loaded fucking question.

"What do you mean?" I question in a small voice.

"There are no wrong answers here," is all he says.

I exhale a sigh, then make an effort to slow my breathing like I've learned over many years of panic attacks. "I feel...heavy. Like my shoes are filled with concrete and bricks have replaced my lungs. My head is foggy and spinning at the same time, and exhaustion clings to me as if I'm covered in molasses I can't wash away."

"Molasses? How...poetic?" His fingers skim the bare skin between my leggings and bra when his grip loosens, and my eyes fly open. I move away, whirling on him.

"How is this supposed to help me fight?"

His expression gives nothing away.

I blow out an exasperated breath, visualizing having the strength and skill to kick his ass. "You are infuriating. Can I hit you again?"

"You can try," he offers dryly. "The way I see it, you haven't actually hit me yet."

I swallow a growl and launch myself at him, grabbing the front of his shirt and shoving as hard as I can. He concedes a few steps, reaching for me, but I duck away from his grasp, slamming my elbow back blindly. I manage to catch him in the chest, snickering when he grunts, but my victory is short-lived when Noah snakes a powerful arm around my waist, hauling my back against his chest and wrapping his free hand around my throat, effectively immobilizing me.

"Fuck," I practically seethe, my pulse pounding in my ears.

"You lash out like that, letting your emotions cloud your judgment, and you'll quickly lose whatever upper hand you might've had." Noah's voice is level, unaffected, his lips right beside my ear as he speaks.

I clench my jaw when his breath tickles the delicate skin there.

"Fine," I say through gritted teeth, swallowing my pride to ask, "How do you suggest I *don't* do that?"

"Get a grip on your emotions."

His hold on my throat eases, though he doesn't let go.

"If you're caught in a position like this, I want you to throw your entire weight into your captor. They'll expect you to try pulling away, so you have a better chance of catching them off guard by throwing yourself *at* them. Push against the floor as hard as you can, using your whole body against the demon's torso. If you can knock their legs out from under them and get them onto the ground, you'll create a window to get free. But that will come with a lot of practice. For now, plan on using the power behind your kick and target pain points—groin, ankles, behind the knees."

I nod as much as I can in his grasp.

"Try it."

Frowning, I say, "It's not going to work when you know it's coming."

His responding chuckle vibrates against my back, and I try to ignore the way that brings heat to my face. He lets me go, and it takes me longer than it should to step away and turn to look at him again.

"I want you to focus on strength training." He nods toward the rack of weights across the room. "Have you lifted before?"

I press my lips together, shaking my head. "Not really. Harper's dragged me to the gym a few times, but nothing substantial."

Noah's expression tells me he isn't surprised, but he doesn't say anything as we walk over and he grabs the two-pound weights, holding them out to me. When I take them, my eyes flick to his. "These aren't heavy. At least give me a challenge, Daniels."

His lips twitch. "I want to make sure your form is proper before we get into the serious lifting."

"Okay." I guess that makes sense.

We go through half a dozen arm workouts with Noah showing me the correct movement, and by the time we're done, my muscles feel like noodles and sweat covers my skin.

So *maybe* the two-pound weights weren't too light…

We return to the mats and sit while Noah gives me a chance to down my water. "Are you going to make me go to a class tomorrow?"

He arches a brow. "I'm not going to make you do anything."

I nod slowly, chewing my bottom lip as I stretch my legs out. "I'm just thinking about how thrilled some of the hunters are going to be with me coming back."

"Why do you say that? Because your boyfriend just became our number one enemy?"

My heart nearly leaps into my throat. "He's not…" My voice trails off, and I frown at my knee-jerk reaction to deny Xander being my boyfriend. But he can't be, especially not now. I resent the hope I had before the mission to be with him once Lucia was gone. It seems impossible now. There are too many unknowns, along with questions I likely don't want the answers to.

"We don't have to talk about him," Noah chimes in. "In fact, I'd much prefer we didn't." His voice lowers. "That whole thing was a disaster."

I nod my agreement. "Noah, I—" I reach for him, wrapping my fingers around his forearm. "I'm really sorry about Elias. He was a good guy and didn't deserve what happened to him."

"You're right." His smile takes me by surprise, and he pats my hand. "We'll have to get you trained enough to be my new partner."

Warmth blossoms in my cheeks, and I decide to play into his quip as I pull my hand back. "I'm not sure how that's supposed to happen when you're going easy on me."

Cue the glimmer of amusement in his gaze. "I'm giving you what you can handle so you'll show up again tomorrow."

What I can handle?

I can't help the flare of annoyance that brings. I get to my feet, flexing my fingers and shaking out my arms. "You're not going to sit there and tell me you know what I can handle better than I do."

The corner of his mouth kicks up as he stands. My attention snaps toward him as he comes closer, and I immediately go on the defensive, my body tensing a second before he attacks. I can't move away fast enough to escape him, and he kicks my legs out from under me. I land hard on the mat, the air knocked from my lungs, and Noah pins me in record time. His thighs trap my hips, and when I try to sit up, he grabs my shoulders and slams me down, holding me there. He opens his mouth to gloat, no doubt, but I snap, "Don't you dare."

He shoots me a smirk, and I use every ounce of strength trying to buck him off. My efforts are futile, which only makes the anger in my chest burn hotter.

"Are you done?" he asks in a voice tinged with arrogance.

Asshole.

I sneer at him, though parts of me are a little too aware of how much he's pressed against me. I'm nowhere near prepared to consider what that means, so I double my efforts trying to get out from under him. Finally, he relents, getting off me and hauling me upright. As soon as my feet are on the mat, I put distance between us.

"I think that's enough for your first day back," Noah says.

I can't agree fast enough.

We grab our jackets and head back to the car.

THE DEVIL'S TRIALS

"You should work stretches into your morning and evening routines. It'll help prevent your muscles from tightening in between training sessions." He slides the key into the ignition, starting the car and backing out of his parking spot. We're near the front gate when he continues, "I also recommend taking a magnesium supplement before bed. It's a natural muscle relaxant and will also help you sleep better. That's another thing—get plenty of sleep. Your mom mentioned that you're taking time off school to focus on training, so you have no excuse not to get enough rest."

I tip my head back against the seat, closing my eyes as we head for the interstate. I'm struggling not to get annoyed with him firing all these things at me, and remind myself that he's trying to help me.

It's safe to say we both have our work cut out for us.

Seven
Xander

I mistakenly thought securing my council would give me, at the very least, the illusion of preparedness to face my first trial. Though considering I have no idea what it will be or when it'll come, being entirely prepared feels impossible. Even after meeting with everyone and discussing past trials, there's still a sense of diving into the unknown.

Since that initial meeting three days ago, I haven't been able to shake the feeling of something missing. It's different from the emptiness in my chest, and my thoughts keep wandering back to the moment I discovered I have a sister. Of course, that comes with the arguably ironic fact of her training to become a demon hunter, and one who already loathes me.

But Harper is the only tie I have to my non-demon family, which has sparked some fascination as I find myself wanting to know more about the sharp-tongued human.

Which is why I send Blake to retrieve her while I wait at the safe house, experiencing what I can only describe as nervousness. I shove it down, tapping into the part of me that is disconnected from any semblance of human emotion until I feel steady enough to face her. Closing off to emotions feels easier now than it did when I was part human, as if doing so as a full demon is more natural. That said, I'm acutely aware the nerves I'm experiencing now didn't announce themselves during discussions with my council. So why is it now, when I'm meeting my sister, that I feel off kilter?

I have no expectation of Harper being anything but furious to see me. That said, I have the confidence to believe I'll be able to persuade her to hear me out. She's not leaving here until she does.

An hour later, Harper's voice has my lips twitching as she curses Blake out from the car to the house. They come through the front door, and Harper's gaze finds mine in an instant when she tears the blindfold off. I stand from the couch, but before I can get a word in, she turns her sharp tone on me.

"What in the ever-loving fuck is this?" she all but snarls, her blue eyes blazing and her cheeks flushed with anger.

Safe to say, Harper had no idea what was happening when Blake picked her up, much less where and to whom he was taking her. The blindfold was a smart move. I don't see us staying here much longer, but Blake wouldn't take any chance of the hunters finding out where we are.

"You think you can summon me with a snap of your fingers, and I'll be cool about being snatched?"

Something about her presence, despite how livid she is, feels familiar. Perhaps it's my new power that makes our blood connection feel stronger. Before discovering we share a bloodline, I had no inkling of our relation, but now it's physically undeniable. I'm drawn to her. There's a sense of protectiveness that I wasn't expecting. Though it's more primal, which isn't going to earn me any points in the brother department, so I keep it to myself. "Harper—"

"I'm not going to tell you anything about Camille," she charges on, as if I haven't spoken. "You've wasted your time and taken a risk the size of your ridiculous ego bringing me here."

I ignore Blake's chuckle, keeping my eyes on Harper as she stops a few feet away. Her dirty blond hair is tied back, and she's wearing the all-black uniform of the hunters—a skin-tight jacket, leggings, and runners—so she was either coming from or going to training when Blake grabbed her.

"That's not why I brought you here," I tell her.

She narrows her eyes and scoffs, her posture rigid with distrust. The race of her pulse and the wisps of dark fear rippling off her call to the part of me she loathes the most. "I don't believe that for a second."

"While I want to know about Camille," I offer, "the reason I brought you here is to learn about *you*."

She blinks at me, her lips parting silently. Then she clamps her jaw shut, swallowing hard. "Is this your idea of a reunion? Because I don't give a fuck what your psychotic mother said. You and I are *not* family."

A tinge of discomfort spreads through my chest as her words land there. She has every right to feel that way. To resent and despise the blood we share.

Blake slips out of the room, offering us some privacy, though I'm sure he's close enough to intervene if needed. Like if Harper attempts turning me to ash with the obsidian blade strapped to her thigh.

"Would it make a difference if I told you I had no idea what Lucia did to your parents?"

"Are you still a demon?" she shoots back, and I have my answer.

"Because of our father, I wasn't completely."

"Don't," she snaps, her voice pure venom. "Joshua Gilbert was *my* father. Not yours."

I lower my gaze for a moment, exhaling a breath. Perhaps bringing Harper here was a mistake. When I look at her again, my mouth drops into a frown at the shaky hand she now has hovering over her dagger. "I'm not going to hurt you, Harper, but I'm also not going to let you use that on me."

"Fuck you." Her jaw clenches when her voice breaks. She's clinging to a mask of anger, but talking about her parents is clearly a pain point. Still, I'm surprised her fear has all but disappeared. So there must be some part of her that trusts I meant what I said about not hurting her.

Harper steps forward, pinning me with a glare. "If you didn't exist, my parents would still be alive."

A low growl rumbles in the back of my throat and I falter unreservedly toward violence in response to her accusation. Suddenly, I'm crossing the space between us, wrapping my fingers around her throat, and squeezing until she begs for air.

I blink to find Harper still staring at me from several feet away, her eyes brimming with malice, and I grit my teeth against the vision of attacking Harper, despite knowing it wasn't real.

With a sigh, I say, "I can't bring them back and I can't tell you why my mother manipulated your father into giving her a human son. He was merely a pawn. Same as I've always been."

She folds her arms over her chest. "Is that why you killed her?"

"It's why I was determined to send her back to hell like we planned." Holding her gaze, I continue, "I killed her to save Camille."

"Ever the white knight," she remarks in a mockingly dry tone. "You saved her only to leave her in the dark, driving her to flee the state."

My brows tug closer at the tension unfurling in my chest. I can only think of one place she'd go. "She went to New York."

THE DEVIL'S TRIALS

Harper's eyes narrow. "I told you I wasn't going to tell you anything about Camille."

I could point out that she just did, but I shrug, reigning in the thoughts that want to race around everything related to Camille. What she's doing, where she's staying, when she's coming back.

"So, what's your plan now?" Harper's voice cuts in and pulls my attention back to her.

"That's not an easy question to answer," I say in lieu of giving her any real information. Because I know what comes next, but I won't risk that getting back to the hunters. We may share blood, but there's a good chance Harper and I will never trust each other. At least not fully.

Harper laughs, and that alone sounds like an insult. "Why don't you do what's best for everyone and turn yourself over to the organization?"

My brows lift. "To be slaughtered?"

There's a pause where Harper appears conflicted by that, as if maybe she doesn't want me to be killed. It's gone in an instant, replaced with a hard mask of coldness as she shrugs.

Instead of pushing that point, I veer the conversation toward the two of us again. "You know," I say in a casual tone, "I've always wanted a sibling."

She doesn't miss a beat. "I don't give a fuck."

I immediately challenge her. "Your emotions are running high for someone who claims to be indifferent."

"Stay away from my emotions," she seethes, and her fingers shift closer to her dagger once more.

I hold up my hands, lowering my voice as I shake my head. "Please don't. I didn't bring you here to fight."

Harper pauses, her heartbeat kicking up as her icy facade slips just a little. "Why do you care?" she demands. "Why do you want to know things about me? Whatever twisted idea you have about us bonding or having some kind of relationship isn't going to happen." Her voice cracks and her cheeks go pink, as if she's embarrassed to show anything that could be interpreted as weak. "It can't," she adds quieter.

Everything she said makes sense. Harper is one of the highest skilled demon hunter trainees the organization has seen in a long time. The notion that she could have a relationship with her demon half-brother is laughable. Granted, that doesn't stop me from pursuing it. Perhaps I'm clinging to anything from the newly found—and lost—human part of my life. I can't say for sure what makes me willing to risk whatever comes along with getting to know my sister, but the desire to have her in my life is something I can't ignore.

"What would it take for you to drop this pretense of hatred and give me a chance?"

"What pretense?" she shoots back, then presses her lips together for a moment before exhaling a heavy sigh. There's a stretch of silence before she finally says, "If I agree to a *brief* conversation, will you agree to let me leave?"

I consider mentioning that I could just as easily force her to stay, but I don't see that encouraging the civility I'm after, so I nod instead of voicing a response.

"Fine." She huffs out a breath and crosses the room, dropping onto the couch. I follow, sitting a comfortable distance from her so she isn't tempted to bolt. "What do you want to know?" she asks, an air of reluctance in her words.

"Everything," I offer, then amend my answer when she rolls her eyes to, "Okay, anything you're willing to share, then."

After pursing her lips in thought for a moment, she says, "I grew up in Seattle. My parents moved there to be closer to my grandparents when they found out my mom was pregnant with me. They took care of me a lot when I was younger, while my parents were on missions with the organization."

"Were your grandparents hunters as well?"

Harper surprises me when she laughs. "No. They've always been anti-government to an obnoxious degree. They also don't trust any sort of big establishment. You should have seen my grandad the day I showed him online banking."

My lips curl into a faint grin as an odd sensation spreads through my chest. "I can imagine."

"It has to be a generational thing. They'd rather keep their money in coffee tins at the back of their closets and pay every bill with cash."

"But they were supportive of your parents being hunters? Of you?"

"For the most part," she comments with a shrug. "They appreciated that the organization exists to protect people." She pauses, her brows pinching closer. "To protect humans."

THE DEVIL'S TRIALS

"Hmm." I scratch my jaw. "And when did you meet Camille?"

"Our paths didn't cross until we were fifteen and hunter training started. We instantly became inseparable—we were meant to be hunting partners before her sister was killed and she left the organization." She swallows visibly. "But you knew that part already."

I nod. "And your parents were killed a couple of years later."

Harper presses her lips together, dropping her gaze, and murmurs, "Yeah." The unevenness of her voice makes me think I've made progress with her, even if it's marginal.

Perhaps that is why I say, "I'm sorry."

Harper looks at me again, arching a brow, but doesn't reply.

"For not being there," I continue. "For not being your brother when you needed one most."

"What the fuck do you expect me to do with that?"

I shrug at her defensive tone. "I have no expectations here, Harper. I'm figuring this out alongside you."

She glances toward the kitchen as Blake struts toward the fridge, then frowns before she says, "I need to go."

"Not on my account, I hope," Blake purrs.

Harper barks out a laugh. "Please." Her eyes cut back to me. "The hunters have been watching me closely since..." She trails off, clearing her throat. "Are you going to stop me from leaving?"

Shaking my head, I say, "I keep my word, Harper. You're free to go. Blake will take you home."

"I can get there myself," she interjects, standing from the couch.

"You have no idea where you are," Blake points out with a grin that certainly doesn't help the irritation on Harper's face.

She shoots him a deadly glare. "Fine. Take me home."

I get up to pull her attention away from Blake, wanting this interaction to end on a positive note. "Will you let me see you again?"

Her brows draw together as surprise fills her eyes faster than she can attempt to mask it. "I...don't know."

"Think about it," I offer as we walk toward the door.

She exhales a sigh, briefly meeting my gaze. "Okay." She turns her attention to Blake again. "And you—" she says, crossing the room toward him "If you try the shit you pulled today again, I will take great pleasure in cutting off your dick and shoving it down your throat."

With that, she walks out of the house, leaving the door open.

Blake doesn't tear his gaze away from Harper until she reaches his car, then he lets out a low whistle. When he turns to me, the hungry glimmer in his gaze has me shaking my head.

"Watch it," I warn, caught off guard by the possessive urge filling my chest. It has zero place there, and I have absolutely no right to feel any sort of way about Harper. But that doesn't change the strange tightness in my lungs at her leaving.

His lips curl into a grin. "Sorry, mate. I can't help that your sister threatening my most prized asset so violently is such a fucking turn on."

I roll my eyes and go back to the couch as Blake leaves to take Harper home, locking the door behind him.

My gaze drifts from the TV to the window in the kitchen, where the wind stirs the trees beneath an overcast sky, threatening rain. I turn up the volume on the TV as an attempted distraction, and yet I can't stop myself from replaying Harper's words over and over in my head.

You saved her only to leave her in the dark, driving her to flee the state.

...leave her in the dark...

...flee the state.

Harper's presence effectively disturbed the mental block I've been building, and it's my own damn fault.

No matter where my mind goes, it always circles back to Camille.

Eight
Camille

I never thought I'd be a person who goes to the gym when they can't sleep, but after spending over an hour tossing and turning, I figure a workout can't hurt—despite it being nearly two in the morning. Since my first training session with Noah yesterday, my muscles are a bit sore, though less so after following his advice about stretching.

My footsteps echo throughout the underground parking garage as I walk toward the private gym connected to the building. I shiver against the chill, wishing I'd grabbed a jacket on my way out, and wrap my arms tighter around myself as I pick up my pace.

I freeze and suck in a breath at the sound of a car door slamming. Whipping around, I half expect to find someone standing there, and my hand immediately goes to where the dagger Harper sent me *should* be. Too bad I didn't think to arm myself to walk to the gym on the property.

I exhale a steadying breath and turn to keep walking—only to come face-to-face with Blake.

"Fucking hell," I breathe, nearly choking on nothing.

He offers me a dazzling grin. "Not quite, love." He cocks his head to the side, surveying my face, and a bit of his blue hair falls forward.

When did he have time to change the pink?

Now is *so* not the time to worry about that.

Why is he here?

"Long time no see," he says casually, as if him showing up here in the middle of the night is completely normal. "How've you been?" It was only two weeks ago that Xander killed his mother and became king, though it still feels like yesterday.

I swallow hard, still catching my breath. "What do you want, Blake?"

"Me personally? Nothing."

I stiffen.

"He wants to see you."

Before I can stop myself, I ask, "Why didn't he come himself?"

Blake frowns briefly. "I'll try not to be offended by that." He flicks a piece of lint off the shoulder of his black peacoat and sighs. "Xander asked me to come. The logistics of his new role don't allow him to move as freely as he'd like. Since the shift of power, he has a king-sized target on his back, courtesy of your lovely little organization."

My eyes narrow. I want so badly to snap at him that the hunter organization isn't *mine*, but I bite my tongue, caught up on the whole 'king-sized target' comment. I can't help the pit of worry expanding in my stomach. Xander killing Lucia and taking the throne didn't make me stop caring about him.

I wish it was that simple.

"You're concerned," Blake muses, a glint of something akin to surprise in his eyes.

"I—" I clamp my mouth shut. He'd see right through my lie, anyway.

Blake steps in closer. "I'm making sure he's taken care of. I will always make sure he's all right, by whatever means necessary."

My mind goes back to when Blake and Xander ambushed me in New York the last time I was here—to the moment Blake seemed dangerously human, speaking of how he cared about Xander. If I trust anything when it comes to Blake, it's that.

"How'd you even get in here?" I ask, glancing around the silent garage.

He shrugs. "I might've snapped the lock on an emergency exit door. It was easier and less noticeable than breaking in through the front entrance. I was going to make my way to your apartment when I saw you come out here. Perfect timing, by the way. Saved me a trip upstairs."

I shoot him a glare, irritation prickling along my neck at his flippant tone. "I'm not going anywhere with you. If Xander has something to say to me, he can say it himself. Have you demons never heard of phone calls?"

Blake cocks his head to the side, a glint of amusement in his eyes. "You'd like me to ask the king of hell to give you a call, then?"

Shaking my head adamantly, I finally find my voice and say, "What exactly does it mean for Xander to be king? It doesn't seem like the type of position to come with a job description."

Blake's lips twitch, and he leans against the side of a car. "Well, *technically*, he's not *officially* king yet."

THE DEVIL'S TRIALS

I frown. "Right. The trials."

He waves a hand nonchalantly. "Yeah, but as soon as he passes, he'll be sworn in by the royal guard and take the throne for *realsies*."

I stare at him for several beats. These prerequisites seem like the type of thing that hunters should know about, though it isn't something I remember from my first stint with the organization. Nor does it seem like something I'd forget had it been taught, which invites the question of why. Either there's a reason the hunters higher up in the organization don't lecture the trainees about the royal succession in the demon world, or they don't have the history themselves.

"Demon got your tongue, love?"

I scowl, crossing my arms over my chest. I should tell Blake where to go—though that's less of an insult to a demon—but I find myself asking, "So that's what Xander's doing now? The trials?"

"Not yet. He had to select his council first." Blake must see confusion when he looks at me, because he adds, "His support system."

"Oh." I hate the pit of jealousy in my stomach. The nagging feeling of being left out. It has no place with me, and yet I can't shake it.

"You're looking a little deer-in-the-headlights. Shall I stop?"

I shake my head again. "What happens if he doesn't pass the trials?"

I'm surprised when his expression softens. As if he's concerned about what telling me will do. "Camille—"

"What happens, Blake?" I push.

He sighs. "He'll be remanded to hell, where he'll spend the rest of his life. He won't be able to come topside and will patrol the deepest, most depraved parts of the underworld."

My chest constricts as I fight the urge to look away, to hide the burn of tears in my eyes at the thought of Xander being in that position. I swallow past the lump in my throat and force out, "I can't see him."

Blake pushes away from the car, stepping into my personal space, and grabbing my wrist when I go to move away. "No?"

My pulse spikes with panic at the way Blake's eyes darken. They don't go black like I'm waiting for them to, but the grimness in his expression is still unsettling. "People will immediately wonder where I am and look for me. I can't leave the city," I insist.

And I'm definitely not ready to see Xander. Our last encounter is still too fresh. Too painful.

"Right. Because you're so busy with hunter training," he taunts in a low voice. "What happened to never going back to that life?"

Xander must've told him about my past. It shouldn't surprise me, and to be honest, it doesn't. Not really. I don't love the idea of Blake having any information about me, but I suppose there are more consequential things to worry about right now.

"What *happened?*" I echo incredulously, pulling my wrist free from his grasp. "My boyfriend turned out to be a royal demon and literally became the king of hell in front of me!"

"He did that to save *your* life."

"You think I don't know that? That I don't think about it every day since it happened?"

His eyes narrow. "And your first instinct was to rejoin the hunters?"

"I don't have to explain myself to you," I snap, resenting the tremble in my chin. "Now, if that's all—"

"What should I tell him?" he asks, raking a hand through his hair. His tone is back to casual, any trace of a serious expression gone from his face. *Talk about emotional whiplash.*

I open my mouth to say, what? I have no idea. I wasn't prepared to see Blake, much less send a message to Xander.

"Nothing," I finally say, my heart beating so hard I feel it in my throat. "Just...take care of him."

He nods. "I'll be in the city for a couple of days, so if you change your mind, you know how to reach me."

"Go to a cemetery and draw a pentagram in the dirt?"

Blake lets loose a surprised chuckle. To be fair, the dry remark came out of nowhere. I have his number saved in my phone, so I don't bother changing my response.

Without another word, Blake walks in the opposite direction, and I continue toward the gym. When I steal a glance over my shoulder, the demon is gone.

Exhaling a steadying breath, I use my building fob to unlock the door to the gym, slipping inside and stopping dead in my tracks when my eyes land on a shirtless Noah doing bicep curls across the room.

Fuck.

What if he heard me talking to Blake?

What if he'd caught us in the garage?

THE DEVIL'S TRIALS

My mind spins with what-if scenarios that make my anxiety spike, but then he glances up, catching my gaze in the mirror and looking shocked to see me.

"What are you doing here?" The words tumble from my lips before I can stop them.

"I could easily respond to that with some hilarious quip, but then you'd call me an asshole." He sets the weights down and turns to face me. "I want it on the record that I took the high road in this instance."

I fold my arms over my chest as he approaches and deadpan, "How big of you."

The corner of his mouth kicks up. "I didn't expect to have a late-night workout partner."

"Couldn't sleep," I offer, uncrossing my arms and pocketing my keys.

Noah nods, his eyes roaming over my face as if he's searching for something there.

"What?" I ask, suddenly feeling squirmy under the weight of his gaze, especially when I'm fighting to keep mine from dropping to his bare chest.

Wait, what?

The mental ping pong from Xander to Noah throws me off kilter, and the surge of conflicting emotions does nothing to ease my anxiety.

"Nothing," he murmurs, and I realize then how close he's standing when his breath skates across my cheeks, making heat bloom in them.

"Why are you here so late?" I ask, unable to stand the brief silence.

"It's the only time I know for sure I'll have the place to myself." Amusement flashes across his features. "Well, *usually*."

"Right," I mumble, going to step back. "I can go."

Noah moves swiftly, catching my wrist and holding me in place before him. "That's not what I meant."

My breath catches, my gaze dropping to where his fingers wrap around my wrist. "I, um, I'm not really in the headspace to train. I think I'm just going to go back upstairs."

When I go to pull back, Noah doesn't release me.

My eyes fly to his, where I find concern mixed with a hint of suspicion that kicks my pulse up.

"Noah—"

"What is going on with you tonight?"

I immediately shake my head. There's no way I'm going to tell him about seeing Blake. Certainly not about thinking of Xander every minute I'm awake, my only reprieve from him being when I'm asleep. "Nothing."

"Bullshit," he says, though his voice isn't harsh. He's worried about me, which has the risk of leading to questions I really don't want to answer. Except I know he won't let it go.

Before I can consider what a terrible idea it is, I'm on my tiptoes, planting my mouth on his.

Noah stiffens...and then he's kissing me back.

Noah is kissing me.

The crisp, sandalwood scent of his cologne overwhelms me as he buries his fingers in my hair and I drape my arms over his shoulders. My eyes fall shut of their own volition, my mouth moving with his and my heart lurching when his other hand curls around my hip and tugs me against him.

Shit, shit, shit. What am I doing?

I tear my lips from his, gulping down an unsteady breath as I blink quickly and back toward the door. Wiping my mouth with the back of my hand, I shake my head at a stunned-looking Noah before spinning around and fleeing the gym, my cheeks flaming and my stomach heavy with guilt.

I practically sprint through the garage, not stopping until I'm in the elevator going back to my floor. I pull my phone out of my pocket, willing my hands to stop shaking as I fumble through a text to Harper.

> I know it's late but I need to talk to you.

She hasn't answered by the time I reach my apartment, so I resign myself to pacing the living room. My head doesn't stop spinning even as my pulse slowly returns to a somewhat normal pace. Pausing in the middle of the room, I can't help but lift my fingers to my swollen lips.

Fuck. Me.

Pressure unfurls in my chest. It's brought on by the dark tendrils of guilt that the kiss even happened, but more so that I enjoyed it. It was meant to be a distraction. I was desperate and panicked. I didn't want Noah pushing me and then spilling about Blake coming to see me. There would've been zero chance of me convincing Noah to not report that to the organization. And considering what Blake told me about the council and the trials, Xander has enough to deal with.

THE DEVIL'S TRIALS

I shouldn't be worried about that. I've tried not to care. But I...can't do it. I can't just turn off what I feel for him because he broke my heart.

I fucking wish it was that easy.

I drop onto the couch and grab the closest pillow, pressing my face into it and groaning.

Tonight has been an utter shit show. Why couldn't I have fallen asleep and avoided seeing Blake and kissing Noah?

My phone buzzes, and I shift to pull it out, relief flooding through me when Harper's name fills the screen. I answer the call, but she speaks before I can get a word in.

"What happened?" Concern is heavy in her voice, and I immediately feel bad for my text.

"I'm okay," I rush to say. "I mean, I'm not, but everything is fine."

A beat passes before she asks, "What the hell does *that* mean?"

I take a deep breath, then spill my guts about kissing Noah.

"Ohhh." She drags out the word. "I understand why you're freaking out, but to be completely honest, babe, I don't see a problem. You wanted to kiss him. You've wanted that for nearly a decade."

"Correction—I *wanted* that. Nearly a decade ago."

"Right, well, whatever. It happened. Do you want it to happen again?"

I know the answer in my gut, yet I can't help but think of how my life would be different if I were in love with Noah instead of Xander.

"Did I lose you?"

"No, I'm here. You know, just spiraling about my life choices," I grumble, pulling at a loose thread on the pillow in my lap.

"Speaking of...I kind of saw Xander."

My stomach drops and clenches at the same time. It's an odd mix of sensations that makes me wince with discomfort, sitting upright. It takes me a second to find my voice. "What happened? Why did you see him?"

It's Harper's turn to sigh. "Well, Blake—I've since made it my mission to ruin his life if it's the last thing I do on this earth—snatched me off the street and dragged me to see Xander. Because apparently texting or calling didn't occur to either of them. I don't know. At first, I was livid—scared out of my mind, too, but I think I did a decent job of masking that with anger. But then, Xander and I actually had a decent conversation."

I sit in stunned silence for a few beats. "How do you feel about it?" I much prefer talking about Harper instead of what happened in the gym.

69

"I'm torn between wanting absolutely nothing to do with him and being somewhat curious. You know I've always wanted a sibling, but the king of hell is definitely not what I was expecting. Talk about a painfully ironic example of 'be careful what you wish for.'"

I chuckle at her dry tone. "Maybe it's not something you need to figure out immediately?"

"Yeah," is all she says, her tone distracted.

"Well, since you shared that you saw Xander, I guess I better tell you that I saw Blake tonight."

"Hold the fuck up. *What?*"

"Uh-huh. He's in New York."

"I'm on my way. I'll kick his ass straight back to hell for bothering you."

A faint grin curls my lips. Harper will never stop having my back, even from a different state. "He came to tell me that Xander wanted to see me. Actually, he came to bring me back to Seattle, apparently. Though he didn't snatch me off the street and force me to go with him, so I'm not sure what Xander actually told him."

Harper curses. "Don't get me wrong. I miss the crap out of you and want to see you so badly, but I'm glad you told him off and that he didn't pull some shady shit on you like he did to me."

"You and me both," I say around a yawn. "I should go and try to get some sleep. You should, too. What are you even doing up right now?"

"Late-night training session and then a bunch of us went for drinks."

"Keeping busy, as always. Hopefully, you can take a break to visit me soon. Do you have Thanksgiving plans?"

"Is your dad cooking?"

I laugh. "I haven't talked to him about it yet, but probably?"

"Then I'm there," she says without missing a beat.

"I see how it is," I tease. To be fair, my dad's cooking is amazing, so I can't fault her.

"I'll book my trip soon and send you my flight details. Until then, keep me posted on all of the things, yeah?"

"You, too."

After we say goodbye, I haul myself off the couch and drag my ass to bed. Burying myself under the covers, I curl onto my side and pray the exhaustion clinging to my muscles will allow for sleep to take me before my thoughts can spiral all the way out of control.

Nine
Xander

The last time I enjoyed a restful sleep was when I spent the night in Camille's bed. That warmth and comfort have never felt so far away. I haven't longed for something this human in...well, ever. Of course, that makes it happening in this instance more concerning, considering I've never been less human than I am now.

I try to shake off the unsettled feeling as I shuffle out of the bedroom in search of coffee and find Blake in the kitchen, shirtless, and making...I want to say pancakes?

"Did you leave me any coffee?" I grumble, leaning against the counter opposite him.

"And good morning to you," he says with a wry grin, whisking the bowl of batter in his hand. He pauses to pour coffee into a mug and sets it in front of me. "There's a very pressing matter we need to discuss."

My brows lift as dread gnaws at me. Instead of doing what I want, which is taking my ass back to bed, I ask, "What's that?"

"Well, you know what tomorrow is."

I take a sip of my coffee, waiting for him to continue because I genuinely have no idea—nor do I particularly care.

"It's Halloween, mate."

"And your point?" I ask hesitantly.

"Hear me out. Things have been all doom and gloom around here for a hot minute. In light of that, I want to throw the most amazing Halloween party anyone has ever attended." Before I can respond, he quickly adds, "I even bought you a costume."

I nearly choke on a laugh at how ridiculous he sounds. "You did what?"

"Please hold." He leaves the room in a blur of movement, coming back a few seconds later with a large paper bag. Shooting me a grin, he pulls out a bright red set of devil horns and a sparkly red tail.

"Fuck off," I grumble at him.

"So that's a 'no' to the party, then?"

I send a glare in his direction.

He pouts, dropping the costume back into the bag and leaving it on the counter as he returns to the stove, pouring pancake batter into the waiting pan.

With his back to me, he says, "Being that I'm not trying to kiss your ass, because you've already crushed my amazing party idea, I'm going to go ahead and tell you that you look like shit."

I rake a hand through my hair, pressing my lips into a tight smile as I tap my fingers against the side of my mug. "Thanks, Blake. You're such a pal." I take a drink of coffee, taking a moment to enjoy the warmth spreading through me.

"I'm not going to ask, and you're not going to fight me. After we finish devouring these pancakes, we're going to feed the other hunger I'm sure is clawing at you."

I exhale a sigh, peering down at the darkness of my mug. I'm not going to argue, because he's right. I need to be at my strongest to face the first trial.

Once breakfast is ready, Blake sits next to me at the counter, drowning his pancakes in maple syrup.

I shove a forkful of pancake into my mouth and nearly groan. As irritated as I am, Blake makes a damn good breakfast.

I point my fork at him. "Are you planning on putting on a shirt?"

He glances down, smirking when his head lifts. "Does my semi-nakedness bother you?"

I chuckle. "Hardly. But we're trying to keep a low profile, remember?" Which also makes me think the party was meant as more of a joke, or Blake figured the costumes would provide enough of a disguise to be safe.

"Ah, yes. I suppose my inhumanly impressive abs are rather—"

"Okay," I interrupt and get up to take my plate to the sink. "Let me get changed, and we'll go."

"Actually," he says, "we have to wait until tonight."

"But you just said—"

"I know, I know." He flicks his wrist, waving me off. "I just had a brilliant idea."

THE DEVIL'S TRIALS

My eyes narrow. "I'm afraid to ask."

Blake shrugs. "So don't. Just trust me."

He knows I do, which is why I don't respond to that, instead saying, "Can you gather the council? I want to strategize before the trials start."

The corner of his mouth kicks up, and he nods. "Excellent. Give me half an hour."

True to his word, thirty minutes later, we're sitting around the living room. It's too small for the seven of us, but we're making it work. Blake, Francesca, Greer, and Roman squeeze onto the couch, while Jude takes the chair in the corner with Declan perched on the arm, leaving me standing in front of the unlit fireplace.

"I appreciate you coming on short notice," I tell everyone.

"You don't have to thank us," Greer says, tucking a stray copper curl behind her ear. "We're here for you. For whatever we must do to get you from here to your throne."

"It is our duty and our privilege," Declan offers, resting his arm on the back of the chair near Jude's head.

My gaze slides to each member of my council, taking in their solemn expressions. "Most of you have lived in our world and among our kind longer than I have. And until now, I've been plagued by a part-human existence, which made my experience…challenging."

"Are you concerned that experience will impede your ability to face the trials?" Roman asks, causing Blake to glance sideways at him, his eyes narrowing slightly.

"It certainly won't help," I mutter, leaning against the mantel and sliding my hands into the pockets of my jeans.

Francesca sighs. "You need to let go of your human life."

I look at her as Jude chimes in, "She's right."

"He knows that," Blake says before I can.

"The trials are to test your ability to be the demon king." Greer's voice is level, and she folds her hands in her lap as she continues, "A human wouldn't survive. And you won't survive unless you let the human part of you go, completely and permanently."

"I have." The words are out of my mouth in an instant.

"You've embraced your demonic traits, have you?"

My eyes narrow at Francesca. "You'd like to test me?"

She purses her lips, then shakes her head. "Just making sure."

"Based on the history of the trials we have, the first is the easiest test you'll face," Jude explains, then warns, "Don't let that fool you into letting your guard down. It will be designed to do just that. You must give in to your newly strengthened demonic nature to be successful. Tune out everything else and follow your instincts."

I nod. "Understood."

"Besides that," Francesca says, "the best way to prepare is by feeding to ensure you're also at your strongest physically."

Blake shoots me a grin. "Oh, I've got that part covered."

The sky is dark when Blake and I pull into a nearly packed dirt parking lot at...a barn?

Unbuckling my seat belt, I turn to him. "I'm confused."

"Remember when I reminded you about what today is?"

I arch a brow at him. "Yeah?"

"Well, Halloween means 'haunted house.' What's better than feeding on one human? How about a building full of them?"

Huh. This might actually be a halfway decent idea.

"It's a fucking demon buffet," he adds with a satisfied grin.

Offering a short laugh, I say, "Nicely done."

We get out of the car and join the crowd heading toward the barn. It's a tall, wide building with a cornfield on one side and an apple orchard on the other. There are lights strung through the trees and ominous music plays from a loudspeaker. The air is crisp, and I get a whiff of apple cider and popcorn as we pass a concession stand. Overhead, the moon shines bright in the dark sky, casting the property in eerie light. It works in the attraction's favor, if the distant sound of screaming is any indication.

Blake and I join the line, and he hums the tune of a classic Halloween favorite under his breath as we get closer to the entrance of the barn, where a machine is creating a thick curtain of fog between the waiting patrons and what lies ahead.

Heartbeats pound in front of and behind us, and I practically salivate at the sound. Though in tandem with the anticipation is a thin veil of nerves. The thought of failing my impending trial twists my gut into knots. It has me reaching into myself and shutting down the part of me that remembers what it's like to feel those all too human emotions. As my pulse levels, my focus homes in on the reason we're here.

THE DEVIL'S TRIALS

A couple of guys wearing jackets marked STAFF wave us forward. I peg them to be high school age based on their scrawniness and the blemishes spattered across their faces. Blake and I exchange a glance, and his eyes, already glimmering with excitement, darken with hunger.

We step through the fog, and it takes a second for my eyes to adjust to the dark. Wood floors and bits of hay crunch under my shoes, and I chuckle at the next round of screams that comes from ahead. The humans are drunk on adrenaline—likely some booze as well—and their fear is *intoxicating*. Even from a distance. I already know how energized I'll be once I've fed. How much stronger. This is exactly what I needed. Leave it to Blake to figure that out before me.

Ominous music mixes with periodic crashes of prerecorded thunder, and Blake claps me on the back, shooting me a grin as his eyes go fully black. "I'll catch you on the other side. Happy hunting, mate," he says before disappearing in a blur of movement.

I continue through the entrance set up as a graveyard, the damp air filled with a musty, earthy smell from the dirt arranged to look like fresh graves. A system attached to the rafters above fills the barn with flashes of white light as I venture deeper.

The first room is a massacre scene. A masked man revs a bloody chainsaw, grinning maniacally at the bodies scattered around him. He steps closer as if he's going to come at me, and I keep walking, pressing my lips into a smile as he follows me to the next scene, grumbling "What the hell?" under his breath.

Instead of wasting time walking through the different horror scenes, I close my eyes and listen for an erratic pulse and thundering heartbeat. I focus on the closest one and open my eyes, moving through the barn faster than any of the humans can track—the pitch darkness helps, though they couldn't see me at this speed in the light, either.

When I spot my target, a growl of satisfaction rumbles in my chest. It's a middle-aged woman, and it looks as if she's here with a group of friends who left her behind. She seems frozen in place off to the side as she fights with the fear instilled by the hoax surrounding her. Even under a thick hoodie, I can see the uneven rise and fall of her chest as she gets close to hyperventilating.

I strike without hesitation, snaking an arm around her waist and pulling her behind an animatronic. Her scream is lost in those of the others in the barn, her face draining of color when she spots the endless black in my eyes. Fear pours off her in waves that I drown myself in. Energy and power crackle through me at a near-dizzying speed. I feel stronger almost immediately, relishing in the terror reflected in the woman's wide eyes. Tears fall down her cheeks as pathetic little whimpers escape her trembling lips. She sways on her feet, but I catch her before she can collapse.

"What..." She blinks, and more tears wet her face. "Why is this happening?" she cries, her brows drawn together. "This was supposed to be fun."

"Your friends ditched you," I mutter, keeping my arm around her waist. "How's that supposed to be fun?"

She shifts away as she shakes her head, leaving us a few feet apart but still concealed by a stack of hay bales. "You're not part of the attraction, are you?"

I cock my head to the side, my eyes flicking between hers. They appear clearer now. I've fed on her fear, which didn't eliminate the emotion entirely, but it seems to have lessened it. "I am," I lie smoothly, shoving my hands into my pockets. Keeping a low profile is still important with every hunter in the organization after me, so my prey needs to believe this encounter was part of what she paid for. "Clearly, I'm not very good."

She backs away more, nodding slowly and chewing her bottom lip. When she turns without another word and hurries away, I don't stop her. I got what I came for. It's the first time I've fed on a human since I became a full demon. The act of feeding itself felt easier, effortless even. The energy racing through my bloodstream is incredible. My muscles feel stronger, my senses crisper, as if I've just awakened.

Is it the act of feeding without the guilt of a human soul?

If that's the case, I should have destroyed my soul a long time ago.

Instead of overthinking it, I make my way through the rest of the barn and meet Blake at the exit. His eyes are alight with amusement and satisfaction.

"Come on," he says. "Let's grab some cotton candy and bask in the lingering fear of these pathetic little humans."

As much as I don't want to hang around here, there's something to be said for absorbing multiple sources of fear at once without having to work for it, so I don't argue.

THE DEVIL'S TRIALS

We continue around the grounds, walking through a corn maze and past several photo ops Blake insists on stopping at.

"Too bad it isn't Halloween year round," Blake comments as we approach the section of the farm set up with different food trucks, and I nod my agreement. It certainly made hunting for prey easy.

Walking up to the first vendor without a line, my eyes narrow as I recognize the demon on the other side of the counter.

"Ah, shit," Blake mutters, noticing Dominic the same moment I do.

"Your first trial commences now," he says, handing over a glass of dark amber liquid. "Drink the poison and face what lies on the other side."

I take the glass without hesitation, glancing over at Blake, who looks less than pleased. To be fair, I'm not thrilled about it either, but with the power zipping through my veins, at least I'm at my strongest.

Blake takes my arm, pulling me away from any prying eyes. We find a quiet spot along the side of the haunted barn, and I bring the glass to my lips. The liquid is thick and bitter on my tongue, and I force it down with a hard swallow.

It makes my throat tingle and my gut fill with heat. The night air feels cooler as my vision blurs, and I barely hear Blake wish me luck before reality slips from my grasp.

A dim hallway materializes around me, and after a few moments of my limbs feeling like static, the ground solidifies beneath my feet.

I stand in the doorway of an unfamiliar bedroom, but I know exactly where I am. My eyes find her immediately, standing at a dark window with her back to me and wearing a long-sleeved light gray pajama set.

"Camille."

She whirls around to face me, her expression pale with shock as I walk into the room, stopping a few feet from her. "Xander," she breathes, and her features sharpen. "How did you get in here?"

I open my mouth to explain, but stop myself before the words form. I glance around the room, searching for something to confirm if this is a dreamscape, or a hallucination brought on by the royal guard's poison.

"You need to leave," she insists, snaring my attention again. "If he sees you—"

"Who?" I cut in sharply.

She blinks, folding her arms over her chest. "Noah. He's in the shower."

Those words shouldn't feel like a dagger to the gut, but they steal my breath just as viciously. My molars grind as I bite back a growl, stepping closer to Camille.

"Come with me," I tell her in a low voice.

Her lips fall into a frown. "Where?" She shakes her head as if to herself. "No. No, I'm not going anywhere with you."

I cock my head to the side, searching her gaze. "But you want to."

Her pulse ticks up. "I don't."

Before I can call out her lie, the doorknob rattles across the room, and we both turn to face it. I clench my hands into fists, straightening and preparing to take on the hunter.

Except when the door opens, it isn't Noah.

I clench my jaw, my head spinning as I fumble for words. Only one falls out. "Mother."

The late queen of hell glides forward, her black eyes locked on me, and says nothing. She's dressed in a floor-length crimson gown, her dark hair pin straight. Her appearance is flawless, as always. Which is unsettling for so many reasons.

The most prominent being the last time I saw her, she was a pile of ashes at my feet.

This is a hallucination, then. That much I know for certain.

Still, I ask, "What are you doing here?"

Lucia's eyes flick between me and Camille before she sighs. "Cleaning up your mess, as usual, my son."

I grab her wrist before she can make a move toward Camille, recoiling inwardly from the ice-cold feel of it against my fingers. "I don't need you to do that. I'm handling it."

She laughs, and I stiffen at the condescending sound. "You're 'handling it'?" she echoes, shaking her head. "You'll never be able to do what needs to be done when it comes to her, Xander. The human girl will be your weakness as long as she's breathing."

Camille stays silent, her expression unreadable. Nothing but the rapid beat of her heart gives away her fear of the situation. Which makes me think that perhaps Camille is experiencing this trial alongside me. And if this is real for her, if the royal guard is somehow controlling her dreamscape. That puts her in very real danger.

"I did what needed to be done, which is why you're no longer here."

THE DEVIL'S TRIALS

Her eyes narrow, and she pulls her wrist free. "You believe yourself strong enough to sit on my throne?" Moving at preternatural speed, she grabs Camille, sinking her nails into her throat, making Camille yelp in pain and gasp for air. "Prove it."

No sooner are the words out of her mouth does an obsidian dagger materialize in my hand. I glance down at it, my jaw working.

The options are clear. Lucia or Camille.

It's not the first time I've been faced with the choice, but unlike the last time, I'm being judged by those who will determine my future. If I kill Lucia for a second time, I won't be able to lie my way through an explanation because I'm being watched this time. But if Camille is truly here somehow, and I kill her...*Fuck*. I don't have time to figure it out for sure. I can't hesitate—that's exactly what the royal guard is expecting me to do. They're testing my weakness.

I have to believe this isn't real for Camille. That, like Lucia, she isn't actually here. I swallow the fear clogging my throat, reaching into myself and latching onto my newfound ability to switch off my emotions.

And then I let the dagger fly.

It finds its target in Camille's chest, and her eyes pop wide before they roll into the back of her head as bright crimson seeps through the front of her shirt.

Lucia steps away, letting Camille's lifeless body drop to the floor, and laughs loudly. "Hmm. Perhaps I was wrong." Her eyes find mine once more. "Congratulations, Xander. You have passed your initial ascension trial."

I don't have a moment to process anything as the scene darkens, and the floor gives way under my feet, swallowing me whole.

The ground is cold and damp when I blink my eyes open and find myself propped against the side of the haunted barn. It's quiet now. The only sound is the soft chirping of crickets and steady breathing next to me.

I glance at Blake when he murmurs, "Welcome back."

We stand, and I groan and the ache in my limbs. "How long was I out?"

Blake shrugs, checking his watch. "Hmm. A couple of hours?"

It barely felt like ten minutes.

"And you stayed with me the whole time?"

JESSI ELLIOTT

He arches a brow, nodding. "Well, yeah. I couldn't leave you slumped over out here. Someone could find you and would probably think you drank too much and passed out." He nudges my shoulder with his. "We couldn't risk having the cops called and your trial disrupted, so I kept watch to intervene if necessary. Nothing came up, though, so we're good." He tilts his head to the side, searching my face. "We are good, right? You passed?"

"I did." There's a burst of pride in my chest, but it's tainted by the lingering pressure in my lungs.

"Dominic came by after you passed out. He told me your first trial would reveal your greatest weakness and force you to face it," Blake says as we walk to the car, his brows furrowing. "So what'd you see?"

"I'd rather not talk about it. I need to do something now."

"Do I want to ask?"

"Probably not."

Blake lets loose a heavy sigh. "Well, one trial down. Only two to go."

I chuckle softly, but it sounds more tired than humorous. "Ever the optimist. Thanks, Blake."

"Anytime, mate. Now I hope this thing you need to do won't take long, because we're going out tonight to celebrate."

I don't bother arguing with him about the party, but I do say, "We can celebrate tomorrow."

As soon as we get back to the house, I shut myself in the bedroom and drop into the armchair in the corner. Closing my eyes, I focus on my breathing. I've never dreamwalked from such a distance, but with my new power, it should be something I can do—so long as Camille is sleeping.

If she's not dead. If I didn't just kill her during my trial.

I exhale a harsh breath, shoving that thought away. I need to focus if I'm going to do this. I recall a conversation I had with Camille when she told me about a breathing technique to work through a panic attack and ground herself. I follow the steps she shared, inhaling through my nose and holding it, then letting it out slowly through my mouth. After repeating the exercise a few times, my nerves settle enough to focus my thoughts. I visualize going to her, finding her waiting for me.

The room spins behind my eyelids, but I keep them shut, gripping the armrests on either side of me as I continue breathing deeply until I feel the familiar pull of being transported into someone else's subconscious.

THE DEVIL'S TRIALS

I blink my eyes open and find myself in another unfamiliar space. I stand from the couch and follow the sound of a steady heartbeat I'd know anywhere. The relief flooding my entire body nearly throws me off balance.

I didn't kill her.

I cross the room in a blur, pausing at a closed bedroom door before reaching for the handle and letting myself in.

Camille is standing at the window like she was in the hallucination, except I don't have a chance to speak her name before she turns to find me walking toward her.

"What are you doing here?" she says in a breathy voice, her heart racing, and looks around the room with a calculating gaze. She shakes her head, her brows pinched. "This isn't real."

I cock my head to the side, regarding her curiously. I expect her to bolt at any moment. That, or take a swing at me. Considering the way we left things, neither would be surprising—or unwarranted. "You're asleep," I tell her, "but this is real."

Camille hesitates, crossing her arms over her chest. "How?"

"We're sharing a dreamscape."

She squeezes her eyes shut. Rubs them. Blinks them open. She continues staring at me without a word.

"Still here," I offer wryly.

She shakes her head, her expression shrouded in disbelief. "Are...are you in New York?"

"No." I shake my head for extra measure.

Her back stiffens, and she takes a step away from me. "I don't understand. You're over two thousand miles away. How are you in my dream?"

"With the power I have now, there are fewer limitations on my abilities, meaning I can dreamwalk from a distance."

"Okay, that explains the *how*. Sort of. What about the *why*? To flaunt your newfound power? Because you can?" Her pulse ticks faster with each pointed question.

It's impossible to ignore and offers a challenge to move closer. *I wonder how close she'll let me.*

"What if it's because I wanted to see you?" The question leaves my lips before I can clamp my damn mouth shut. Being this close to her, even in the realm of unconsciousness, is a test...in a lot of ways.

Camille clenches her jaw, her gaze hardening. "You—"

"I had my first trial tonight," I cut in smoothly before she can attempt to throw me out.

Her posture doesn't relax when her eyes leave mine. She glances down at her feet, then past me to the doorway. "What does that have to do with me?"

"You were there. At least, a hallucination of you was."

Her eyes snap back to me. "Me? Why?"

"I had to face my weakness—my humanity." *You.* If the thumping in my chest and the deep-rooted sensation of longing are any indications. I've done a halfway decent job of blocking out these feelings, but being so close to the focal point of them is proving to be something I'm not sure I'm strong enough for.

"Your humanity," she says in a low voice, her eyes dancing over my face as if she's searching for it there. Slowly, she shakes her head. "I watched you abandon your humanity when you drove that dagger through your mother's heart."

I ignore the barbed wire weaving through my rib cage. "We've all made choices." Closing the remaining distance between us, I lower my voice and speak into her ear. "I'd face any consequence if it meant keeping you safe. Take my queen. Take my soul. As long as you're breathing, nothing else matters."

Her chin quivers, and she blinks quickly. The look of disbelief that splashes across her features makes me go utterly still. There's a short intake of breath and then, "You lost your soul?"

She didn't know.

"I thought..." My voice trails off. It doesn't matter now.

"Is that why you're doing this?" Her voice is small, growing more detached with every sentence. I can feel her slipping away from me. "Is that why you're fighting for the throne? Because you want it now that you don't have a moral compass to tell you right from wrong?" Her heart beats like the wings of a hummingbird just trying to survive.

I wet my lips, knowing whatever response I offer isn't going to please her. "I don't know what you want me to say."

"The truth!" She exhales a heavy breath. "Did you know killing Lucia would kill the human part of you, too? Was it all part of your plan to become king?"

My brows lift. "Is that what you think?"

"I don't know what to think." Desperation creeps into her tone, and I can tell by the way her jaw tightens that she loathes it. "I'm fucking lost, Xander."

I find myself nodding in agreement, fighting the urge to admit that I often feel the same. Raking a hand through my hair, I slide my hands into the pockets of my jacket. "And you thought you'd find yourself in the Big Apple?"

Camille blinks at me, hesitating before she comes up with, "I don't have to explain myself to you."

I nod. "I wasn't asking you to."

"Then what *are* you doing?"

Good fucking question.

I exhale softly through my nose. "I didn't kill Lucia for any reason other than to stop her from killing you. There wasn't time to consider the consequences or consult a moral compass. Whether or not you believe my intentions were in the right place is up to you."

Her heart pounds like a drum, her hands balling into fists at her sides. When she starts blinking faster, her gaze darting about, and sweat dotting her brow, I realize she's tumbling toward a panic attack.

"Stop," I say in a low voice. "I can see you spiraling. The guilt is clear on your face."

Her jaw works, and she whispers, "You shouldn't be here."

"Are you asking me to leave?"

"I should," she murmurs.

"Are you?" I repeat.

"No." She swallows hard, her eyes glassy when she looks at me. "I'm asking you to let me go."

Pressure clamps down on my chest.

"Camille—"

"We both knew this wouldn't work. What we were doing was reckless before, but it's nothing short of impossible now, and we both know it."

I rub the stubble along my jaw. "Is that why you ran away and rejoined the organization you vowed you'd never return to?"

"No," she snaps, her pulse ticking faster. "Why did you send Blake after me, anyway?"

I purse my lips, then tell her, "He was in New York already."

She stares at me, searching my face as if she's trying to figure something out. "That doesn't answer my question."

Instead of crafting a not-entirely-truthful answer, I offer, "I wanted to see you."

"Okay." She looks as if she wants to say more, but doesn't know what or how to articulate it. The tendrils of uncertainty are floating off her like ribbons of darkness, even within the dreamscape. The fear woven in them calls to me, and if it were anyone else, I wouldn't hesitate to feed on it. But I can't. Not with Camille. I've taken enough from her.

"I can feel everything you're experiencing right now. The fear, the anger, and that pull you still have to me." I steal the remaining distance between us in the time it takes Camille to blink, tracing my fingers along the side of her face. When she stumbles back, I catch her wrist with my other hand, pulling her close.

"Let go," she breathes, her hands pressed to my chest.

I dip my face and speak low in her ear, my fingers lingering against her cheek. "We both know that's not what you truly desire, *mo shíorghrá*."

Ten
Camille

My breath catches, but I manage to shove away from him and pull my wrist free of his grasp. "Why are you doing this?" I demand, my hands shaking at my sides until I tighten them into fists. I keep my eyes locked on the king of hell to be, waiting for him to answer my question.

He looks the same, but different. Power emanates from him like a warning. It's impossible to ignore and even more impossible to escape. He's dressed uncharacteristically formal—besides the leather jacket—in a navy button-up, black slacks and dress shoes, with his hair tousled stylishly. His chiseled features are sharper but his eyes...they're the same deep, warm brown ones I fell for.

He shrugs. Fucking *shrugs*, as if this means nothing to him.

Maybe it doesn't.

I open my mouth, but whatever I was going to say vanishes. I regret wanting to see him, and I sure as hell resent missing him. I lick the dryness from my lips, meeting his darkening gaze, and whisper, "Where did you go?"

Xander shakes his head, arching a brow at me before he says, "You're the one who left."

"That's not what I mean." I bite the inside of my cheek, struggling to continue looking at him. "I don't know who you are anymore. You...you're a stranger."

"Good." His voice is harder now. Cold. "A stranger to you is exactly what I need to be."

Pulling free of his grasp, I shoot back, "To be king?"

Xander hesitates before nodding.

This emotional back and forth is giving me whiplash. It's clear in his tone and the expressions he's failing to hide that I'm not the only one struggling. I just want it to end. If distancing himself from the parts I fell in love with is what he needs to do in order to succeed in the trials, fine. But I can't be part of it.

"Fine," I say in a resigned tone, swallowing past the lump in my throat. I close my eyes, focusing on breathing steadily, willing myself to wake up. I doubt it'll work, but I have to try.

There's a soft brush of knuckles against my cheek before I'm overcome by the sensation of the floor disappearing from under me. Instead of fear flooding through me, I'm filled with relief, and I fall willingly.

Waking with a start, I sit up in bed, looking around my bedroom. Grounding myself. My heart is still racing, and I reach around blindly until I find the lamp beside my bed, switching it on and grabbing the glass of water on the nightstand, chugging it to soothe the fire in my throat. I set the empty glass down and run my fingers through my hair, taking deep breaths until my pulse returns to a normal rhythm.

I check the time on my phone with a sigh. It's just after one in the morning. Adjusting my pillow, I curl onto my side and attempt to get comfortable again.

Sleep evades me as I turn over the dreamscape conversation with Xander. I'm left feeling betrayed all over again, but knowing what he gave up so I would live has also planted a seed of guilt in my chest.

I would've felt better if he'd been angry and blamed me. His blatant indifference to the outcome of killing Lucia—his newfound motivation to pass the ascension trials and take the throne—makes me regret putting my faith in him on a whole other level.

I was blinded by my feelings for him. They tricked my gut into believing he could be trusted.

And I let it happen.

I can't trust Xander.

I can't even trust myself.

So where does that leave me?

After a restless night, I struggle to get out of bed and get ready in time to meet Noah in the parking garage. Of course, there's also the matter of that kiss we shared in the apartment gym two days ago. I haven't seen or spoken to him since, and I have no idea how to broach the subject. Or if I even should.

"Are you ready to tackle a group class today?"

THE DEVIL'S TRIALS

So, I guess we're not going to talk about it.

"Sure," I say automatically despite the way my stomach dips and my pulse ticks faster. I'd much rather have another private class with Noah but I can't keep putting this off. I need to train with other novices, and the sooner I start the easier it'll be.

"What's with you this morning?"

"Nothing."

"Liar."

I sigh. "I didn't sleep well, that's all."

"Oh? Is there something you want to talk about?"

"Not with you," I say without missing a beat.

He sucks air through his teeth. "Ouch, Cam. You wound me so deeply."

Heat floods my face. "No, that isn't—I only meant—"

"Relax," he says with a chuckle. "I'm messing with you. I get it. We're not exactly friends, and I'm sure you have plenty you'd rather talk to, which is fine."

"Just Harper, really,"

He nods. "Have you spoken to her much since you got here?"

"Uh, well, I called her the other night. After, um, you know."

"Do I?" he asks. "I think you need to refresh my memory."

"Can you not be an ass about this? Please?" I feel the weight of his gaze as he glances over at me, though I don't meet it. I keep my eyes trained forward, watching the skyscrapers turn into shorter, more industrial buildings spaced further apart.

"Sorry." His attention returns to the road. "We don't have to talk about it if you'd rather not."

"Really?" The relief in my voice is almost embarrassing.

"I don't want to make you uncomfortable. If you think it would be better to forget it happened then we will. Is that what you want?"

My throat suddenly feels tight, and I press my lips together as I consider how to respond. Aside from the initial comment, Noah is being incredibly considerate about the whole thing. "Honestly, I don't know. I wasn't in a good headspace that night and I shouldn't have kissed you."

Noah nods. "I understand. So we leave it in the past and focus on your training. Sound good?"

"I don't..." I trail off, fumbling for the right words. "How are you being so reasonable about this?"

He turns onto the private road leading to Ballard. "It's simple. Your success here is more important than how I might feel about our kiss."

My eyes widen. *How he feels?* "I'm not sure what to say."

"I guess there's a first for everything," he teases.

Same old Noah.

I scowl halfheartedly, though his quip does make me feel a bit better. "Ha-ha. So funny." Letting loose a breath, my tone is sincere when I say, "Thank you."

"You bet." He drums his thumbs against the steering wheel.

The rest of the drive to Ballard is quiet. We go through the security checkpoint, and Noah waves to the guard at the gate and drives through as it opens.

After we park in Noah's spot, instead of going into the private training room, he guides us into the main building through the front entrance.

This place was custom built by the organization to be a training facility, so we're met with a security checkpoint the minute we walk through sliding doors. Noah flashes his badge at the hunter behind the desk.

We walk through a set of metal detectors, and Noah swipes his badge at another door. There's a buzzing sound, and then it slides open, granting us access deeper into the building.

I follow Noah, my pulse ticking unevenly as my eyes dart around. There's not much to see past the plain gray walls and shiny linoleum floors. It doesn't smell like anything—not like a gym or an office building. I get the occasional whiff of Noah's cologne, and weirdly, it brings me a bit of comfort, though I have little energy to explore that.

The training facility I started at in Seattle was much smaller than this. The time I spent there was in classes on one side of the facility. I never made it to the physical portion of hunter training, which is precisely why it's going to kick my ass now.

We come to a fork in the hallway, and I follow Noah down another corridor. There are solid black metal doors on either side with placards on each—offices, I think—and past them is yet another door.

Noah taps his badge against the panel beside it, and the door slides open, revealing a room that looks like what we trained in before, but easily three times the size.

Cardio machines and weight racks line the perimeter of the room, leaving the middle a wide-open space with mats. Small groups of peo-

THE DEVIL'S TRIALS

ple mingle around the space, while a few others are warming up on the treadmills and stationary bikes. There's a section of hooks in the wall adjacent to the doors, so I hang up my jacket and bag, then head over to the treadmill at the end of the row to warm up.

Nerves coil tightly in my stomach as I feel the weight of eyes on me, and I try to ignore them and focus on the display screen of the treadmill as I increase the speed to a light jog. I knew my first group class would be a challenge for my anxiety, and I cling to knowing it'll only be an hour as if it's a life raft.

Noah walks around the room and says good morning to the trainees before jumping on one of the bikes himself. Part of me wants to glance around the room, but my apprehension gets the best of me and I keep my eyes forward until I finish my warm-up.

When Noah calls everyone to the center of the room, I keep my eyes on him, afraid the other trainees are going to judge me for being here. I shouldn't assume they know who I am, but I've gotten so used to being the black sheep of the Morgan family. The well-known disappointment within the organization.

And that was all *before* I got involved with Xander.

Noah drones on about the importance of always being aware of your surroundings, and I look away from him as he moves on to talk about stretching after a training session.

It's a repeat of what he told me during our first private session, and the importance of the reminder isn't lost on me.

I finally get the nerve to glance around at the other class members while their attention is glued to Noah. There's a good mix of guys and girls, and a lot of them appear younger than me, which makes sense considering this is basic hunter training. There are close to two dozen trainees, and they're listening so intensely to Noah, I have to press my lips together to keep from snickering. He must love this gig. All of these people looking at him with such awe and respect. It's a buffet for his ego.

Noah crosses the room and grabs a black bin off a shelf I hadn't noticed before, carrying it back to the center of the room and dropping it with a loud thud. The obsidian daggers inside have the class shifting, either nervously or excitedly, on their feet.

"Everybody take a dagger," Noah says in a level voice.

"Are we going to learn how to fight with one today?" one girl asks.

Noah laughs. "You're lucky I'm letting you touch it today. So no. But I do want you to know how it feels. The weight of it in your palm."

Once each person has a dagger in their grip, I step forward. Noah plucks one out of the box and holds it out to me, hilt first. "Just like riding a bike," he says under his breath so only I can hear.

My lips twitch as I take the dagger. "Right." I step back and wait for further instruction with the rest of the trainees. I catch one of their gazes and am rewarded with a spectacularly dirty look before I glance away from the girl. Evidently my concern about ruffling feathers by being here wasn't entirely unwarranted. *Super.*

I try to distract myself by passing the dagger from hand to hand before holding it in my dominant one, curling my fingers around the hilt. The metal is cool against my skin, and I frown at how normal such a lethal thing can feel in my grip.

It isn't unbelievably heavy, which makes the weapons easier to transport and secure to different limbs. Most hunters are inclined to strap them to the outside of their thigh just above the knee where they can easily grab it out of its sheath. I've also seen some hide others at their ankles or waist or between their breasts.

I don't want to be the type of person who has a dagger strapped to every inch of me. One has to be sufficient—two max.

Noah gives the class a few minutes to converse over the wonder that he just bestowed upon them before he kicks the box and says, "Good. Now put them back."

"What was the point of that?" a guy to Noah's left grumbles, dropping his dagger back into the bin.

"I want you to be familiar and comfortable with them when you're prepared to wield them."

"When are we going to be ready?" someone else asks.

Fuck, these trainees are eager.

Whereas the idea of actually having to use the dagger in my grip threatens to shoot anxiety through my veins like wildfire. It brings me back to the night Xander and I were attacked. I had no choice but to use his dagger and kill that demon. Even now that I know it was a twisted way for Xander to steal my trust, I still hate thinking about the fact that I took a life.

That demon would've done the same to you.

THE DEVIL'S TRIALS

I swallow hard, willing the memory to fade as I return the dagger to the box.

Noah spends the next hour going through several techniques to block attacks, walking through each step and picking a different person to use as an example. Most are thrilled to jump into practice, while I stand off to the side, paying close attention to the movements and how each person who goes up against Noah doesn't stand a chance. When his eyes shift to me and the corner of his mouth kicks up, my stomach dips.

No. Please—

"You're up, Cam."

"Uh, I'm more of an observational learner."

His brows lift. "That wasn't a suggestion. Get over here. Unless, of course, you'd like to continue wasting our time."

My eyes narrow as heat fills my cheeks, and I bite my tongue to keep from cursing him out as I trudge forward, feeling too many sets of eyes on me.

"Ready?" he asks, any trace of amusement gone from his expression.

"Sure," I deadpan.

Between one breath and the next, Noah moves swiftly, putting himself behind me as he locks an arm around my neck and the other around my waist, effectively immobilizing me. I'm trapped against his chest, and he drops his chin to the top of my head.

"What do your instincts tell you to do at this moment?" he asks loudly enough for the class to hear.

"Scream," I offer plainly, "but I know that's useless."

Noah makes no move to let me go. "Your instincts can be clouded by emotion, including fear." His grip tightens, and I suck in a breath, unable to ignore the fluttering sensation in my stomach. "Which is why we drill this training into you," he continues, "so you don't have to think. You'll act without hesitation and, ideally, avoid a situation like this."

"I get that," a girl with bright red hair speaks up, then asks, "But what would you do if you ended up in this situation?" She's wearing a matching soft blue workout set, which stands out against the sea of black outfits around her. I like her already.

Noah's responding chuckle vibrates against my back, and I press my lips together, cursing this stupid exercise. "I wouldn't be in this situation."

I roll my eyes, trying to pull away instantly.

"Nope," he murmurs, "we're not done yet." He clears his throat, speaking to the class again. "If Camille had a dagger, she would do her damn best to get her hand around it and stab wherever she could until I let go."

He finally does, and I immediately take a huge step away from him, my chest rising and falling faster than it should.

"The very moment you get free, you need to attack. Don't give them a second chance to capture you."

Without thinking, I strike out with my fist. There's a fleeting moment where I think I'm going to get a shot on him, but he dodges at the last second, his gaze sharp, focused.

"Plant your feet wider apart," he instructs, his eyes locked on me as if we're the only people in the room.

I adjust my stance and throw a punch before he can bark another order at me. This time I aim lower, my fist connecting with his ribs, and am met with a satisfying grunt. Pain flares across my knuckles, but it's worth it for the impressed look stealing over Noah's features.

My god, it's as if I'm fifteen all over again.

I shouldn't give two shits about impressing Noah, and yet...

Whirling away from him, I blurt, "Who's next?"

Without waiting for a response, I return to where I was standing before getting called on.

Try as I might, I can't shake the weird bubbly sensation in my chest. And every time Noah's eyes land on me over the next hour, I look away. It's ridiculous, and I want to kick myself every time it happens.

"Take a five-minute break. When you come back, pair up."

I make a quick trip to the bathroom and gulp down half my water bottle, catching eyes with the redhead I noticed earlier. I try for a friendly smile, and relief floods through me when she returns it and approaches.

"Hey, I'm Sierra. You're Camille, right?"

"Yeah. It's nice to meet you."

"You, too," she offers, propping her hands on her hips. "Partners?"

I laugh softly, nodding. "Sounds good."

"I haven't seen you here before," she comments as we wait for the rest of the class to pair up.

"Uh, yeah." I panic over how much to say and land on, "I left the academy for a while and I'm just coming back to it."

THE DEVIL'S TRIALS

Her brows lift. "Why'd you leave?"

She doesn't know?

I glance around the room. Maybe these trainees are too young to recognize who I am. Frankly, that would be ideal.

"Sorry, I didn't mean to pry or anything. I was just curious. You can absolutely tell me to get lost."

My gaze flits back to Sierra. "No, no, it's fine. I'm just not used to people being involved with the organization not already knowing." I lick the dryness from my lips. "My sister was killed by a demon a little over five years ago. I left after that."

She frowns, her arms falling to her sides. "I'm so sorry. That's awful." The sympathy in her gaze makes my chest tighten, but I manage a nod and a faint smile.

"How did you get involved with the hunters?" I ask, desperate to shift the focus of our conversation to her.

"Family legacy," she offers.

"I understand that."

She nods. "Are your parents hunters as well?"

"Oh, um, yeah," I stumble through my response. I'm used to everyone around the training facilities knowing who Rachel and Scott Morgan are. "They sort of run this place. Well, my dad does. My mom runs HQ in Seattle."

Sierra's eyes widen. "Holy shit. That's...wow. I can only imagine the pressure you feel being here."

"Yeah, just a little." I fight the urge to throw my arms around her, because that's probably a little weird for a girl I just met, but the relief singing in my veins makes me want to hug her. I was expecting everyone here to know who I am and immediately hate me, so finding someone who doesn't feels special.

"Can I ask you something?"

"Sure?" I offer hesitantly.

Her eyes twinkle with amusement. "I get the feeling you've known Noah a while?"

I nod. "He was ahead of me the first time I was enrolled in training, and now he's sort of mentoring me. He also works pretty closely with my parents, so I've always had to deal with him in some capacity."

"Makes sense. I've just never seen him act like he did with you today."

I arch a brow, that odd fluttering returning to my stomach. "What do you mean?"

Sierra purses her lips. "I don't know. It's like he can't decide if he loves or hates you."

I almost laugh, though I'm still conflicted about the conversation Noah and I had on the drive here. "I think it probably depends on the day."

Her lips twist into a grin. "Fair enough. Anyway, are you nervous about the novice assessment next week?"

I blink at her, shaking my head. "The what?"

She cringes. "Oh, shit. Sorry. I just assumed you already knew. We are tested monthly at this level. If you fail more than one, you're out of the training program."

"What kind of test?" I ask, wiping my palms on my thighs as I lick the sudden dryness from my lips. I'm torn between my nerves and being pissed at Noah for not telling me about this during our first training session a few days ago.

"It's a physical exercise to test our strength, focus, and retention of the lessons we've learned here. They're basically like high school midterms and finals, but hands-on."

"Have you gone through them before?"

Sierra nods. "A few times. I always stress majorly and don't sleep the night before, but luckily, I've passed every time."

I nod along. "That's good."

She smiles and pats my shoulder. "You'll be fine. You're a hunter prodigy *and* working with Noah? I'm sure you're going to make the rest of us look bad."

I manage to fake a short laugh as Noah calls the class back into session. "Yeah, I wouldn't be too sure about that."

Eleven
Xander

Seeing Camille in the dreamscape last night was a stark reminder of what I lost to save her, and I wasn't expecting the sense of grief and longing that came from being in her presence. They're dark, sticky emotions I thought I left behind when I embraced my demon side completely. As it turns out, that doesn't seem to be the case—at least where Camille is concerned.

And while I crave her fierce determination to resist me, I also take pleasure in witnessing her struggle against her own feelings. Because she is mine, and deep down she knows it as well as I do.

I'd rather spend another night in a dreamscape with her, but there isn't a chance in hell Blake will let me out of this party to celebrate completing the first ascension trial.

By the time we reach downtown, it's pouring rain. The sky fills with lightning every few minutes, a clap of thunder following close behind.

As we circle the block several times, I consider telling Blake to drive home. I'm not really in the mood to party in a loud room full of mostly strangers. Though I suppose this is the type of thing I need to get used to. As king, someone will always want a piece of me. I add that to the list of negative consequences from my choice to kill Lucia and force myself to accept whatever tonight will be.

Blake finds an open spot on the street and parallel parks before cutting the engine. "The others are already at the bar."

My gaze cuts to him, ready to remind him of our intention to keep a low profile. I trust he's scoped the place out, which is why I haven't flat out refused. Yet. "Who did you invite to this thing?"

He laughs. "Your council. They want to celebrate with their king."

I'm not sure what pushes me to point out, "I'm no one's king yet."

"Semantics," he says with a flick of his wrist. "Let's go have a drink—or five—and if not celebrate, then at least forget the reason behind all of your broody vibes."

"I'm not—"

His brows lift before I can get the sentence out.

"Fine," I grumble.

He grins. "Excellent. I also have a team of trusted acquaintances to watch our backs so you don't need to be concerned about a hunter ambush or any other trouble. You can let go and have a good time. Get blindingly drunk without worrying about finding yourself on the sharp end of an obsidian dagger."

I chuckle at that.

We hurry through the rain and into the building vibrating with bass-heavy music.

Blake and I immediately walk to the bar and order, the twenty-something bartender pouring me a scotch and sliding it across the counter with a polite smile.

I return it, thanking her before turning away to survey the crowd in the dark.

Demons and humans alike dance with reckless abandon, filling the space with a heady mix of desire and arousal, mixed with alcohol, perfume, and sweat. It's fucking tempting to let myself get lost in it, and I could—so damn easily.

Jude and Greer are dancing together near the edge of the dance floor, their cheeks flushed with warmth and beer in each of their hands. Spotting me, they lift their bottles in cheers.

I return the gesture, taking another drink of the smooth liquor.

Declan and Roman have found a quiet corner booth, where they sit and sip from whiskey glasses while making conversation.

Before I can start toward them to join, Francesca saunters up to the bar, ordering herself a vodka soda and clinking her glass against mine. She's wearing a skintight black dress that stops just above her knees and sleek black boots with a heel that puts her almost at eye level with me.

"To the new king of hell," she murmurs before taking a sip.

I chuckle, meeting her glimmering gaze over the rim of my glass as I take a drink. I don't bother correcting her—she knows I still have to pass the other trials. "Right."

THE DEVIL'S TRIALS

"Dance with me?" she purrs in my ear.

My brows lift before my gaze flicks to the dance floor, then back to Francesca, her emerald eyes filled with anticipation and sparkling with gold shadow. "I'd rather not."

She frowns. "We're supposed to be celebrating. You should have fun. You *do* remember what that is, don't you?"

I narrow my eyes, setting my drink aside and pulling her in swiftly. Her floral perfume assaults my senses, and my lips graze her ear, an air of warning in my tone as I murmur, "What game are you playing?"

Her responding laugh is lyrical. "One you'll enjoy immensely if you let yourself, I promise."

I find myself clinging to that promise. I don't give a fuck about fun. What I need more than anything is a damn escape. So I let her pull me toward the cluster of warm, writhing bodies. I lose myself in the music, not flinching when Francesca wraps her arms around my neck. I drop my hands to her waist as she grins at me, and suddenly we're fifteen again. Finding comfort in each other when everything else was literally hell.

I lose her attention for a moment as her grin widens and her expression darkens with something I know all too well—hunger.

Before I can speak, she slips out of my grasp and dances away. I turn, my gaze following her through the dark crowd until she finds her prey. It's a lanky guy who can't be much older than me, and the second Francesca gets her claws in him, he's a goner. She leans up, speaking into his ear, and his face pales, his eyes going wide and near-vacant with fear.

A quick glance around the room tells me most of the demons are feeding. The music is so loud the humans' screams are drowned out, which makes it the perfect feeding den.

I watch for several beats, finding I have no desire to step in and help the humans. In fact, the pull to feed my own hunger is inescapable. I wasn't aware of how much the first trial sucked away my energy until now. I suppose being surrounded by humans doesn't help. It'd be like a human going grocery shopping on an empty stomach.

I move through the room in a blur, coming up beside Francesca. A growl tears from her lips before she realizes it's me. Her eyes flicker between their normal color and endless black before staying dark. She grabs the front of my shirt, tugging me closer, and I reach out with my senses to feel the white-hot fear pouring off this guy.

JESSI ELLIOTT

His mouth has fallen open in a silent scream and his eyes are bloodshot as tears spill from them, soaking his blanched cheeks. His fear transforms into energy as it sinks into my skin, and I close my eyes, relishing in the way it takes over my entire body, washing away every worry and care lingering in my chest.

I only pull away when Francesca laughs, opening my eyes in time to watch the human sink to the floor, the front of his pants soaked with piss.

"Well, that's disappointing," I mutter with a sigh, stepping over his unconscious body, then offer my hand to Francesca to do the same.

She slides her fingers through mine without looking back at our discarded prey as we return to the bar. She motions for the bartender, who comes over immediately, and asks for a bottle of top-shelf tequila.

"Fran—"

"Fucking finally!" Blake interrupts, throwing his arm around my shoulders. "We're doing shots, right?"

I glance between him and Francesca, then mutter, "It would appear so."

Francesca grins, unscrewing the bottle cap and taking a long swig before passing the bottle my way. Without overthinking it, I take a shot, letting the liquor burn a path from my tongue to my stomach, warming it along the way.

Blake goes next, then smacks a loud kiss against Francesca's cheek before shooting me a salute and sauntering back into the crowd.

"He's so weird," Francesca says with a laugh, swallowing another mouthful of tequila before the bottle ends up in my hand again.

I shrug, taking another long drink as my head swims pleasantly. "At least it's mildly entertaining."

"True," she offers, tossing back her third shot.

Several shots later, we're on the dance floor again. I've fully lost myself in the music and alcohol, and while the escape is devastatingly fleeting, I cling to every damn second of it. It's a weak attempt at numbing the chasm in my chest that, despite feeding and drinking half a bottle of tequila, hasn't lessened as I hoped it would.

Francesca leans into me, sliding her hands up my chest and leaning on her tiptoes. I dip my face so she can speak in my ear, loosely hanging onto her waist. "Where are you?" she asks.

I lean back to look at her, shaking my head. "I'm right here."

"No, you're not."

THE DEVIL'S TRIALS

I cock my head to the side. "What—"

She huffs out a sigh and grabs my hand, pulling me through the crowd. I let her for the sole reason of not wanting to be surrounded by all these fucking people any longer.

We walk down a hallway, past the washrooms, and into a private lounge at the back of the bar. There Francesca slams the door shut and crosses her arms over her chest as she stares me down.

"Why do I feel as if I'm about to be scolded?" My tone is heavy with amusement as I scan the room.

It's small but furnished with two maroon leather couches and a glass coffee table, along with a matching, fully stocked bar cart off to the side.

"Is it working?" she asks, not a hint of sarcasm or humor in her voice.

I shake my head, perching on the armrest of the couch closest to me. "Is *what* working, Francesca?"

"This distraction from whatever has you so twisted up."

I chuckle. "Since when is partaking in shots and feeding a code for distraction?" I don't move as she steps closer, but I lower my voice and add, "I'm simply following your lead."

She drops her arms back to her sides. "You forget how long I've known you, Xander."

I stand, shooting forward until I'm right in her face. "No, you seem to forget who you're speaking to."

Francesca blinks at me. Her cheeks are flushed, though that could be a combination of the drinks and my proximity, or perhaps frustration based on the pinch of her brows. Still, she doesn't back down.

Not a chance," she murmurs, her long, dark lashes shadowing her high cheekbones. "So if you want a real distraction from the trials or the oh-so *tragic* loss of your soul, I assure you I can provide one."

The back of my neck prickles at her suggestion. While Francesca and I have, at times, been there for each other like that, it was a long time ago. She isn't who I want now.

Perhaps she's what you deserve, a feminine, hauntingly familiar voice croons at the back of my head. *A monster, just like you.*

I recoil from the thought, putting distance between us.

"Seriously?" She arches a brow at me.

Holding her gaze, I speak firmly. "Whatever happened between us stays in the past where it belongs."

JESSI ELLIOTT

Francesca studies my face in the silence stretching between us. "You don't want me?" Her doubt-filled tone raises my hackles, as if telling her nothing is going to happen between us now isn't convincing enough.

"I don't," I say firmly, so as to not leave anything up to interpretation.

"You used to." She prowls closer again. "Especially when I did that thing with my tongue on your—"

"Enough," I cut her off, my tone sharp. "You wanted a spot on my council, and I gave you one. I thought we had an understanding of what that meant and what it didn't. Do I need to clarify things for you?"

She scowls. "Of course not. I'm simply trying to be there for you. To help you keep your head clear of certain *distractions* so you're at your strongest for the remaining trials. You don't need to be an ass about it."

I grind my molars at her insinuation, though I can't refute it. "We should go back to the bar," I finally say, walking out of the room without waiting for her.

I wave the bartender over and point to a bottle of scotch on the middle shelf behind her. When she hands it over, I turn away, unscrewing the bottle and taking a long swig. The burn is immediate, a welcome distraction from the storm brewing in my chest. As I tip the bottle to my lips again, the room fades into a blur of sounds and moving bodies. With a deep sigh and another burning shot, I close my eyes and resign myself to get lost in it.

Twelve
Camille

"I have a bone to pick with you," I tell Noah the next morning when we meet at his car. I didn't bring it up on the drive home from Ballard yesterday because I wanted to give myself a chance to cool down instead of snapping at him. I had hoped that sleeping on it would diffuse my anger at being blindsided by news of the hunter tests.

"Uh-oh," he says with a grin, getting behind the wheel and setting his travel mug of coffee in the cup holder.

"I'm serious." I buckle my seat belt as he starts the car. "When were you going to tell me about the tests? That seems like something my mentor should have brought up to me instead of finding out from someone in class."

He sighs as we drive out of the parking garage. "I wasn't trying to keep it from you. I was waiting until you were ready—"

"There you go again with that shit," I interrupt in a snippy tone. "You don't get to—"

"Actually, I do." He cuts me a look before returning his attention to the road. "I'm your mentor. I decide what you can and can't handle, and when, based on what I see in class and our private lessons. I hate to break it to you, Cam, but you have a long way to go until you're ready to be tested."

I recoil as if he just smacked me across the face. My cheeks flame with embarrassment and my eyes burn. I stare out the windshield, willing myself not to cry, but all I want to do is curl into a ball and hide.

"When I think you're ready, we'll talk about it," he adds.

I can't bring myself to respond. I have no idea what I'd say, anyway. I can't refute his words, and I hate that. So, I pull out my phone and send Harper a text.

> Are you around today? I could use a chat and I miss you.

JESSI ELLIOTT

Her reply comes a minute later.

> Heading to class now and training right after. Can I call you tonight? Unless this is an SOS, in which case, I'll ditch my lecture.

I chew my lip, typing out a quick response.

> All good. Noah and I are heading to Ballard now. Give me a shout when you're home.

I pocket my phone and turn up the music, hoping to fill the silence without having to talk.

When we arrive at Ballard, Noah parks in his designated spot near the private training building, and we go inside. I guess he's not teaching a class today, which means this session is going to be one-on-one. *Awesome.*

While I don't love being surrounded by the other trainees, some who look at me as an enemy—or the girl who slept with the enemy—spending time alone with Noah right now gives me nearly as much anxiety.

I dive into my usual warm-up, finding it slightly easier than the first day after ensuring to stretch after my shower last night and when I woke up this morning. Once I'm finished, I meet Noah on the mats, propping my hands on my hips and asking, "What's on the lesson plan today?"

"I want to work on defensive maneuvers. Let's start with the basic ones we've already gone over as a refresher, then we'll move into the more complex ones and the transitions into offensive moves."

Noah attaches padded gloves to his hands and holds them up for me. I spend a few minutes hitting them as directed with closed fists. When my eyes drift upward, he's already looking at my face.

"What?" I grumble.

The corner of his mouth kicks up. "Your face gets all scrunched up when you concentrate."

I scowl. "Quit making fun of me." I land a harder punch against his gloved palm.

"I'm not making fun. It's cute. And I'm glad to see you're getting stronger. You have a good amount of power in your punch."

I should be focused on his compliment of my strength, but the stupid butterflies in my stomach flutter at him calling me cute.

You're still pissed at him, I remind myself, my eyes narrowing when he throws off the gloves and starts circling me, moving at an easy pace.

"What are you doing now?"

"Focus," he says in a level tone. "Don't let me get behind you."

With a sigh, I narrow my gaze and kick out, attempting to knock him off his feet, but he darts away easily.

It's embarrassing how quickly he can sneak behind me. Even more so when he sweeps my legs out from under me and takes us both to the ground, pinning me beneath him. It knocks the air out of my lungs, stunning more than hurting me. He swiftly straddles me to trap my hips between his, gripping my wrists tightly with both of his hands and holding them above my head, effectively immobilizing me. My heart slams against my chest, my pulse erratic and my eyes darting between his. He licks his lips, and when his gaze drops to my mouth and stays there a moment too long, panic hits me like an ice-cold tsunami.

He's going to kiss me.

And I could easily let him. Except...it isn't fair to him. Not really. Not when there's someone else who I want so completely that it makes me physically ache.

"You can't kiss me." The words tumble out of my mouth in a rush, and Noah freezes above me.

Silence stretches between us, the furrow in his brow making me frown. My heart still pounds so hard I can feel it in my throat, but we're frozen in this moment.

"Why not?"

I shake my head, wanting to look away from him as my eyes burn. "Because I still—" My voice cracks. I clear my throat and open my mouth to try again.

"Because you still love him," Noah offers.

When I don't respond, Noah releases and rolls off me, standing and offering me his hand. I take it, and as soon as I'm upright, he lets me go. "Let's take a break."

"What? Why?"

He scratches the back of his head. "Why?" he echoes. "Because it's clear your focus is in the wrong place. And I get it. That's not me shitting on you. But I can't be sure you're in the right headspace for training to fight demons when you're thinking about—"

"I'm not," I cut in, and he gives me a doubtful look that slices deep into my chest. "I'm sorry. Maybe I'm just...You're right. I'm not in the right headspace." I don't elaborate. Something tells me Noah won't be too keen on hearing about my dream walking experience with Xander. Honestly, I'd rather not relive it at the moment, either. "I think I just need some air."

He nods. "Take a walk outside. I have to check on something in the main building, anyway. Meet me back here in ten minutes." He doesn't wait for me to respond before crossing the room and tapping his badge against a security panel beside the door. He pulls it open, and I get a quick look inside an empty hallway before the door slams shut.

I exhale a heavy breath and walk to the door to the parking lot, where I stand outside and take measured breaths until the pressure in my chest eases some. Leaning against the cold exterior of the building, I close my eyes, timing my slow inhale, then hold it for the same amount of time before letting it out.

"You can do this," I tell myself, reaching for the door handle and walking back inside.

The rest of our lesson is tense, but I focus on Noah's instructions. We go through the defensive routine he showed me at the start of our session at least a dozen times over the next hour, and while I feel I'm getting better at it, he gives no indication of my progress.

The drive home is painfully quiet, and Noah sends me a curt, "I'll talk to you later," when we get back to the apartment before we part ways.

I curse myself the entire walk from the elevator to my place, slamming the door behind me with a loud groan to the empty entryway, then make sure to lock the door before I trudge through my living room and into the bathroom to take a shower.

Standing under the hot spray of water, I scrub my scalp and skin until everything is tingling and smelling of my coconut body wash.

Why is this so fucking confusing?

Why did I have to meet Xander in the first place?

A wave of dizziness rushes over me, and I press my forehead to the cool shower tile, focusing on my breathing. Inhaling slowly, holding it for a few seconds, and exhaling.

The more I consider it, the more I can't stop myself from wondering... If Xander and I hadn't met that night at Hallowed Grounds, would fate have brought us together another time?

Except, it wasn't fate. Xander orchestrated that night to get close to me in service of his mother's agenda. Though at some point it became more than that, which makes considering my life without Xander nausea-inducing to the point I reach to shut off the water and get out of the shower.

I'm getting changed when there's a soft knock at my door. I consider ignoring it for fear that it's Noah. But when the knock comes again, I tug on a hoodie and pad to the door, looking through the peephole to find my dad standing in the hallway sporting a casual navy polo shirt, jeans, and loafers.

Opening the door, I smile at him. "I didn't know you were coming by."

He steps inside, wrapping me in a hug that pushes the nausea away almost completely, instead filling my senses with the woodsy scent of his aftershave. It's the one he's always used, and the smell brings me a semblance of comfort. "Just wanted to check in, kiddo." He kisses the top of my head. "I like having you in the city. Being able to drop by and see you is nice. I wish I had a chance to come before now, but things have been a bit more chaotic at the office lately."

"Yeah, I'm glad you're here," I say, doing my best to ignore the unspoken reason for his chaos at work. "I, uh, don't have much in the way of groceries, but we could order something if you want to stay for lunch?"

"I'd love that."

Half an hour later, we're sitting at the small dining table eating takeout from the Thai place around the corner.

"How are you liking this place?" Dad asks, taking a sip of water as he glances around the apartment.

Luckily, it came furnished with the basics. As much as part of me wants to decorate and make the space feel more like mine, I don't know how long I'm going to be living here. That, and I really haven't had the motivation to put in any effort.

I push the noodles around my plate. "It's nice, but I miss Harper." I've never lived alone—I was with my mom until my first year at the University of Washington. It's only been a couple of weeks, but I've already decided I don't enjoy being alone so much. It's practically an open invitation for my anxiety to rear its ugly head.

"That's understandable," Dad says with a thoughtful smile. "I'm sure she misses you."

I manage a small smile in return. "Have there been any developments...?" My voice trails off. I don't think I can bring myself to say the words, but, thankfully, Dad understands what I'm asking.

He shakes his head. "Things are quiet, which isn't a good or bad thing at this point. What *is* good is that the number of demon attacks has decreased since the queen was executed."

Considering Lucia was responsible for many of them, it makes sense.

I nod, forcing myself to lift a forkful of noodles to my mouth. I chew slowly, reaching for my glass of water as Dad clears his throat.

"Do you want to talk about it? I know—" He pauses, as if he's debating how to craft what he wants to continue. "You were involved with Xander before all of this happened."

I stare at my plate. "I'm not sure what to say. The head of the hunter organization doesn't need to hear about his daughter's feelings for a demon."

"Camille," he says in a voice that makes me meet his gaze across the table. "I'm not asking in any official capacity. I'm asking as your father because I'm concerned about you."

The tears that prick my eyes aren't surprising, but I still try to blink them away before they can slip down my cheeks. Pressing my lips together against the words desperate to escape, a fiery pressure builds in my chest until I can't hold them back a second longer. I suck in a sharp breath. "I'm not ready to give up on him, Dad, and that scares me. I'm terrified the person I fell in love with is gone. That he doesn't care about me anymore."

His brows knit as he sets his fork on his plate. "And if he doesn't?"

"I can't imagine anything hurting more than this, but I'm scared that it would." I lean back in my chair, tearing small pieces off the napkin in my lap.

"You underestimate your own strength, kiddo. I'm not saying it would be easy, but I have no doubt you'd handle it with grace."

"I don't want to, though," I admit quietly, unable to grasp a false bravado at this moment. "I don't want any of this."

He offers me a sympathetic smile. "I know."

Dad heads out after lunch, and I tidy up from our meal. My thoughts spiral as I load the dishwasher and only get worse by the time I'm finished, causing me to gravitate to the bottle of tequila I bought the day I moved in.

A few hours later, I'm sitting in the dark living room squinting at my phone instead of adjusting the screen brightness—because that makes more sense. Obviously.

THE DEVIL'S TRIALS

Curled up on the floor in front of my coffee table, I giggle to myself, then hiccup and cringe at the threat of my poor decisions making a reappearance all over the floor. Tequila sounded amazing when I was trying to forget everything that has me waking up with a heavier weight on my chest each day. But now as it sloshes around my stomach? Not so much.

I tip my head back against the couch cushion and scroll through my contacts. Instead of calling Harper like I should, I'm tapping the name I should've deleted as soon as I decided to come to New York.

He's not going to answer.

I don't even know why I'm trying to call him.

You miss him, a treacherous voice in my head croons. I shove it away with a groan as heat spreads through my limbs, drowning me in a pleasantly heavy warmth.

This is a bad idea. Way worse than drinking half a bottle of tequila by myself in the dark.

I need to hang up.

The line keeps ringing. Each chime sounds louder, to the point I wince at the next one.

I'm going to hang up as soon as I can convince my hand to move.

More ringing.

I'm about to pull the phone away from my ear when his voice slams into me with the weight of a thousand bricks.

"Camille," is all he says, and it's painfully sobering.

I stare at the ceiling as it swirls above me, then squeeze my eyes shut. My heart thumps so hard I can feel it in my throat.

Opening and closing my mouth, I finally manage to force out, "Hi."

Fuck. Me.

I should've hung up the damn phone.

"What are you doing?" His voice is deep, sending a shiver skating over my flushed skin.

What am I doing?

Logic seems to launch itself out the window as I pry my eyes back open and blow out a breath, which turns into a whiny sigh-like noise. "I'm sitting on my living room floor, questioning the rug I bought the other day." I run my fingers over it. "It's super soft, but I don't think it really goes with the space, y'know?"

There's a stretch of silence. Then he asks, "Are you drunk?"

"Camille." My name acts as a warning. I'm not sure what for. Scratch that. I don't fucking care what for.

"I'm..." My voice trails off as I run my finger along the edge of the coffee table, completely forgetting what I was going to say. Or maybe I had no idea where that sentence was going from the start. Or this conversation. "I shouldn't have called you," I mumble, scrubbing my free hand down my face. "Why? Why do I keep making these bad—no, these *terrible*—decisions when it comes to you?"

"I can't answer that," he says in a level voice.

"I should go now."

"If that's what you want."

That hits a nerve, and I let out a humorless laugh. "None of this is what I want."

There's a soft sigh through the phone. "Camille—"

"No," I snap as tears prick my eyes, only fueling the swirl of emotions in my chest. "You had to go and ruin everything. And you know what the worst part is? I can't even hate you for it." I swipe angrily at the tears that escape my eyes, thankful he can't see them. See how easily I'm falling apart. "You saved my life and fucking ruined it in the same heartbeat." I choke on the lump in my throat and grit my teeth against the pressure building in my chest. All I want to do is scream.

"This isn't a conversation to have right now."

I laugh too loudly. This isn't a conversation we should have, period. I shouldn't be talking to him at all. Realistically, I know that. But getting my head and my heart on the same page these days is...challenging.

"What conversation should we have right now?"

He sighs, though it doesn't sound irritated exactly. Sad maybe? "What are you doing?"

I hum a pitchy tone, hugging the tequila bottle to my chest. "Making a new best friend. His name is Jose Cuervo."

"Hmm. I have a feeling you're not going to appreciate that particular friendship later on."

"I'm not thinking about that," I ramble, grabbing a throw pillow off the couch and lying on the floor, tucking it under my head.

"What are you thinking about?" he murmurs.

I close my eyes, inhaling slowly, then exhale a heavy sigh. "Too fucking much, *your majesty*."

THE DEVIL'S TRIALS

A giggle slips free, and I slap my hand to my forehead, making my head spin.

"I understand more than I'd like to."

His subdued tone makes my chest ache, and I sniffle softly, whispering, "I miss you. That's really what I'm thinking about—all the damn time. That, or how much I *shouldn't* be missing you and all the reasons why."

There's a beat of silence before he says, "You're right," and fuck if that doesn't feel like a dagger to the chest.

What was I expecting him to say? That he misses me too?

Don't be so naive, I chide myself.

"I know that," I bite back.

"You should go to sleep."

"So you can invade my dream?" I shoot at him.

He exhales a soft laugh, but his tone isn't joking when he says, "Because you sound tired."

Anger bubbles in my chest, rising swiftly. "Careful now. Don't want to make it seem like you give a shit about a weak little human."

I sit up and immediately wish I hadn't when the room starts spinning and bile coats my throat.

"I answered your call, didn't I?"

I hate the way his words steal the breath from my lungs. I press my lips together, my pulse thrumming. Instead of fumbling through a response, I drag myself upright and shuffle through the apartment to my room, where I fall into bed.

The line is quiet as I pull the blankets around me, willing my stomach to settle as I stare at the swirling ceiling.

"I've never been so physically and emotionally exhausted and yet so wired I can't sleep."

"The tequila should help," he remarks dryly, and I almost laugh at how normal our conversation feels right now.

I close my eyes, trying to convince my muscles to relax as I roll onto my side and hug a pillow to my chest. "Will you stay with me?"

"Do you remember what I said to you before we stormed Lucia's compound two weeks ago?"

My breath hitches as I'm transported back to that day.

"For as long as you want me, I'll be by your side. The gates of hell couldn't keep me away from you."

I swallow past the lump in my throat, thankful he can't hear the race of my pulse. "Seems that's exactly what they're doing," I murmur before I can stop myself.

"Need I remind you that you're the one who left Seattle?" His tone is level, unbothered, which irks me further.

"Yeah, after you went all 'it's not you, it's me' on me. What should I have done, Xander? Bowed to you like that room full of demons did?"

There's a gruff sound on the other end of the phone, something akin to a growl that brings the warmth back to my cheeks.

"We had a plan," I rush to add. "When that was derailed, I panicked. I did what I had to do to protect my sanity." I hug the pillow tighter and admit, "I'm hanging on by a thread most days and I make no apologies for what I've done to keep my head above water."

"I'm not asking you to."

"Good."

"Good," he echoes with a hint of amusement.

I sigh. Even this ridiculous banter is making me long for what we had before everything went to hell. "I should...I'm going to hang up now."

"Okay," he says.

The pang of disappointment that surfaces when he doesn't try to continue the conversation makes me blink my eyes open. I reach for my phone, my finger hovering over the button to end the call.

"Camille?"

My heart lurches, and I whisper back, "Xander?"

"Sweet dreams, *mo shíorghrá*."

I'm caught off guard by the rush of tears that burn my eyes, and I quickly disconnect, kicking myself for calling him to begin with.

One of these days, I'll learn to fight my weakness.

Better yet, I'll conquer it altogether.

Thirteen
Xander

Since reaching Camille in the dreamscape two nights ago, I've had a curiosity about another, newer connection. Since learning I can dream walk without being close to my target, there's a chance my other abilities—like tracking—are enhanced, and I can track down Harper.

Before discovering our relationship, I had no inkling of our shared blood. Perhaps if I had any link to my human family, I would've felt a bond with Harper before I discovered she was my half-sister, but Lucia ensured I never did. There's an absence where I expect to feel resentment, and I shrug it off.

Grabbing my jacket from the foyer closet, I nearly run into Blake coming through the front door.

"Where have you been?" I ask, pulling on my jacket.

"Checking on the bar," he explains. He hasn't spent much time there since everything went down with Lucia. I suppose he has employees taking care of his business while he's not around, though I've never asked.

"Everything okay?"

He nods. "Where are you headed?"

I slide my hands into my pockets, preparing myself to have him try to warn me from going to see Harper.

Instead, he spins his key ring on his finger with a grin. "Let's go."

Blake drives toward a suburban neighborhood on the outskirts of the city, while I sit in the passenger seat with my eyes closed.

I focus my breathing, pushing my senses out until something like an internal GPS flares to life in my gut, singing in my blood with gentle vibrations. I press my lips together at the new sensation, giving Blake directions as I follow the invisible guide from connecting to the Gilbert bloodline. It's as if I'm seeing the road light up in my mind, and the surrounding details get clearer the closer we get to Harper.

Ten minutes later, we turn onto a dark, quiet street, and the faint sounds of fighting reach me. Blake pulls over, and I'm out of the car before he has it in park. I find Harper in an abandoned park, facing off with a group of demons.

Her heart pounds as she surveys the scene, her dagger gripped tightly in her hand. Her opponents are low-level demons who appear human, save for their all-black eyes. They're practically salivating as they close in on her, and a growl tears from my throat as an odd sense of possessiveness comes over me.

I'm moving in an instant, putting myself between the group of demons and Harper.

"Get the fuck out of my way, Kane," she grumbles from behind me, and feeling her fist connecting with my shoulder blade makes my lips twitch. Even when I'm saving her life, she wants to fight me.

I ignore Harper as the demons in front of me exchange wary glances with one another. "You know who I am?" I check, and once they all nod, I continue, "This hunter is off limits. Is that clear?"

There is hesitation, but slowly they each acknowledge what I've said, though none of them appear too happy about it. Confusion and resentment roll off them in dark, smoky waves, making their expressions grim, though I don't acknowledge it.

"Good. Now leave."

The demons disperse in a matter of seconds, and I turn to face Harper, who's sliding her dagger back into the holder at her thigh. When she lifts her gaze to mine, her eyes are narrowed, and she crosses her arms over her chest.

At least she isn't pointing her dagger at me. I'd like to think that means we've made progress in the her wanting to kill me department.

"What the hell was that?" she demands, her pulse still racing.

I dip my face to meet her gaze. "I think you mean 'thank you.'"

"Fuck no. I needed that hunt to expedite my graduation."

My brows lift. "You were going to take on all six demons yourself?"

She scowls. "I'll try not to be insulted by the surprise in your voice."

"My apologies for evidently underestimating you."

"You can take your apologies and get the fuck out of here."

THE DEVIL'S TRIALS

I ignore that and say, "Aren't hunters supposed to work in pairs?"

Several beats of silence pass between us before she says, "I'm not working...officially."

"Interesting," I muse.

Harper's posture straightens as she glares at me. "How am I supposed to hunt demons if you have them refusing to engage with me?" She exhales an annoyed sigh, letting her arms fall back to her sides. "I mean, it's certainly not impossible, but it's far less fun when they're running away because they're more scared of pissing you off than being hunted by me. You see my problem?"

I press my lips together in an attempt to mask my laugh, and she shoots me a murderous glare. I hold up my hands in defense. "And here I thought you'd be grateful to have your big brother's protection."

Harper glowers at me, and the fury in her eyes almost makes me regret baiting her. Almost. "Don't hold your breath." She cocks her head to the side, her lips twisting into a cold smile. "Actually, go ahead."

I can't help but chuckle. "Oh, come on, Harper. You don't truly want me dead."

Hunter-in-training or not, Harper is still human. There *should* be some instinctive part of her that recognizes me as a danger, and yet it's clear she isn't afraid of me. If it were anyone else, that'd be a problem I would swiftly be fixing, but with her...I'm glad she doesn't cower or tiptoe around me. It's entertaining, to say the least. It also gives me hope that perhaps down the line we can have some kind of relationship that doesn't involve her itching to dagger me with an obsidian blade.

"No?" she challenges.

I arch a brow, shrugging. "That would be far more convincing if your dagger was in your hand instead of strapped to your thigh."

She rolls her eyes. "Whatever. Aren't you supposed to be off ruling the demons or something?"

"Or something," I say wryly, not offering any details. Harper is my enemy, same as I'm hers, and information is a powerful thing that I can't let slip into the wrong hands.

The distrust in her eyes claws at my chest. It feels wrong. More so is knowing there's little I can do to change it.

"Are you stalking me now?" she asks in a cold tone. "How'd you find me here, anyway?"

"Coincidence?" I offer, and she shoots me a dry look before I continue, "I found you, because as much as you'd prefer to ignore it, we share blood, which ties us to one another."

The color drains from her face, and she steps back, as if on instinct. "What the fuck? So, you have some weird ability to track me?"

I hesitate before answering, "To put it simply."

A muscle ticks along her jaw for a moment before she blows out a breath, fogging the air in front of her face as she glances around and shakes her head. When her gaze returns to me, she says, "Were you looking for me then?"

I nod. "It's not exactly easy with your entourage of hunters. I've had to be very careful and make sure you weren't with any of them. How'd you give them the slip?"

She crosses her arms again. "Don't worry about it."

"You're concerned about my interference when it comes to graduating your precious organization, but ditching the team doesn't seem very conducive to your fast-track plan. Sounds like self-sabotage to me."

"That's funny, I don't remember asking you," she shoots back.

I let silence hang between us for several beats. "What's your target?"

"What?"

"How many demons do you need to kill to graduate?"

Her brows knit. "I...Why? Going to round them up for me?"

I shrug, the corner of my mouth kicking up. "Maybe." The thought of bringing Harper onto my council shoots to the forefront of my thoughts. The idea is wild, and has never been done in the history of demonic monarchies. I started my to-be reign by making history...perhaps I should continue to.

Plus, having someone on my side from my own bloodline could be beneficial. If nothing else, I'd have her carry out punishment under my rule to save me from doing it while earning points with her organization. We'd need to figure out the logistics of how the demons would be rounded up for her to hunt without raising suspicion from the royal guard or the hunters.

They will need to have committed an act of treason so I can justify their executions.

"That doesn't make any sense," Harper says, unimpressed. "You're the king of demons. They're your people—you're meant to protect them."

"I'm not king yet." I'm not sure what possesses me to add, "Have you and Camille not spoken? I would've thought she'd report to you when I saw her after the first trial."

Harper crosses her arms again—she does that a lot around me. "Of course we have. But she's been a little preoccupied with being sick. She's been in bed for two days, probably since you saw her."

My brows lift. "What—?"

"I don't mean to break up the playdate at the park," Blake interrupts as he approaches, "but you shouldn't be out in the open like this." His attention travels to Harper. "Hello, love."

"Bite me."

"Hmm. Tempting."

She scowls, reaching for her dagger again, but I step in front of her, snaring her attention away from wanting to kill Blake.

"What's wrong with Camille?"

Her expression softens slightly at the mention of her best friend. "She's sick with some brutal flu, but I'm sure Noah will take care of her."

A growl tears from my throat at the thought of that damn hunter anywhere near her.

Harper rolls her eyes, snapping her fingers in my face. "You don't get to go all alpha male, jackass."

Blake whistles under his breath as I back away, barking, "Go home," at Harper. "We'll finish this conversation later."

I don't wait for her response before going to the car with Blake on my heels. He takes one look at me and sighs. "We're going to New York, aren't we?"

Fourteen
Camille

I shoot upright and nearly fall out of bed with dizzying nausea, then stumble to the bathroom across the hall with my hand clamped over my mouth. Getting the lid of the toilet up just in time, I fall to my knees and empty my stomach into the bowl. I heave until there's only bile left, my throat raw and my temples throbbing. My skin feels hot and cold at the same time. I'm sweating and shivering, and I feel as if I've been hit by a truck.

Groaning, I rock back until I'm sitting on the floor against the wall adjacent to the toilet. I tip my head back and press a hand to my clammy forehead as I take slow, measured breaths in through my nose and out through my mouth.

I don't know how long I stay there before I manage to crawl back to bed, and when Noah comes banging on my door sometime later, I barely find the strength to pick up my phone and text him. I'm not going to let a little sickness get in the way of training—he'd never let me live it down.

> Be right out. Just need a quick shower.

It's probably just me, but I can't help worrying that I reek of vomit.

He calls me immediately, and when I answer and try to speak, my voice is all but gone.

"What's the matter with you?"

"Nothing," I croak. "Give me ten minutes." I pull the phone away from my ear as I'm gripped with a coughing fit. I squeeze my eyes shut against the pressure in my temples. My eyes burn, and I will the bile rising in my throat to recede.

"Are you sick?"

"I am the vision of health," I lie, entirely unconvincing. Still, I add, "I'll be right out."

THE DEVIL'S TRIALS

"The hell you will. I'm not letting you train in this condition. Stay exactly where you are. I'll see you later."

"Noah—"

"I mean it, Camille. I'm not arguing with you." He hangs up before I can, in fact, attempt to argue. If only I had the strength to get out of bed, I might try to fight him on it. Instead I leave my phone on the nightstand and roll over, curling into myself as my head continues to throb.

I lose track of the day, and the next time I blink my eyes open, I find Noah sitting in a chair at the end of my bed. He must've dragged it in here from the living room.

"What are you doing?" I ask, my voice still ragged.

He glances up from the book in his lap, and the corner of his mouth kicks up. "Sleeping Beauty wakes," he teases, nodding toward the nightstand. "I brought you some stuff."

I look over and find a water bottle, cold and flu meds, cough drops, and my favorite chocolate. My chest swells, and I press my lips together before I can let out a sound of surprise. "Thank you," I finally say, glancing at him again. "What time is it?"

He checks his watch. "Just after two in the afternoon."

My brows lift. "How long have you been here?"

"A couple hours. I stopped at the drugstore on my way back from Ballard this morning."

"And you let yourself into my apartment."

He nods. "Your dad gave me a spare key when you moved in."

I exhale a humorless laugh, shaking my head. "Of course he did."

"You should try to eat something."

I close my eyes again. "Not hungry."

"I understand, but you need to keep your strength up, so what can I get you?"

I keep my eyes closed, pulling the blankets up around me. "You don't have to take care of me, Noah," I mumble into my pillow as I hug it to the side of my face, enjoying the cool fabric against my flushed skin.

"Would you prefer Scott be here? I can call him, if you want."

I groan. "No, I don't want him to worry about me. Besides, I'm fine."

"You're sticking with that party line?"

"Don't call my dad, Noah."

"Fine, I won't. But tell me what you want to eat."

I pry my eyes open, squinting at him. "Are you going to hand feed it to me, too?"

He laughs, then pats my leg and stands, leaving his book on the chair. "I'm going to make you some toast. Try to stay awake for the next five minutes, yeah?"

I stifle a yawn. "No promises."

I spend the next few days in bed, sleeping on and off for hours at a time. My dad stopped by to bring food yesterday. I couldn't avoid him finding out I was sick when he texted and asked me to come over for dinner. I guess I could've lied, but I felt like I'd done enough of that lately and it hasn't gotten me anywhere good.

After managing to stomach a piece of toast with peanut butter, I take a heavy dose of cough syrup and a painkiller for my headache, then doze back off.

I haven't been able to kick this wicked fever, and the sweats and chills happening at the same time have to be the worst part.

I'm not sure how long I manage to stay asleep this time, and when I open my eyes, my vision is blurry. Noah is sitting on the end of my bed, and—wait, no…I blink until the dark figure comes into focus. I must still be asleep, because it isn't Noah sitting there.

It's Xander.

Too many thoughts attempt to process at once, making my already fuzzy head inundated with static. I squeeze my eyes shut and—

"I'm here, *mo shíorghrá*." His voice is soft, and the bed shifts as he moves closer. "Open your eyes."

I blink until his face is clear, swallowing against the fire in my throat. "What…are you doing here?" My voice is low and hoarse, my temples still pounding with pressure. Even if I wanted to throw him out, there's zero chance I have the strength. I barely have the energy to force myself into a sitting position.

His gaze stays locked on my face. "Harper told me you were sick."

I frown, reaching for the glass of water on my nightstand and downing half of it. "I didn't realize the two of you were on speaking terms."

He inhales through his teeth. "More or less."

Setting the glass down, I look his way again and say, "You didn't need to come."

THE DEVIL'S TRIALS

Xander lowers his gaze, his shoulders rising and falling with a sigh, as if his being here is as hard for him as it is for me. "I did. I had to know... that you were okay."

I ignore the way his words kick up my pulse as I cling to my mask of indifference. "Never better."

"Camille—"

"Why didn't you use that dreamscape trick again? I've been sleeping more than I've been awake."

"I just needed to see you. For real."

My eyes narrow. "How did you even get in here?"

"I stopped at the office in the lobby and got a key from the building manager. Nice guy."

I have a feeling he didn't just hand it over willingly, but I don't have the energy to push that line of questioning. "You don't get to just show up here. Or show up in my dreams. It's not fair." I turn my face away, coughing into my shoulder until my temples are throbbing again.

"I know," he says once the room is silent. "You deserve so much more than what I've given you. More than I could ever give you. But when Harper said that you were sick and Noah would look after you, something in me snapped." Xander shifts closer, and my breath catches when his hand lands on my knee over the blankets.

The butterflies I thought were long dead flutter to life in my stomach as I watch Xander's thumb brush back and forth. Even with layers of fabric between our skin, I feel him like I've felt no one else. He's ingrained in me somehow—I think he always will be.

"That sounds awfully like jealousy," I point out, feeling far too glib about it. I'm going to blame the fever.

His lips twitch. "Feels like it too, and I don't much care for it."

"I thought losing the human part of you would change things."

He nods. "It did. As it turns out, I don't need a soul to feel certain things. I guess I should've known that after being friends with Blake all these years. He's the most emotional person I've ever met, and there's no chance that bastard has a soul."

I sit in silence, trying to keep up with everything he's throwing at me. I haven't let myself consider that Xander could have feelings for me without a soul, but hearing this, I can't stop myself from thinking about the possibility.

"As conflicted as I am most days, my feelings for you haven't changed, no matter how hard I fight them."

I immediately want to kick myself. I'm being too vulnerable around him, but I can't seem to stop. It's like it's always been—feeling connected to him, *longing* for him, even after all he's done. Even when I know I absolutely shouldn't.

So why the hell do I still feel this way?

He squeezes my knee. "You can't fight the soulmate bond."

Soulmate.

Xander's words are a violent kick to the gut, knocking the air from my lungs in a vicious *whoosh*.

My rib cage ignites with fire, my eyes springing tears as I stare at the most powerful demon in the world sitting on my bed.

Soulmate.

"You're my…" I trail off, my voice cracking as my vision blurs.

Soulmate.

My heart cleaves in two as an unbearable weight falls onto my chest. I swallow hard, trying to dislodge the lump in my throat as I grip the blanket in my lap until my knuckles turn white. I try to calm my racing thoughts, but can't make sense of anything through the fog in my head.

I haven't heard the term outside romance books or considered the possibility of soulmates being real. And yet, there's a burst of warmth in my gut that tells me it's true. "What does this mean?"

The pain etched in his features digs deep into my chest, only made worse when he says, "I don't…Our bond was broken when I killed Lucia and lost my soul."

I try to take a deep breath, but my lungs constrict, and I choke on a gasp. The room spins, and the bit of food I managed to eat earlier threatens to make a nasty reappearance.

"That's what I've felt," I whisper and lift my hand to my chest, pressing my palm against the pounding there. As crazy as the notion of us being connected by an otherworldly bond is, I can't deny the certainty that seizes me. "There's been this…physical absence of something I can't put my finger on, no matter how hard I try. That must be it."

"I'm sorry." He pulls his hand back, and I feel the loss of his touch more profoundly than it seems should be possible. "You don't deserve the pain of—"

THE DEVIL'S TRIALS

"Loving you?" I blurt, my chest seconds away from bursting with all the emotions at war in my tattered heart. "Believe me, there are many times I've wished I could stop."

Is the soulmate bond what's kept me from being able to walk away from Xander even when I know I should?

I resent the idea, especially when this isn't the first time I've been forced to face the possibility that my connection to Xander might be what I thought it was.

I pull my knees to my chest, wrapping my arms around my legs. The urge to bury my face in my hands or scream into a pillow has tears spilling down my cheeks before I can blink them away. Here I am, once again having the rug pulled out from under me, questioning everything I believed about my feelings for Xander.

"How long have you known?" I ask in a low voice. I can't hide it if I tried—I'm fucking drained.

Xander sighs softly. "I think we should save this conversation for when you're well."

My jaw clenches, and I shake my head. "*When*, Xander?" My voice cracks. "When did you know we were soulmates? Was it after the first time we kissed? After we slept together?"

He looks away for a minute that seems to last forever before his eyes meet mine again, and something inside me cracks wide open when he says, "I knew the moment my mother was going to kill you."

I stare at Xander, my heart pounding in my throat and my stomach twisted in so many knots, I fear the nausea is going to lead me to vomit as I try to wrap my head around that. The room falls silent, save for the beating of my heart—it's so intense I can feel it in my throat.

He discovered we were soulmates moments before he lost his soul. He was faced with the harsh reality of losing me at the hands of his own mother, and something must have snapped into place.

I try to think back to that horrific day, to recall what I was feeling. If perhaps part of me knew it then, too. But everything is dark and fuzzy and painful, and I don't want to feel any of it. Paired with the rush of emotions, I feel as if I'm having an out-of-body experience. Like maybe this isn't real, just another dream he's appearing in.

Xander's gaze holds mine, and with each second that ticks by, I find it harder to keep the space between us. Before I know it, I'm shifting my legs so I can move closer and wrap my arms around his neck. His arms come around me without hesitation, and I bury my face in his chest, the rapid beat of his own heart against my ear making my eyes burn. He slides his fingers into my hair, cradling my head, and I have no idea what's happening or what it means, just that I don't want it to end. Because learning about the bond between us also means knowing it was destroyed when Xander lost his soul.

And that's fucking devastating.

"What does this mean?" I ask again, my voice small, hesitant. I'm torn between wanting to know more and just living with the knowledge I've already gained. What else is there to know? I'm not sure it even matters now—I can't be soulmates with someone who doesn't have a soul. I guess I'm naively hoping he'll say otherwise.

Xander's chest rises and falls as he sighs. "You already know."

Of course I do. And yet, my stomach still sinks.

"Right," I whisper.

Demons don't have souls. They *can't* have soulmates.

The hunter organization would have us all believe that demons can't experience something as pure as love, but I don't believe it. Blake is the most obvious evidence that demons can feel and care and *love*. I've seen it in his loyalty to Xander, and even in the way he's spoken to me.

Blake is not a monster, and neither is Xander—not to the people who are important to them.

Xander guides my head away from his chest, tipping it up and pressing his lips to my forehead. I close my eyes, pulling in a shaky breath as the tension in my temples softens, then fades completely.

I pull back, breathing, "What was that?"

He blinks, his expression confused as he shakes his head.

"My headache. You kissed me, and it's just…gone."

His brows lift. "I don't think I've done anything like that before," he muses. "It must be another development in my power. Demons are fallen angels, after all. I suppose healing abilities make sense to some degree."

"Maybe we are still connected somehow," I offer, my skin tingling at the thought.

His fingers slip free of my hair as he shifts away, his jaw set tight. "If that's the case, you'll be in even more danger as I work through the trials to ascend the throne."

THE DEVIL'S TRIALS

I swallow, my throat raw from coughing for days. "Good thing I'm in demon hunter training, then." I sigh, shaking my head. "I never thought I'd say that."

Xander's expression darkens. "It's more complicated than that. You'll be a target, a liability."

His words slice deep into my chest, feeling more like an attack than they should. I resent the way my chin quivers, and I clench my jaw against the tears threatening to form. I loathe how weak I feel in this moment, in front of him.

Maybe he was right—now isn't the time to talk about this.

"I think you should go," I tell him, unable to meet his gaze.

"You're upset," he observes, his brows drawn together.

"I'm sick," I say instead of admitting the hurt gnawing at me. It's not untrue, though I am better physically than I was a few days ago. "I just need to sleep," I add, hoping he'll take the hint and leave.

Xander nods but doesn't move from his spot on my bed.

I sigh despite the twisted part of me that finds comfort in his proximity. It begs the question of a lingering connection, even in the absence of Xander's soul. Maybe if I was more awake, clearer-headed, I'd ask about the possibility, but, instead, I say, "You're not going anywhere, are you?" My eyelids grow heavier, staying closed longer with each blink.

He tilts his head to the side, surveying my face. "I'm not leaving until you're feeling better."

Left with no energy to fight him, I stretch my legs out and pull the blankets up around me as I try to get comfortable. "Stay out of my dreams," I grumble at him, turning onto my side to face away from him, and close my eyes as I exhale a slow breath.

I think he chuckles, but I've sunk too far into the warm, comforting cloud of unconsciousness to hear his soft reply.

Fifteen
Xander

Camille is right. I shouldn't be here. I should have left—no, I shouldn't have come at all. I should be building my strength for my next trial, not using it to cure a human headache.

Except, I couldn't stop myself from coming. I had to see Camille, to know for myself that she was okay.

Even now, there's some innate anchor that stops me from walking out of her apartment and getting on a plane to Seattle. Luckily, Blake has connections at a local private airport, which made getting here discreetly possible. Public transport isn't ideal with a government agency actively hunting me.

My attention drifts around the room, taking in the space that Camille hasn't done much to personalize. She's only been here a couple of weeks, and I'm sure has spent most of that time training before falling ill. So the basic bed, dresser, nightstand setup makes sense, and the chair near the end of the bed appears to have been brought in from the dining space in the other room. The thought of Noah sitting there, being with Camille, makes my molars grind.

Because he's better for her than you are, Lucia's voice croons at the back of my head, driving the torment deeper into my bones.

I recoil from it, rolling my shoulders to force the tension out, and check my phone for any messages from Blake. When I don't find any, I send him a quick update, and stand from the bed, walking out to the kitchen to see what I can find to make for Camille. Something tells me she hasn't eaten much these last few days.

After scouring her kitchen, I make a plate with avocado toast, bacon, and strawberries, pairing that with a glass of orange juice and a cup of lemon tea. I look up at the sound of her phone chiming and find it on the coffee table in the living room.

THE DEVIL'S TRIALS

My eyes narrow at the message from Noah.

> I'm about to leave Ballard. Need me to grab anything on the way and stop by?

I type out a response and hit send without thinking about it. I'm not about to have this prick interrupt my visit and attempt to throw me out. As much as I loathe the arrogant hunter, killing him would hurt Camille. It's the only thing refraining me from doing so.

> Feeling much better. No need to stop by. I have everything I need.

I switch her phone to silent and leave it in the kitchen.

Carrying breakfast to Camille's room, I set everything on her nightstand, turning and brushing my fingers along her cheek.

"You need to eat something," I murmur, tucking her hair behind her ear. Her skin is still warm, but I think she's kicked the fever.

She stirs, making a soft noise that twists my heart. The urge to crawl into the bed and pull Camille into my arms makes me oddly lightheaded, and I frown at the sensation, trying to will it away. It feels dangerously weak, as if I've lost control of myself in her presence. I don't want to think about what that could mean, though there's a pit of dread in my gut that tells me I already know. When I had a soul, Camille brought out the human part of me. Now that I'm a pure demon...she makes me weak.

That should be cause for concern. It *should* drive me to put distance between us, because the last thing I need in the wake of my trials is weakness. And yet, I can't bring myself to leave her. Not in this condition, not right after learning the truth about our connection.

I'm a monster but I don't *want* to be when it comes to her.

If that's the only piece of my humanity that remains, I'm going to cling to it for as long as I can, and hope to hell it doesn't sabotage my ascension. And the voice inside my head that says I can't have both—Camille and the throne—is one I want to prove wrong.

That desire doesn't eliminate the truth of her being a target of very dangerous and powerful demons. Even without a soul, I still love her, ruined soulmate bond be damned. And for something we didn't know existed until it was broken, I refuse to give it so much power over me—over *us*.

Camille blinks her eyes open, and when they connect with mine, the pace of her heart kicks up.

"You're here," she says, her voice hoarse and low, sleep clinging to it. "I thought it might've been a dream."

My lips curve upward. "I'm here." I nod toward the food. "Eat."

Her brows tug closer. "Bossy."

I exhale a short laugh. "I'm trying to take care of you."

"Are you going to feed it to me too?"

"You'd like that, wouldn't you?"

So easily we've fallen into amusing banter, and I delight in the way her pulse quickens as she reads into the question.

She glances over at the plate of food, smiling faintly. "Thank you."

"You're welcome." I sit on the side of her bed as she shifts upright and scoots toward the headboard, crossing her legs.

"Did you eat?" she asks, reaching for a strawberry.

I shake my head. "I'm not worried about me."

She frowns. "Do you want—"

"You need to eat and regain your strength so you get better," I cut in smoothly, keeping my eyes on her.

Pausing mid-chew, her gaze connects with mine. She finishes and swallows before she says, "You should be preparing for your trials not here being a caretaker for a human with the flu."

I pick up the glass of orange juice and hold it out to her. "They're not really something you can prepare for. I'm fine right here."

She takes the glass and sips on the juice. "Xander, I don't have the energy to argue or fight with you. What are we doing?"

"Pretending," I offer. I'm aware of how quickly this conversation can descend into Camille attempting to throw me out, and I'd much rather avoid that. I'm not going anywhere.

"We've been here before. You know as well as I do that whatever pretending we do is limited. We can only ignore who we are for so long, and the longer we do, the worse it is for both of us."

I lick my lips before asking her, "Is that why you want me to leave?"

Her gaze falls to her lap. "You know exactly why."

I do but, "I want to hear you say it."

She exhales a heavy sigh. "We went our separate ways after you killed Lucia. You being here, taking care of me, it's nice but it's also uncomfortable. A painful reminder of what we can never truly have, save for these fleeting, stolen moments that get more dangerous each time."

THE DEVIL'S TRIALS

I nod my agreement.

She continues in a quieter voice, "Your part of the soulmate bond might've vanished with your soul, but I don't think mine did. So this, you being here, feels like the universe is punishing me for something I didn't even do. Like you killing the queen of hell disrupted some kind of balance, and I'm paying for it. Same as me almost dying at the demon queen's hands and you losing your soul to save me has you paying for it.

"If we are—*were*—soulmates, it definitely feels like we're being punished for breaking that bond, even though we had no idea it existed."

Her words stir something in my chest, and I frown briefly. "I'm not sure what to say to that."

She shakes her head, setting the glass back on the nightstand and instead of eating the food I brought in, she slides back under the blankets, meeting my gaze. Her eyes are tired, drooping more with each blink. "You don't need to say anything. We both have things we have to live with." The sound of defeat in her voice weaves through my rib cage and strikes my heart with a power that steals my breath as I watch her slip away from me all over again.

Sixteen
Camille

I startle awake to the sound of a door slamming shut. Groggy as I am, my pulse races as I sit up and get out of bed. The room sways, reminding me that I've been mostly bedridden for days, and I grit my teeth against the swimming in my head.

"Get the fuck out of here before I do everyone a favor and kill you instead." Noah's venom-filled voice forces me to keep moving, using the wall to keep steady enough to make it out to the main living area where he's facing off with Xander. My gaze bounces between the two, then drops to the dagger clutched so tightly in Noah's fist that his knuckles are white. Panic seizes me, and somehow I'm moving forward and putting myself between them with my back to Xander.

"Stop," I say to Noah. "Please."

His jaw is sharp, his expression wild and dark with the promise of violence against the demon behind me. Blood rushes through my ears and heat seems to fill my pores as my heart beats erratically. There's no chance I'm strong enough to stop them from fighting each other if that's what's going to happen—so that *can't* happen.

"Get out of my way, Cam," Noah barks, his gaze locked on Xander.

I shove against the hunter's solid chest, but he doesn't budge. "Noah, *stop.* You're not going to brawl in my living room."

Finally, his eyes drop to my face, and he says, "Is this why you haven't answered my texts since yesterday?"

I frown, not remembering the last time I even looked at my phone. The days have blurred together. I'm not sure how long Xander's been here—maybe a day? Two? I've been so out of it, sleeping on and off, I feel as if I've entered the twilight zone by this point.

He doesn't wait for me to answer. "When you didn't pick up the last two times I called to check in, I got worried so I came over and knocked.

THE DEVIL'S TRIALS

You didn't answer, so I let myself in and found this prick in your kitchen." His eyes flick between mine. "Tell me you didn't know he was here."

I press my lips together. I'm not going to lie to him.

"Son of a bitch, Camille."

When I wince at the sharpness of Noah's voice, Xander moves closer, a deep growl rumbling in his chest. "Watch your tone," he warns.

"Go to hell," Noah seethes.

I sway on my feet, closing my eyes at the dizziness filling my head. "Please stop this." I'm speaking to both of them.

"You need to sit down before you fall over." Noah's voice sounds far away, echoing as though he's talking to me from the bottom of a well.

I can't seem to make my eyes open as my breathing quickens, and I reach out for anything to steady myself when my legs start shaking.

Xander catches me around the waist as I fall against him.

My ears ring, my throat seemingly clogged with cotton, and I feel uncomfortably warm and clammy. He gets me to the couch, then there's a cool cloth pressed to my forehead and a glass of water held at my lips.

I manage to pry my eyes open to find Xander sitting next to me and holding the cloth, while Noah perches on the coffee table, tipping the water glass back so I can drink from it.

A few minutes later, I've cooled down and feel marginally better. Still weak, but the feeling of collapsing and passing out is gone.

Silence stretches between the three of us, though the tension between the demon and hunter hasn't gone away. I doubt it ever will. I still don't know how to feel about Xander being here, which was only made more complicated by Noah's drop in, and if I was smart, I'd take this opportunity to kick Xander out.

At least I'd have Noah to back me up and physically remove him if needed, yet the words refuse to form on my tongue. Part of me wants him here even though I know deep down it's the wrong choice. My heart strongly disagrees.

Noah's phone chimes, and he sits back, pulling it out of his black jean jacket pocket and cursing at the screen. "I have to go." He sets the water glass on the table beside him, his eyes shifting briefly to Xander before returning to me.

"It's okay. I'm fine," I attempt to assure him.

His eyes narrow slightly. "I shouldn't leave you here with him."

"I'd never hurt her," Xander chimes in before I can respond, his voice low, as if he's holding himself back from biting Noah's head off.

Noah scoffs. "It's a little fucking late for that, *your majesty*."

"*Okay*," I cut in sharply. "That's enough."

Noah stands, keeping his eyes on me. "Keep your phone with you," is all he says before stalking to the door and slamming it shut behind him.

"It's always so nice to see him," Xander remarks dryly.

I sigh, falling back against the cushions. "What did you say to him before I woke up?"

"Nothing. He came in, saw me, and demanded I leave, as if he owned the place—and you."

The air between us feels charged, and I shift away from him as my nerves have the hair on the back of my neck prickling. I can't forget that, at his core, Xander is a predator. He'll be king of the underworld soon enough—a monster. Even when he's sitting in my living room or making me tea to help me feel better. He's a walking contradiction to what a demon is supposed to be, and what I know them to be. Which makes our connection even more difficult to navigate.

Xander's eyes flick between mine as he surveys my face. His attention is all-consuming, and I have no room to deny that it still affects me. "Are you afraid of me?" he asks, and my eyes narrow at his curious tone.

"Should I be?" I ask, fishing for *anything*—a speck of reassurance, a hint that holding out hope for us isn't as completely insane as I fear it is.

"Some would think so, but I hope you aren't."

Emotion clogs my throat, elevating the confusion filling me with the urge to run away from this interaction. "You do?"

He dips his face, lowering his voice. "I hope that whatever has happened doesn't change that you know, even with everything you aren't certain about, that you will never come to harm at my hands."

I turn my face away again, blinking to clear my vision, and bite my tongue as I will myself not to shed a tear in front of him. I don't know how to tell him that Noah is right—he's *already* hurt me. Because how can I do that when what he did to hurt me is also what saved my life?

It takes me a short eternity to find my voice. "I find myself questioning what I think I know too often these days."

He chuckles as if he understands, and for a moment—a split fucking second of pure bliss—I forget it all.

THE DEVIL'S TRIALS

He's cooking me dinner. Kissing me for the first time. Keeping my anxiety at bay on the Seattle Great Wheel. Bringing me to new levels of pleasure and making me feel like the only person in the world.

All too quickly, those warm flashes of memories disappear, and I'm left with the cold, hard truth that we will never be those people again. We can't be. And hell, I wish I'd known before we kissed for the last time, because it's all I can do not to think about it right now.

My breath gets lodged in my throat as Xander lifts a hand to my face, capturing a rogue bit of hair between his fingers. I don't breathe as he gently tucks it behind my ear, letting his touch linger at the pulse along the side of my neck.

I resent the shiver that zips through me, and even more, the desire to lean into him. I should move away and put distance between us, but I don't move. My face heats and my lungs scream for air as I continue staring at his chest.

"Breathe, *mo shíorghrá.*"

My body obeys his gentle command, and I inhale deeply, greedily sucking in air until my chest stops burning. I shake my head, as if that will clear the dizziness. "You really should go now." There's a trace of desperation creeping into my voice. I can feel my control slipping with each passing moment as the pressure between my ribs intensifies.

Xander tilts his head to the side, and I think I see a flicker of disappointment in his gaze when he asks, "Do you want me to leave?"

No. "Yes."

"Hmm. I don't quite believe you."

"That sounds like a you problem."

His lips twitch. "There's that snark of yours."

I ignore that, instead saying, "Why are you being so difficult?"

"Because I'm not ready to leave," he answers simply.

"*Why?*"

His eyes meet mine. "Because I miss you."

I miss you.

The words land hard and fast, stealing the air from my lungs. There's no hiding the way my pulse races as I play those three little words over and over, resenting the spark of hope they ignite in my heart.

"How is that possible?" I whisper instead of doing what I should do, which is walk away.

My feet are blocks of concrete—I'm not moving anywhere. Would Xander stop me if I tried to leave? A twisted part of me hopes he would. That he'd fight for me and for us.

"Losing my soul didn't destroy the part of me that cares for you." He exhales a humorless laugh. "It would make this a lot easier."

I bite my bottom lip to keep it from trembling. There are too many emotions going to war inside me, the overwhelm has me close to tears, and I fucking hate that. "What does that mean?"

He lets silence stretch between us for a moment before he sighs. The hopelessness in that sound punches a hole through my chest. And then he says, "My heart is human and it remains yours." His expression softens, and that's my only warning before he's reaching for me, his hands on my hips tugging me into him.

I suck in a breath before his lips crash against mine. I lose myself in seconds, and the only thing that exists is him. His touch and his lips on mine, damning me to want him even now. Even when it hurts so deeply.

Xander makes the sound of the back of his throat that makes my heart slam against my rib cage, and suddenly I'm not sure if my hands on his chest, gripping his shirt until it's wrinkled, are to push him away or pull him closer.

A strangled whimper escapes my lips, and he swallows the sound as his tongue darts into my mouth, sweeping along mine. He deepens the kiss, tipping my head back with one hand while the other remains curled around my hip. My eyes slip shut as I'm overcome with sensations, our lips moving in sync, our tongues dancing. Our bodies know each other. It feels natural. Right.

Except the pressure in my chest and the fear clogging my throat are always-present, painful reminders of how wrong it is. So why can't I seem to remember that when I need to the most?

Lucia told me Xander's feelings for me were his weakness, and moments like this only prove my feelings for him are mine.

I finally find the strength to push him away and suck in a shallow breath, pressing my hand to my chest. I can't stop my fingers from drifting to touch my lips as they tingle. I can't decipher the expression on Xander's face when I focus on him again, and before I can speak, he says, "Are you okay?"

I shake my head. "You don't get to do that anymore."

THE DEVIL'S TRIALS

"What? Kiss you, or care about you?"

"Xander." I drop my hand back to my lap, knowing full well my expression is pleading with him to go.

He was able to get past my defenses all too quickly, and with one kiss, it feels as if it ruined the distance I put between us. Whatever wall I thought I'd built crumbled in an instant.

How could I be so weak?
Why did I let him get close again?
Why did I let him kiss me?
Why did I kiss him back?

I feel like I just failed a test I wasn't allowed to prepare for.

Seventeen
Xander

Camille's unsteady heartbeat fills the space between us. Her pupils are blown, her skin flushed, and her expression darkened with an enticing mix of anger and lust. There's a spark of fear there too, though it doesn't seem directed toward me—rather what my being here makes her feel. Which only makes me want to stay longer.

"You're making this so much harder," she says.

"I've tried staying away from you." It's not entirely true. That said, I could've stopped her from leaving Seattle—I *wanted* to despite it being a terrible, dangerous idea for both of us, which is ultimately why I let her go. And if I came to her, either in person or by dreamscape whenever I thought about her, she'd realize how often I've resisted the urge to do just that.

"Says the guy who traveled across the country because I have the flu. This coming after you used your freaky demon power and waltzed into my dream."

Fair enough. My lips twitch, and a car horn blares in the distance outside the apartment window. "Yes, well, you're stepping on the point I'm trying to make."

"That your self control sucks?" she offers in a sarcastic voice, briefly allowing me to forget every wretched reason for us to be apart. There are no demons or trials or hunters standing between us. There's just *us*.

"I seem to recall you kissing me back a moment ago," I say with a lilt of challenge in my tone.

She doesn't miss a beat. "Further proof of your bad influence on me."

I shift closer, lowering my voice as I speak into her ear. "Then let me corrupt you."

Her pulse jumps, and I devour the heat of her nearness as she leans toward me, making my nerve endings tingle.

THE DEVIL'S TRIALS

I can't deny that I crave her surrender.

"Xander," she breathes, turning her face and brushing her lips against my cheek. "*No.*"

I don't move a muscle. "See?" I offer in a soft voice. "You're stronger than you think you are."

She pulls back to look at me. "If that were true, you wouldn't be here at all right now."

The corner of my mouth kicks up. "Nothing in this world could keep me away from you."

"And the underworld?" Her eyes flick between mine, glimmering with an emotion I could easily mistake as hope.

I'd make you its queen—my *queen.*

The words get stuck in my throat. As deeply as I desire that, the danger that lies down that path isn't something I'm ready to face, let alone subject Camille to.

So all I say is, "That's complicated."

She sighs, wetting her lips. "Of course it is. We keep going in circles." Her gaze falls away from mine, and her voice is quieter when she asks, "When does it end? Will it ever?"

"I don't know," I answer honestly, frowning at the discomfort it unfurls in my chest. It shouldn't. None of this should affect me. If it were anyone else, it wouldn't. But even after losing my soul, Camille holds power over me she doesn't realize—and that's probably for the best.

Camille nods, slowly standing from the couch, and I keep a close eye on her to make sure she's steady enough on her feet to not fall over. "I'm going back to bed and I need you to be gone when I get up."

"I'll go," I tell her, standing. "But tell me one thing first."

Her brows scrunch together, her voice tired when she says, "What?"

"Do you love him? The hunter?"

Her lips part as her heart skips a beat, then races. There's a moment of heavy contemplation etched in her features and then she says, "I could."

My eyes narrow a fraction. She likely doesn't notice, but I feel the tension in my temples. The next words spring from my lips before I can snap my mouth shut. "Do you love me?"

A muscle feathers along her jaw, and she swallows hard. "Love shouldn't feel like this, Xander. I...I can't *breathe* around you. You're all I think about, all I dream about—even when you're not actually there.

I still want you, still feel drawn to you. I don't know if that will ever go away, but...when I think of what kind of relationship we could have—our future—I can't see anything. It's just darkness. And that terrifies me." With that, she walks out of the room, leaving me staring after her.

Her words light a fire in my gut, and I ache to go after her. To take her in my arms and claim her in every way possible, damn the consequences.

But that's not the reality we exist in.

Camille is training to hunt demons, and I'm going through trials to ascend the throne as their king.

We'll never be the safe option for each other.

As I leave Camille's apartment, I wonder if the celestials who created our soulmate bond saw this coming.

I'm not ready to return to Seattle, so I check into a tiny B&B on the Upper West Side, much to Blake's dismay. I understand my second trial could come any day and the royal guard can find me wherever I go, which also makes staying with Camille any longer reckless. I've taken a big enough risk coming here as it is. I need to get my head in check and focus my energy on ascending the throne.

"I'm going out for drinks with Stephen and Will," Blake says once we're in our suite. "Do you want to come with me?"

I shake my head and drop my duffel bag onto the bench at the end of the bed. "Enjoy yourself. I'm going to shower and call it a night."

"How exciting." He digs through his own bag and pulls out a fresh collared shirt and quickly changes into it. "You should give room service a call. Maybe they'l send up a cute delivery person for you to snack on."

I roll my eyes despite the intrigue that stirs in me. After spending time with Camille and healing her, I should feed. Making a mental note to take care of that before we leave New York, I tell Blake, "Try not to stumble in here at three in the morning and wake me up by tripping over your shit."

He shoots me an unimpressed look on his way to the door. "Two times that's happened, and you'll never let me forget it."

I chuckle as he leaves, the door clicking shut behind him.

After a shower, I turn on the TV and lie down to decompress. The relief I felt seeing Camille recovering from her illness has done nothing to stifle my nerves surrounding the trials. My time with her was a fleeting distraction, even as tainted as it became by Noah's presence.

THE DEVIL'S TRIALS

Exhaling a slow breath, I close my eyes and tune out the soft audio from the TV. I could give Harper a call and update her on her best friend—not that I doubt she's keeping close tabs on it from Seattle herself—but I find myself wanting to test my abilities, especially after healing Camille. I was able to reach Camille in a dreamscape from Seattle, but maybe our unique connection made it possible.

Only one way to find out...

I visualize Harper's apartment while letting my muscles relax, focusing on the beat of my heart as it pumps blood through my body. Blood I share with my half-sister, and how I was able to track her the other night in the park.

Without warning, the room spins behind my eyelids. I grab for the blankets on either side of me, but the sensation is gone as quickly as it came over me. And then I'm falling. Gritting my teeth, I prepare for an impact that never comes. The loss of gravity vanishes, leaving me standing upright in the middle of...Blake's bar. The scene isn't quite accurate—the shelves behind the bar are empty and the walls are bare and dark. Evidently I don't have the strength to build this dreamscape with as much detail as the actual establishment.

"Harper?" I call out, frowning as I glance around at the tables with their chairs stacked on top. Crossing the quiet bar, my eyes narrow as I catch movement in my peripheral and turn to find Harper throwing a dart at the board near the back of the room.

She glances at me over her shoulder, scowling. Her disappointment in seeing me is plain as day on her face, but I walk over to her anyway.

"I wasn't expecting to find you at Blake's bar." I lean against a wooden pillar, folding my arms over my chest as I regard her curiously. "Have you actually been here before?"

Harper turns away from me and throws another dart, hitting the second ring from the bullseye. "What are *you* doing here?" she asks without answering my question. *Interesting.*

"Testing a theory," I offer.

She throws her last dart, sighing when it doesn't land where she wants. Facing me, she says, "Drop the mysterious shit. Why are you in my dream?"

"I came to New York to make sure Camille was okay. Just so you know, she's doing better."

Harper steps closer, matching my crossed-arm stance and shooting me a bland look. "You're an idiot."

I chuckle. "I won't argue with you there."

She stares at me, suspicion darkening her gaze. Her eyes search my face as if she's trying to figure something out. Finally, she says, "You need to let her go, Xander."

A muscle feathers along my jaw, and I push away from the pillar to stand in front of her. "I tried."

"Try *harder*."

I frown as she fades in and out like a hologram, as if I'm losing my connection to her. Ignoring the subtle lightheaded feeling I'm getting, I step closer, our shoes nearly touching. "I can't."

Her eyes dart between mine, her heart beating faster. "Can't or *won't*?"

I bite back a snarl. "She is *mine*."

Harper's hand comes flying toward my face in an instant.

I catch her wrist before her palm connects with my cheek, gripping it tightly. It's fair to assume that my eyes are fully black based on the horror in Harper's expression.

"Loving you is going to get her killed," she snaps, tears swimming in her eyes. "Don't you understand that? Or do you just not care anymore?"

I lean in until her fist is pressed between us and I can feel each ragged breath she exhales. My voice is low when I say, "You need to be careful right now. There are very few I care about—"

"Oh, give me a fucking break," she interrupts coldly, pulling away, further proving I'm not as strong here. "You're being reckless and pompous and selfish and—"

"I think that's enough adjectives," I cut in.

Her expression turns incredulous, and she reaches toward her thigh for a dagger that isn't there. She glances down, then exhales a slow breath. "You wanted to build some kind of relationship between us, but let me be very clear. If you hurt my best friend one more time, I don't care who or what you are." She lifts her chin, meeting my gaze. "I will kill you."

I don't have a moment to respond before the dreamscape falls apart, plummeting me into darkness.

Eighteen
Camille

The worst of my sickness seems to have passed a few days later. My energy still isn't at one hundred percent, but I can't keep spending all day in bed if I want it to improve—that goes for my health and my hunter skills.

After a shower, I throw on my comfiest sweats and shoot Harper a text to see if we can catch up. No more than five minutes later, my phone rings.

I answer it on speaker so I can finish making my cup of tea. I'm still slightly dehydrated, and my throat is a desert, so I'm downing as much liquid as I can.

"*Camiiiii*," Harper sings into the phone. "How are you feeling?"

"Better," I say, taking a sip of my tea to coat my throat. I set my mug on the coffee table, then pull a blanket off the back of the couch, draping it over my lap as I sink back into the cushions. "Things were…really shitty, to be honest. I've never felt that awful."

"Geez, babe. I'm sorry I wasn't there to take care of you."

"It's okay," I'm quick to say. "Noah was actually really helpful."

"He took care of you, then?"

I ignore the warmth that fills my face. "Um, yeah."

"Weird tone," she muses. "Did something happen?"

Blowing out a breath, I pluck at the blanket. "Not really. I just wasn't expecting him to be so, I don't know, caring? It was kind of nice to see that side of him, considering he's annoying me most of the time or barking orders at me in training."

"Right," she murmurs.

"*Anyway*," I say pointedly. "I didn't want a call to talk about Noah."

"Fair enough. Whatcha wanna talk about then?"

I chew my bottom lip, grasping for a way to explain what happened while I was in what I thought to be a fever dream. "Are you sitting down?"

"Uh, should I be?"

I cringe. "Probably."

"Okay, you're starting to freak me out."

"This is a conversation I wish we could have in person, but I don't think it can wait. I can't keep it to myself, or it's going to drive me crazy."

"Uh-huh. Not making me feel any better over here. What's going on?"

I take a deep breath, then blurt, "I saw Xander."

Silence stretches between us.

"Harper?"

"I know," she finally says. "He told me after he was there. I'm sorry. I shouldn't have said anything to him about you being sick. I really didn't think he'd get on a plane and go there." With a sigh, she adds, "I guess I should have realized he would."

"Don't apologize. It was hard to see him but also, um, enlightening?" My pitch increases as if I'm posing it as a question.

"Care to explain that?"

I hesitate, unsure how to dive into the whole soulmate thing. The longer the line is quiet, the more I overthink it.

"Cami, the silence really isn't helping me stay chill."

"Sorry. I'm still processing this so I'm not entirely sure how to talk about it." I take a deep breath, then swallow past the emotion threatening to clog my throat. "Xander is...or, um, *was*...my soulmate."

Now she's the silent one. Finally, she says, "What did you just say?"

"Yeah. Soulmates. Wild, right? I had no idea they were even real until I lost mine."

"I never believed they were real, but I guess it makes sense for you two. And for people like my parents or Phoebe and Grayson."

My lungs constrict at the thought of them—of Harper's parents and our friends, all lost in the war against demons. "I think so, too. It's at least part of what drew me to Xander and made it so impossible to walk away, even when I knew I should."

Harper exhales heavily. "But he—"

"Doesn't have a soul anymore," I finish for her. "I know. Our bond broke when he killed Lucia."

"When he..." She trails off, cursing under her breath. "I can get on a plane today. Just say the word, and I'll ditch class and throw some shit in a duffel bag."

THE DEVIL'S TRIALS

"It's okay," I insist. "As much as I miss you, I just need to throw myself back into training and keep trying to move on." Even as I say the words, part of me knows how impossible they are. There's no moving on. Especially not when there's so much unresolved with Xander.

"You don't expect me to believe that, do you?"

I sigh. "I'm still trying to get myself to believe it."

"Are you going to tell Noah?"

My eyes widen. "I don't know." Why would I? None of it affects my training, so I'm not sure there's any reason to tell him I had and lost my soulmate. I'm trying not to think about it—and failing miserably. "He hates Xander so deeply, and telling him about my celestial connection to him won't help that." Considering the mere thought of talking to Noah about anything involving Xander is kicking my pulse up, that's something I'm definitely going to avoid.

"That makes sense."

"And it took everything to keep him from killing Xander while I was sick," I add, cringing at the memory.

"Wait a minute. Noah knew Xander was there with you?"

"Oh. Um, yeah. After they puffed their chests at each other, they took care of me together."

"Holy shit," she says. "Talk about a *hot* fever dream."

"Not helping," I mutter. "Plus, *ew*. Your half-brother, remember?"

She groans. "Still trying to forget."

I lean back into the couch cushions. "Right. So, by that I take it you don't want to talk about how things are going between the two of you?"

"Thank you for asking. Seriously. But no."

"Okay," I say gently. "But you know whenever you want to talk about it, I will put aside whatever I feel about him and be there for you, just like you always are for me."

"I know and I really appreciate that."

I smile, though she can't see it. "Of course."

"I suppose you're freaking about this whole soulmate thing, huh?"

I exhale a laugh, but it's forced and shaky. "Pretty much. Because if I lost my soulmate, is that it for me? Do I only get one? Can I even be truly happy with someone else?"

The myriad of questions prompt a deep spiral into dark thoughts I'm wholly fighting to avoid. I didn't learn about the existence of soulmates until I lost mine, and if that isn't a monumentally cruel joke from the universe, nothing is.

Harper sighs. "Well, that answers my question of whether or not you believe in soulmates."

I pause, closing my eyes and letting out a slow breath. "I do. I wish I didn't, because maybe that would make this easier, but I do. And I have no idea what to do about that."

"You do whatever you need to be okay. I have your back no matter what, you know that."

"Thanks, Harper."

"And I expect a daily check-in from here on out. Even if it's just a quick text. Okay?"

"Of course," I say. "But back to you. I don't want this to just be about me."

Harper laughs softly. "I would very much rather it be."

I frown despite her not being able to see me. "What's going on there? Should I be worried?"

"No need to worry. Promise."

I reach for my mug, taking another drink of tea and hoping the peppermint will help settle the unease in my stomach. "Harper—"

"Look, I have to head out for training, but we'll talk later. I'm glad you're feeling better."

With a sigh, I concede. "Thanks." I'm not going to get Harper to talk about something she doesn't want to. She's even more stubborn than I am. "Talk soon. Love you."

"Love you more," she says before ending the call.

It takes another full day before Noah agrees to let me train again. Once he clears me, we head to Ballard early in the morning and go into the main building for a group class.

After warming up, I walk toward the middle of the room where the rest of the class is congregating.

"Hey, Camille," Sierra says. Today she's dressed in a matching soft pink workout set and black sneakers, her hair twisted into two French braids that fall just past her shoulders. She offers me a warm smile, putting me at ease instantly, and at that moment I realize why.

She reminds me of Phoebe.

THE DEVIL'S TRIALS

"Hey," I say in greeting and return her smile.

"We missed you in class the last few days."

"Thanks," I tell her, slightly caught off guard. When I decided to return to training, the last thing I expected to do was make friends. That said, I'm grateful for the kindness Sierra has shown me. She likely has no idea just how much.

"I have to confess something," she says in a near-whisper as Noah walks around the perimeter of the room while the rest of the class finishes their warm-ups.

My brows shoot up my forehead. "Oh?"

"After we spoke the other day, I asked around about your family."

I stare at her, my stomach sinking, then repeat, "Oh."

Sierra's expression falls. "I'm sorry! I didn't think anything of it, but when you told me who your parents are, I couldn't help myself."

I nod slowly.

"Can I ask you something?"

I blow out a breath. "Sure, I guess."

"What brought you back to the organization?" she asks in a gentle, almost hesitant voice.

"She was fucking the prince of hell," a deep voice cuts in before I have a chance to respond, snagging my attention as a black-haired guy who can't be much older than twenty squares up with me. "Sorry, I should have said, the *king* of hell."

My eyes narrow as my muscles lock up. "Excuse me?" *Who is this guy?* He clearly knows who I am...I resent the tears burning my eyes and threatening to spill over. I want to fight back, but my fight or flight has kicked in and rendered me useless in the fight department. My lack of skills would likely be a detriment.

"You shouldn't be here," the guy sneers, his hazel eyes blazing with a wild mix of distrust and anger that has my gut twisting uncomfortably.

"What's Cody talking about?" Sierra asks, concern etched into her previously soft features.

I turn my attention to her, hesitating before I say, "I *was* in a relationship with Xander Kane *before* I knew who he was." *And somewhat after*—but they don't need to know that.

She blinks in surprise, pulling her bottom lip between her teeth as her gaze shifts between me and Cody. "Oh, um, that's—"

"Irrelevant to today's exercise," Noah cuts in, and I stiffen at the sound of his voice at my back. "You're with me," he snaps at Cody. "Let's go."

The smugness drops from the trainee's face, replaced by a nervousness that makes my lips twitch. He walks away with Noah, and I exhale a low breath, waiting for Sierra to bail.

"He's such a dick," she says, readjusting her ponytail.

"Cody or Noah?" I ask with a faint grin.

Sierra chuckles, bumping her shoulder with mine.

With the class paired up, Noah uses Cody to demonstrate each drill, and I find likely too much enjoyment in watching the guy get his ass handed to him over and over in front of his peers.

I expected some of the trainees to be less than thrilled to share a class with me, but I can't say I was prepared to handle a direct attack like Cody's. That was probably naive of me.

I'm glad the rest of the session is uneventful. I focus on each drill, practicing my footwork and blocking as Sierra goes on the offensive, and then we switch positions.

By the time we wrap up, my limbs are noodles, and I feel as if my entire body is covered in a layer of sweat. While I've never looked forward to a shower more in my life, I also feel a sense of accomplishment. I caught Noah watching us a few times, and the pride in his expression spurred me on, making me feel as though I've made genuine progress despite the setback of getting sick.

"What are you doing later?" Sierra asks as we head out of the training room.

I swallow a mouthful of water from my bottle. "Not sure. What's up?"

"A few of us are going to grab pizza at Two Boots in the East Village." She shrugs on her jacket, zipping it up. "You should come."

I chew the inside of my cheek, glancing sideways at her as we make our way to the entrance of the training facility. "Are you sure?"

"Absolutely." She shoots me a reassuring smile. "Don't worry, Cody isn't invited."

Nodding, I say, "I don't want to cause any issues." I wasn't expecting any social invites. I'm not here to make friends. Though if we're going to keep doing group exercises, it might be a good idea to at least be friendly with the rest of the trainees.

Sierra waves away my concern. "It's not a problem." She keeps walking toward the front doors, pausing to look back when she realizes I'm not beside her. "Aren't you coming?"

"I got a ride with Noah, actually. We live in the same building."

"Oh, that's convenient."

I laugh. "Not the word I'd use, but sure."

She walks back to me, pulling her phone out. "Here. Send yourself a text so we have each other's numbers, and we can meet up tonight."

I take it and send a quick message before handing it back.

"Awesome!" She slips her phone into her pocket and smiles at me again. "See you later."

"See you later," I echo before she walks away. I wander back to the training room to find Noah, pausing outside the door when his voice reaches me. It's deep and harsh, and I press my lips together when I realize he's talking to Cody.

"...I suggest you focus on the reason you're here."

"I am," Cody insists. "That doesn't change the fact that she shouldn't be. How do we know she isn't a spy for the demons?"

"That's not your concern."

"Evidently it's not yours, either."

"Watch it," Noah snaps. "You disrupt another class of mine, and you're out. Do I make myself perfectly clear?"

There's a stretch of silence before a low, very reluctant, "Yes."

Tension unfurls in my chest at Noah standing up for me. I'm not entirely sure why he felt the need—I can take care of myself just fine—but I can't ignore the piece of me that is grateful for it.

I feel weirdly...*protected*.

Heavy footfall makes me quickly shift back from the doorway seconds before Cody storms through it, throwing a vicious scowl in my direction.

I have a crude retort on the tip of my tongue, but bite it back as Noah walks out, catching my gaze.

"He's not worth it, Cam."

"I know," I force out, glancing after him despite myself.

Noah claps me on the shoulder, and I wince at the ache in my overexerted muscles. "Come on," he says with a chuckle. "I'll take you home."

I stare at myself in the bathroom mirror after drying my hair and applying a bit of makeup. I'm not sure if I'm trying to talk myself into going tonight or trying to talk myself out of it. I don't know who besides Sierra is going and I don't bother asking, considering I don't know anyone's name anyway.

She texted to make sure I was coming, and I didn't want to let her down by bailing. Especially when she's the first potential friend I've made since reenrolling at Ballard Academy—because Noah most definitely doesn't count.

As it gets closer to when I need to leave, I find myself pacing, tidying random things, even fluffing the couch cushions. I'm doing anything to keep busy enough to prevent my thoughts from sabotaging me into thinking tonight is a bad idea. These are new potential friends. I should be excited to hang out with them, and I am. But there's also a voice of doubt that refuses to leave me alone, trying to convince me these people will never actually want to be friends with the girl who fell in love with the devil.

I stop in the middle of the kitchen, pressing my hand to my chest and swallowing past the sudden dryness in my throat. I fell for Xander before he became king—before I knew he was a demon. Even after the way we met, it didn't take long for feelings to develop, and while I could easily over-analyze why it happened that way and drive myself crazy, it won't change anything. And that makes the chasm in my chest feel bigger with every breath.

When I walk into Two Boots at the corner of Avenue A and East Third Street, I'm immediately overwhelmed by bright red booths, teal, mosaic-decorated walls, and the mouthwatering aroma of freshly-baked dough and of cheese. My stomach growls, reminding me I didn't eat nearly enough for lunch after this morning's vigorous workout.

"Camille!" Sierra's friendly voice snags my attention from the glass case of pizzas, and I find her in a booth across the room with some of the other trainees from this morning, a few girls and a couple of guys.

I swallow my nerves and approach them, wiping the dampness from my palms on my pants and forcing what I hope appears to be a pleasant smile as I offer an awkward wave. "Hey, everyone."

Sierra smiles at me before going around the table and introducing me to each person. No one immediately seems upset at my presence, and the

THE DEVIL'S TRIALS

guy Sierra called Paul slides out of the booth and offers me his seat, while he grabs a chair from a nearby table. He has soft brown eyes and matching floppy curls—definite teddy bear vibes, which really contradicts the whole demon hunter thing.

"Thanks," I tell him with a more relaxed smile, then add to everyone, "I'm Cami." I glance around the booth as they introduce themselves.

Sierra sits across from me, and beside her is a girl with chest-length, straight black hair and purple glasses named Zara. On her other side is Wyatt, a thick-muscled guy with sandy blond hair, tied back at the nape of his neck. He offers me his hand when I sit, and I reach across the table to shake it.

Sitting across from Wyatt is a girl who looks closer to my age named Florence. She leans forward to shoot me a grin and says, "Call me Ren."

The last trainee is Brynne, who sits to my right. She's a curvy redhead, though her hair is darker, a cherry red, whereas Sierra's is more of a burnt orange.

With the introductions out of the way, we order a variety of pizzas to share. Wyatt all but demands a meat lover's, while Zara politely orders a vegetarian, which seems to amuse him as he rests his arm along the top of the booth behind her. I'm not sure why I'm surprised to find a demon hunter who doesn't eat meat, but I remind myself there are plenty of reasons for someone to choose that lifestyle. None of which affect me or my choice to devour slices from both kinds of pizza.

We chat about training as we stuff our faces with cheesy goodness, and I find it shockingly easy to feel as if I belong here. To pretend, at least. All my worrying from earlier feels insignificant now. I don't think I've had so much fun since...the last date Xander and I had. The moment the thought crosses my mind, my stomach dips, and I press my lips together at the memory.

By the time our group walks out of Two Boots, it's well after dark. Wyatt, Brynne, and I head down the sidewalk as I zip up my sweater against the chilly evening air. The others headed in the other direction toward the parking garage a few blocks away, while we opted for the subway. The street is quiet, save for the distant sirens, which are a constant in the city that I've quickly gotten accustomed to.

"I'm glad I came tonight," I say in a casual tone. "It was really nice to meet you guys."

Wyatt offers a wide grin and drops his arm around Brynne's shoulders. "You say that like you're surprised."

Casting him a sideways glance, I laugh. It's so genuine the sound is almost foreign, but it brings a pleasant warmth to my chest. "To be honest, I sort of am. Not everybody is super keen on me being around."

Brynne frowns. "Yeah, I heard what Cody said."

I clench my jaw, waiting for her to mention something about my relationship with Xander. About how awful and delusional I am for being with him when I was.

But she doesn't. Instead she says, "I suppose I can understand where the reservations lie, but he didn't need to be a dick about it."

Wyatt snorts. "Pretty sure that's his default personality."

I only nod along, because what else am I supposed to do? I understand the others' reservations, but there's not much I can do about them. I can't change who I am or what happened. As much as I wish I could.

"Anyway," Brynne drawls. "We'll see you at training tomorrow, right?"

"Absolutely. I—"

A deep, marrow-chilling growl cuts her off, and Wyatt throws himself in front of her seconds before a demon charges into my line of sight from behind a row of parked cars. My stomach drops as I get a flash of his appearance in the dim streetlight—olive-toned skin, short salt and pepper hair, and an unfortunate tweed suit jacket. In human years, I'd guess late forties. Of course he moves with a preternatural speed that's impossible to track, so he's mostly just a blur of beige.

Oh, for the love of—I reach for where a dagger should be before I realize I'm not actually a hunter, and those daggers we got to hold in training are safely stowed at the academy.

Wyatt rears back and catches the demon in the jaw. It makes a sickening crack, but the demon only cackles, amusement darkening his gaze. He makes no effort to put an end to this encounter quickly. *He wants to play with his food*, a warning voice whispers in the back of my mind, entirely unhelpful.

"Fuck," Wyatt growls, reeling back and shaking out his hand. "Do either of you have—"

"No," I snap, my heart thumping in my chest so hard I can feel each rapid beat in my throat. "We should go. Yeah, we should definitely run."

Never run from a demon. They relish the chase.

THE DEVIL'S TRIALS

"Cami, you know—"

"What else are we supposed to do?" I cut Wyatt off.

He continues facing off with the demon, who dances around as if he's savoring the moment before he attacks and shreds us all to ribbons. And the knowledge that he very easily could makes my blood run cold.

My muscles lock up, making each movement jerky, and the ground beneath my feet feels harder somehow, as if I'm not wearing shoes. Fear does weird things to your perception, and I don't have time to analyze why my body feels all out of whack right now.

I slowly make my way around the demon while his attention is snared on Wyatt. If I can tackle the monster from behind, maybe—*just maybe*—the three of us can take down this one demon. Damn, I wish I had more confidence in my abilities, but I really am the newest of newbies in this arena. "I don't know how long you two have been training, but I'm definitely not prepared to go up against—"

The demon launches forward, swiping out with dirty, claw-like fingers, and Wyatt barely ducks in time to avoid a nasty gash across his throat. He kicks the demon's legs out from under him, but before he can get his fingers around the demon's throat, it head butts him in the face.

Wyatt yelps in pain as blood sprays from his nose and he falls backward, hitting the pavement. He holds his hand to his face as red leaks through his fingers and scrambles upright, but the color is drained from his face, and he sways on his feet.

The demon straightens, peering between Brynne and me, and my heart stops. He grins slowly, and I see death in his all-black eyes. No matter what I do, there's a very good chance none of us are going to make it out of this alive.

Terror steals the air from my lungs as Brynne steps closer, her shoulder bumping against mine. We're both breathing hard and fast but neither of us are running away. I think we both know the moment we turn our backs on this monster, we're dead. My hands shake at my sides, and I ball them into fists. If this is it, I refuse to go down without a fight. And despite the fear clinging to my skin like a film, one fleeting thought brings me a semblance of comfort in the midst of it all.

I'm going to see my sister again.

A sharp whistle to the side captures the demon's attention as well as the rest of ours. Wyatt mutters a breathy, "Thank fuck," as relief floods through me at the sight of Noah crossing the lot toward us, wielding a dagger and a downright wicked grin.

Okay, I can kind of see the 'hunter god' thing as he gets closer, and now is *not* the time to be staring at him. Though, evidently, he's not as concerned with this demon as the rest of us are. And considering he has a weapon that can destroy the monster, I suppose that's fair.

The demon turns his back on us, cackling as he saunters toward Noah. I start moving without fully realizing what I'm doing. I throw my arm around the demon's neck from behind, hauling him backward, then jump on him, using my full body weight to take him to the pavement, where I smack his head against it. A low growl rumbles through him as Noah closes the rest of the distance between us.

"A little help here?" I nearly snarl at him, struggling to keep the demon beneath me. I squeeze my thighs, using every ounce of strength I have to hold him down.

Noah's voice is far too easygoing when he says, "I'm kind of curious to see where this goes."

"Do *not* fuck with me right now, Daniels."

"You seem to be doing just fine."

"I swear to—"

The demon bucks me off, and I fall to the side, wincing as the pavement bites into my skin through my sweater. Noah sighs, and I scowl at him.

Within seconds, the demon is in my face, wrapping his fingers around my throat and squeezing until I gasp.

Everything happens so fast.

Noah yanks the demon off me, then steps closer, offering me the dagger. "Earn it, and you can keep it," he says as he pulls another out of the inside pocket of his jacket. Wyatt and Brynne hang back, I guess figuring they're not going to be much help without weapons.

I take the dagger as Noah moves with a lethal grace to swipe his outward, slashing the demon across the cheek. It hisses in pain, baring its mouthful of fangs, and charges at Noah, who dances out of the way. The two of them go head-to-head, both getting in some nasty blows. When Noah skids across the pavement and loses his bearings, the demon flashes in front of him, catching him by the throat and knocking the dagger out of his grip.

THE DEVIL'S TRIALS

I'm moving forward before I can think about it, my grip sure and my target locked in. There isn't a moment of hesitation in my muscles as I slam the dagger into the demon from behind. The obsidian blade slices too easily through skin and muscle as I hold my breath and grip the hilt so tightly my knuckles turn white.

A sickeningly guttural sound fills the air as he whirls around, and I yank the dagger out of his back only to slam it as hard as I can where I hope his heart is as nausea ripples through me. The demon's all-black eyes go wide, nearly bugging out of his face, and then it turns to ash at my feet, the dagger clattering to the pavement as I stand there gasping for breath.

Wyatt and Brynne holler their praise from behind me, but I barely hear them over the rushing of blood in my ears. The pressure in my chest tightens to a near unbearable amount, and I shake my head as my sight starts to get fuzzy. Nausea floods in now and I hurry across the lot, slipping between two buildings to keep myself out of view just before I empty the contents of my stomach onto the ground.

My throat burns when I swallow, and I suck in a sharp breath as someone gathers the hair from around my face, holding it back. I relax slightly the moment Noah's scent reaches me but I still shove him away, wiping my mouth with the back of my hand.

"I'm fine," I grit out.

He lets out a harsh laugh. "Right. Forgive the fuck out of me for trying to make sure you're okay. What an ass I am."

My stomach drops, and I stand there staring at his chest as my heart pounds in mine. I exhale a shaky breath. "I'm sorry, okay? I'm not used to you taking care of me." The absolute last thing I want is to look weak in front of Noah. I don't even want to think about what's going through his head at me getting sick after killing a demon.

He steps in closer, dipping his chin and lowering his voice. "There is no shame in this. The moment taking a life becomes easy is when I'm going to start worrying about you."

I lean against the cool brick exterior, tipping my head back to look at him. "I get to keep the dagger though, right?"

The corner of his mouth kicks up, and he reaches into his back pocket, retrieving it. "I should tell you no, considering you ran off without it, but here." He hands it to me, and I slide it into my sweater pocket.

"Come on. Let's go home."

Let's go home.

The words land oddly in my chest, trapping the air in my lungs for too long before I can force out, "Where's your car?"

"Just a few blocks over."

I nod slowly. "Why? I mean, what were you doing out here?"

His expression doesn't change. "Patrolling."

Arching a brow, I say, "Right. You just so happened to be patrolling where I was hanging out."

"Something you want to ask me?"

Warmth spreads through my cheeks despite the cool night air. "You're keeping tabs on me."

"Is that a question?" His tone is laced with an irritating mix of amusement and condescension, and I roll my eyes.

"I guess it's a good thing you were here," I mutter.

"Sure, but you did pretty well yourself." His eyes lighten with something akin to pride. "You're going to be the talk of the class tomorrow."

My eyes widen, and I immediately shake my head.

"Relax," Noah says before I can speak. "I asked Wyatt and Brynne not to say anything before they took off."

The rigid lock on my muscles lessens, and I nod. "I'm not trying to make a name for myself here, Noah."

"I'm aware of that," he says in a level tone. "Now, can we go, or do you want to keep hanging out in this alley that suddenly smells like vomit for some reason?"

I punch him in the shoulder. "Asshole."

We don't say much in the way of talking about what happened on the drive home, which I'm thankful for. Instead of leaving me in the elevator, Noah rides up to my floor and walks me right to my apartment.

"I'm here. I'm alive. You did your ever-so brave duty. You can go home now, thank you."

He folds his arms across his chest, holding my gaze. "Do you want to talk about what happened?"

I frown, hesitating before I ask, "Tonight or the other day when you went all macho guy?"

"Why do I get the feeling your answer is the same for either?"

"Maybe you're more perceptive than I give you credit for, Daniels."

THE DEVIL'S TRIALS

He nods, lips quirking. "Got it. Well, offer stands." He starts to turn away, then pauses, looking at me again. "It doesn't have to be me, but it should be someone."

I nod as I pull my keys out and unlock the door, stepping inside.

"Cam?"

I turn back to Noah, my brows lifting in question.

"We need to report the demon attack to HQ, and I think you should be the one to do it. Call Rachel and explain what happened. I'm sure she'll be pleased to hear it from you—considering it was your hunt."

Panic strikes me at the speed of light. "Oh no." I shake my head for extra measure. "Can't you just say you did it? I really don't want to make this a bigger thing."

He slides his hands into his pockets. "I get it. But we have to handle it by the book." His voice softens when he adds, "It'll also help your reputation within the organization for people to know you're taking things seriously."

I hate the idea. More so, I hate that he's right.

With a heavy sigh, I say, "Okay, I'll call her."

He shoots me a smile as he turns to walk back toward the elevator. "See you in the morning."

I close and lock the door, then fall back against it, briefly closing my eyes as I let out a heavy sigh.

What a fucking day.

I pull my phone out to get the conversation with my mom over with, sighing when it goes to voicemail. She's probably asleep already. Instead of leaving a message, I end the call and try Harper.

"*Helloooooo,*" she sings into the phone. "You're up late."

"Yeah..."

"What's with the weird tone?" Concern fills her voice. "Did something happen?"

"Uh, well, I went out with some people from training tonight, which was fun, but when we left the restaurant, there was sort of a demon attack."

"Sort of?"

I walk to the couch and drop onto it, propping a throw pillow under my head. "Okay, there *was* a demon attack, and I...killed the demon."

There's a stretch of silence on the line, and if I didn't hear Harper breathing I'd think the call dropped.

"Fuck. That's really intense," she finally says. "I'm sorry, babe. Were you hurt?"

"No. I...I'm fine."

"Are you though?"

"Not really," I answer honestly.

"Do you want to talk about it?"

"Not really."

"I understand," she says. "If you decide at any time that you do, I'm just a call away. I don't care what time it is."

"Thanks, Harper," I say, my bottom lip trembling as my eyes burn. "You are the best friend I could ever ask for. I appreciate you so much."

"Don't worry, babe. I know. And right back at you. Get some rest, and we'll talk tomorrow, okay?"

I sit up, swallowing past the lump in my throat. "Sounds good."

We hang up, and I get off the couch, walking into my room. I leave my phone on the nightstand and slip into the bathroom to shower before bed.

The moment I step under the hot spray of water, I can't hold back tears. They fall down my cheeks as my shoulders shake, and I choke when I try to stifle a sob. The pressure in my rib cage has me sliding down the shower tile wall until I'm sitting on the floor, pulling my knees to my chest.

I'm still crying when the water loses its warmth nearly an hour later. I've been so overwhelmed by everything since Xander killed Lucia three weeks ago, and it's all I can do to let out the emotions I haven't been able to deal with otherwise.

After I turn off the shower and get ready for bed, I send my mom a to-the-point message.

> Hey, Mom. I don't remember the official procedure for submitting information about a demon attack, so please consider this my report. I was with a group of other trainees tonight at Two Boots in the East Village and ran into a demon when we were leaving. Noah showed up and gave me a dagger which I used to kill the demon. No one got seriously hurt and I'm home now, just heading to bed. If you need any other information, let me know, but otherwise, I would really prefer not to discuss it. And please don't tell Dad. I want to do that myself.

I switch my phone to silent and leave it face down on my bedside table. I figure I've given my mom the pertinent information and let her

THE DEVIL'S TRIALS

know I'm safe, so anything else can wait until my head doesn't feel like scrambled eggs.

Sleep doesn't come easily once I'm under the covers. I'm not sure how long I spend tossing and turning before I finally drift off.

When I open my eyes to find myself standing on the quiet sidewalk near Two Boots, my jaw clenches tightly as my gaze drops to the obsidian dagger in my hand.

Because living *this nightmare wasn't enough.*

A deadly growl snaps my attention upward, and I narrow my eyes at the tweed-wearing demon I killed mere hours ago. His mouth is full of fangs and twisted into a sadistic grin, and his eyes are completely black.

Soulless.

He lunges for me, and I stumble back, gripping the dagger tighter as my pulse kicks up.

This isn't real.

I'm dreaming.

It doesn't matter. I'm not about to let this monster get the best of me.

He cackles maniacally. "You have no idea what you're in for, princess."

I grit my teeth against the nausea swirling in my gut and fight the urge to roll my eyes at the cliché line.

Thunder crashes overhead, and I suck in a breath. The demon uses that opportunity to advance once more, but I refuse to let myself lose focus, even as the skies open and rain pours down on me, chilling me to the core. As soon as he gets close enough, I aim for his rotted heart as I slam the dagger into his chest for the second time.

He snarls in pain, gasping for air as rainwater spills down his cheeks and blood as black as his eyes stains the front of his shirt. Except he doesn't turn to ash like he should.

I blink quickly through the downpour, trying to focus my vision, my panic cresting as the demon before me changes.

A scream tears its way up my throat when the demon on the other end of my dagger is no longer the unknown one I killed.

It's Xander.

I'm back in Seattle less than a day and Harper is blowing up my phone with angry texts about leaving Camille alone. I admire the fierceness in which she wants to protect her best friend, and I can't help but consider how useful that could be on my council. For many reasons once I take the throne, but also for Camille should she decide to continue living in my world.

While I may be able to convince Harper to join me, other demons won't look too kindly upon a hunter being part of the king's council. We'd have to keep it secret—same with our shared bloodline. I'm not even sure the rest of my council would get on board without some guarantees being made, namely that Harper won't attempt to dagger them. While keeping it from them might be easier, I don't want to. These people are my support system. If they don't agree with my decisions, they are welcome to accept dismissal from my council.

There will have to be some level of mutual trust for an arrangement with Harper joining us to work, and that'll likely be as difficult as passing the ascension trials.

Instead of brainstorming the arrangement further by myself, I type a to-the-point message to Harper and hit send.

> Where are you? I want to meet.

Her reply is immediate.

> And I want an all-inclusive trip to somewhere sunny. We don't always get what we want.

I can't help the grin curling my lips.

> I do.

> So fucking arrogant. What could you possibly want to meet about?

THE DEVIL'S TRIALS

> Come find out.

> If I say no?

> Do you really want to play this game with me?

> I don't want anything to do with you. I thought we established that already.

One step forward, three steps back.

> The reason for this meeting is mutually beneficial. You have my word, Harper.

> Your word means nothing.

I ignore the slice of pain that brings to my chest. It's a flare of heartburn that tells me that I care more about what Harper thinks of me than I realized.

> Give me a chance to make it mean something.

Her response comes after several minutes of me staring at my phone, and I have a feeling she made me wait intentionally to make a point. To keep me on the hook until she was ready.

> Meet me at my apartment in an hour.

> Not happening.

> What, you don't trust me?

> As much as you trust me.

> Touché.

> You suggest a place, then.

I send her the address to Blake's bar and wait for her to refuse me. So, imagine my surprise when her reply pops up a few seconds later.

> Fine.

> See you in an hour.

I don't expect another response and I don't get one.

Blake shuts the bar down so Harper and I can meet without prying eyes or risk being overheard, and busies himself in the back office.

I'm sitting in one of the round booths when she walks inside, her combat boots echoing on the old wood floor. I get up to greet her, quickly locking the door.

She eyes me warily, her heart rate increasing as she shrugs off her rain spattered jacket and tucks it over her arm. "Starting off by locking me in? You're not earning any points here."

I offer a wry smile. "You're free to leave anytime. The locked door is to keep anyone else out."

Nodding slowly, she shifts back and forth, glancing around the relatively small space. It's mostly open floor for dancing, with a few high-top tables near the bar and booths around the room. The lights are on but dim, giving the room a warmer feel.

"Would you like something to drink?"

Her eyes flit to mine. "Are you drinking?"

"Probably not, but I'm buying, so feel free."

She shakes her head. "No one likes to drink alone."

I chuckle. "Fair enough. Do you want to sit?"

"I guess. Is this going to take long? I have about a million chapters to read for normal human classes. Cami deferred her semester, but I didn't."

"Only a million?" I try for a joke, but she doesn't look enthused, so I move on and gesture to the booth I'd been sitting in before she arrived.

Once we sit down, she clasps her hands in front of her on the table. "You called this meeting."

"I did."

"It's not every day you're summoned by the king of hell." She leans back against the cushions, keeping her sharply focused gaze locked on me.

"Not king yet, but I appreciate your confidence in me."

She scoffs. "Whatever. Get to the point, or I'll get gone."

I hold up my hands in mock surrender. "Easy. I want to offer you a deal. I had planned to the night we met in the park, but after you told me about Camille—"

"You went all creepy ex-boyfriend and stalked her across the country," Harper cuts in snidely.

I ignore that and continue, "You have the skills and potential to be a strong asset."

Her brows lift. "An asset to what, exactly?"

"Me."

She barks out a laugh. "You have got to be kidding me." When I don't join in, her expression hardens. "Holy shit, you're serious."

"Quite."

Harper stares at me, processing what I've said. "I'm going to need more to go on here."

"You need experience and demon hunts under your belt to graduate training, and I'd rather delegate the task of killing my own kind."

She purses her lips, her forehead creasing in thought. "Just so I'm clear what's happening here. Are you suggesting...we work together?"

I nod. "Would you consider it?"

"Making a deal with the devil?" she mutters as if to herself before speaking louder. "What do you get out of this?"

Closing the distance between us, I lower my voice. "I get out of killing. You may not believe this, but I don't particularly enjoy it." Soul or no, the act of taking a life doesn't bring me anything.

She eyes me suspiciously. "Right. Isn't that what your lackey is for? What's his name? Brent? Brody?"

I chuckle. "Blake is occupied with other responsibilities. Besides, many demons take issue with killing their own. Which is where you come in."

"What, you want me to be the devil's executioner? Your personal hunter?" She frowns at the words that spill from her lips a second later.

"If you want a title, sure. I'm offering you a position on my council."

Her heart beats faster, and she swallows hard. "If anybody found out, it wouldn't be good for either of us."

I press my lips together in consideration. "So no one finds out. We keep it to ourselves—and Blake, because I tell him everything."

"Is this the part where you ask me to keep it from Cami?"

I scratch the stubble along my jaw. "No, I won't ask you to do that."

"Good, because I won't. I've always talked to her about training, even when she wasn't part of the organization."

I acknowledge that with a subtle nod. "You've spoken to her about training since she started again?" The question is out there before I can stop myself, ignoring the dull sense of discomfort in my gut.

She hesitates and then shrugs. "A little. She's been taking classes at Ballard along with extra private sessions with Noah and—Get that look off your face. You're not allowed to get angry that he's involved. That he's helping her. He stuck his neck out for your asinine plan that went sideways, and quite frankly, we're lucky he was there. If he hadn't been, I can't say that we would have made it out alive."

I grit my teeth at the pressure in my chest, the possessive urge to snap back at Harper, despite knowing full well she's right.

I have no right to be angry over another man being close to Camille and helping her with something I can't. But that doesn't change the rage simmering in me, because even if Camille doesn't know it, some greater power—the stars or universe or whatever—decided she was mine, same as I was hers.

Of course, killing Lucia stole what was left of my soul, destroying the otherworldly bond between Camille and me. It didn't, however, take away the all-too human feelings I developed for her.

I don't need a soul to love Camille Morgan.

I'm suddenly torn between relief that I can still feel the most important part of the humanity I thought I lost completely, and dread, because on some level my life as the king of hell would be easier without the attachment of emotions.

Perhaps also easier if I was no longer capable of love.

I push the thoughts away and focus on Harper again. "I need an answer. Do we have a deal?"

Her pulse jumps, and she swallows. "I need time to consider it."

"I'll give you three days."

"You'll give me whatever I need," she snaps back. "Including a plan so we can make sure no one finds out *if* I decide to join your council. Also, contingencies in the event someone does." She shakes her head, as if she can't believe she's saying the words, much less considering it.

"Of course. Should you come under suspicion with the hunters, I won't hesitate to take the heat. You can blame me, the evil demon half-brother, who preyed upon and manipulated you to act against your will to do my bidding."

Her eyes narrow. "I'll try not to take offense to you thinking I'm so *weak* you could manipulate me."

"I don't think that," I say without missing a beat. "But your organization has no idea what I'm capable of, and we can use that to our advantage if needed."

"Right," she says hesitantly. "If I agree to this—and that's a huge *if*—we need to prevent that from happening at all costs."

THE DEVIL'S TRIALS

I nod in agreement. "And it's probably best you don't attend council meetings unless absolutely necessary."

She arches her brow at me. "I don't see why you'd need a hunter at your meetings, so let's just go ahead and put that under the 'not going to happen' column." With that, she slides out of the booth.

My lips twitch as I follow her. "Very well." I won't call on Harper to fulfill her side of our arrangement until I take the throne, so we have time to hammer out the rest of the details she doesn't appear to be in the mood to discuss right now. "I'll see you soon."

Harper rolls her eyes, muttering under her breath about the insanity of our conversation as she leaves.

TWENTY
CAMILLE

I've slept like shit since I killed that demon a few nights ago. Training has felt more real—not that I wasn't taking it seriously before, but getting a taste of what we're learning *outside* the classroom has fundamentally shifted my outlook on the whole thing.

For every one demon that doesn't immediately pose a threat to humankind—like Blake, and I'm sure some of Xander's other friends—there are at least a dozen that do. That's what I keep reminding myself each day as I get ready for training. Taking that life saved countless others.

Yet the pit in my stomach always feels heavier as I stand in the middle of the training room surrounded by other trainees, including the group from Two Boots.

Noah has us practicing with obsidian daggers, much to the delight of most of the class. Target dummies are set up around the room, and I step closer to the one I'm sharing with Sierra, wrapping my fingers around the dagger.

Before I can take a shot, Noah pops up seemingly out of nowhere, shaking his head. "You're not gripping it firmly enough." He moves closer, his combat boots scuffing against the linoleum floor as he comes behind me. "You need to lift your arm higher, unless you're trying to slice through the demon's gut, which won't kill it but will piss it off. Don't mess around—take the kill shot immediately."

I bite back a scowl at his tone that grinds my gears, and adjust my grip, making sure my stance is correct, with my feet spaced shoulder-width apart to keep me steady.

"Are you waiting for something?"

What is his deal?

I thought since he was with me to hunt that demon things were better, but clearly he's still pissed about what happened while I was sick. I knew

THE DEVIL'S TRIALS

he wasn't happy I didn't send Xander away, but he's seriously holding resentment over it? It could be something else, but his attitude toward me in particular feels intentionally cold and he's never acted like this in class before now.

"Noah—"

"Do not hesitate," he cuts in. "You do that, and you're dead. I know you know that, so *focus*."

My cheeks burn. After the demon attack, I thought I'd proven to him that I've improved since he started training me, but he's treating me like... like he did Cody the other day. I'm not prepared to explore why, but that notion lights a fire in me, filling my veins with a scorching determination.

I focus my attention on the dummy in front of me, turning out the rest of the class as they continue practicing on their targets. Sierra shoots me a thumbs-up from my peripheral, and I move, shifting into the offensive stance Noah drilled into me yesterday. I lunge forward, striking out with the dagger and slamming it into the marker on the dummy's chest where the heart would be.

Sierra cheers, sending a grin in my direction, but before I can return it, Noah shoves the dummy out of the way and steps toward me.

"What the hell?" I mutter.

Noah glances between me and Sierra. "This isn't a game."

"We know that," I snap back, feeling oddly defensive over him yelling at Sierra. I can take his crap, but she shouldn't have to just for being nice to me.

His gaze focuses on me. "Really?" He briefly shifts away, yanking my dagger from the dummy's chest.

"What are you doing?" I demand.

He offers the dagger, and I take it before he says, "Defend yourself."

I stumble back when Noah advances, shaking my head. "This is ridiculous," I hiss at him. "Why—"

"Demons won't give you an opportunity to prepare for their attack," he bellows for the whole class while keeping his eyes locked on me. "You need to be alert at all times. Focus and *fight*."

The training room fades away, and it's just me and Noah. I can't let myself consider the onlookers and what they're thinking or I'll end up running in the other direction, and I don't want to even imagine how that'll affect my reputation around here.

JESSI ELLIOTT

My heart thumps hard, and I focus my breathing, steadying my stance as Noah's brows furrow in concentration. We circle each other for no more than ten seconds before I press forward, refusing to allow him the upper hand. I throw a jab with my non-dagger-wielding hand, but Noah is fast, shifting out of reach before countering with a kick to my ribs that sends me backwards and knocks the air from my lungs. He isn't using his full strength, otherwise I'd be guaranteed a few broken ribs, but my cheeks are flaming with embarrassment for getting thrown on my ass so fast.

Ignoring the throbbing in my midsection, I roll onto my stomach and get to my feet before he can advance on me again.

Do not hesitate.

His voice rings clearly in my mind, and I latch onto it, shooting toward my target.

Noah's eyes widen briefly when I slam my elbow into his gut, and I don't back down. Don't give him a chance to recover. I strike harder, faster. A kick to the groin, a punch to the jaw. My moves are less precise, but based on the rapid rise and fall of his chest, they're good enough to work.

When he lunges for me, instincts I wasn't sure I had take over and I lift my arm to block his fist from connecting with my face. The impact shoots pain down my forearm to my elbow, and I grit my teeth, hissing out a sharp breath.

He presses forward to strike again, but I jump out of the way, my muscles burning at the sudden movement, and whirl around to kick him hard behind the knees. Excitement fills my chest with pressure as he hits the mats, and I shoot forward, wrapping my arm around his neck from behind and pressing my knee into his back. He grunts at the attack, and I nearly fall to the side when he grabs for me as he rolls onto his back. I steady myself just in time and throw my full weight into him, keeping him against the mats.

Heart pounding, I straddle him, trapping my arm over his throat to immobilize him as I position my dagger over his heart.

Holy shit, I just took down Noah.

His expression is an interesting mix of shock and pride, and the corners of his mouth creep upward slightly, as if he's fighting a smile. Reaching up, he taps my arm, conceding.

The class erupts into cheers and clapping, and I grin so hard my face hurts as I catch my breath.

THE DEVIL'S TRIALS

"Okay," he mutters, clearly less impressed with the class's response.

I shoot Noah a smug look before pushing to my feet, leaving him to get up himself as I tuck my dagger into the waistband of my leggings. My stomach sinks when I catch Cody's glare, but I steel myself and instead of turning away, I smile at him. Nobody is going to ruin this moment for me, least of all some guy I don't even know.

"That was epic," Wyatt says, clapping me on the back when he and Brynne come over with Sierra and a girl I recognize from class but can't recall her name.

"Seriously," the girl says. "And this after you kicked demon ass the other night. Word travels fast around here—you're a total rockstar."

My brows lift, and I glance around the small circle of trainees. Noah had asked Wyatt and Brynne not to say anything, but—

"Sorry," Sierra sing-songs. "I couldn't help it. Your peers should know how amazing you are."

I shake my head, laughing softly. "I'm very much a work in progress, but thanks."

More people come over, offering their praise and congratulations. I struggle to keep up and smile back at everyone as tension prickles along my neck.

The room feels warmer, and my pulse kicks up as each breath becomes harder to take.

Noah calls the class back into order, and I use that opportunity to slip out of the room, grabbing my water bottle on the way. In the hallway, I lean against the wall and down a few mouthfuls, wiping the back of my hand across my forehead to dry the sweat forming there. The pressure in my chest worsens, and I try to calm my breathing, struggling through the dull ringing in my ears.

I shouldn't be shocked that all the attention—despite it being positive—on something I'd rather forget triggered a panic attack, but I need to get it under control.

I close my eyes, going through my tried and true breathing exercise until I pull myself out of the haze of anxiety. I blink them back open and sip on my water, waiting for my heart rate to return to normal. I'd rather sit the rest of the class out to avoid more comments, but I still have a long way to go and I need the training. Today was a victory, a clear marker of progress, but I need to stay focused.

JESSI ELLIOTT

I repeat that to myself a few more times as I walk back to the training room and hope it's enough to keep the anxiety at bay for the rest of class.

That evening, shortly after six, I walk over to my dad's condo a few blocks away for dinner. His place smells like an Italian restaurant when he opens the door to greet me with a warm smile and tight hug. The savory aroma of garlic and butter permeates the air, making my mouth water as we go into the kitchen.

I sit on a barstool at the island counter as my stomach grumbles. "Whatever you're making smells incredible."

"I've been on a pasta kick lately," Dad says. "I hope you like rigatoni."

"Pasta of any shape is perfect. I don't discriminate."

Dad laughs, tossing the dish towel over his shoulder. "Excellent." He looks like he just got home from work, wearing a black dress shirt and slacks with his hair tousled but still neat, professional. Not so professional are the fuzzy slippers on his feet. They're the ones I got him for Christmas last year, and I love that he actually wears them—I wasn't sure he would.

"I'm making the pasta in a vodka sauce you're going to love. I also have garlic bread in the oven and a salad on the table."

"That all sounds great. Thanks, Dad."

"My pleasure, kiddo." He grabs a wooden spoon off the counter and turns to the stove, stirring the pot. "Tell me how things are going at Ballard. I've been looking forward to hearing about your experience so far."

I'm reaching for the bottle of Riesling, unscrewing the cap and pouring each of us a glass before I say, "It's been...a lot." I take a sip and settle into my seat. "I'm constantly reminded of how behind I am, which has sucked, but I've made a few friends. I really didn't expect to, so that aspect is nice."

He glances at me over his shoulder. "Training with Noah is going well?"

"I think so. As well as it can be." I run my finger through the condensation on my wineglass. "What has Noah told you?"

Turning off the stove, he carries the steaming pot to the sink to drain the water. "He's kept me updated, but I want to hear from you."

I press my lips together, watching him mix the pasta into the sauce. "It's hard. Some of the trainees don't exactly like me being there because of my connection to the demon world, so there's a level of distrust

THE DEVIL'S TRIALS

because of that. Not everyone is mean, though. There's one girl, Sierra, who's become somewhat of a friend."

"That's great to hear." Dad pulls a couple plates down from the cupboard and dishes out the pasta.

"Yeah." I follow him to the dining table, carrying our glasses of wine and taking the chair across from him.

After a trip back to the kitchen for the garlic bread, we're digging into our food and sipping our wine.

"This is phenomenal," I tell Dad around a mouthful of pasta.

He smiles. "I'm glad you like it. Don't get too full, though. There's tiramisu for dessert."

"I'm coming here every night from now on," I say, only half joking.

Dad laughs. "You're welcome anytime."

I take a sip of wine before asking, "How are things going with you?"

"Busy at the office as usual, but nothing I can't handle."

I arch a brow at him. "You say that as if you have a normal job instead of hunting demons."

"I'm trying to be considerate of what I share with you," he explains in a gentle tone.

The knots in my stomach announce themselves with an uncomfortable tug. "Is there something I should know? Something about Xander?"

His brows furrow. "Nothing in particular. We're monitoring the number of demon attacks as usual, and nothing has appeared out of the ordinary. The Seattle team scoured the apartment Xander used to live in but found nothing to lead them where he's hiding out."

I chew the inside of my cheek, setting my fork down beside my empty plate. "Before you ask, I have no idea where he is."

"I wasn't going to ask, kiddo. I didn't expect you to know, as I hope you haven't been in communication with him."

I nod slowly without offering a real answer. I don't want to lie to him.

"How about dessert?" Dad asks, picking up on my discomfort.

"Yes, please."

Dad clears the table and brings out dessert. Halfway through and another glass of wine later, I find myself asking, "How many demons have you killed?"

He sets his glass down, swallowing then clearing his throat. "Unfortunately, I can't answer that. It's not something I've tracked over the years."

"Oh. Not even a ballpark?"

He laughs, shaking his head. "Why do you ask?"

"I don't know. I guess I've just been curious about the family legacy within the organization since returning." I drop my gaze to the table, adding quieter, "And since killing a demon a few nights ago."

"You did?"

I glance over at him, nodding. "I asked Mom not to say anything so I could tell you myself."

Eyes that remind me of my own glimmer with pride. "Congratulations, Camille. That is a significant accomplishment. There are very few trainees who have a real demon hunt on their record before they graduate from a training academy."

I poke gingerly at the tiramisu with my spoon, unsure what to do with the new sensation bubbling in my chest. I'm not used to praise from my parents. It takes a few seconds too long, but I finally find my voice and say, "Thanks."

"I understand it could have brought up some complicated emotions for you, but it will get easier."

All I can do is nod as I cling to those words.

It will get easier.

I hoped the wine I had at dinner would help me fall asleep, but it's clear that isn't the case when I'm still staring at the ceiling an hour after I crawl into bed.

Maybe it's the dessert conversation that's been playing on a loop in my head since. Recalling the pride in my dad's eyes as we discussed my first demon hunt. I'd already gone through it earlier in the week when I spoke with my mom in Seattle to report the attack.

At first, I was adamantly against it—I just wanted to forget the whole thing. But Noah managed to convince me to handle it by the book, citing that it would also help my reputation within the organization, and I couldn't argue with that.

It felt wrong to enjoy the sense of accomplishment brought on by my parent's approval. It threatens to open a can of worms I'm really not in a place to deal with, so I pop in my headphones and attempt to fall asleep to my ambient music playlist. And after another hour of tossing and turning, I eventually slip into restless sleep.

THE DEVIL'S TRIALS

The silk sheets beneath me are so soft and warm, I never want to leave the comfort of this bed. I curl onto my side, hugging a pillow to my chest and sighing softly at the faint scent of sandalwood permeating the air. I don't think I've ever felt so relaxed.

Which is probably why it takes far too long to realize I'm not alone.

Some innate part of me senses him before I even see him. Blinking my eyes open, my next breath still gets caught in my lungs when my gaze connects with Xander's where he lounges across the room in a dark wingback chair.

I sit up and immediately panic when the air feels cool against my bare skin. I glance down, and heat fills my cheeks at the tank top I fell asleep in. Gathering the sheets, I rush to pull them up to my chest. My heart still beats too quickly as Xander's lips twitch and his eyes darken with a hunger that makes my throat go dry.

"What is this?" I ask, glancing around the unfamiliar bedroom. There isn't much to it aside from the bed, chair, and an unlit fireplace. There are two closed doors across the room near Xander, as well as another to my left. The walls are a deep green that remind me of a forest, paired with dark wood floors and black drapery over the windows along the wall to my right.

Xander stands from the chair, approaching the bed at a languid pace as I white-knuckle the sheets. His eyes are locked on me as I take him in. The shadow of stubble on his cheeks and along his jaw, the casual, all-black ensemble of jeans, and a crew neck sweater under his leather jacket.

He shrugs off the jacket, dropping it on the cushioned bench at the end of the bed before coming around the side closest to me and leaning against the wall. His demeanor is relaxed and unbothered, basically the complete opposite of mine. I'm half-tempted to scramble off the bed and make a break for the door, but I have little faith in my control of this scenario. Xander brought me here—it's probably not up to me when I get to leave. That, and I didn't put on pants before I went to bed, and I'm not about to give Xander a show of my lace panties.

"Why am I here?" I ask in a low voice when he doesn't answer my last question. "Is this a trial?"

He shakes his head, a wisp of unruly curls falling across his forehead.

My brows scrunch together at the urge to brush his hair back. "Then what—"

"I wanted to see you." His gaze lowers to where I still have the sheets in a death grip. "You can relax."

I shake my head, keeping the sheets against my chest. "Do you really need to be in my dream right now? I've had a long week and just want to sleep."

Color me surprised when Xander's expression softens, and he nods. "Harper told me what happened."

"The two of you are on speaking terms, then?" I ask, not knowing how to tread when it comes to that relationship. Harper still doesn't really talk about having a new demon brother, and I won't push her to.

I can't decipher the look on his face before it vanishes, and he cocks his head to the side. "I've found it depends on the day."

I press my lips together to stifle a quiet laugh. "Yeah, that sounds like Harper."

He offers a warm, genuine smile that makes a soft dimple appear, and it almost has me forgetting that none of this is real. Maybe that's why I don't move away when he comes closer, sitting on the side of the bed and angling his body toward me as he toes off his shoes. His eyes flick between mine, and the longing in them urges me to close the distance between us. My pulse ticks faster, and I swallow, trying to ignore the faint throbbing at the apex of my thighs.

Xander licks his lips, and I watch the movement too damn closely. I can't even pretend I didn't, so when he smirks, I just shake my head, exhaling an uneven breath.

"This is a bad idea," I murmur.

He leans toward me, his breath skating across my cheek in a featherlight caress. "What's that?"

My eyelids flutter, and it's suddenly a challenge to keep them open. To deny what my body craves even while I'm unconscious. "You know what."

Dipping his face, his lips brush my neck, his stubble lightly scratching the delicate skin just below my ear. "Hmm, I don't think so." The amusement coating his words like sweet honey only fuels the fire burning hotter in my core.

"Xander," I say in warning. It's more for me than him. Because if we cross that line again, I fear it will mean something different this time.

"Tell me to stop, and I will." There's a challenge in his voice. He knows I'm still drawn to him. That I still long for him in ways I can't explain.

THE DEVIL'S TRIALS

My heart thumps in my throat, and I can't make the words form on my tongue. I close my eyes, my teeth sinking into my bottom lip for a moment before I whisper, "This is a dream...It isn't real."

He pulls back and lifts his hand to snag my jaw, tipping my head back to meet his gaze. "What about this doesn't feel real to you?"

I stare back at him, hating that I don't have any room to respond, because his point landed exactly where he intended it to. Everything about this dreamscape feels dangerously real, most notably the longing and desire filling my veins like electricity.

Xander rests his forehead against mine, sliding his fingers from my jaw into my hair, where he cradles the side of my head. "Will you continue to deny yourself what you want?"

It's called self-control, and I'm quickly losing my grasp on it.

As if on cue, the pulsing at my core grows stronger, more impossible to ignore. My pulse continues its wild pace, and before my thoughts can spiral further out of control—because *what the fuck am I doing?*—I grab the front of his shirt, wrinkling the cotton in my grip. "Just so we're clear, this is a one-time thing." Even as it leaves my lips, I don't believe it.

Xander's responding chuckle tells me he doesn't either.

"We both know this doesn't work in the real world." I'm not sure if I'm trying to convince him or myself. Regardless, I have little faith in the effectiveness of my words. We both want this, to get lost in each other, even when it's devastatingly fleeting.

In the space of a heartbeat, Xander moves onto the bed, bracing himself over me, his hair falling forward as his gaze meets mine. My legs are trapped between his thighs, and my heart thunders in my chest. He leans in, his lips level with my ear when he murmurs, "As you so cleverly pointed out, we're not in the real world right now." He kisses the pulse at my throat, stealing my breath, and my fingers slide into his hair, tugging gently. I guide him to my mouth, where our lips meet in a searing kiss that all but assures mutual destruction. And there's not a single fiber of my being that cares.

I kiss him hard, not caring if our lips are bruised in the process. I put every ounce of anger and fear and longing into it, wrapping my arms around his neck and pulling him onto me so our bodies are flush. The weight of him on top of me sets my skin on fire with need, and when his knee presses between my legs, it takes everything in me not to grind against it like some wanton fiend. With only a thin layer of silk sheets between him and the ache at my core, my head spins, making my thoughts hazy with lust.

His tongue darts out, tracing my bottom lip before pushing into my mouth and grazing mine. He deepens the kiss, his fingers sliding into my hair, while his other hand glides under my tank top. "Tell me you want this," he murmurs against my lips, palming my breast.

As if there's any room for denial at this point.

"Yes," I whisper, warmth cascading over me as I arch into his touch.

Xander breaks the kiss and shifts down the bed, taking the sheets with him. When he realizes I'm bare from the waist down, his eyes darken with lust, making my stomach dip.

I fight the urge to cover myself—it's nothing he hasn't seen before—and swallow past the dryness in my throat as Xander wraps his hands around my ankles and slowly spreads my legs open, keeping his eyes locked with mine. My cheeks and chest flush with heat when his gaze drops to my core and he drags his tongue over his bottom lip. Sliding his hands up my legs, my skin tingles in their wake, and when his breath teases the most intimate part of me, a shiver races through me. I inhale shallowly, struggling to come to terms with how this dream feels so damn real. The most powerful demon in existence is between my legs, mere inches away from feasting on me.

His mouth closes around me, and my thoughts scatter. I grip the sheets on either side of me, pressing my lips together as I lose myself to the sensations he's wringing from my body. His tongue circles and pulses, and when he eases a finger inside me while sucking the bundle of nerves nestled there, my hips jerk and a moan slips from my lips.

Xander plays my body like an instrument. Teasing and caressing in all the right places to bring me new levels of pleasure. I never want to leave this bed, this dream, this moment. I can't think about anything except the feel of him, his tongue and fingers, and when my core tightens around him, I moan his name and fall apart with euphoria.

I force my eyes open in time to watch him lean back and catch my gaze, his lips, glistening with my release, curl into a devilish smirk.

Holy shit, that should *not* be as hot as it is.

My chest rises and falls quickly as I work to catch my breath, and Xander slides off the bed, undressing with a smooth grace that makes it

THE DEVIL'S TRIALS

impossible to look away. His lean muscle ripples with the movement of removing his shirt and pants, and perhaps I should feel embarrassed by the way my mouth waters, but I don't. Not here, not with him.

I do my best to keep my eyes on his face, but when he crawls over me, I can't help when my gaze drops between us. My pulse kicks up as anticipation floods through me, and Xander chuckles, pressing a chaste kiss to my lips. He nudges my legs apart again to settle between them, and the blunt head of him teases my entrance.

He snags my chin, trapping my gaze with his. "You still want me?"

"*Always.*" The word tumbles from my lips before I even realize what I said. Xander's eyes widen in time with mine, and he pushes into me completely, stealing my breath anew. I clench around the sudden invasion, reaching for him and bringing his mouth to mine. Our lips crash together, and he pulses inside me, groaning against my lips. I drape one arm around his neck and slide my other hand between us to work my clit as I adjust to the fullness of him.

"You feel so good," he murmurs, trailing his lips along my jaw before he pulls halfway out and then thrusts back in with a shallow grunt.

"Keep going," I urge, overcome by the all-consuming need to be undone by him once more.

"With pleasure." He pulls back, then slams into me. Over. And over. And over, until I'm writhing beneath him, panting in between moans.

"Like that?" he checks in a voice deep with arousal, rolling his hips to hit a spot deep inside me that has my head spinning.

"Yes," I breathe, "Don't stop."

"No chance in hell, *mo shíorghrá.*"

I race toward my second orgasm, my core tightening as it crests, and I hold him against me as pleasure explodes in my core. Crying out my release, I moan when his lips find mine again, quieting the sounds with a kiss that I feel all the way to my toes as they curl into the mattress.

Xander doubles his efforts, thrusting harder and faster as his breathing grows shallower. He breaks the kiss and buries his face in my neck as his body tenses, and he growls against my collarbone, announcing his own climax.

It takes a minute for either of us to move. Xander pulls out, making me shiver at the sensation it brings, and trails kisses along my shoulder, pushing down the strap of my tank top that miraculously stayed on.

"What's this?" His voice is deep, curious.

"Hmm?" I ask hazily, my head still all warm and cloudy with post-orgasmic bliss.

"You have a tattoo?"

Realization dawns on me when he pulls back to look at my face. The other time I was naked with Xander I wasn't exactly in a position where he'd see it... "Oh. Yeah. I forget it's there sometimes." The intertwined flowers on my back along my shoulder blade—a reflection of my and my sister's birth months—was a spur-of-the-moment decision we made walking past a tattoo shop one summer in high school. It would've been a lot cooler if I didn't have to call our mom and beg her to come sign the waiver. Danielle had been old enough, but I was still a minor. Even still, it's one of my favorite memories.

Xander drops down beside me, and we lie on our sides, facing each other as I tell him the origin story of the floral ink.

"That's nice," he says softly.

I nod, smiling. "Don't get any ideas, though. I don't think Harper is there yet."

He chuckles. "I still have hope I'll win her over. I just need time."

My brows lift. I can't help but wonder what's pushing him to continue trying to build that relationship. It begs the question of just how lost his humanity is if he's willing to work for that connection. "For what it's worth, I think you're making strides."

His lips curve into a small smile in response.

We lie in silence for a few minutes. My eyelids feel heavier with each blink, and I snuggle into the blankets around us, the pillow under my head feeling extra comfy.

Xander shifts closer and lifts his hand to my face, brushing his fingers along my cheek and using his thumb to tilt my chin up to look at him. "You're mine," he murmurs. "Soulmate bond or no, there's no one else for me."

My stomach dips, and I struggle to understand the sudden burning in my eyes or the urge to reach for him and echo the sentiment. But something stops the words from forming on my lips.

It's undoubtedly true—I'm his as much as he's mine.

And that has the power to destroy us both.

Twenty-One
Xander

"*You still want me?*"
    "*Always.*"

That single word holds all the weight in the world, and I cling to it too fucking tightly as I get ready to meet Blake. I was supposed to be at his bar an hour ago to discuss the newest member of my council, but I slept through all of my alarms. Being with Camille inside a dreamscape for so long last night took more power than I'm used to exerting—and it was worth every second.

I send Blake a quick text to let him know I'm on my way, and shrug on a jacket after noticing the overcast sky outside my window. Rain is almost guaranteed on any given day. Such is living in the Pacific Northwest.

When I get to the bar, I find it surprisingly busy for a Monday afternoon. I ruffle the bit of rainwater out of my hair as I step inside and approach the bar, where one of Blake's employees is pouring a tall glass of beer.

"He's in the office," she says, barely giving me a glance. She's human and she knows the man she works for isn't, but that's the extent of it.

I offer a nod as I move through the patrons waiting to get their drinks. Walking down the hallway, the sounds from the bar quiet, and I tap my knuckles on the door before letting myself into Blake's office. He's lounging on one of the couches with his computer on his lap and a small cup of what smells like espresso in his hand.

"Nice of you to finally get your ass out of bed, you royal sleepyhead."

My lips twitch as I cross the room and drop onto the couch across from him. I nod at the laptop. "What are you doing?"

"Well, you see, I do run a business when I'm not defending your ass." He sips his espresso before setting it on the coffee table between us. "My accountant has been asking for a bunch of shit and wanted it last week."

If I put her off any longer, she's going to think I'm committing tax fraud or something."

I arch a brow at him. "Such human problems."

He snorts. "You're telling me." Blake sits up, closing his laptop and facing me. "What's going on with you, though? You never sleep in."

I scratch the back of my neck, genuinely unsure how he'll respond to what I'm about to tell him.

"Oh, fuck. I know that look, mate. What did you do now?"

I exhale a humorless laugh. "My council is gaining another, potentially controversial member."

Harper hasn't officially accepted the position, but it's only a matter of time. I may not yet have all the skills of a royal, but persuasion has always been a strength of mine.

"Don't keep a bloke in suspense. Who is it?"

There's a moment of hesitation before I tell him, "Harper."

A look of disbelief crosses his features. He sits back. Rubs his jaw. "Are you sure about this?"

I nod. "You won't convince me otherwise."

"I won't try. I just want to make sure you've considered every angle. I'm only looking out for you."

It's moments such as these where it's all too easy to forget Blake is a demon. Some of his mannerisms—his genuine concern for me—feel so damn *human*.

"I appreciate that and I understand. This wasn't a decision I made lightly. But with such an already complicated relationship, there wasn't much else I could do if I wanted to continue building something with her."

"So, you do, then? Want a relationship with her?"

"She's...family." The word tastes odd on my tongue and sits heavy in my chest as I replay it a few times in my head. I've never had anyone I *wanted* to explore a familial relationship with, and I can't let this one go without attempting to make it work.

"Fair enough, mate. So long as she doesn't get in the way of anything—your trials, for example—then I'm all for bringing the little hunter on board."

I catch the subtle look of hunger in his gaze and exhale a deep sigh, leaning back against the throw pillows. Blake has made no attempt to mask the attraction he has toward Harper, and I don't have any right to play the protective big brother, so I clamp my jaw shut against the warning that sears my tongue.

"Have you decided how you'll tell the others?"

"Provided Harper agrees—"

My words are cut off by a loud crash from the bar, quickly followed by heavy footfall and screaming.

Blake and I barely exchange a glance before we're moving, though he tries to stop me at the office door.

"You should—"

"You're not telling me to stay put," I growl at him, ripping the door open, and then we're both moving down the hallway at breakneck speed.

"Bloody hell, you feel that?"

The fear. It floods the bar like a tsunami. Together with the bone-chilling screams of terror, it's a demon's playground.

Blake and I enter the bar, and in seconds, chaos erupts around us. Glass shatters and wooden furniture is destroyed. My first thought is hunters, but my stomach plummets a moment later when I realize it's not members of the wretched organization.

We're being attacked by demons.

The sharp scent of blood permeates the air, mixed with sweat as humans attempt to flee in any direction, knocking over furniture and people in their path.

Blake jumps into action without hesitation, grabbing a low-level demon off a human and snapping its neck in a brutal maneuver. I scan the room, my blood running cold as I come to the stark realization that these demons aren't attacking to feed—this is a massacre.

Human bodies and demon ashes, litter the floor and booths. Most are dead or very close to it, their skin so pale it appears gray and their clothes tattered and bloodied.

I stalk toward a group of demons converging on the bartender, who's attempting to stand her ground behind the bar with a knife in her grip. Her eyes are wild with fear and determination, her pulse pounding erratically as her hand shakes.

I whistle sharply to get their attention, and the three dark-haired demons whirl around and snarl at me, their mouths full of razor-sharp fangs and their eyes completely black. There's not an ounce of humanity in these creatures. They're here to slaughter—but *why?*

The one closest to me lunges forward, clawed fingernails swiping at my face. I bat him away with a brutal backhand, and he growls in pain, spitting black blood onto the wood floor. Blake's going to have a time getting the place clean after this.

Before the demon can get up, I slam my boot into his windpipe, crushing it with ease. Those black orbs widen as he gasps for breath he'll never get to take. I haul him upright and snap his neck, then shove him toward his cohorts.

My temples throb with pressure, and the constant screaming as people attempt to flee and end up fighting for their lives isn't helping. Taking inventory of the demons still standing, it's immediately clear how severely outnumbered we are.

I bite back a snarl, shooting forward to grab the other two demons before they can reach the bartender. "Unless you'd like to end up like your friend, get the fuck out of here." I don't relish killing my own kind but I won't stand for this senseless brutality.

The older of the two spits in my face, and I see red. Rage whips through me like a tidal wave, and I lose control of myself in an instant. I meet his gaze as I slam my fist through his chest, wrapping my hand around his warm, beating heart.

And then I rip it out of his chest.

He gasps and gargles for a few seconds as he collapses, then goes completely still.

I hold his heart in my palm, watching it twitch as my lips curl into a cruel smile, and I offer it to the other, slack-jawed demon. "Hungry?"

His face pales, and he sputters out, "N-no."

I shrug. "Too bad." Moving too fast for him to escape, I shove his friend's heart against his lips, forcing the organ into the demon's mouth even as he thrashes, attempting to get away.

I vaguely notice the bartender bent over, vomiting into the sink. With a sigh, I drop the mangled heart and snap the other demon's neck, wiping my hands on my pants.

"On your left, mate," Blake shouts over the noise. Though, it's quieted significantly, considering most of the patrons are dead. Music still plays over the sound of ragged breaths and unsteady heartbeats, but the sense of a battle ending seeps into the room—and we mostly definitely didn't win this one.

THE DEVIL'S TRIALS

I turn just in time to be on the receiving end of a sucker punch to my jaw. I snarl at the female demon with ice-blond hair and sharp cheekbones. She has otherwise normal features, so she's a higher pedigree than most of the low level demons we—Blake mostly—have taken on here.

"Traitor," she snaps, rearing back for another attack.

"Lovely to meet you too," I bark, snatching her fist before it can meet its mark. I hold it in a grip that would crush a human's, and she grits her teeth. "Care to explain who's responsible for this attack?"

Despite the discomfort in her features, a smugness fills her gaze as her deep red lips curl into a cold smirk. "He will never allow you to ascend the throne."

My brows lift, and I cut a glance over to Blake. The demons he was facing off with have stopped trying to fight. The ones left standing converge on where I'm standing near the bar, and Blake is at my side in a blur of movement.

"What the hell are you talking about?" Blake demands, his jaw sharp enough to cut glass.

"Xander Kane is a traitor to our kind," one of the males shouts in a deep, jagged voice. He has smears of black blood across his face, dripping from his lip and a cut above his eye, courtesy of Blake. "He committed an act of treason that will not be ignored."

Ah, so these must be what's left of Lucia's fan club. Excellent.

"The royal guard—" Blake starts.

"Has been compromised. That much was perfectly evident when they dismissed Marrick's claim to the throne."

I school my features into a mask of indifference, but shock crackles through my veins like electricity. Lucia's psychotic lover—and Francesca's father—has always loathed me. It comes as no surprise that he's threatening my reign, though I can't say I expected him to make a play for the throne.

"If Marrick is so enraged by what happened, where is he now? What's taken him so long to act?" I pose the question to no one in particular. "Should he take issue with my ascension, he is welcome to make that known to my face."

The eldest demon of the group cackles. "What do you think this was, boy?" He steps forward, shouldering past two younger demons. "This was merely a taste of the carnage Marrick will bring should you continue your pathetic attempt at ascending. We all know you're too human to rule. Give up now, and save us all the wreckage that will ensue should you refuse."

Blake laughs harshly. "If Marrick wants a war, you tell that prick to wage it himself. Sending a horde of low-level demons and you lot is as amusing as it is pathetic."

The demon's eyes narrow, flicking toward Blake before returning to me. When they meet mine, dark arrogance glimmers in them, making my back straighten.

"My mistake. I wrongfully thought you cared about the hunter who shares your blood."

Blake snarls at the same time I lunge forward, grabbing the demon by the throat. Evidently, word has spread about my relation to Harper.

"Let me be very clear," I say in a low voice. "You—"

"Don't bother with your threats," he wheezes out. "It's very simple. You are going to abdicate the throne to Marrick...or he will very slowly, very painfully end the life of your sister. Of course, he'll only kill her after a long period of torture until every bit of her pathetic human mind and body is broken."

My fingers dig into the bastard's throat, breaking the skin. Black blood drips down my hand, and his breathing becomes shallow as I lean in. "If Marrick wants a war, he's fucking got it. No one threatens what's mine."

When a few of the other demons step forward, Blake growls deep in his throat, his eyes going black as he moves with lethal grace.

I hear his heart beat faster as he attacks without mercy, snapping necks left and right.

Something came over him at the threat of Harper's life. I can't say I fully understand it, but I certainly share the sentiment. That said, I want to be smart about retaliation. We'll plan an attack Marrick won't see coming. He'll find out soon enough exactly who he's dealing with.

I'm not the half-human teenager he used to know.

I am a *king*.

"Leave here now," I say in a low, hard voice, shoving the demon away from me. "If I see your face again, I'll rip it from your skull."

He looks as if he's going to keep fighting, but a subtle glance around the room makes it clear he's the one outnumbered now. With one last snarl in my direction, he disappears through the space where the bar's

THE DEVIL'S TRIALS

front door used to be. Now it sits in a broken mess on the floor, ripped from its hinges.

I step over bodies to approach Blake. His expression is grave, his face smeared black with demon blood.

He exhales deeply. "What's your plan now, mate? What are we going to do about Marrick?"

My lips curl into a slow smile as my pulse settles into a normal rhythm. I meet Blake's gaze. "*I'm going to fucking destroy him.*"

Twenty-Two
Camille

Noah is at my door half an hour before we typically meet in the parking garage. I open the door with my toothbrush still in my mouth.

"What are you doing here?" I say around a mouthful of minty foam.

"Your first test is today."

An anxious pit blossoms in my gut, and I back away from the door, leaving it open and hurrying to the bathroom to spit out the toothpaste. After rinsing my mouth, I return to the living room, where Noah is perched on the arm of the couch.

"I don't get any notice?"

"What do you think this is?"

I shoot him a look. "That's not what I mean, and you know it. A few days to prepare would be nice."

He nods. "I'm sure it would be."

I cross my arms, exhaling a harsh breath. "Okay. So—"

"Let's go," he interrupts. "I'll explain how it works on the way."

Without waiting for me to respond, he stands and walks out of my apartment. I tug on my shoes, then grab my bag and jacket on the way out, cursing Noah under my breath as I hurry to catch up before he gets on the elevator.

He doesn't say anything until we're in the car driving toward Ballard. "Your test will be administered by my supervisor."

My brows inch closer. "Why aren't you doing it?"

"Mentors don't score their mentees. It's an organization-wide policy to ensure fair testing."

I nod. "I guess that makes sense."

Noah turns the heat down a little as we speed up to merge onto the interstate. "The test is a combination of mental and physical exercises that are meant to evaluate how you respond under pressure."

THE DEVIL'S TRIALS

"Will I be running through drills like we do in training?"

"Not quite. You'll be expected to use what you've learned in those drills, but the test is a simulation of a demon attack."

My next breath gets caught in my throat and pressure clamps down on my chest as I stare at Noah, while he keeps his attention on the road. "So I'm fighting a fake demon?"

"Trust me, you won't be able to tell that it isn't real. The government invested an obscene amount of money in the technology to create a life-like rendition."

I swallow past the dryness in my throat, wringing my hands in my lap. "You watched me successfully kill a *real* demon less than a week ago. Can't that be used to evaluate my progress instead of this test?"

All through high school and college so far, exams have been a major trigger for my anxiety. Having to face them now in an environment I already feel profoundly uncomfortable in has my heart rate steadily increasing as we get closer to Ballard.

"No, for the same reason I can't evaluate your test."

I exhale slowly, nodding. "Do I get to bring a dagger in?"

"Anything you're allowed will be provided. I'll be watching from the observation room above the testing center."

I'm not sure if that's meant to make me feel better, but my skin still feels too hot, my upper lip dotted with sweat. I reach over and open my window a crack to get some air, closing my eyes to concentrate on controlling my breathing. I need to keep the anxiety at bay so I can focus on recalling what I've learned in training.

Too soon, we're walking into Ballard's main building. Instead of heading for the usual training room, Noah leads me to what appears to be a clinic waiting room on the opposite side of the facility. The space is lined with white plastic chairs and a registration desk. Half of the chairs are taken by other trainees, some of which I recognize from class, and others who are strangers.

Wyatt sits across the room and offers me a smile and wave, which I return before turning to Noah.

"Take a seat while I sign you in," he instructs. "And I'll see you after."

I nod then walk over and sit next to Wyatt, who's dressed in black joggers, sneakers, and a muscle shirt, his hair gelled back. "Did you know about the test before this morning?"

He shakes his head. "I found out when I showed up. They test us all on different schedules so no one really knows when they'll get called."

"Oh," I mumble, wiping my hands on my thighs. "Are you as freaked as I am?"

He chuckles. "Ehh, yeah, probably not, but this isn't my first test. I imagine it's yours?"

"Uh-huh," I admit, "I didn't get this far when I was in training years ago, so it's all new to me."

Offering a wide grin, he says, "Don't sweat it. You'll do great, especially after training with Noah since you got here."

I blow out a breath and force a smile. "Thanks. I hope so." I catch Noah's gaze across the room when he steps away from the registration desk. He sends me a nod before leaving the room, the door clicking shut behind him.

"Camille Morgan, proceed to the testing center," the woman behind the desk calls out, and my pulse races as I grip the armrests tightly.

"Hey," Wyatt says to snag my attention, then assures, "You've got this."

I nod silently, getting to my feet. "Good luck with your test," I tell him, and then I'm moving across the room in a daze, my heart thumping erratically in my throat.

The door buzzes when I get close, swinging open automatically. I step into a cold, empty hallway, my running shoes echoing off the concrete floor with each step. After a short eternity, I reach a set of metal double doors. There's a digital countdown above them, indicating that I have thirty seconds until they open.

I can do this, I tell myself. *I have to do this.*

Watching the timer tick down, I inhale through my nose, hold it, and exhale through my mouth a few times.

10, 9, 8, 7, 6...

My stomach drops as the timer runs down.

5, 4, 3, 2, 1

An alarm rings and the doors slide open, revealing an empty room with white walls and floors and harsh overhead lighting.

I swallow hard, steel myself, and step inside.

The door closes immediately behind me, leaving me alone in the silent room. The lights hum with energy, and I take a tentative step forward. A panel in the floor opens in front of me, a small platform rising from it with

THE DEVIL'S TRIALS

a single obsidian dagger on top. I snatch it up and whirl around to scan the room. It's still empty.

I move around slowly, looking over my shoulder every few seconds as my pulse pounds. Coming to a halt in the middle of the room, I shiver at the eerie silence and the frigid temperature.

A low, guttural growl rumbles behind me, and I don't have a second to prepare before a solid boot slams into my back, launching me forward and sending the dagger clattering across the smooth floor.

I barely manage to catch myself in time to avoid face planting, my knees taking the brunt of the impact, and wince at the pain shooting up my thighs.

I push myself up and run for the dagger, the hair on the back of my neck standing straight. I feel the demon stalking toward me, and the moment I have the weapon gripped tightly in my hand, I whirl around to face—

No.

No, no, no.

My lungs constrict, and I stumble back, stomach clenching painfully.

"Camille." Xander's deep voice slams into me, stealing my oxygen.

I squeeze my eyes shut.

This isn't real.

"You knew it would come to this."

My eyes fly open to find Xander circling me like a predator would its prey, his eyes solid black and his lips curled into a wicked smirk.

Fuck, this simulation is terrifyingly real.

He comes at me, and I barely jump away in time to avoid him grabbing me. His responding snarl flips something on in me, and I close my hand into a fist, letting it fly toward his face. When it connects with his jaw, sending him stumbling back a few steps, I suck in a breath and pursue him again with Noah's voice ringing in my head.

Do not hesitate. You do that, and you're dead.

Of course, I wasn't expecting to face a disturbingly realistic simulation of Xander for my first test, but maybe I should have. And something tells me I have Noah to thank for that detail.

Xander dodges my next attack, moving around me with incredible speed, and I spin on my heels to keep up. Except I'm not quick enough and don't have time to duck before his boot slams into my stomach. I make a strangled sound and clutch my middle, panting and trying to push through the dull ringing in my ears. It's a good thing I didn't have a chance to grab breakfast this morning, because I'd probably be coughing it up right now.

"You can do better than this," the simulation of Xander taunts, sauntering forward as I back away, still trying to catch my breath.

"Shut up," I mutter, wiping my forehead with the back of my hand.

"I'm disappointed," he pushes, his eyes glimmering with smugness.

"I said, *shut up.*" I jump into action, launching myself at him again, the cool metal hilt of my dagger biting into my palm. I use the discomfort to focus and center myself.

Slashing across his chest, I wince as Xander growls in pain at the obsidian that slices his skin, and my eyes drop to the tip of my blade now coated with black blood that drips onto the pristine white floor.

In the space of a heartbeat, Xander knocks the dagger out of my hand and closes in, baring his teeth like an animal and sneering at me. He cocks his head to the side, those black orbs studying my face—for what, I have no idea.

And then he laughs.

The sound chills me to the marrow of my bones and sends nausea rolling through me like a tidal wave.

"Oh, Camille." He inhales slowly, then sighs. My eyes widen when his flicker to their normal brown, but everything in me tenses when he murmurs, "You're dead."

Those words shoot adrenaline straight into my veins, but I struggle to channel the surge of energy into fighting the soon-to-be king of hell. The man I love. *My soulmate.*

Xander lunges before I can, slamming into me and taking us both to the ground. I gasp, the air knocked from my lungs, and grit my teeth against the flare of pain in my tailbone.

A shudder ripples through me, and I stare up at him, my heart beating so hard it burns. Tears of fear and anger blur my vision as Xander snatches the dagger off the floor and raises it. He's poised to strike, and I can't move. He has me trapped beneath him, with his thighs on either side of my hips and my hands pinned above me.

My eyes fall closed, my shoulders shaking with silent sobs as fire licks up my throat.

THE DEVIL'S TRIALS

I wait for the pain to come, but instead, the weight of Xander on top of me disappears.

The simulation is over.

I just failed my first hunter test.

Silence fills the room once more, and I blink my eyes open to stare at the industrial ceiling as my heart continues pounding against my rib cage. My pulse spikes, and I sit up when the doors slide open and Noah walks in, his expression grim.

I get to my feet on shaky legs, sweat coating my skin as the cool air chills me to the bone.

Noah stops a few feet from me, tension screwing his features. "What was that?"

I clench my jaw, willing the burning in my eyes to fade. "I'm sorry," I croak, shame filling my voice.

He shakes his head. "I don't even know what to say."

I drop my gaze, dipping my chin as it quivers. "You and me both." I swallow past the lump in my throat and press my lips into a tight line.

"Camille, this is serious. If you fail your next test, there's nothing I or your parents can do. You'll be kicked out of the training program."

I don't say anything. I can't. All I can do is stand there and will myself not to burst into tears.

Noah exhales heavily. "I can tell you're not in the headspace to discuss this now. I'll take you back to the apartment and we'll talk about it later."

I'm getting out of the shower an hour after I get back from my test when my phone chimes from the vanity. I pull on my robe and wrap my hair in a towel before grabbing it and finding a message from Harper.

> Hey, babe. Just checking in. You around today?

> Hey! Sure, what's up?

> Don't freak out, but things have gotten a bit complicated here. Turns out being related to the heir to the throne in the demon world puts a bit of a target on your back.

My stomach plummets and my legs suddenly feel unsteady. I walk into my bedroom and sit on the end of my bed before calling her.

She picks up on the first ring and quickly says, "I'm fine."

"What happened?" I demand.

"Take a breath, Cami. Nothing happened to me. Xander and Blake ran into an issue with some demons that were supporters of Lucia."

I swallow hard, my pulse beating in my throat. "What does that have to do with you?"

She sighs. "Apparently her bitter ex-lover, Marcus or whatever, is pissed Xander is taking the throne and is trying to use me to threaten his way into the position instead."

I chew my thumbnail, my knee bouncing as I quickly try to visualize my schedule. It's only Tuesday, and I'm supposed to have training all week, but this is more important.

"Did I lose you?" Harper asks with a short laugh.

"No, I'm here. Just…hang on." I pull the phone away from my ear and put it on speaker before logging into my flight app.

"What are you doing?"

"Booking a flight."

"You don't need to come to Seattle. I'm perfectly safe. Besides, I'm going to be in New York with you in two weeks for Thanksgiving."

"Of course, I do. This is my—"

"Don't you dare say fault," she cuts in firmly.

I sigh. "I was going to say, 'this is my job as the best friend—to be there for you.' If you can truthfully say that you wouldn't do the same for me, I won't come."

There's a beat of silence, and then Harper groans. "Fine. Send me your flight info when it's booked, and I'll pick you up at the airport."

"Will do. And, uh, how much of this have you shared with the organization?" I'll have to see my mom while I'm there, and if this comes up, I want to know what, if anything, is safe to talk about.

"About that…" She trails off. "I haven't really. There's some other stuff at play that I'll explain when I see you, but no one knows this psycho demon put a hit on me. Well, except for Xander and Blake. Probably Xander's council members, too."

"I feel like I missed a bunch of chapters here, but okay. I'll see you soon and we can talk about everything. Preferably over drinks. And tacos. And cookie dough. These are necessities." Especially when I tell her I failed my first hunter test. The thought of that conversation makes my stomach hurt.

THE DEVIL'S TRIALS

"Of course." Harper offers a soft laugh. "I fucking love you, babe. Have a safe flight."

"Love you," I echo before ending the call. I toss my phone onto my mattress and exhale a shaky breath. The back of my neck prickles with unease, like the beginnings of a panic attack. I do my best to shove it away as I pack a duffel bag with some clothes and toiletries.

Traveling has always been a pain point for my anxiety. It's not about being away from home so much as it's being stuck somewhere—like a giant metal tube with wings in the sky—and knowing I can't leave.

It's fine, I tell myself. *You can distract yourself with cheesy sitcoms for the six-hour flight. You* want *to do this.*

I manage to get a grip on the doom spiral and stop it, or at least pause it. I book my flight using points, then send the identical text to both Noah and my dad.

> I'm going to Seattle for a few days to visit Mom and Harper. I'll let you know when I'm back.

Dad texts back first.

> Everything okay, kiddo?

Based on his response, I have to think he hasn't been informed about my test result. Same with Mom, otherwise she would've called to yell at me, I'm sure.

> Yeah, all good. I just want to see Mom before Thanksgiving because I'll be in NYC this year.

> Sounds good. Enjoy your time in Seattle. Please send me your travel itinerary. Love you.

> Will do. Love you.

I'm not sure if I'm surprised or a little disappointed that Noah doesn't answer by the time I get to the airport two hours later, but I can't worry about it. Noah being an ass is very low on my list of problems right now.

Harper meets me at arrivals when I land in Seattle, and we hug harder and longer than I think we ever have before getting in the car, damp from the light rain.

I wait until we're out of the heavy airport traffic before turning to her. "Okay, spill."

Her lips twitch. "Spill what, exactly?"

"All of the things," I say in a light tone, trying to keep the stress of the conversation to a minimum for as long as possible.

She blows out a breath, drumming her fingers against the steering wheel. Her cobalt nail polish is chipped, which is normal considering the training she does on a daily basis. "Shit, I don't even know where to start." Casting me a quick glance, she adds, "Maybe you should talk first, then I can after we've had many, *many* drinks."

"And you think I know where to start?" Between the demon kill, that wild dream with Xander, and my monumental failure this morning, there's no shortage of drama.

"Okay," she says. "Any developments on the Xander front?"

I chew my bottom lip, pulling my legs onto the seat and tucking them under myself to get comfortable. "I, uh...sort of had dream sex with him a couple of nights ago."

Her eyes pop wide. "You did *what*?"

"It wasn't real," I say in a desperate voice, as if that'll make it better. I haven't stopped thinking about it since. It felt so *real*.

And so fucking good.

"I don't even—How did that happen?" she demands, shaking her head in disbelief.

I shrug. "Same way it does in the conscious world?"

"Right." Her tone sounds distracted, like she's still doing mental gymnastics to figure it out. "Are you back together then?"

"No," I answer too quickly.

"Are you sure about that?"

I groan. "I'm not sure of anything, Harper. That's part of the problem."

"If it makes you feel better, I'm right there with you these days." She reaches to turn the heat on. "I didn't think I wanted any kind of relationship with Xander. But then...I don't know. It feels like I'd be losing a brother all over again if I toss away the opportunity to at least try with him, you know?"

"I understand." Her words pull at my heart, making my chest tighten. All I want to do is hug her, assure her everything is going to work out even though I have no idea if it's true.

THE DEVIL'S TRIALS

"If I do that, though, I'm forced to face a lot of things I've never considered before, like if it's possible Xander could be a decent person and someone I *want* to know despite being a demon."

I nod. "Which, of course, goes against everything we're taught by the organization."

"Right." The unease in her voice makes me frown, because there's not a thing I can do about what she's struggling with. Hell, I'm struggling with the same thing. "So, that's where I'm at," she continues. "But we'll chat about that and everything else later, once you've had a chance to visit with your mom."

Harper drops me off with the promise that she'll pick me up when I'm ready to leave. I leave my suitcase in the car and walk up the driveway to the house I grew up in. I haven't seen my mom in almost a month and haven't been back here in far longer so I climb the front steps and ring the doorbell.

My eyes widen at the deep sound of a bark.

When did Mom get a dog?

Thirty seconds later, footsteps approach from the other side of the door, and I adjust my purse strap on my shoulder as I wait.

Mom opens the door with a smile, using her knee to keep what looks to be a fluffy golden retriever from bolting outside. "Come in, come in." She ushers me inside while keeping the dog back, then closes the door.

"Who's this?" I ask, bending to pet the dog so it'll settle down.

She steps back, smiling at the dog as I scratch behind its ears. "I rescued him last week when the shelter put out an urgent call to rehome him."

"What's his name?"

"Hawkeye."

His ears perk up at the sound of his name, his tail wagging back and forth across the floor where he sits.

My brows lift. "Like the *Avengers* character?"

Laughing softly, she shakes her head. "Try forty years earlier. Hawkeye was the captain in *M*A*S*H*."

"Well, he's adorable. The dog, I mean." I stand, hugging my mom. "It's good to see you."

She squeezes me back. "You too, honey." When we lean apart, she asks, "How was the flight?"

"Good. Harper picked me up."

Mom nods, and we move into the living room to the right of the entryway, where a steady flame fills the gray stone fireplace, heating the small space. "I didn't make anything for dinner because I didn't know when you'd arrive, or if your flight would be delayed, and I figured you'd want to go out with Harper."

"That's okay," I insist, feeling a little out of bounds with this conversation. I've never been incredibly close with my mom—less so after Danielle died—but seeing her out of her element too brings me some comfort. We're navigating this new chapter of our mother-daughter relationship together, and it might be uncomfortable at times, but I find I'm grateful for it.

We sit on opposite ends of the couch, while Hawkeye curls up on the floor at Mom's feet.

"How are things?" she asks, a little hesitant.

I shrug. "Complicated, but that's nothing new. Training has been the single most humbling experience of my life. I didn't realize a person could be so out of shape, but I sure as hell am."

The warmth from the fireplace contrasts the look on her face, and my stomach sinks when she sighs. I've heard that sound many times before. She's disappointed.

"I've spoken with Noah several times since you went to New York."

I fight a cringe as my stomach drops at the thought. It doesn't surprise me, but I say, "Oh?"

"He's concerned you're not as far along in training as you should be. I am as well after learning you didn't pass your first test."

Well, shit. So, she does know. I guess the silver lining here is that I don't have to tell her myself.

My brows slam down, and I clench my jaw. "I don't suppose he told you about me kicking his ass in training yesterday?"

She shakes her head. "That's good to hear, but my concern stands." Her tense expression doesn't fade. "If you don't pass your next test, you'll be dismissed from the training program."

I know that, I want to snap but instead I just blink at her. This is just about the last conversation I expected to be having. I also hate the burning in my eyes and the growing pit in my stomach. I wouldn't have cared about this a month ago, but now...

"What am I supposed to do with that?"

THE DEVIL'S TRIALS

"Work harder," she offers. "Train more. You deferred school to focus on training, but it doesn't sound like you're dedicating enough time to it. I know you can do better than this, Camille."

I swallow, forcing down the lump in my throat. "Okay, well thanks for the vote of confidence?" I sit back on the couch, exhaling a sigh.

Mom leans over and pats my knee. "Talk to Noah. He's your mentor and wants to help you succeed in the program."

"Is that why he told you about how miserably I'm failing?"

She frowns. "He was worried it would chase you away from training if he tried to talk to you about it."

I scowl at that.

"Can you blame him?"

Instead of responding to her question, I say, "I'll talk to him when I get back to New York." A pit forms in my stomach at the thought of that conversation, and I immediately recoil from it.

Mom nods. "Will you be here long?"

I press my lips together, shrugging. "I haven't really decided." I startle when the dog shifts on the floor, forgetting he was there.

She chuckles, moving to pet his head.

"I still can't believe you got a dog. You never let me and Danielle have pets growing up. What does he do while you're at headquarters all day?"

"He comes with me," she says with a faint grin. "He has a bed beside my desk."

I choke on a laugh. "I can honestly say I wasn't expecting that."

Mom joins my laughter, then makes a soft sound of contentment.

"What?"

Her gaze meets mine. "It's nice to see you, that's all. I miss my daughter." The emotion in her tone brings tears to my eyes. My relationship with my mom has been less than ideal since Danielle died and I left the organization, but maybe with my return to it, we can repair the rift between us. This is at least a good start.

Pressure blooms in my chest, and I stumble over my response. "Oh, um...I miss you too. Things have been a little hectic since I left, but I'm sorry I haven't made more of an effort to keep you in the loop with everything. I'll do better."

She lifts her hand to my cheek, smiling softly. "I understand. Maybe you'll come home for Christmas this year?"

I can barely think a day ahead, much less a month and a half, but I nod anyway. "That sounds good."

When Harper picks me up, she comes bearing a bottle of wine, a roll of cookie dough, and tacos from my favorite restaurant downtown.

"I am absolutely in love with you," I tell her as I pull the passenger side door shut, leaning over the center console to smack a loud kiss against her cheek.

She laughs as she pulls out of my mom's driveway, turning up the music a bit, though not too loud we can't talk. "You best keep me out of that love triangle of yours." Her tone is light and teasing, but I can't help my responding cringe. "Sorry," she singsongs. "I couldn't resist."

"It's not a love triangle," I insist as we drive toward the interstate. We could drive through the city, but even after the commuter rush, this way is easier.

"Then what would you call it?"

"A series of poor decisions?" I offer, dragging a hand down my face. "I'm still figuring it out."

"Hmm, that sounds like code for 'I'm not letting myself think about it so I don't have to deal with it.'"

"Why do you have to call me out like this?"

"Trauma bonding." She shoots me a grin. "Because you can bet your ass I've been doing the same thing since you left for NYC."

I stretch my legs out and fold my arms over my chest, exhaling heavily. "So we both have something we don't want to talk about."

Harper opens her mouth to respond, but the sound of an incoming call fills the car. My eyes widen slightly at the caller ID on her display screen.

"Why is Blake calling you?"

"I really don't know, and you know what? I care even less." She hits decline, and the music comes back on. For a few seconds anyway, and then Blake calls again.

"Maybe you should answer it?" I offer.

She makes a sound of annoyance as we get on the interstate and she answers the call. "What?" she snaps.

"That's not a very nice way to start a conversation, love." His deep, accented voice is filled with amusement.

Harper glances my way, rolling her eyes. "I'm busy. What do you want?"

THE DEVIL'S TRIALS

"That's a dangerous question to ask," he taunts, and Harper grips the steering wheel tighter. No one seems to be able to get under her skin like Blake.

"I'm going to chime in and suggest you get to the point," I say.

"Well, hello to you too, Camille. Lovely to hear your voice."

"Is there a reason you're being extra annoying?" Harper asks.

"Just keeping things fun."

Muffled voices on the other end of the phone snag my attention. *Is Xander with him?*

"*Anywayyyy*," he says, drawing out the word. "I'm calling to see if you've decided—"

"No," Harper cuts him off in a panic.

He sighs. "Xander wants an answer."

"You can tell Xander to go to hell."

Blake chuckles. "Yeah, that's not the insult you think it is, love."

I watch the whole exchange with a frown. *What is going on right now?*

"I'm not dealing with this right now. I'm going to enjoy my time with my bestie, eat tacos and cookie dough, drink too much, and I'm most definitely not going to think about you or Xander for a second."

He whistles. "You wound me so flippantly. But that sounds like a good time. Should we meet you—"

"Goodbye, Blake," she says in a firm tone before ending the call, exhaling a harsh breath.

"Do I want to ask?" I angle toward her while she keeps her attention on the road.

"Uh, probably not." She signals to get off the interstate and slows to a stop at a traffic light.

"Okay. Should I be worried?"

She looks over at me. "I'll explain everything once we get home. You'll want the tequila."

Unease blossoms in my chest. "I'm going to be really bummed if I lose my appetite, because the tacos smell divine."

With a short laugh, she turns her attention back to the road, and we're moving again.

Being back at the apartment I lived in before fleeing to NYC is weird. Almost as though I never left and also like I've been gone far longer. It's an odd mix of feelings as I walk inside, wheeling my suitcase behind me.

JESSI ELLIOTT

Everything looks the same. Harper hasn't changed anything since I left. It still smells like our favorite citrus candle. The throw blanket I crocheted last summer is still draped over the back of the couch. The wall in between the windows in the living area is still covered with our photos. Nothing is out of place. I'm not entirely sure why, but that brings me a sliver of comfort, maybe because it means I can come back and it'll feel like home.

Once we're settled on the couch with our food and drinks, I pin Harper with a look until she starts talking.

"Before I say this, you should know that I still haven't made up my mind about the whole thing."

My brows lift. "Okay?"

She chews her lip, looking away as if she can't stand to hold my gaze when she says, "Xander asked me to join his council."

"He *what*?" I demand, shaking my head. "That doesn't make sense. You're not a demon."

Harper finally looks at me. "I know that. *He* knows that." She plucks at the blanket draped over her lap. "He wants a hunter."

I blink at her, trying to wrap my head around what she's saying. "I feel like I'm missing something here. Why does Xander want a demon hunter on his council?"

She swipes up the bag of tortilla chips and munches on one. "He doesn't want to kill demons—even when it's required of him in an underworldly political capacity—and I need to in order to graduate. In theory, it could be a mutually beneficial arrangement. But I don't know. It also seems absolutely insane when I say it out loud."

"Yeah, kinda," I offer unhelpfully.

"Guess I don't have to ask if you think I should do it," she mumbles, pulling out another chip, and the disappointment in her features has me reaching for her.

I rest my hand on her knee and squeeze. "My hesitation comes mostly from the danger associated with the role. I trust that you've thought it through and you'll make the best decision for you. I've got your back no matter what you choose, you know that."

Harper groans, letting her head fall back against the couch. "If I accept the role, I could very well be kicked out of the organization if they find out. I'm pretty sure this is unprecedented, so I don't even know what the punishment for something like this would be."

"You'd be killing demons. The way I see it, you're still doing your duty under the organization's vow to protect humankind."

"Right, but they haven't been known to hire, uh, independent contractors. If they discover I'm working for both sides, my loyalty will harshly be called into question."

I relate to her concern more than I should as I consider what could happen if I even attempt to pursue *something* with Xander. And she's absolutely right about being questioned. At its core, the hunter organization is a division of the government, and its members agents of it.

"I wish I could say I'm optimistic this has the potential to change the way the organization views demons. That maybe a partnership between the hunters and the monarch could be good for both sides. But I'm not naive. If my superiors learned I was hunting demons the king of hell assigned to me, I'd be hauled into headquarters and interrogated."

I don't want to agree with her. I'd much rather be naive and believe the arrangement Harper is considering with Xander could breed change between opposing sides of a centuries-old war. Except trust is far too high an order for the humans and demons.

"I think you need to be okay with the possibility of being exiled from the organization if you're going to accept Xander's offer. Ask yourself if you'd still want the role on his council if that happens."

Harper sits straighter, swallowing hard. "I enrolled to help people. Sure, the government salary and benefits would be helpful when I graduate, but this just feels…bigger?"

I offer what I hope is a supportive smile. "I know what you mean."

"I'm not saying I think I can change the world or anything, but I'm willing to take the risk and try to at least make things better."

"That's really brave," I tell her in a thick voice. I wasn't expecting the lump of emotion in my throat, and I swallow past it to continue, "And it sounds like maybe you have decided, even if you're not ready to say it."

She inhales slowly, then lets out a shaky breath. Her eyes meet mine, and she gives a little nod. Fear steals her expression, as if she just realized the impact of her decision, and I pull her toward me, wrapping her in a tight hug. Her heart thumps in her chest where it presses against mine, and I smooth a hand over her hair.

"Everything is going to be okay." The reassurance is as much for me as it is for her. We both need it right now. "Whatever happens, we'll deal with it together." I pull back, cupping her cheeks in my hands and hold her watery gaze. "Besides," I say in a forced humorous tone, "we have the devil on our side."

A startled laugh escapes her lips, and she lifts her hands to cover mine as she blinks away her tears. "Does that mean you've made a decision about him too?"

My stomach dips, and I press my lips together. "I don't know," I finally say, letting my hands fall to my lap.

Her brows lift. "You know enough to have dream sex with him."

I smack her shoulder with the back of my hand, groaning at the heat in my cheeks as the memory comes rushing back. "I knew I shouldn't have told you that."

She laughs again, this time sounding more genuine. "Your mistake."

I open my mouth to spill about the hunter test I failed, but the words don't form. I can't bring myself to tell her—not now. "Yeah, my mistake."

"Come on. Let's call it a day and fill the pits of stress in our guts with food and alcohol like people do for their mundane problems."

Twenty-Three
Xander

It takes more effort than I care to admit to stay away from Harper's apartment when I know Camille is there. According to Blake, she came yesterday after Harper told her about the threat Marrick sent. It doesn't surprise me that she jumped on a plane and came to support her best friend. Camille is practiced at putting the people she loves first, even when it's difficult or dangerous.

I'm not sure how long she's staying. I shouldn't try to see her despite the pull in my chest to go to her, but it's harder to ignore with her close by. That alone begs the question of just how thoroughly losing my soul affected our bond. Does it go deeper than either of us initially thought it could?

It doesn't help that Blake is gone all day, leaving me to spiral and seriously test my willpower to stay put. I go for a long run until my calf muscles burn, then stand under the hot spray of the shower until my skin is pink.

I relive the night we spent together only a few days ago and can't help but wonder if she's done the same since it happened. The thought of Camille still caring for me chips away at the stone wall in my chest, which has the beast grumbling with irritation. Taunting me with accusations of humanity and weakness.

Blake comes back to my apartment long after dark, bringing reports of a demon in Seattle who's leaking information to the hunters about a previously *secret* feeding tavern because of a personal vendetta he has with the owner of the establishment.

These places have become more prevalent in the last year or so, with humans seeking them out to let demons feed on them willingly. For some demons, it takes the fun out of the hunt, but others appreciate the low effort of it. But now that the hunters have been made aware of them, they'll act swiftly to shut them down. 'Kill demons and keep humans in the dark about their existence' is their unofficial motto, meaning they're going to be all over this.

"What's the motive here?" I say to Blake as I pour myself a glass of scotch from the bar cart I insisted on when I moved here following our stint at the safe house.

"Besides mutually assured destruction?" He shrugs, sipping the cup of tea he made when he arrived. "Greer suspects he's trying to make a statement about the demon world being unsafe under your reign."

I set my glass down, a muscle ticking in my jaw. "Do we have eyes on him?"

Blake nods.

"Let's go," I say without hesitation.

"Yes, my king." He shoots me a wink, and I respond with an icy glare, making him grin as we leave the apartment.

Blake drives to the industrial part of the city, humming along to the music he's playing. "There's an old warehouse out here that a bunch of demons turned into a nightclub of sorts years ago. So far, the hunters haven't been alerted to it. Fran and the others are already there, along with the royal guard, waiting for your arrival."

"What the fuck is the guard doing there?" I glance out the window, stretching my legs out in front of me.

His expression is grave as he turns the music down. "This is your second trial, mate."

A low growl rumbles through my chest. "Since when do they insist on watching?" And would I have failed whatever this trial is if I hadn't decided to go after this demon?

He taps his thumbs against the steering wheel, keeping his eyes on the road. "Since now." His gaze slides toward me briefly, and he says, "With Marrick rousing doubt about you among the demons who will listen to his shit, they want to oversee the rest of the trials."

"Great." I deadpan as discomfort tugs at my gut. Nothing like an audience of judges to kick up the pressure. My brows draw closer, and I turn to look out the window. Now that we're in the second half of November, the days and nights are colder, though at least the rain from earlier today has stopped. The sky is clear, the complete opposite of how my thoughts feel as I go over what I'll have to do tonight.

THE DEVIL'S TRIALS

Blake turns off the main road, and the storefronts transition into warehouses. We pull onto a laneway at the end of the road and drive for several minutes until we arrive at the building. The parking lot is dark but filled with vehicles, and the warehouse is vibrating with the music playing inside.

We get out of the car and start toward the front entrance, where two thick muscled demons stand on either side, bowing their heads the moment they recognize me. They open the double doors, beckoning us inside. The music is immediately louder, paired with the scent of booze and people as Blake and I walk through the dimly lit entrance toward the crowd. We move into the massive, wide-open space filled with dancing bodies and a stage at the front, where a DJ performs. Colored strobe lights flash through the otherwise dark room, and smoke machines near the stage give the room a haze that some appear to think is an invisibility cloak with how openly they're groping each other.

Shaking my head, I square my shoulders, schooling my features into something cool and indifferent. Despite the increased beat of my heart, I slow my breathing and tap into the confident, twisted part of me that relishes the spark of excitement in my chest at the thought of doling out punishment in front of an audience. Of showing them what will happen should they attempt to act against my reign.

My eyes land on Greer and Jude, who have climbed onto the stage and are speaking to the DJ. A moment later, the music cuts off, and the crowd boos, hollering at him to turn it back on.

"Apologies for the interruption," he says in a thick Australian accent. "It seems we have a very special guest in the house tonight who requires your attention for a moment."

People start searching the dark room while the lights continue flashing, and several offer short gasps when their eyes land on me.

While I haven't spotted the royal guard, I know they're here. I can feel the utter weight of their presence, sight unseen.

I move to the front of the room as the crowd parts and stand with my arms crossed and the weight of countless gazes on me. I inhale a slow breath while the demon I'm here for is dragged forward by Francesca and Jude. He appears middle-aged, with short black hair, thick-rimmed glasses, and a permanent scowl twisting his lips. His navy dress shirt is wrinkled, and his black jeans are ripped, though I can't tell if they are meant to look that way, or if he got into a scuffle with my council. It doesn't matter much.

I meet his hate-filled gaze. "What's your name?"

"Fuck you," he seethes, a mixture of anger and fear surrounding him in a plume of darkness.

"How unfortunate," I say flatly, and a few of the demons snicker. Blake's eyes glimmer with amusement from where he stands off to the side, though he doesn't speak. "Do you know why I'm here?" I ask.

He lifts his chin, evidently deciding not to answer.

"Very well." I inhale slowly, nodding at Francesca and Jude, who force him to his knees. "I am giving you one and only one chance to provide a reason for your actions. Why is it you believe you can act without consequences while putting our kind at risk of exposure?"

"I don't have to explain myself to *you*," the demon snarls, disgust dripping from each pointed word.

Francesca snarls, grabbing the accused by the back of his head and fisting his hair. "That is to be your king. You will address him as such—with respect."

"He is not *my* king."

I level my gaze with his. "I don't care how you feel about me. You've been colluding with the hunters and putting your own kind at risk."

The demon cackles. "If our queen still sat on the throne, she would have stopped me before I had the chance." He attempts to turn and face the crowd, but Francesca and Jude hold strong. The bastard continues his tirade with, "This pathetic excuse for a demon is not fit to rule our kind! Do not continue this blindness to his shortcomings! He will destroy—"

I move forward in a blur, grabbing the demon's chin and forcing his gaze to mine. I know what needs to be done, what *I* have to do. Perhaps that's why my heart is beating violently and sweat beads above my upper lip. Because even as I stare into his eyes, all I can think about is Camille. What she would think and feel and say if she saw me like this. I'm being the monster she hates, not the man she cares for, and I despise that more than the actions of the demon in front of me.

Glancing up, I catch Blake's gaze. His brows are pinched together as he watches, shaking his head subtly at my hesitation. He glances between me and the demon, the look in his eyes urging me to act. *You're fucking this up*, he says without speaking, his posture tense and a muscle feathering along his jaw.

The whole exchange takes a mere few seconds, but the pressure in my chest grows tenfold. I can barely breathe, and my grip on the demon before me falters as my fingers cramp.

Fuck, fuck, fuck.

I can't—

Jude clears her throat, and my eyes snap to her to find her expression mirroring Blake's.

I adjust my grip, digging my fingers into the demon's jaw as I exhale a harsh breath. I swallow past the dryness in my throat and give myself over to the monster that beckons deep in my chest. The pit in my gut numbs, the heavy guilt on my shoulders about punishing one of my own dissipating as I block out each emotion until nothing remains.

The distrust and rage on the demon's face slips into something closer to panic, *fear*. I can't say what he sees in my pitch-black eyes that makes his face pale, but my lips curve into a grin as energy sparks through my veins. I've never fed on a demon before. Perhaps this is a perk of my new position. But that's not what this is about.

Tension fills the room, though no one dares utter a word. Pulses race, and faces are filled with varying degrees of anticipation.

"I could kill you," I purr. "End your miserable existence right here. But that would be far too mild a punishment for putting my people—your *own*—at risk. Instead, I'm sending you home."

The relief that passes over his face is short-lived when my lips curl into a smirk that has him trembling.

"W-wait," he blurts, his pulse racing.

I hold his chin in an ironclad grip that makes him hiss in pain. "No, no. The time for pleas of mercy is long past. There will be none of that. You will return to hell and endure the next five hundred years confined to a cell without a single soul to feed on." The terror in his eyes feeds the monster in me. "There's no need to worry. You won't be all alone with your wretched thoughts. My friends will ensure your trip to the underworld is consumed by your worst fears on a delightful loop for your viewing pleasure."

"What?" he squeaks pathetically, and I chuckle at the shift in his demeanor as I release him, stepping back. For someone content to curse me out with insults only a few minutes ago, he looks as if he's about to pass out or shit himself.

"Let this be an important lesson," I say in a deep, level voice, addressing the entire room now. "You will face severe punishment should you defy me or put my people in jeopardy." I nod at Francesca and Jude, my voice gravelly with disgust when I order them to, "Get him out of here."

The demon is dragged through the crowd, kicking and shouting more profanities as the other demons watch with differing expressions of shock and trepidation.

Once he's gone, Blake steps forward and stands beside me, swiping the microphone off the DJ stand. "Now that business is taken care of, let's get back to the party!" He returns the mic and gestures for the DJ to turn the music back on. Bass fills the room a moment later, and I head for the exit with Blake on my heels.

He catches up to me in the parking lot and claps me on the back. "Care to explain what the fuck that was?"

I bristle, shrugging his hand off as part of me relishes in the energy zipping through my veins. It craves the sensations brought on by my display of power. It's an odd contrast to the ache in my chest, pounding in time with the music we left behind. "I punished him."

"You should have killed him, Xander."

I whirl around, my hackles up at the need to defend myself. "There are fates much harsher than death. He got exactly what he deserved."

His expression hardens as he shakes his head. "You better hope the royal guard agrees. They expected an execution. If they decide what you did wasn't enough, they'll deem this trial a failure."

I ignore the tightening in my chest, hissing out a sharp exhale. "Considering the royal guard hasn't been explicit with their instructions for these damn trials, I don't see how they can call this a failure."

Blake steps in front of me, gripping my shoulders. "You knew you were supposed to kill him. I saw it in your eyes. So why didn't you?"

I grit my teeth, narrowing my eyes at him. "I don't see how it matters. It's done."

He digs his fingers in, lowering his voice to murmur, "Your humanity is showing, mate."

"Watch it," I growl at him.

THE DEVIL'S TRIALS

"You need to hear this, though I get the feeling I'm not saying anything you don't already know."

"*Blake.*" His name is a warning. I know what he's about to say, and once it's out there, I won't be able to ignore it any longer.

He sighs, shaking his head. "She's always been your weakness."

I knock his hands off me and grab the lapels of his jacket. "Enough."

Blake's eyes darken, matching the blackness I'm certain fills mine by the way I feel my control slipping. "It's my job to keep you alive," he says. "To get you through these trials and onto the fucking throne. You don't get to lose your shit on me for doing exactly that."

Letting go of him, I step back, clenching and unclenching my fists while my heart thumps in my chest. Before I can speak, Rupert leads the other council members from the building to where Blake and I are standing. His eyes shift between us, calculating, and I hold my breath.

"That wasn't the performance we expected from you, Xander."

I nod curtly. "I understand, but the loyalty that demon betrayed is worth far more than his life. His punishment ought to measure up, don't you agree?"

Rupert glances over his shoulder to the others. Dominic and Malachi exchange a glance, while Lorraine keeps her eyes locked on me.

"While an execution would've been a far more entertaining show," she says in a level tone, "I believe the punishment was...adequate."

Dominic nods, sliding his hands into the pockets of his navy peacoat. "Agreed. Perhaps your display will dissuade others from acting in the same manner."

"That's the idea," I offer.

"Very well," Rupert speaks up. "We will grant you this success."

My eyes slide to Malachi, who hasn't said a word, but his expression is impassive. He seems to be taking a backseat in this decision. Regardless, I bow my head to them all. "Thank you."

In seconds, the four of them disappear in a cloud of black smoke, leaving Blake and I alone for a brief moment before the rest of my council joins us in the parking lot.

Francesca is the first to approach, her eyes filled with the question they all no doubt have. When I offer a subtle nod, her crimson lips curve into a grin.

"Nicely done."

JESSI ELLIOTT

Blake remains silent as the rest of the group congratulates me on successfully completing my second trial. That silence continues as we drive back toward my apartment, and I don't bother attempting to break it.

I'm mentally and physically exhausted—it's a bleak contrast to how I was feeling in the moments I dealt that demon his fate in hell. I miss the spark of power. But I know the minute I speak, Blake is going to be down my throat about letting myself show any fragment of weakness. Of how being around Camille seems to have dragged my lingering humanity to the surface despite believing it died with Lucia.

I couldn't take a life, but I could damn it to an eternity in the underworld. The pit in my gut tells me I don't feel entirely pleased about that, but at least the demon *deserved* the punishment he was given.

Something tells me I won't get so lucky during the final trial, and that leaves a chill deep in the marrow of my bones.

Even now, when my future in the demon world depends on passing the trials, I can't stay away from the one who jeopardizes it all.

Twenty-Four
Camille

After Noah canceled our private session yesterday to attend a meeting with the other mentors in the organization, we head to Ballard early today to get in a few exercises before class starts.

I hang up my coat and bag, then hop on the treadmill to warm up. When I'm done my usual ten minutes at no incline, I meet Noah on the mats in the middle of the room so we can run through the defensive drills I have memorized at this point.

"What did Harper say when you told her about the test?" he asks, blocking my punch with his padded glove.

I pull my arm back and lower my gaze, resenting the warmth of embarrassment in my face. "I haven't told her yet."

"Really?" He doesn't bother hiding the shock in his tone. "Why not?"

My eyes snap back up to meet his gaze. "I didn't tell her because I'm sick of everything being about me. Harper deserves a best friend who's there for her as much as she is for them. So when I visited Seattle, I kept it to myself."

He nods, rubbing his jaw. "That was almost two weeks ago."

I sigh heavily. "I'm aware, thank you."

"Are you going to tell her?"

"Why do you care so damn much?" I snap.

I've managed to keep my attitude surrounding the test out of my training sessions with Noah for the past couple weeks—mostly—but the more he pushes, the harder it is not to yell in his face.

His brows inch up his forehead. "Easy, Cam. I'm just—"

"You're just what?" I interrupt with a jagged tone. "I get you're pissed that me failing my first hunter test looks bad on you being my mentor, but maybe if you hadn't got the organization to use a simulation of Xander, I would have passed."

He steps closer, looking down at me. "I didn't tell them anything. Your history with that prick isn't a secret." His eyes flick between mine. "You thought... Why would I try to sabotage your first test after working my ass off to prepare you for it? In what world does that make sense?"

My stomach fills with knots, and I struggle to hold his gaze as my eyes burn. "I'm sorry," I force out, pressing my lips together.

"I am, too. Obviously, you think very little of me if you believe that's something I would do."

I shake my head, blinking back the tears. "I said I was sorry, Noah. I shouldn't have thought that, but the whole thing really screwed with me, okay? So, I am really sorry. Sincerely. You've been so helpful and supportive, and I probably don't tell you enough how much I appreciate that."

His expression softens, a hint of a smile playing on his lips. "You definitely don't." He reaches for me, squeezing my shoulders. "Despite the setback, you *are* progressing. We've only been working together for a month, and after such a long break, you're readjusting better than I thought you would."

I blink at him. "Thanks?"

He chuckles. "I know it hasn't been easy dealing with some trainees not being happy to have you around, especially when you aren't thrilled to be back in training, but all of this will get easier."

"Yeah?" I mutter. "When?"

He releases my shoulder, tweaking my chin before dropping his arms back to his sides. "I bet it'll be sooner than you think."

I shrug, blurting the first thing that comes to mind. "Maybe if you can convince the organization to let me redo the test that would help."

Noah arches a brow. "Is that what you want?"

I find myself nodding, the idea of redeeming myself too enticing to pass up. "If that's a possibility, I want to take it."

"Okay," he says, pulling his phone out of his back pocket. "I think I can make that happen." He leaves me to hit the punching bag while he slips out of the room to make a call, and when he returns ten minutes later with a smile curving his lips, a nervous fluttering erupts in my stomach.

"Are you sure this is what you want?" he asks, coming to stand next to the punching bag. "If you don't pass a second time—"

"You think I'm going to fail again?" I cross my arms, which turns out to be quite an awkward movement while wearing boxing gloves.

THE DEVIL'S TRIALS

He offers me a pointed look. "No, but I understand how nerve wracking tests can be for some people. I just want to make sure you're ready."

I tug the gloves off and toss them into the bin. "I'm ready."

Something akin to pride flashes in his gaze. "Good. Because you'll be fighting your pal Cody. I just arranged this class to be observed by my superiors, so the fight will count as your evaluation."

My heart beats faster, and I swallow three times as my throat goes dry. "Is this a test or a reward?" I say, hoping to cover up the anxiety wading to the surface.

Noah laughs. "Hang onto that confidence, and you'll do just fine."

Class starts half an hour later, and I quickly greet the few trainees I consider friends at this point before Noah explains the one-on-one practice tests we're doing today.

Of course, for me it isn't practice, but he and I are the only ones who know that. Well, us and the representatives from the organization who are observing from the security feed, according to what Noah told me as the class filed in.

We're split off into pairs, and when Noah calls out my name followed by Cody's, my muscles tense. The vicious look on Cody's face makes my pulse tick faster. He's been at this longer than me and I'm sure would love nothing more than to knock me on my ass, but I'm not going to let that happen. I'm going to use every bit of training Noah has taught me, because failure is not an option.

The training room falls silent when Noah calls me and Cody onto the mats. Sierra shoots me a supportive smile that I struggle to return as I walk forward.

Cody meets me in the middle of the mat, smirking. "Don't hold back, demon fucker," he says under his breath. "I'd hate to utterly embarrass you here."

I grit my teeth against a snarky response. *He isn't worth it*, I tell myself, steadying my stance as I hold his cold gaze.

Noah commences the fight with a loud whistle, and my focus narrows on Cody. He's wicked fast, I'll give the asshole that. He launches himself at me without a second of hesitation, and I jump back instinctively, sucking in a breath as he circles me.

His next attack is a swift grab for me that I barely manage to sidestep, and I nearly trip over my own feet in an attempt to put distance between us and regroup so I can flip to the offensive maneuvers I've been practicing with Noah.

Cody comes at me again, the animalistic grin on his mouth sending a cold shiver through me as I move out of his grasp. His hands swipe at empty air as I dart around him, but he recovers in an instant, whirling to face me.

"Not bad," he grumbles, nostrils flaring. "But you'll have to do a lot better than that."

I offer a mockingly sweet smile. "Touché."

His fist comes flying toward my face, and I duck just in time to avoid it connecting with my jaw. I drop low and kick out, knocking his legs out from under him. When he hits the mats with a loud *thud*, I resist the urge to make a comment about him skipping leg day at the gym.

Cody scrambles upright before I can attack him on the ground, growling obscenities at me as he charges forward. I shift backward, but not fast enough to avoid a hit to my shoulder. Pain flares all the way to my fingertips, and I suck in a breath at the sharpness. I block his next attempt, twisting away before doubling back and driving my knee into his ribs then my elbow into his throat. He coughs violently, his eyes popping wide, but I don't back down. I jump onto his back as sweat rolls down my temple, throwing my weight into knocking him back to the ground, the impact reverberating through the mats.

This time, I don't give him a moment to get up. I grab his dominant arm and pin it above his head at an angle that threatens dislocation should he move. Still he struggles, but I have the full weight of my body against him. My breath comes in short, shallow pants, my heart beating hard against my rib cage as I hold Cody where I want him.

I pull in a deep breath, then use every ounce of strength I've built to flip him onto his back. His eyes widen, his chest heaving as I throw myself on top of him, pressing my knee just above his groin and my dominant arm against his throat, effectively immobilizing him. He grits his teeth, scowling as he struggles beneath me, knowing he can't move enough to get free.

I hold his gaze, relishing in the triumph of taking him down and witnessing the look of defeat in his eyes.

The blare of Noah's whistle fills me with a dizzying mix of relief and pride as I climb off Cody to leave him on the mats, breathing hard and no doubt cursing my existence.

THE DEVIL'S TRIALS

Sierra, Brynne, and Wyatt rush over and slap me on the back, offering their congratulations. They have no idea what this victory means for me, but their excitement only adds to the warm fuzzy feeling in my chest.

My gaze finds Noah's as the next two trainees take the mats. He offers a nod and a grin that tells me I passed the test, and that paired with the pride in his eyes has me floating on a cloud of warmth and accomplishment for the rest of class.

I've never been happier to endure New York City traffic than I am the next morning picking Harper up from JFK. I borrow Noah's car and meet her at arrivals, and there are squeals of excitement as we squeeze each other so hard I can't breathe, but I don't care. I saw her only two weeks ago in Seattle, but with everything going on in both our lives, moments like these feel as if they hold more weight. More importance.

Once we're in the car heading toward my apartment, Harper turns to me. "So what's the plan?"

"Uhhh..." I drag out the word. "That's a pretty loaded question these days." Since I passed my reevaluation yesterday, I decide I don't need to tell Harper I failed the first test. My position in the program is secure for now, so there's no sense in making her worry for nothing.

She playfully punches me in the shoulder. "I meant for my trip. What are we doing for Thanksgiving?"

"My dad's cooking, which you'll be happy about, and I don't know besides that. Noah is probably going to come over. We'll eat and drink too much, maybe watch the parade. I haven't really thought too much about it. I'm just glad you're here."

She grins at me from the passenger seat.

Groaning under my breath, I hesitate before saying, "Why are you looking at me like that?"

"Are we going to talk about how you feel about Noah coming to dinner? I've refrained from saying anything about you driving his car. This is his, right?"

I exhale a short laugh, nodding. "He would've had dinner with my dad whether I was here or not."

Noah's family lives out of state, so he typically spends holidays either by himself or with my dad. He's known my family for most of his life. He's practically part of it by now.

After we drop Harper's things at my apartment, we meet up with Noah in the lobby and catch a cab to my dad's place so we don't have to worry about driving.

Dad's in the kitchen when we arrive, an apron tied around his waist and his reading glasses on as he studies the tablet in his hand, glancing between it and what appears to be some type of casserole.

"Hey, Dad." I walk over and give him a half hug, leaning up to kiss him on the cheek.

"Hey, kiddo." He smiles in greeting at Harper and Noah. "Would you believe me if I told you I have been in the kitchen since seven o'clock this morning?"

I laugh fondly. "Yeah, I would actually."

"Everything smells amazing, if that helps," Harper chimes in, and my dad shoots her a wink. My eyebrows lift when her cheeks go pink, and she dips her chin before glancing away.

"Is there anything we can help with?" I ask, refusing to explore the weirdness of that moment. I think my head would explode.

Dad shakes his head, waving us away. "You guys relax in the other room, watch the parade, help yourselves to a drink. Everything will be ready in an hour or so."

Harper, Noah, and I saunter into the living room, where Dad's flatscreen is already turned on to the Macy's Thanksgiving Day Parade. Harper flops onto the couch with a content sigh, grabbing a blanket off the back and wrapping it around herself, while Noah and I converge at the bar cart in the corner of the room. I glance over at the screen every so often to see the floats—several oversized animals followed by Santa's sleigh, which has always been my favorite.

"Whiskey sour?" Noah asks, bumping my shoulder with his. The hint of his cologne tickles my nose with the subtle scent of rain and mint, and I can't help the tentative smile that curls my lips as I nod. It's a small thing, but Noah remembering my drink of choice fills my stomach with a faint fluttering sensation.

"Once you two are done flirting like I'm not here, I'd love a margarita."

Before I can speak, Noah laughs, glancing at Harper over his shoulder with a teasing, "Do you want me to flirt with you, Harper?"

"Please, oh please," she deadpans, her gaze sliding to me as Noah turns back to make my and Harper's drinks.

THE DEVIL'S TRIALS

I shoot her a look that she ignores, reaching for the TV remote to turn up the volume. "Did you connect with your family?" I ask, watching him make Harper's drink after mine.

Noah's family doesn't know about demons or that he hunts them and trains others to as well. They only know he works for the government, and he wants to keep it that way.

"Yeah," he says casually, "I called my mom and sister this morning. They were getting ready to host my aunt and uncle along with their kids for dinner, and my dad was outside putting lights up."

I choke on a laugh. "Christmas lights?" The holidays were never a huge thing in my house, decorations even less so. I appreciate why Noah's mom likes having them up far ahead of the actual holiday. More time to enjoy them.

"Christmas lights," he echoes with a nod and rolls his eyes, though his tone doesn't allude to annoyance when he says, "Mom insisted. My dad's lucky she didn't want the tree up already too." He finishes making my and Harper's drinks before we join her on the couch, and I end up sandwiched between them as we drink and watch the parade.

Not long after, Dad calls us to the table in the dining space attached to the kitchen, and I slip out of the room when my phone rings with a call from my mom.

"Happy Thanksgiving," she says in a warm voice. "How's your visit with Harper going? I know she was looking forward to it."

"We're having a great time," I tell her, walking the length of the hall.

"I have to say, I miss having you in the same city. Even though we didn't spend much time together while you were here, knowing you were close made me feel better."

"I'm safe here," I insist. "You and Dad made sure of that when you put me up in the same building as Noah." As much as I hated it at the time, it's grown on me. Having him close is convenient for training, and while I'd never admit it aloud, it does make me feel safer knowing he's there.

"Of course, I know that," she says.

"Noah's going to eat all the food if you don't hurry up," Harper hollers from the other room.

Mom laughs. "Go enjoy your dinner."

"Are you doing anything special tonight?" I ask, slowly heading back toward the dining room.

"Pizza and Pinot curled up on the couch with a movie and early to bed. I have back-to-back meetings in the morning."

I frown at the thought of her spending Thanksgiving by herself. Mom's always been more introverted, but still. "Sounds nice." I try to make it sound lighthearted, but she must hear something else.

"Don't worry about me. This is my ideal evening. Holidays lose some of their magic as you get older. I've learned to make them days where I do things that make me happy, which is exactly what I'm doing tonight."

That makes me feel slightly better. "I'm glad to hear that." This conversation is one of the easiest I've had with my mom in...well, too long. I don't want it to end, but my stomach is also grumbling like crazy. I lean against the doorway to the dining room with my back to the table.

"And I'm glad to hear you passed your test. You're lucky you have a mentor willing to stick his neck out for you. Most trainees don't get a redo, and Noah fought for you to get one."

I cup the back of my neck with my free hand as my heart rate climbs. *Noah fought for me.* "Yeah, thanks. I know, he's—"

"Cami, come on," Harper yells.

"I better go." I press my lips together, then add, "I love you."

"I love you," she echoes before we say goodbye and end the call.

Exhaling a slow breath, I swallow and blink away any trace of tears before walking into the dining room and taking my seat across from Noah.

Dad raises his wineglass. "A toast to an enjoyable holiday season. And a special congratulations to Camille for passing her first hunter test."

Harper squeals, while Noah and Dad offer warm smiles.

"Thank you," I murmur with a blush, and we all take a drink before diving into the meal.

As I predicted, we all eat too much. I sit back in my chair, groaning with discomfort as I rest my hand on my stomach. Everything tasted so good, we all went a little overboard.

"I don't suppose anyone wants dessert?" Dad asks, finishing his glass of wine.

Harper's hand shoots up, and when I laugh, she says, "What? Everybody knows you have a separate stomach for dessert."

After a slice of apple pie and a couple more cocktails as we watch *A Charlie Brown Thanksgiving*, the three of us say goodbye to my dad and get a cab back to my apartment.

THE DEVIL'S TRIALS

When the elevator hits my floor, I slug Noah on the arm, grinning when he grunts in surprise. "Why don't you come hang for a bit? We can keep drinking." I'm quite enjoying the pleasant buzz I have going on.

He chuckles. "Why not?"

"Woo hoo," Harper belts out as she dances down the hallway toward my apartment.

We end up sitting on the floor in the living room while some cheesy Christmas rom-com plays in the background, and we take turns drinking from a bottle of tequila. Safe to say, it's more fun to drink with friends than alone.

Harper gets up, mumbling, "Gotta pee," as she walks out of the room.

Noah exhales a sigh, then goes to stifle a yawn.

"Oh, I'm sorry. Are we keeping you up, grandpa?"

"Kind of, actually. Yeah. I think I'm going to head back to my place."

"Fine." I pout. "Party pooper."

"I don't consider sitting on the floor taking shots of tequila on Thanksgiving as much of a party."

"Whatever." I roll my eyes, setting the bottle on the coffee table with a heavy *thud.*

"See you later, Harper," Noah calls out as we stand, and I walk him to the door. Instead of leaving him there, though, I follow him to the elevator.

He arches a brow at me as we wait for it to reach my floor. "I can get the rest of the way home on my own," he comments in an amused tone.

"Hmm, are you sure about that?"

His lips twitch. "I think I'll be okay."

"Fine, fine. I was just trying to be nice. I know you and I don't really do that, but I thought with it being the holidays and everything..." My eyebrows tug together, and I clamp my mouth shut, because *what am I even saying?*

The haze of alcohol is starting to wear off, and I don't enjoy that it's brought the pressure back to my chest. Instead of letting him go when the elevator door slides open, I get on and press the button.

He just shakes his head and laughs under his breath as we ride in silence for the short trip from my floor to his.

When we get to his apartment, Noah pulls out his keys and unlocks the door, peering over at me curiously. "Well done. You ensured I made it home safe and sound."

"Yeppers." I nod for extra measure.

He regards me strangely, and it makes my stomach dip. Then he asks, "What is going on with you?"

I watch his lips move as he speaks, and my pulse ticks faster as I'm overcome with the memory of us kissing. Of the way his lips felt on mine, soft yet firm, and how being with him has somehow made me feel safe amidst all of the chaos.

"I...don't know," I admit with a sigh.

When Noah's eyes dart between mine, I can't seem to stop myself from leaning up on my tiptoes and planting my mouth on his.

He stiffens for a moment before his arms come around my waist, and he kisses me back. As soon as he does, though, it's as if a bucket of cold water is poured into my veins.

What am I doing?

I was with Xander a couple weeks ago, and now I'm kissing Noah again? My head spins with confusion, and I pull away, pressing a hand to my mouth.

Noah just stares at me, his eyes flicking between mine. He shakes his head. "You told me I couldn't kiss you again."

He's right. Fuck, I hate this whole thing. I fumble with something to say, some explanation that will make sense. "I...I know. I just—I got caught up in the moment, and you know, I drank—"

"Don't do that," he cuts in more firmly, snaring my gaze. Any lingering amusement is quickly replaced by something colder as he says, "Why did you kiss me?"

Why did *I kiss him?*

I swallow hard, then blurt, "Because it makes me feel better."

Noah laughs humorlessly. "Well, okay then. I'm glad I can make you feel better."

I frown, my heart still thumping hard in my chest. "You're mad."

"Hey, if you want to use me to forget about him, by all means, go ahead. But the least you could do is let me know."

"What are you talking about?" I ask in a small voice, feeling painfully sober and wishing now that I'd said goodbye to him at my door and let him leave.

"Do you want to kiss *me*, or do you just want to forget about the person you actually want to kiss but can't?"

THE DEVIL'S TRIALS

Heat floods my cheeks, and I bite my tongue. Obviously I'm not going to tell him I *did* kiss Xander, or anything else we did. "I'm sorry. I shouldn't have..." My voice trails off, and I shake my head. "I didn't mean to upset you. This isn't—Whatever you and I have been doing, whatever is between us, it has nothing to do with him." I take a deep breath, exhaling slowly, as if that'll settle the anxiety crackling beneath my skin like static. "Look, I don't know what we're doing—"

His mouth is on mine in an instant, swallowing the rest of my sentence. I make a sound of surprise against his lips as my eyes shut of their own volition, and he grabs my hips, nudging his door open with his boot and guiding me inside. He kicks the door shut without breaking the kiss, and we keep moving through his apartment. My heart pounds in my chest as heat flushes through my whole body, and I fist the front of his shirt, kissing him hard. My senses are completely consumed by him. His closeness. His minty, fresh rain scent, even. It brings me comfort and sends my heart racing in tandem.

One of his hands slides up my side, cupping the side of my face, and he tips my head back slightly, deepening the kiss. His thumb skates across my cheek, gentle and grounding, and a tsunami of emotions slams into me, making my eyes burn.

Noah pauses, breaking the kiss. "Camille—"

"I'm fine." I pull in a shaky breath. When I try to kiss him again, he turns his face away, and my stomach drops. "Sorry." Looking away, I try to take a step back, but he holds me in place as I sniffle. My voice cracks when I say, "You don't deserve this hot and cold from me." I blink quickly to force the tears back, but my quivering bottom lip gives me away. "Sorry," I repeat.

"Hey," he murmurs. "Look at me." He uses a finger to lift my chin until our eyes meet. "You want to stop, we stop. No questions asked."

I swallow past the lump in my throat, my pulse thrumming. "I—I can't do this."

Part of my heart will probably always be drawn to the life Noah could offer me, but I can't let go of my feelings for Xander.

A muscle feathers along Noah's jaw and his shoulders drop with a sigh. "Then we won't."

Silence stretches between us for a long moment. "I should go," I say quietly, afraid my voice is going to break.

"Yeah," he agrees. His tone is distant and he won't meet my gaze.

Without another word, I walk out of his apartment and hurry to the elevator. Once I'm back at my place, I close the door and fall back against it.

Harper rushes over from the living room. "Oh, *babe*."

She knows. Of course she knows.

I catch my bottom lip between my teeth and let my head thump against the door as I groan.

"Do you want to talk about it?" she asks.

"I feel like I can't breathe," I tell her, my chest rising and falling faster as my skin prickles with the dreadfully familiar sensation of an oncoming panic attack. "I'm so fucking scared I'm making one monumental mistake after another."

Resting her hands on my shoulders, she meets my gaze and says, "Inhale and exhale slowly. You're doing your best, and no one is faulting or judging you here."

We take a few measured breaths together, and my racing pulse slows to a somewhat normal pace. "I could see myself with Noah. He drives me nuts but I'm also constantly impressed by him. There's a trust for him that comes from our history, which is inherently comforting, but it's...not enough."

Harper presses her lips together, nodding. "Right. Because you're in love with the devil."

I stare at her.

You're in love with the devil.

Harper is right. I do love Xander. Soulmate bond or no, at some point I moved past catching feelings for Xander to falling irrevocably in love with him.

Allowing myself to admit it only complicates things further. I love Noah, too. I had feelings for him before I met Xander, which makes me feel worse.

I'm worried I'm making a huge mistake with Noah.

I'm scared Xander is going to break my heart.

Worst of all, I'm terrified that whatever we feel won't be enough to save us from destroying each other.

Twenty-Five
Xander

I've never attended a Thanksgiving dinner, let alone prepared one for a group, so I'm not entirely sure what led me to think doing so for my council was a good idea. Blake jumped on board the moment I mentioned it and had invites sent out before I could change my mind.

"We should meet with them anyway, so why not do it over a feast?" he'd said, and I couldn't argue with him.

As I stand at the sink, rinsing and peeling a ridiculous amount of potatoes, I severely wish I had.

Blake walks into the kitchen wearing a bright red apron with the phrase kiss the chef printed above the outline of lips. "How's it coming?" he asks, setting down the grocery bags he carried in. "Having fun yet?"

I shoot him a bland look, and he grins before starting to unpack the rest of the things we needed for dinner. "The turkey has been in the oven for a little over an hour," I tell him, pulling a knife from the block on the counter behind me before turning back to the island to chop the potatoes.

"Excellent," he beams. "Fran's grabbing the pie on her way over after she picks up Declan."

I nod, finding it somewhat strange that Declan would be coming with Francesca instead of his partner. "What about the others?"

He pulls out a bag of carrots and a large head of broccoli. "Roman and Jude are coming together of course, and Greer is visiting a friend in Tacoma, so she'll head here on her own after."

"Sounds good."

And hopefully everyone will be gone before nine.

That hope goes out the window an hour after Roman and Jude get here and Francesca and Declan haven't arrived. Greer shows up shortly after them. The food is ready, and the table is set. The others are half an hour late. Then an hour. Blake calls Francesca several times, and it keeps going straight to voicemail. Same with Declan's phone. Greer paces the living room, texting and calling, trying to get ahold of him.

"I'm going out to find them," I announce, shrugging on my jacket. I was hoping to avoid tracking them using the blood connection we made. It'll take a toll on my energy, which isn't ideal ahead of the next trial—especially not knowing when it'll be—but I'm left with no other option.

Just as I straighten from lacing up my combat boots, there's a loud crash in the hallway. The others rush forward as I open the door, and my gut sinks as a bloodied and bruised Francesca collapses. I catch her before she hits the floor, and she groans in pain as I scoop her into my arms and carry her inside. Her head falls against my chest, damp with water from the rain outside and tinged black with blood.

"She's barely alive," Jude says in a grave tone.

Blake curses, and I've never heard his voice so livid. He's vibrating with rage, his eyes flickering black as he keeps them locked on Francesca.

I lay her on the couch as gently as I can. Dark makeup is streaked down her pale, tear stained cheeks, which is the least of my concerns when her lip is split and bleeding down her chin and one of her eyes is nearly swollen shut. Her knee-length dress is shredded across her waist, her sheer tights ripped almost entirely off her legs, which are spattered with bruises like the ones on her arms.

Roman disappears and comes back with a warm, damp towel. Jude takes it from him and sits on the edge of the couch, leaning over to clean up Francesca's face. She continues making sounds of discomfort, and her heart beats faster, her non-injured eye filling with tears when Blake asks her what happened. She shakes her head, whimpering, and I exchange a look with Blake, who looks ready to slaughter whoever did this.

"Tell us what happened," Jude says.

Francesca shudders, tears rolling down her cheeks as her shoulders shake with silent sobs.

Jude stops cleaning her face and holds her still by her arms. "Easy, darling. Take a breath."

She sniffles, then inhales and exhales slowly a few times as the rest of us wait for her to speak. "We—" Her voice breaks, and she tries to clear her throat, wincing as if it hurts. "We went to the market to get the pies and when we were walking back to the car...They came out of nowhere." Her chin quivers, and she stops talking, shaking her head again.

THE DEVIL'S TRIALS

"Hunters?" I ask, a muscle ticking in my jaw and my temples throbbing from the tension.

Francesca sucks in a breath. "N-no."

My brows tug closer as the pit in my stomach grows. "Then who?"

Her attention lands on me as she licks her lips. She swallows hard before she's able to force out, "My father."

Fire bursts in my gut, and I bite back a growl.

Marrick is a dead man.

"Francesca," Greer speaks up in a small voice, keeping herself pressed against the wall. "Where is Declan?"

She doesn't look at Greer, but it's written all over her face.

He's dead.

"No," Greer snaps frantically, moving toward the couch as she demands, "Where is he?"

Roman catches her around the waist, holding her back, and she completely loses it. It takes both Roman and Jude to haul Greer out of the room, and she continues screaming from the bedroom upstairs after the door slams shut.

Blake helps Francesca upright on the couch, then sits next to her. "Talk to us, Fran. Marrick did this to you?"

She exhales an unsteady breath. "His cronies. My father has never done his own dirty work." Reaching up with a shaky hand, she touches her lip and sucks in a pained breath. "He watched as they beat me and called me a traitor for aligning myself with you." She sniffles, and the utter brokenness in her features gnaws at me. This is my fault.

"He won't get away with what he did to you," I vow to her, perching on the coffee table in front of the couch to face her and Blake. "Or what he did to Declan." Greer's screaming upstairs has quieted. I'm not sure how Jude and Roman settled her down, or perhaps she cried herself dry.

Francesca's voice is so uncharacteristically small when she says, "He was going to let them kill me, Xander. But he…he needed someone alive to send you a message."

"What message?" I snarl, though the anger isn't directed at her.

"He wants the throne and he'll do whatever it takes to make sure you don't take it." She winces at the movement as she reaches for me, grabbing my hands where they're clenched in my lap. "Everyone you care about is a target."

221

My back straightens, my whole body going taut. I can't help immediately thinking about Camille and Harper in New York.

I glance toward Blake, a silent message passing between us, and he nods in understanding.

"I, um..." Francesca starts, then trails off, dropping her gaze to her lap.

"What is it?" I ask, focusing back on her.

"It's going to sound insane." She inhales slowly, lifting her head and looking at me. "Years ago, when we were still in hell, I overheard a conversation between Marrick and Lucia. They were discussing the future of our kind following the eradication of the hunters."

"They had a plan?" Blake asks.

Francesca shakes her head. "Not quite. What I heard...It didn't make a lick of sense, but my father was adamant, convinced this was the answer to any threats they would face."

"Just tell us what you heard," Blake says, shoulders tense.

There's a moment of hesitation before she continues. "My father seemed to think he could gather an army of demons that were loyal to him by default."

Blake makes a sound of disgust deep in his throat. "How exactly could he guarantee that?"

Francesca's brows knit, and she exhales an uneven breath. "By transforming humans into demons to form an army."

My stomach drops as dread floods into my chest, seizing my lungs in an ironclad grip.

"*Make* demons?" Blake echoes. "Is that what you just said?"

"I've never heard of it happening," I say, trying to ignore the nausea swirling in my core. "But that doesn't mean it isn't possible. I don't think we can rule it out at this point."

Francesca nods. "Other creatures inhabiting this world can turn humans into their kind. Who's to say demons can't do the same?"

"If Marrick can turn humans into demons and force their loyalty, this just became a much bigger problem," Blake says, raking his fingers through his faded blue hair.

The tension in my chest burns hotter, morphing into something violent. My hands curl into fists, and I inhale slowly. "If Marrick wants a fight, I will give him a war he'll have no chance of surviving. He'll wish he'd been at the compound to perish alongside Lucia."

THE DEVIL'S TRIALS

Blake and I leave Francesca to rest on the couch while we go to the kitchen. My thoughts are racing, blood rushing through my ears as I struggle to ground myself.

I haven't felt this out of control since the day I killed Lucia.

Jude and Roman enter the kitchen, leaving Greer asleep upstairs.

"What do we know so far?" Roman asks, glancing between us.

"You heard what Fran told us?" Blake checks, and Roman nods.

"I spoke to an old friend of mine in California," Jude says. "Marrick was living there for a while before he joined your mother's council, and it seems he's returned."

"This has been confirmed?" Blake asks from where he stands next to me, arms folded over his chest.

Jude nods. "He's been spotted several times."

"It makes sense," Francesca chimes in weakly, and we all turn to her in the living room as she continues, "We have family in Los Angeles. He could be hiding out there."

"I don't think he's hiding," Roman adds in a low voice, his jaw tight. He turns to me. "Your mother had a lot of support in California. Marrick is most likely recruiting demons who will fight alongside him against you taking the throne."

I rub my jaw, leaning against the counter. "How does he plan to turn humans into demons?"

"Who bloody knows?" Blake grumbles.

"I've come across centuries old literature that spoke of the process as a myth," Jude offers with furrowed brows.

The knots in my stomach grow and tighten, making me shift my stance at the pang of discomfort. "How is this the first I'm hearing of it?"

"There's no way to say for certain if it's been done before because, if I remember correctly from the writings, you cannot discern a born demon from a created one."

"Well isn't that just fucking peachy," Blake huffs.

"And you believe Marrick has access to this information?" I ask.

"I think it's safe to say he does," Roman says. "You know how close he was to your mother. How obsessed he was with pleasing her. She wanted demons to rule the human world, and he'd do anything to give her that."

I loathe Marrick with every bit of my soulless being, though I suppose I can understand doing whatever it takes for the love of a woman.

Glancing between Roman and Jude, I say, "I need you to dig for more information. Find out if this is truly Marrick's plan. And if I can leave it to the two of you to take care of Greer—"

"Of course," Jude interjects smoothly. "We've got it covered."

The two of them go back upstairs, speaking in hushed voices about where they'll start looking for answers.

I grab the bottle of whiskey from the bar cart and pour two generous glasses, sliding one across the counter to Blake before downing mine. I exhale a deep sigh as the liquor burns a path to my stomach. "No one in the inner circle is safe. I need you to do something for me."

He nods, sipping from his glass as he stares down at the phone in his other hand. "I'm already booking a flight. You stay and make sure Fran gets better. She needs to feed and keep resting. I imagine Greer will also need both of those things."

"I'll make sure they're taken care of." My voice sounds detached, an eerie reflection of how I'm starting to feel. I glance at the kitchen island, at the spread of untouched food Blake and I spent hours preparing.

He sets his phone on the counter, giving me his full attention before asking, "When I get to New York, what do you want me to tell them?"

"It doesn't matter. I don't care what you say so long as you bring them back with you."

"Of course, but I also don't think we should stay in Seattle. Too much has happened already, it's no longer a viable or smart option." He takes another drink. "I was already in the process of arranging a new place for after you complete the trials when Marrick started causing problems."

My brows lift, and I lean against the counter, folding my arms. "A new place where?"

"Vancouver. It's a nice house. Out of the way so it's private enough, but still close to a handful of portals for any necessary trips home." He scratches the stubble along his jaw. "I think you should head to Vancouver with the others, and I'll meet you once I've collected your girls."

I rub my eyes with my thumb and finger, sighing.

"We're going to figure this shit out, mate."

"There's nothing to figure out. Marrick is going to find out what happens when you threaten what's mine."

He whistles softly, finishing his drink. "Spoken like a true king."

Twenty-Six
Camille

Harper has only been here for three days but she has to go back to Seattle tomorrow. Between needing to finish her own training and figuring out things with Xander and his council, she can't stay any longer. As bummed as I am, I understand.

I get up early and sneak out to pick up breakfast from the café a few blocks away. It's a small, family-owned place that makes the most amazing egg and cheese croissants and cinnamon rolls. Not to mention, their chai latte is top tier—probably the best I've ever had. It keeps me coming back.

The street is still quiet, and it's cold enough that my breath fogs the air. I hug myself tighter, tucking my hands under my armpits to keep them warm as I pick up my pace.

I only slow to cross the street, glancing both ways before I step off the sidewalk.

From nowhere, a body collides with mine, shoving me backward away from the street and under the awning of a closed floral shop.

My pulse skyrockets, and when my brain catches up and I recognize Blake's face, my eyes narrow sharply. "What the fuck are you doing?"

"Long time no see, love."

I try to shove him away, but he isn't going anywhere. "Is that the only greeting you know?" I mutter. "And I saw you less than a month ago. What do you want now?"

"Here's the deal," he says in a voice void of his usual flippant humor, which puts me on edge immediately. "You and I are going to take a little trip. We can do it the nice and easy way, which includes a first-class flight, or—"

"I'm not going anywhere with you," I cut in as I try to put distance between us, and my heart beats harder as panic pours into my chest.

JESSI ELLIOTT

Blake grips my shoulders, pinning me against the brick exterior of the shop. With a sigh he says, "For the record, I really didn't want to do this the hard way."

I open my mouth to, what? Scream? But Blake is faster. His eyes go black as he pulls a hand off my shoulder. Then his fist is flying, slamming into the side of my head and sending me toppling into darkness.

My head is throbbing something fierce when I open my eyes. I sit up against a mountain of unbelievably soft pillows and blink quickly, desperate to orient myself, but my surroundings are unfamiliar. The room is dim, lit softly by lamps on the nightstands on either side of the king-size bed I'm on.

I glance down, frowning at the black silk sheets as my panic crests, and I scramble off the bed, wincing at the splitting headache taking residency behind my eyes.

Fuck, fuck, fuck.

I was walking to get breakfast for me and Harper when Blake ambushed me on the street. The bastard knocked me out.

Whipping around, my eyes land on a window, and I rush toward it in search of some clue as to where he brought me.

The night sky outside is so clear I can see the stars, making me think we're not in New York, and the moonlight reflects off a small pond. I can't see anything else but trees, and as the reality of being kidnapped settles in, the back of my neck tingles and my throat goes dry. My eyes burn with unshed tears as I fight to stay grounded in reality.

Panicking won't help the situation, but the pressure building in my chest evidently didn't get the memo. Each inhale is shallower than the last, and I cross the room in a hurry on unsteady legs, reaching for the handle of the first door. Throwing it open, I find a simple yet modern, four-piece bathroom that smells faintly of citrus and mint.

After splashing cold water on my face, I reach for a towel to dry my hands and brush the inside pocket of my jacket. My breath catches at the hard outline of my dagger.

I've been carrying it since Noah tossed it at me during the demon attack outside Two Boots.

I return to the bedroom, torn between relief and insult, considering Blake obviously didn't think I was enough of a threat to disarm me.

THE DEVIL'S TRIALS

Scanning the space, I bypass the sitting area and go right for the other door. An odd mix of dread and excitement zips through me when I turn the knob and the door opens. I guess I was expecting it to be locked.

Taking a deep breath to center myself, I pull the dagger from my jacket and slip out of the room, ready to dive into a fight.

The hallway is empty.

I deflate, exhaling slowly and peering around the area. The walls are neutral and decorated with modern works of art. My footsteps are quiet on the dark wood, and I squint a little at the lighting above.

I'm going to make Blake pay for this damn headache.

It's brighter out here, the contemporary fixtures hanging from the high ceiling drowning the space in crisp light.

I do my best to ignore the thumping in my head as I continue down the hall, my grip on the dagger making its solid metal hilt bite into my skin.

I'm halfway between the bedroom and the top of a staircase when a shiver zips up my spine.

I freeze, holding my breath. Alarm bells blare in my head, which doesn't help the throbbing behind my eyes, but there's nowhere to run. I won't make it out of here, and the certainty of that makes my jaw clench.

I know it's him before I whirl around.

My eyes lift to Xander's immediately, my muscles locking as I take him in. He looks the same as when I saw him in New York, except he's clean shaven, his hair tousled just right. He's also dressed more formally than I'm used to, in a light gray dress shirt under a black suit jacket and matching slacks. His attire is impeccable. *Royal.*

He regards me with a curious glint in his eyes, cocking his head to the side. "Going somewhere, *mo shíorghrá*?"

"Kitchen," I lie without missing a beat. "I'm feeling snacky."

Xander chuckles. "Try again."

I slink back, my eyes narrowing. "Was I meant to stay in that room? Maybe you should've locked the door. Better yet, is there a dungeon in this place you'd like to cage me in?"

He steps toward me, and it takes everything in me not to bolt. My posture stiffens, and he notices, frowning briefly. "I'm not going to lock you up."

I swallow hard, glancing past him, back the way I came. I don't think that's the way out of here...I need to get to the main floor. I need to get to the stairs I was heading for. So I have to keep him talking, distracted, and then make a break for it. "I can leave then?"

His brows tug closer, a muscle feathering along his jaw. "No."

I blink at him, shaking my head. "You see why that might be a problem for me?"

"You're here so I can ensure your safety."

"Why?" The question leaves my lips before I can snap my mouth shut. In the time it takes me to blink, Xander closes the remaining distance between us. I suck in a sharp breath and stumble back, but Xander catches my wrist, plucking the dagger from my grip.

That maneuver sets off something in me, and I lunge forward, slamming my fist into his jaw. His head barely moves, and pain flares across my knuckles as I curse at him.

Still I try again, but he catches my fist in his hand, using that grip to push me back until I hit the wall. He cages me in, moving faster than I can follow. Between one moment and the next, he tucks my dagger in the waistband of his slacks and has my arms pinned to the wall above my head. I continue to struggle, lifting my knee to try and sock him hard enough he'll let go of me, but he dodges each of my attempts with an ease that has anger burning hot in my chest.

"Stop fighting me," he says in a level voice, his chest pressed against mine, invading my senses with his proximity and a hint of aftershave.

"Let me go," I pant, gritting my teeth, but don't stop trying to free my wrists from his grasp.

"I will once you settle down."

I give one last fruitless attempt to break free, shooting him a dark look before I stop fighting. My chest rises and falls quickly against his as I catch my breath. His eyes roam over my face, bringing heat to my cheeks, but I force myself to hold his gaze when it meets mine. Slowly, he frees my wrists, and I drop them back to my sides, clenching my hands to keep from slamming them into his chest. It won't do any good, but the urge is strong nonetheless.

"Why did Blake bring me here?"

Xander takes a small step back, giving me room to breathe. "Let's not have this conversation in the hallway."

I scowl. "I don't give a fuck where we are. I want answers. Now."

His lips twitch. "I've missed your sharp tongue."

THE DEVIL'S TRIALS

That trips me up, and I stare at him for too long before I cross my arms over my chest. "Xander—"

He catches my elbow, drawing me toward him and guiding me down the hall toward the room I came from. I don't protest, but the second we're behind the closed bedroom door, I start in on him, my anger from before still simmering just beneath the surface.

"What am I doing here?" I demand unsteadily, following him as he crosses the room toward the sitting area.

He gestures to the couch he stands behind. "Sit down."

I don't. Instead, I repeat, "What am I doing here, Xander?"

"Sit down, Camille." His tone is sharp, and it cuts into my chest, reminding me exactly who he is. Why I shouldn't be anywhere near him.

I turn on my heel and cross the room toward the door. I can't be here any longer.

"Don't walk away from me," he calls out, igniting something in me.

I whirl around, and suddenly tears are blurring my vision. "I should have walked away from you the moment I found out what you are!"

He stumbles back—he actually recoils—as if I hit him.

I exhale an uneven breath, meeting his gaze, and ask once more, "What am I doing here?"

"Camille—"

"What do you want?" I snap.

"You."

The air leaves my lungs in a vicious *whoosh* as I take an instinctive step back.

Xander sighs. "There are things happening in my world that could put you in danger, and I needed to make sure you were safe."

Too many emotions shove forward, making it hard to breathe, and I swallow hard. Walking back toward the sitting area, I keep a healthy distance between us. I'm not entirely sure what makes me say it, but the words are out of my mouth before I can't stop them. "Tell me everything."

He walks around the couch and sits, waiting until I take the armchair furthest from him, putting the glass coffee table between us.

"There is a very old, very powerful demon that has made it his mission to destroy me. Marrick was quite close with my mother and agreed with her vision to eradicate the hunters. From the second I made a play for the throne, he's been vehemently against my reign."

I wipe the dampness from my palms on the armrests, keeping my gaze locked on his face. "What does that mean exactly?"

"Marrick will do everything possible to ensure my downfall, which means you're not safe."

My eyes widen as my heart beats faster. I can't help the jumble of racing thoughts as I try to sort through everything being thrown my way. I want to ask what I have to do with Xander's downfall, but honestly, I'm too afraid of the answer. Instead, I say, "So you decided to have Blake knock me out and bring me—" My gaze shifts to the window before I look at him again. "Where are we?"

"Vancouver."

I blink. "Vancouver..." My voice trails off. "Why?"

He shrugs. "Staying in Seattle was getting a bit precarious."

"Right. And how long do you plan on keeping me here? I assume I'm being kept, considering you've already said I can't leave."

He sighs. "I'd rather you didn't see it that way."

"And I'd rather not be here, so I guess nobody wins."

Xander cracks a smile. "You didn't miss me then?"

I don't answer, though the jump in my pulse is telling enough, and the smirk on his face tells me he fucking knows it.

"Are you hungry?" he asks next.

I want to say no. Tell him to go away. Because there's no chance of figuring out what's going on in my head with him so close. There's a table filling the space between him and me, but I still feel him *everywhere*. My stomach grumbles anyway, threatening to make a liar out of me if I tell him no. I was on my way to get breakfast when Blake appeared, and I'm not sure how long ago that was.

"I guess," I finally say. "What time is it, anyway?"

He checks his watch. "Eight thirty."

I nod slowly, my anxiety climbing higher as I consider what happened when Harper woke up and I was gone. "How long have I been here? Harper is probably freaking out. I need to—"

"Take a breath," Xander cuts in smoothly. "You've been here less than a day. Blake picked you up this morning, and Harper is heading back to Seattle to the safety of headquarters until she's able to come here."

I think his words are meant to make me feel better, but they don't stop the tingling at the back of my neck or the sense of doom crowding my thoughts. I want to ask him if Harper is involved in my being here. If she accepted the position on his council. But the way my heartbeat is thumping in my throat makes it too hard to form the words.

"Come on." He stands and offers me his hand. "I'll make you dinner."

My eyes drop to his outstretched hand, and I hesitate. I should stand and walk past him, but the urge to feel his touch takes control and has me sliding my hand into his as I get up from the chair.

We walk out of the bedroom and downstairs to the main floor. My stomach dips when I spot the front door, and Xander squeezes my hand, stealing my attention.

"I know you want to try running," he murmurs, his thumb brushing over the back of my hand. "It's in your best interest not to."

I exhale through my nose. "My best interest or yours?" I throw at him. "And don't you have more important things to do besides play house with your would-be soulmate?" I stop walking the second the words are out of my mouth, pulling my hand free from his.

Xander moves to stand in front of me, his face filled with an expression I can't begin to decipher right now. "I wondered when that would come up again."

I shake my head, wishing I could take back what I said as my heart thumps in my chest.

"You'd like to talk about it, then?"

"I really don't."

He cocks his head to the side, his eyes searching mine. "And yet, you brought it up unprompted."

"I don't want to talk about it, Xander," I snap. "Let's just go make dinner and pretend this whole situation isn't fucked up."

"If that's what you want," he offers.

I choke on a humorless laugh. "Don't pretend *any* of this is what I *want*. We've already established that I don't want to be here."

Xander nods but doesn't say anything.

"People are going to wonder where I am. My dad, Noah. Someone will report my absence from training to the organization, and you'll be the first suspect. It won't take long before—"

"There's a nationwide hunt for me?" he offers with a faint smirk.

I scowl at his blasé tone. "There are demon hunters in Canada too, you know."

He shrugs. "They won't find this place, Camille. No one will, which is precisely the point."

Evidently he decides I'm not going to make a break for it, because he keeps walking, leaving me staring after him.

My stocking feet are quiet on the hardwood even as I stomp down the hall after him. I catch up as he reaches a set of double doors and opens them to a combined kitchen and dining room.

I scan the space, immediately noticing a guy standing at the restaurant-grade stove with his back to us. He's stirring something in a massive pot, and whatever it is smells divine.

He turns, wiping his hands on the apron tied around his waist, and offers us a polite smile. "Good evening." He walks around the kitchen island and comes toward us, his pale blue eyes focused on me. "You must be Camille."

I nod slowly, unsure what to make of this guy. He appears to be around Xander's age, maybe a few years older, and has a hint of an accent I can't place. He's dressed in a navy dress shirt with the sleeves rolled to his elbows and black slacks.

"Camille, this is Gio," Xander says lightly, no trace of our previous conversation left in his tone. "He's been a friend for many years."

"Um, hi," I say.

Gio's lips curl into a grin. "Lovely to meet you. Xander speaks very highly of you."

"He does?" I blurt as my brows lift and warmth fills my cheeks. I shouldn't feel any sort of way over Xander talking about me, especially to his demon friend, yet I can't stop the stupid butterflies in my stomach from flapping their wings.

Gio dips his face, making his golden blond hair fall across his forehead, and lowers his voice as if he's sharing a secret. "The bastard doesn't shut up about how wonderful you are. It's really quite annoying." He shoots me a wink before straightening and walking back to the stove.

I inhale a short breath when Xander's hand grazes the small of my back, guiding me toward the dining table off to the side of the kitchen. He pulls out a chair, waiting for me to sit to push it in. Then he rounds the table and sits across from me, his expression unreadable as he takes the dark bottle in front of him and unscrews the cork. Finally, he meets my gaze, asking, "Wine?"

THE DEVIL'S TRIALS

I nod, pushing my glass closer so he can pour. "Thank you," I murmur once my glass is full. I glance toward the kitchen, where Gio continues preparing our meal, then turn my focus back to Xander as he pours his own glass. "Now that you're well on your way to being king you're too important to cook for yourself?"

Gio chuckles but doesn't say anything, keeping his back to us.

Xander sets the wine bottle down, a flicker of amusement in his eyes. "I would much prefer to cook for myself—and for you. I quite enjoy it, as I'm sure you recall. However, as you've already mentioned, I have important things to do, which often means I don't have the luxury of time to do what I enjoy."

I press my lips together. "Hmm."

"Besides, Gio went to one of the top culinary schools in Canada. I don't want his talents wasted while we're here."

Before I can respond, Gio approaches with two dishes, setting one down in front of me and the other in front of Xander.

"You kids enjoy." He pats Xander on the back and smiles at me.

"Thank you," I say, staring at the most mouth-watering piece of roast, paired with steamed broccoli and garlic mashed potatoes. "This smells incredible." My stomach grumbles in agreement as I pick up my fork.

"I wanted to make something fancier—I make a divine duck confit with broccoli rabe—but Xander requested this. Something about it being one of your favorite meals."

"I appreciate it," I tell him sincerely. I have no reason to take issue with Gio, especially considering he's been nothing but kind and just prepared my meal.

He smiles and nods before retreating from the room, leaving Xander and me alone.

We eat in silence for a few minutes, and it feels weirdly...domestic. I can't help but think about the date we had at Xander's apartment in Seattle when he made me dinner.

"What's on your mind?" Xander asks, taking a sip of his wine.

I shake my head to clear it. "Just trying to keep up."

The corner of his mouth curves upward, hinting at a smile. "You don't need to worry, Camille. Everyone in this house is loyal to me, which means you're safe."

I stab a broccoli floret with my fork. "How many people are here?"

"Eight now that you're here. You'll meet the others tomorrow, once you've had a chance to rest."

"Blake's here?" I check.

Xander nods, slicing into his roast and lifting a piece to his mouth.

I drop my fork onto my plate. "Cool. Can I have my dagger back?"

He swallows and offers a short laugh. "Blake was acting on my request."

Arching a brow, I ask, "So you requested he clobber me in the head and knock me out to bring me here?"

His expression darkens. "Not exactly. He knows I wasn't pleased about that part. That said, don't blame him for bringing you here, blame me."

"Can I have my dagger back?" I repeat.

"We both know you won't use it on me."

His confident tone makes my eyes narrow. "Do we?" I taunt, unable to help myself. He doesn't get to win this verbal sparring match.

Xander sets his fork down, holding my gaze. Reaching behind him, he pulls my dagger out and sets it on the table, close enough for me to grab. Then the arrogant bastard picks up his fork and proceeds to eat.

I sit back with a scowl, crossing my arms.

He points at my plate with his fork. "Eat before it gets cold."

"Don't tell me what to do," I grumble, and yeah, it's childish, but it's either that or scream profanities about this whole shit show. I think I chose the tamer option.

After swallowing a mouthful of potatoes, I proceed to down my glass of wine. Because if I'm going to endure whatever this is with Xander, I'm at least going to do it with a buzz.

Twenty-Seven
Xander

Camille's arrival could have gone worse. I expected her to be upset, and it was warranted. I would've much rather gone for her myself and had her come willingly, but there wasn't time to finesse that. What's important now is that she's here and she's safe. With my third trial looming, I can't worry about Camille and keep my focus where it needs to be.

I left her alone last night when she retreated to the bedroom Blake brought her to when she arrived. As much as I wanted her next to me, I have to be mindful of how close I get. I'm so fucking close to the throne, and with just under a month until the winter solstice and the ascension summit, my final trial could come any day. I need to be at my strongest. I can't let any ounce of weakness in.

Camille brings out whatever humanity lingers in me which, by all accounts, is dangerous. Any flicker of vulnerability could mean the difference between ascending the throne and being damned to guard the deepest, darkest pits of hell.

But that doesn't stop me from being drawn to her, especially when she's under the same roof I am.

The others have kept their distance since they arrived. Greer hasn't left her room, so Jude has spent most of her time in there with her so she isn't alone, while Roman and Francesca have been scouring for any information about Marrick's plan to create demons from humans.

I find Camille leaving the dining room and cut into her path with a smooth, "There you are."

"Where else would I be?" she offers with an arched brow, and I can't ignore the way her heart beats faster when she sees me. An ever-present reminder of how I enjoy the way I affect her far too much for a demon who isn't meant to feel such things. That said, I suppose the primal instinct to claim her is far from human...

I tilt my head to the side, trying to get a read on her, though she's learned quite well to school her features. "How are you?"

She blinks at me, a prelude of her wildly unimpressed tone. "Seriously? How do you think I'm doing?"

"Camille—"

"I didn't think I could feel so claustrophobic in such a huge house but I'm trying not to rip my hair out here."

"You're welcome to explore the grounds, though it's a bit cold out there now. Or I'm sure Gio would be happy to give you a cooking lesson. Something to pass the time so you're not entirely left alone with your thoughts." I know how she operates. How easily her own mind can betray her and trigger a panic attack. I'll do whatever I can to prevent that from happening here.

"You want me to hang out with the demon equivalent of a Disney character?" When I chuckle at her frankly spot-on reference of Gio, she punches me in the arm, and I don't stop her. "It's not funny!"

I cough to muffle the sound of my laughter, holding up my hands. "I'm sorry. You're right. I've just never heard someone describe Gio that way, but it's pretty accurate." He'd absolutely agree too—even the demons are nicer in Canada.

"Whatever," she grumbles. "That's not the point."

I nod thoughtfully. "Of course not."

Camille exhales a harsh breath. "You won't let me leave this place, and I'm going out of my mind. I went from training every day to nothing, and it's making me antsy."

"Let me change, and we can go down to the gym together."

"No," she says without missing a beat.

"No?" I can't help the lilt of amusement in my tone that surely matches my expression.

She shakes her head. "I'm not going to train with a demon. Especially not you."

Something in me latches onto the challenge. "Why's that?"

"I don't have to give you a reason. 'No' is a complete sentence."

I whistle softly. "Are you this snarky with that hunter of yours?"

She freezes at the mention of Noah, dropping her gaze as her heart lurches, and she shakes her head as if to herself. Just when I think she's going to refuse me, she looks back up. "Meet me downstairs."

Surprise flares in my chest and my brows lift. "Really? I thought it'd take more convincing. Maybe a bit of quippy banter."

She rolls her eyes and walks past me. "Prepare to have your ass handed to you."

I have no doubt it's a false bravado, but I'm thoroughly entertained by her display of confidence.

After stopping in my room to change into a T-shirt and joggers, I head to the gym to find Camille finishing a warmup on the treadmill. My gaze locks on the green workout set that clings to her and shows off a sliver of her stomach, and I have to bite back a possessive growl as I devour her with my eyes. Her heart is beating steadily, and I can't help the urge to prowl toward her and—

Her eyes meet mine, and my train of thought halts as she swallows hard, stepping off the machine. I start across the gym, and we meet near the middle of the room, an open space with padded flooring.

"Ready when—"

The words aren't out of my mouth before Camille dives into action. She launches herself at me, kicking out hard with her right leg, and manages to hit the back of my knee while I'm still consumed by surprise. I grunt at the shock of contact more than discomfort, then instantly correct my footing and stalk toward her.

"You'll have to do better than that, *mo shíorghrá*," I taunt.

Anticipation flashes in her eyes as her pulse thrums wildly, and she drops to her haunches, lunging forward and effectively taking my legs out from under me. We topple to the mats, and she grabs a fistful of my hair as she straddles my hips, wrapping her other hand around my throat. Sweat dots her brow and upper lip, her chest heaving above me as she visibly tries to catch her breath.

I make no effort to move. My own pulse is ticking faster, blood pumping harder as I fight the urge to abandon our fight for the chance to taste her. Her lips, her skin, her—

Fuck me.

Swallowing against her palm, I murmur, "Impressive."

Her breath catches, and she freezes over me, her gaze snared in mine. I don't wait a moment longer, moving in a blur and flipping us over to pin Camille to the floor. My thighs press on either side of her hips, and I grip her wrists as her pulse jackhammers, though she doesn't immediately attempt to get free. She stares up at me silently while her heart beats like thunder in her chest, her lips parted as she breathes hard.

I could taunt her with the easy victory. Challenge her to fight me off. Instead, I dip my face and capture her lips with mine.

Camille tenses beneath me, but any semblance of resistance is quickly lost as she closes her eyes and kisses me back.

My pulse thrums and energy zips through my veins like the most highly addictive drug as I switch my grip on Camille's wrists to one hand, then bury the other in her hair. Deepening the kiss, my tongue darts out, sweeping across her lips before they part to let me in.

We fight for control of the kiss, no doubt bruising each other's lips as we silently agree to let go of everything else but this moment. The bond between our souls was broken when I lost mine, but I feel as close to Camille as I did the first night we spent together. Even as everything else changed, what I feel for her never has.

I can't pinpoint the exact moment I fell for Camille Morgan, but I know down to the marrow of my bones that I remain entirely in love with her even now.

That stark, quite possibly fatal admission has my heart pounding faster as the distant pang of fear edges me closer to losing myself. The control I have over my desire for Camille frays as I move my knee between her legs, pressing it to her core. I'm immediately rewarded with a gasp against my lips, and I use every ounce of willpower I have to keep from tearing her leggings off and burying myself inside her.

"If we don't stop..." I trail off, voice low and deep with arousal. "It's taking everything I have not to reacquaint myself with every inch of you right here."

Camille pulls her bottom lip between her teeth, blinking her eyes open. I can see the fight she's having with herself. She wants this as much as I do, despite the nagging voice I think we both hear telling us that crossing that line will only lead to more pain.

She swallows hard. "We can't."

Disappointment is a punch to the gut, but I nod. I need to shake the remnants of anxiety crackling through me. I can't think about the reasons my pulse is racing or my chest feels like it's about to explode. Not now. "Perhaps we should get back on task."

Her brows lift. "Wha—"

"You want to show me that you can protect yourself against my kind. So please, go ahead."

She narrows her eyes at me, her cheeks flushing a deeper shade of pink. "You're hardly the best example of an average demon."

The corner of my mouth kicks up as I brace myself over her, leaning closer. "A compliment?"

"Oh yeah, definitely," she remarks dryly.

I chuckle softly, more relieved than I care to admit that she hasn't lost her spark of humor. "Shall I ask Blake or Gio to come down and give it a go with you?"

"If I can beat them, will you let me go?" she shoots back, her breathing returning to a more normal rhythm.

I cock my head to the side, my eyes flicking across her face. "You didn't seem to mind being here a minute ago."

She scowls, bucking her hips in a failed, albeit amusing, attempt to get free. "Xander—"

"No," I cut in, keeping her pinned beneath me as I lower my voice. "I wouldn't let you go." *I won't ever let you go.*

Her breathing turns shallow once more, and she lowers her gaze so her lashes fan the darkness under her eyes. "How long do you expect me to stay here?"

With a sigh, I maneuver off of her, standing and pulling her upright. "That's not a simple question to answer." The situation is only becoming more complicated, and with Marrick attempting to overthrow everything I'm working toward, anyone who means anything to me is caught in his warpath. I haven't decided how to explain all of that to Camille—it's something I'd rather she never have to know, but that's seeming less likely with every passing day.

Camille pulls away from me, concern etched into her hardened features as she regards me coldly. "My parents are going to worry."

I nod. "I'm not saying you're cut off from your loved ones."

"But they don't know where I am, and if they knew who I was with, it would be further cause for concern."

I frown at that. Blake brought her to Vancouver to ensure we can keep her away from the danger coming down the pipeline. I'm not sure what I can say that will help her understand she won't come to harm so long as she's here. "You're safe with me."

There's a deeper flush in her cheeks when her eyes meet mine. "You'd like me to tell the leaders of the demon hunting organization that their daughter is safe with the king of hell?"

I exhale a short laugh. "I won't tell you how to speak to them, I'm only saying that you can. My phone isn't traceable, so call your parents or Harper or whomever you wish." I bite my tongue to keep from suggesting she avoid contacting Noah. It's pathetic and undignified, and I refuse to entertain the notion of jealousy when it comes to that bastard, despite the simmering tension in my chest at the thought.

Camille winces at the offer, chewing her bottom lip. "Right."

I arch a brow at her. "What is it?"

She hesitates, seemingly battling with how to respond before she exhales a sigh and says in a reluctant tone, "Without my phone, I...I don't know their numbers."

I press my mouth shut so I don't laugh again. When her eyes narrow sharply, I hold up my hands. "It's fine. I have Harper's number in my phone. She'll be able to send us your parents'."

"Okay." She peers around the room, as if she doesn't know where to look anymore.

"You're free to use this space whenever you like," I say, feeling as if I need to show her that I'm trying. That as unideal as the situation is, her being here doesn't have to be miserable.

"A prison with amenities," she mutters under her breath as she moves away, wandering toward the stairwell to the main floor.

I follow her, walking a few paces behind. She stops at the bottom of the stairs, her pulse spiking as she whirls around to face me.

"What's the endgame here?"

I fold my arms over my chest, leaning toward her. "I'm more concerned about right now. Keeping you alive and—"

"Ascending the throne," she interjects, her pulse ticking faster as her gaze flits across my face.

"Yes." It's not a secret. My motivations have been clear for a while now. I'm committed to not keeping anything from her, even if it makes her hate me.

Her brows knit as if she's disappointed. "What happens after that?"

"You'll need to be more specific."

She opens her mouth, then pauses and shakes her head. "Never mind."

THE DEVIL'S TRIALS

I catch her wrist as she turns toward the stairs. Her pulse races against my fingers, and when her eyes meet mine, she freezes. "Is there something you want to say to me?" I ask in a low voice.

She only shakes her head again, pulling her wrist out of my grip. "I should call my parents."

When I fish my phone from my pocket and hand it to her, she takes it without a response, then climbs the stairs, leaving me looking after her with a longing that tugs at the remnants of my human heart.

Twenty-Eight
Camille

I find my way back to the bedroom I was put in when Blake brought me here and close the door. After contemplating using the furniture to barricade it, I decide against it and wander to the seating area across from the bed.

I don't feel as though I'm in danger being here but that definitely doesn't mean I'm happy about it. I'm also waiting for Xander to explain what's actually going on. While part of me would much rather stay in the dark and enjoy the ignorance of not knowing, my anxiety isn't having it. I need to know.

I drop onto the end of the bed and find Harper's number in Xander's phone. She picks up on the first ring.

"I'm going to kick your ass to the ninth circle of hell, you fuck—"

"Harper," I cut in, "it's me."

"Cami, holy shit." The relief in her voice is clear. "Are you okay? Xander told me you're with him, and I'll be there as soon as I can, but—"

"Take a breath, Harper. I'm fine. Anxious and annoyed but otherwise okay. You're back in Seattle?"

"Yeah. I got a red-eye and went directly to HQ when I landed."

I inhale slowly before asking, "Have you spoken to my parents?"

"Uh, nope. That's all you, babe. Sorry."

I cringe. "They're going to lose their minds. I don't even know what I'm going to tell them."

"If Noah wasn't expecting you for training at Ballard, you could probably get away with not telling them anything for at least a few days, but he'll want to know where you are when you don't show up."

Groaning, I pull the tie out of my hair and rake my fingers through it. "They're not going to understand, Harper."

"I take it you haven't told them about the whole soulmate thing?"

"Yeah, that's a big no." I wouldn't know where to start with that conversation, considering I still know little about it myself. I fall back against the mattress and stare at the ceiling. "This is so messed up and it keeps getting worse."

"We'll figure it out, babe. If you give your dad a call and let him know you're out of town maybe you don't have to tell him and your mom everything right now."

I drum my fingers against my stomach, turning that over in my head. It sounds like a better idea than trying to explain where I am and why I'm here. That said, there's the added complication of Noah. I'm not sure he'll believe I just left town, and when he's not able to get ahold of me, I don't want him reaching out to my parents.

When I share my worry with Harper, she hums. "I'll tell him you came back to Seattle with me."

"Don't you think he'll see through that? I was just there before you visited me in New York."

"Maybe, but I don't see another option. I think we need to take our chances and cross that bridge if and when we come to it."

She's right. I'm limited in what I can do when I don't want to share information about what's going on here—not that I have much.

"Okay," I finally say. "When do you think you'll get here?"

"I'll try for the next few days. I signed up to teach a few novice classes at HQ and it'll look suspicious if I cancel at the last minute."

"You're staying there, right? You're not alone?"

"Yes. I'm perfectly safe. No creepy, big-bad demon is going to get their hands on me."

"What exactly has Xander told you about Marrick and everything going on? because I know pretty much nothing."

"Maybe you should talk to Xander about that."

I blow out a breath, rolling onto my side and tucking a pillow under my head. "I'd really rather not."

She sighs. "The short version is that Marrick was Lucia's lover and wants to be king. You already know he made threats against me in an attempt to manipulate Xander into passing the crown to him, but when he didn't immediately agree, Marrick attacked his council. He killed one member and severely injured another—his own daughter—to send a message to Xander."

My eyes go wide, my chest tightening, and I have to sit up to take my next breath. "All of this to rule the underworld?"

There's a small stretch of silence before she says, "There's more."

I swing my legs over the side of the bed and plant them on the floor, suddenly needing to feel grounded. "I'm still trying to catch up on what you just told me."

"I know it's a lot. We don't need to talk about it right now."

Sighing, I say, "I'm sorry. Are you sure?"

"Of course. I have to run but I'll see you soon."

"Okay. Harper?"

"Yeah?"

"You know how much I love you, right? You are the most amazing friend I could ever have, and I just need you to know how much you mean to me."

There's a brief silence, and then Harper says in a thick voice, "Right back at you, babe."

Just as we're ending the call, a soft knock sounds at the door. I turn as Xander steps into the room and closes the door behind him, approaching at an easy pace.

"I talked to Harper," I say.

"And your parents?" he asks.

"Not yet. I'm going to call my dad and Harper is going to tell Noah that I went back to Seattle with her to explain my absence from training."

He pauses at the end of the bed, his expression darkening at the mention of Noah before he nods. "Did she say when she'll be traveling here?"

"As soon as she can without raising suspicions of where she's going. Her superiors wouldn't be too thrilled with a family reunion, and the last thing she needs right now is to be considered a traitor by the organization she's worked to be part of for years."

His lips twitch briefly, and he moves closer, dropping down next to me on the side of the bed. "Fair point."

I sit straighter, his nearness putting my senses on high alert. "Are you going to tell me what you've been holding back?"

He angles himself toward me, his palms flat against his thighs. "I can if that's what you want. I also understand if you'd rather not know. If you're able to accept that you're safe here, then you don't need to be burdened with anything else."

I arch a brow at him, as if to say yeah, right.

"Of course not," he murmurs, exhaling a soft but humorless laugh.

"Harper told me about the demon that killed someone from your council." I meet his gaze, frowning at the hardness there. "I'm sorry."

He inclines his head. "Marrick will pay for what he's done. And threatened. And planned. He'll never see his dream of taking my throne."

My throne.

The air of power around Xander has grown stronger in the time since he killed Lucia, but it's moments like this, when he says things like that, he truly seems like the royalty he is.

I catch my bottom lip between my teeth, glancing at my lap as I fumble with how to respond. I understand the sense of territoriality but not to the degree of ending someone's life.

You're playing a different game now, I remind myself. The demon world is dark and twisted, and I need to adjust my perception of things if I'm going to make it out alive.

"So you're going to hunt him down and execute him?"

Xander's hands curl into fists. "Hunting him won't be necessary. He's already sent a warning of what's coming."

My stomach sinks, and something makes me reach for him, covering his fists with my hands. "What's coming?"

His shoulders rise and fall before he turns his face to meet my gaze. "An army that Marrick is building by creating demons."

I tighten my grip on his hands without even realizing it until his eyes flick downward briefly. "*Creating* demons? Is that even possible? I mean, how would that work?"

He shakes his head. "This is the first I've heard of it, but I'm inclined to say yes. Marrick doesn't use empty threats." He turns his hands over, lacing his fingers through mine. "My council is looking into it."

Right. His council. I have yet to meet them—besides Blake, of course—and the idea they know more about me than I do them puts me on edge. Meeting new people is anxiety inducing as it is. With the added layer of tension to this scenario, I'd much rather avoid them while I'm here, though I get the feeling I can only do that for so long.

"Is Gio part of your council?"

"No. Gio refuses to get involved in the politics of our world. He's just a good friend."

I nod. "If Marrick is planning to *make* demons, we need to stop him before he can."

He traces his thumb in a light circle on the back of my hand. "And we will. I don't want you to worry about this."

My brows inch up my forehead. "You know who you're talking to, don't you?"

Xander smiles faintly. "Of course." He shifts closer, brushing my thigh with his as he leans in and lowers his voice. "As much as you don't want to be here, I'm selfishly glad you are."

Heat rises in my cheeks, my lips parting as my eyes dart between his, searching for a hint of what's going on in his head.

"Xander," I murmur.

"Camille," he levels.

"Kiss me."

He releases one of my hands to reach up and cup the side of my face. I lean in to his touch, pulling in a breath before his lips crash down on mine. My eyes shut of their own volition, and I close the remaining distance between us, pulling my hand from his to grab the front of his shirt and tug him in.

Xander snakes an arm around my waist and pulls me onto his lap, deepening the kiss and pushing his fingers into my hair to cradle my head. My heart thunders in my chest as my head spins, and I lose myself to the sensations flooding through me. It's far too easy to push everything else away when we kiss.

I shouldn't want this—shouldn't want *him*—but I can't deny my need for him. Even if I loathe the part of me that does.

Pushing him back onto the mattress, I straddle him as our lips move in sync, just as they always have. I lower myself until my chest is pressed to his, and our hearts pound against our rib cages, desperate to be close to each other.

The pressure in my chest heightens tenfold and my lungs ache, but I don't break the kiss. I'm terrified of what the end of this moment will bring. I'm not ready to face it.

Xander pulls his lips from mine, and I hover over him as we catch our breaths. When I finally open my eyes, I find him gazing up at me with a look so consuming it threatens to steal the air from my lungs anew.

"What are we doing?" I breathe, shifting to move off him.

THE DEVIL'S TRIALS

He catches my hips, keeping me in place, and his hands on me makes my pulse surge. Heat pools low in my stomach, and I gasp sharply when he rolls us onto the middle of the bed and pins me beneath him. The weight of him sends sparks of anticipation racing across my skin, and I already know I'm playing a losing game against my willpower to resist him.

"You're going to tell me what you want me to do," he says, leaning in until his lips brush mine again, "and I'm going to do it."

My entire body flushes with warmth, my throat going dry as I search his expression. *He's serious.*

I press my lips together, lowering my gaze to his chest as I try and fail to ignore the throbbing between my thighs.

"Eyes on me," he says, snagging my chin and lifting my face until our gazes meet. "That's better."

With my heart thumping in my chest, I lick the dryness from my lips. "I thought you were going to do what I wanted."

His smirk is downright wicked. "And what is it that you want, Camille?"

You.

It must be clear on my face, because his eyes darken with the same lust spreading through me at a dizzying speed.

"Tell me you want me," he murmurs.

"I..." My lips part in a silent gasp when he presses a deft hand between my thighs, my leggings the only barrier between him and where I ache for his touch. "Yes."

He brushes his thumb back and forth over my core, tilting his head to the side. "Yes, what?"

My eyes narrow at the taunting lilt in his voice. "I want you. You know I do."

"Hmm." He presses his mouth to mine in the whisper of a kiss, then murmurs, "You're mine."

"Yes." The word tumbles from my lips before I can consider snapping my mouth shut, the muscles in my abdomen tightening.

"Say it." His voice is a smooth, hypnotizing demand I can't ignore, much less deny answering.

"I'm yours."

He slides his fingers to the waistband of my leggings and slips his hand inside. The first brush of his fingers against my core has me sucking in a shuddering breath.

"Is this what you want?" His breath caresses my cheek, his lips brushing along my jaw.

"Mmm," I moan, lifting my hips to guide him closer to where I crave. I slide my hand up his chest, curling it around his neck and tugging him down until our lips meet again.

My pulse jackhammers when he slowly enters me with a finger, using his thumb to tease the bundle of nerves at the apex of my thighs. I make a sound against his lips that encourages him to double his efforts as his tongue flicks along my lips until they part to let him in. He kisses me deeply, bringing me closer to the edge with each subtle movement between my legs.

I lose track of my breath as I give myself over to the pleasure he's wringing from my body. I grip the hair at the back of his neck, tugging it as I circle my hips and whimper as he adds another finger inside me. His lips leave mine, trailing along my jaw and finding the pulse at my throat. He kisses and nips at the sensitive skin below my ear, and I gasp his name as I tighten around him, my only warning as pleasure explodes from my core, leaving me lightheaded and warm.

Even as my heart continues to pound and I catch my breath, I know I need more.

I need all of him.

As much as I'm his... *Xander is mine.*

His face is pressed to the crook of my neck, and when I reach for the button on the front of his pants, he chuckles softly. "What do you think you're doing?"

"I want to say I'm fucking the king of hell, but you have yet to take the throne, so I guess I'm fucking the king of nothing."

I have no idea what possesses me to say that, but the shock on his face when he pulls back to look at me fills me with a smug sense of pride that I latch on to.

His eyes darken, flickering black before returning to their normal brown as he cocks his head to regard me. "Is that so?"

I purse my lips, popping the button open and tugging his zipper down. "You tell me. We've established what I want." My eyes flit between his. "Do you want me, Xander?"

A possessive growl rumbles through his chest, and I shouldn't be drawn to that sound, yet heat fills my face as I hold his gaze. His pupils are blown, his expression dark with lust as he dips his face until his nose grazes mine.

"You," he breathes, "are *all* that I want."

Between one moment and the next, his mouth captures mine with a searing kiss that promises to ruin me for anyone else.

I lose track of time as his mouth explores mine before his lips travel across my body. Our clothes quickly end up on the floor, and when Xander positions himself at my entrance, there isn't a thought of hesitation in my mind. I urge him on until he pushes inside me, stealing the air from my lungs.

Wrapping my legs around him, a moan slips from my lips as he starts to move, and we find a delicious rhythm that has us both racing toward release in minutes.

"Camille," he breathes my name desperately, as if it's a prayer, his voice deep with arousal.

"Don't stop." I lift my hips to meet his thrusts, tightening around him when he hits a particularly sensitive spot. My head spins, my brow dotted with sweat as I slide my hands from his shoulders to his face, cupping his cheeks and bringing his lips to mine.

Our kiss is feverish and desperate, and I lose my perception of reality as the pleasure consuming my body crests, and I cry out, the sound muffled by his mouth on mine.

He continues to thrust into me until his thighs tense as he reaches his own climax, and we cling to each other to ride out the warm, continuous waves of euphoria together.

If this is what being damned feels like, I'll gladly accept my fate in hell.

I'm not sure how long we lie next to each other, my head resting against his chest while he runs his fingers along my hair. I think I'm almost asleep when there's a sharp knock at the door.

"Ignore it," I grumble.

Xander chuckles, then sighs. "You know I can't."

"Xander," Blake says through the door. His tone is deep and serious, setting me on edge immediately.

"What is it?" Xander barks back without moving.

"It's time," Blake responds, "and you're going *home* for this one."

I frown, my stomach sinking as Xander tenses beneath me.

It's time for his final trial.

Xander's chest rises and falls slowly. "Give me a minute."

There's a beat of silence followed by, "We'll be in the car."

Once I'm sure Blake is no longer standing on the other side of the door, I whisper, "I don't want you to go." My eyes burn with the threat of tears, and I don't want Xander to see them. I'm trying so hard to keep the emotions at bay, but the thought of him traveling to the place he grew up fills me with an ice-cold fear that I'm going to lose him all over again.

"I know." He brushes his thumb over my cheek, making my skin tingle. "I don't want to go either."

My forehead drops against his chest, and I inhale slowly. "Tell me you're coming back."

Xander presses his lips to the top of my head, sighing softly. "Of course I am." He pulls back enough to look into my eyes. "When will you realize? Hell won't ever be able to keep me from you, *mo shíorghrá.*"

Twenty-Nine
Xander

After leaving Camille in bed, I shower and dress in record time, then meet my council in the car. Blake is behind the wheel, the passenger seat left empty for me, while Francesca, Jude, and Roman are in the back. Greer is still more than a little on edge after losing Declan, so I opt to have her stay back.

I can only ignore the tension filling the vehicle for so long before I grumble, "What is it?"

Jude sighs from the seat behind me. "You couldn't wait to bed your human fixation until after the final trial?"

"She brings out the worst in you, which is something we needed to avoid," Francesca adds.

The worst being any ounce of humanity in this scenario.

I could lie and call it a momentary lapse, or argue I didn't know when I'd face my last trial, but I don't feel the need to defend my choices. I did what I wanted.

"When were you home last, Fran?" Blake asks to fill the silence after it's clear I'm not going to respond.

We're heading to the portal in the Olympic National Park after I had it scoured for hunters, ensuring we won't run into any upon our arrival in a little under five hours.

"Hmm," she hums. "A few years ago. I found myself lost in this realm and needing a break. Humans are positively exhausting. At least in hell I don't have to be anything but what I am."

Blake chuckles. "You can do that here so long as you don't give a fuck about anything or anyone."

She sighs, the sound intentionally dramatic. "Yes, well, we're not all like you, Blake. That's not as easy for some of us."

"I can't tell if that's meant to be a compliment or an insult."

"Best not to analyze it too closely," I chime in, drumming my fingers against my leg.

By some small miracle, the rest of the drive is smooth and goes by quickly. Once we arrive, Blake parks in the public lot, and we start the trek into the forest. It's an overcast afternoon and there's a bite of coldness in the air that makes me grateful for the jacket I grabbed on the way out the door.

Francesca is dressed impeccably, as always, in a black pea coat, leather pants, and boots with an almost ridiculous heel. Blake and I are dressed in similar black dress pants and shirts, but while my jacket is black, Blake opted for a sandy brown leather zip-up. Paired with his blue hair, some might view his appearance as strange, but Blake's confidence helps him pull off frankly any look, and he knows it.

Jude and Roman are in jeans, hiking boots, and black rain jackets. Roman's hair is combed back neatly, while his sister's is twisted into an intricate braid down her back, as dark as the forest floor beneath our feet.

The leaves crunch under my hikers as we follow the trail into the thick cover of trees, and I swallow past the unease clogging my throat. This portal, at the crossing of Seattle's ley lines, is the same one I came through a decade ago when Lucia decided I needed to be socialized with humans. So I could 'fit in and learn to manipulate them.' Needless to say, it's not the fondest of memories. I was an adolescent already struggling with his humanity versus his demon side. I was never given a chance to discover who I was on my own. My future—my fate—was sealed even before I was born.

Blake leads us off the trail, between the dense trees, until the silence of the forest falls on us. We trudge through the brush, the air damp and earthy. Each breath I take is a plume of fog in front of me as the temperature seems to drop and the air fills with a light mist.

Jude and Roman walk behind, while Francesca stays next to me, the only sound coming from her the steady beat of her heart. My stomach dips, my pulse spiking as we approach two noticeably larger trees that stick out from the others. They're older, their trunks thicker, with massive roots crawling along the forest floor.

Blake stops, propping his hands on his hips, and glances between the trees before turning to regard me. His expression is focused, serious. "Are you ready?" he asks in a level tone, his gaze flicking toward Francesca before returning to me.

THE DEVIL'S TRIALS

I nod before I can hesitate, and Francesca pulls out an obsidian dagger that makes the monster clawing at my chest growl low.

"Relax," she mutters, seemingly unperturbed. "We need your blood to open the portal."

I pluck the dagger from her hand, gripping it tightly until my hand stops shaking. Inhaling slowly, I stand between the two larger trees and open my palm, slicing deeply into my skin as I exhale through my teeth. Fire licks across my skin at the contact of the obsidian, and my jaw works as I fight not to snarl in pain. I turn my palm over, letting the black blood pour from the wound to the forest floor.

Nothing happens at first.

I glance around at the members of my council, who are watching me. Waiting.

And then, the ground starts shaking.

"Do you know what comes next?" Blake asks from my right, while Francesca steps up on my left.

Before I can remind him I haven't been back to hell since I left over a decade ago, the ground opens beneath our feet, and we're falling.

The air rushes from my lungs.

Darkness clouds my vision.

Blood pounds in my ears.

I can't tell which way is up. My senses escape me for what feels like a short eternity. I squeeze my eyes shut as the nausea rolls through me in violent waves. Darkness consumes me, and I have no choice but to let it.

At some point, though, the ground becomes solid under me. Slowly, the darkness recedes and my senses return. Everything rushes into focus, so sharp and fast, it's disarming. The air is thick, smoky, and reeks of sulfur. The trees surrounding us are black as charcoal, and the cloudless sky red like blood.

"I nearly forgot how fucking bleak this place is," Blake comments, brushing dust from the sleeves of his jacket.

I glance around at the desolate wasteland where I grew up. The underworld—or hell—is a mirror of the human world, but...darker. *Sinister.* Everything appears mostly normal at first glance, but look too long and it'll quickly become twisted into your worst nightmare. With demons lurking anywhere and everywhere, the smoky atmosphere is heavy with torment and despair.

JESSI ELLIOTT

Time ceases to exist here, which is to blame for the distant echo of endless screams. Hope is nowhere to be found, and yet, my veins sing with power, as if I've fed on a human buffet of fear.

"How are you doing, mate?"

I turn to look at him and force a blasé smile. "Home sweet home."

He snorts, and we make the trek through the forest, but the parking lot we left in the human world has morphed into a wooden-plank bridge over a wide chasm. Below is a rapidly flowing river of blood, its sharp copper scent burning my nostrils and making my stomach roil.

Being in the human world so long has made you weak, my mother's voice reverberates hauntingly in my head, and I shove it away, gritting my teeth as I step onto the swaying bridge, the first plank groaning under my foot.

"Where are we going exactly?" Jude asks, stepping onto the bridge behind me, and Roman behind her.

"I imagine Lucia's estate is where she left it when she came to the human world years ago. We'll head there until the royal guard decides to grace us with their presence."

We cross the bridge in silence, the river whooshing below us as I attempt to ignore the red mist in the air and coating the thick braided rope guardrails on either side of us.

Roman sighs. "You're not going to make us walk all the way there, are you?"

I keep my gaze trained ahead as we near the other side of the bridge. "What do you..." I trail off as realization dawns on me. "I can portal here."

"Theoretically," Blake calls out. "Your mother could, so now that you're in her position, with the power of the reigning monarch, you presumably can too."

We get to the other side of the bridge, and I exhale a steadying breath. While the surge of energy from being back in hell is undoubtedly beneficial, I've never felt so out of my element.

"We're about to have company, gentlemen," Francesca says under her breath seconds before three demons spill out of the forest no more than twenty meters away.

In an instant, I'm gravely aware that these are high-level demons. They mostly exist in the depths of the underworld and rarely venture topside, choosing to feed on the souls of the damned that are trapped

THE DEVIL'S TRIALS

here for eternity. With appearances more animal than human, my posture straightens as they get closer, their all-black gazes focused on me.

I'm to be their king, I remind myself.

Except they don't bow to me when they get close as they should.

The male in the middle with a mouth full of grotesque, bloodstained fangs snarls a greeting before lunging at me.

Blake dives into action immediately, grabbing him around the waist as he swipes near my face with filthy, wolf-like claws. He throws the demon to the ground with a laugh. "Quite the warm welcome, mate," he tosses over his shoulder at me.

Francesca advances at preternatural speed toward the other male demon, and I follow without missing a beat, not about to let them fight alone. Another move that'd be sure to disappoint my mother. She always expected those loyal to her to fight so she didn't have to lift a finger.

I grab the female demon, wrapping my hand around her throat as she growls at me, her skin ashen gray, like dark granite. She has icy white hair that falls in loose waves down her back, and her black leather bodysuit clings to her narrow frame. This demon is *small-but-mighty* personified. And if she wasn't attacking me, I'd likely appreciate that more.

"Weak human scum," she spits in my face, and I get a flash of the piercings in her forked tongue. She attempts to slam her knee into my groin, but I manage to twist to the side so she hits my thigh.

I tighten my grip, leaning in as I bark, "Stand down or I will *put* you down." When her eyes narrow in defiance, I smile grimly and add, "Go ahead. Allow me to make an example of you."

She seems to consider it. I watch her face, picking up the exact moment she makes a decision. Her mind is made up about me.

A cool sensation ripples through me as I give myself over to the monster lingering just beneath the surface. I grab both sides of the demon's head and twist hard, snapping her neck. Stepping back, I let her body crumple to the ground. Killing demons works differently down here—her body won't turn to ash like it would in the human world. We'll have to sever her limbs and burn the pieces to ensure she doesn't come back as a low-level demon.

I clap my hands together and exhale a sigh as I turn toward the others. Blake and Francesca each hold a demon by the throat as I walk closer, gravel crunching under my boots.

"Perhaps we can discuss why you saw fit to attack your king," I offer in a level tone. I may not be king yet, but I'm fucking close enough. "Alternatively, I have no problem if you'd prefer to join your snake-tongued friend in eternal nothingness. Your choice."

Slowly, both of them bow their heads, and when I nod at Blake and Francesca to release them, they sink to their knees. Jude and Roman, who were covering our backs, walk forward to stand with us.

"Forgive us, my lord," one of the males says in a low, gravelly voice. He appears older than the other, maybe early forties, and has short, salt and pepper hair with a matching beard.

"Tell me," I say as they keep their gazes trained on the ground. "Should I expect more greetings such as yours?"

The younger demon looks up first, meeting my gaze. When he opens his mouth to respond, his teeth are shockingly human, though his ears are slightly pointed, as if he could be one of the fair folk. Maybe in another life he was.

"Was the welcome into the monarchy topside friendlier than down here?" The serrated edge to his voice makes my lips twitch.

"That's truly how you want to speak to me after I just killed your friend for disloyalty?"

He chuckles. "Not a friend."

"You have two options," Francesca chimes in. "Respect your king, or I'll kill you myself."

The demon doesn't look at her. Doesn't take his eyes off me. "We all wondered when you might take the throne. Some of us didn't think you ever would. I personally don't think you're cut out for it."

"And why do you think your opinion matters?" Blake asks, and I can see the muscle in his jaw ticking. He's itching to fight, but despite the adrenaline rush of battle, I would rather not have to kill another today.

I wave Blake off, flicking a glance toward the other demon who still has his head bowed. "Rise," I tell them both, and they get to their feet. "You don't share the same fear of me your acquaintance here does."

He shrugs. "I don't fear death."

"Death is not what you would have to look forward to if I end your life here. Have you forgotten that because you do not have a soul, once you die in hell you're damned to an eternity of nothing but darkness—and I mean that quite literally."

THE DEVIL'S TRIALS

"Are you waiting for me to beg for my life?"

"No," I say honestly. "I wouldn't wait. If I was going to kill you, I would have. I want to make it clear how things are going to go moving forward. Lucia ruled for a long time, and near the end of her reign did so with the promise of power over the human world. I can understand why that might be appealing to many. That said, I'm not continuing my mother's legacy."

"And you wonder why many aren't pleased with you. We are loyal to our ruler to an extent. However, a lot of demons are not supportive of a half-human king."

"He isn't human," Jude speaks for the first time, her voice sharp.

"Taking the throne meant sacrificing his soul," Roman adds. "He's as much a demon as any of us now—and more powerful than all of us."

I glance to the less combative demon as he clears his throat.

"What is your plan then?" he asks.

"To fulfill my duty," I answer simply. "To enact punishment on those who deserve it."

"Will you return to the human world then?" the snarky one asks. I can't quite pinpoint his angle. He seems to despise me, but in an oddly playful way.

"I plan to, yes. There is still the issue of the demon hunters."

"And do you believe eradicating that issue as your predecessor would have is not the right idea?"

"Lucia's plan is not mine," is all I say. "Now—" I nod toward the demon I killed. "I leave it to you to deal with this."

"Of course," the older demon says, bowing his head again before grabbing the elbow of the demon next to him and pulling him away. He holds my gaze for a beat longer before the two of them walk back toward the body.

The five of us continue on our way, heading for Lucia's estate. Once we're under the cover of trees, we stop, and Francesca folds her arms over her chest, asking, "Do you know how to portal?"

"In theory. Of course, I haven't done it before." From what I know, it *should* be as simple as closing my eyes, focusing on where I want to go, and *poof*, I'll end up there.

"No time like the present to give it a shot," Blake says with a grin in my direction.

I nod and direct everyone to join hands as I close my eyes. Physical contact will make it easier to ensure I don't portal away without them as I visualize the parlor in Lucia's estate. The massive stone fireplace with crackling flames that never seemed to run out of firewood, and the antique chest set that sat between the dark leather couches.

Without warning, the world tilts, and I hold my breath as everything starts to spin. Seconds later, the ground is solid beneath me once more, and I blink my eyes open, releasing my friends as we all look around to the place I remember from years ago.

"Easy peasy," Blake says and claps me on the back, grinning wide. "Nicely done, mate."

"Well, I don't know about you guys, but I need a drink," Roman adds.

"I'm with you there," Jude agrees immediately, linking arms with him and Francesca, and the three of them walk to the brass bar cart in the corner of the room in front of a floor-to-ceiling window draped with heavy blue velvet curtains.

"How does it feel to be back?" Blake asks in a quieter voice.

I exhale a sigh. "This place never felt like home, but the familiarity of it amidst the final trial is oddly comforting."

"Fair enough. I'm going to get myself a drink. You want one?"

I shake my head. "I'm going to take a beat."

"Do you need—"

"All good."

He eyes me for a moment, then nods.

I leave them and walk the estate grounds, then head toward the small village I frequented as a child. The old cobblestone streets are quiet, most of the shops closed.

There is no day or night here, and I don't recall how the operating hours of these places work.

I pass one shop I don't recognize—an art store. I'm stepping inside before I can stop myself, a small bell above the glass door ringing to announce my arrival.

I browse the small space for what can't be more than a few minutes and pause as my gaze connects with the young woman behind the front counter. She has soft brown eyes and matching hair, twisted into a braid over one shoulder. The woman offers a faint smile and a subtle bow of her head, and I just stare at her.

THE DEVIL'S TRIALS

I feel as if I should know who she is. She seems familiar, like an itch of a memory that refuses to form enough to comprehend. To make any sense of.

When she turns to reach for something on the shelf behind her, the dim light catches her bare shoulder, revealing a tattoo of two intertwined flowers. It's simple yet unique and I...*I've seen it before.*

Recognition hits me like a blow to the gut, and my back stiffens. There's suddenly a chill in the air, and my neck prickles with unease.

But it can't be...can it?

I blink, but the tattoo doesn't go anywhere—of course it doesn't.

The shopkeeper turns back around, and the gentle similarities are so painfully obvious the second time I look at her, I find myself moving closer.

"Danielle." Her name flies from my lips, the disbelief clear in my tone.

Her eyes dart across my face. "You know who I am?"

I release a surprised breath. "I do."

Her lips curl into a faint smile. "I guess I should be flattered. Or nervous." She offers an awkward laugh, tucking her hair behind her ear. "Should I be nervous?"

Shaking my head, my brows knit as I regard her, still unsure *why* I'm seeing her. "How are you here?"

"Um..." She glances toward the shop door before meeting my gaze again. "That's kind of a complicated answer." Confusion flickers across her features. "I'm sorry, I know who you are because, well, everyone here does, but how do you know me?"

I pull my gaze away, unsure how to navigate the situation. If I didn't know better, I might believe that *this* is my final trial. But considering it's the first time I'm seeing Danielle, her being part of my hell loop wouldn't make sense.

"Camille—"

"You know my sister?" she cuts in, eyes widening with a mix of shock and concern. "How?"

"That's kind of a complicated answer," I echo her previous response.

Danielle crosses her arms over her chest, her expression hardening. Hell, even her mannerisms are similar to Camille's. She opens her mouth but before she can get a word out, the front door opens, and none other than the royal guard files inside with their sights set on me.

"We're here to deliver you to your final trial."

JESSI ELLIOTT

My eyes narrow, tension filling my upper body, but I nod. I knew this was coming. I'm as prepared as I'm going to be. "Very well," I finally say.

"We need to finish this conversation," Danielle says in a firm tone.

"Of course," I agree. "I'll return once the trial is complete."

She nods. "Uh, good luck?"

I exhale a short laugh. "Thank you. I'll see you again."

"When you're king?" she asks, her eyes on mine.

I nod. "When I'm king." I pull my gaze away, moving toward the door as my thoughts drift to the human I left and how I'm going to explain this to her.

A month ago, I thought Camille was my future. Escaping Lucia's clutches after we chained her in hell, and starting a life for myself with the fiery, compassionate human I couldn't—I *can't*—seem to live without.

Instead I lost my soul saving my soulmate and now have the responsibility of ruling an entire race, which just so happens to be the part of me I despise the most.

My stomach plummets as I follow the guard out of the shop, leaving Camille's sister behind. My insides are in knots, my palms sweaty as I try to picture what my hell loop will be. There are endless possibilities, which makes preparing nearly impossible. That said, the finish line is in sight. I just have to get through this final test.

I may not have a soul anymore, but I still have my heart—a tether to my humanity. Though more than before, I find myself wishing I didn't. That I could switch off the emotions plaguing me.

So do it, a deep voice at the back of my head taunts. *Turn it off and become the monster you're meant to be.*

I exhale a harsh breath, crossing the empty town square as the sky above darkens. We're heading toward a stone building that resembles a courthouse, with wide concrete steps and pillars on either side of the massive wooden doors.

I start up the steps, then freeze at the sound of my name being shouted. I turn, half expecting to find Danielle coming after me, and my blood runs cold when my eyes connect with Harper's.

No, no, no.

She isn't supposed to be here.

I close the distance between us and grab her upper arms. "What are you doing?" I demand.

THE DEVIL'S TRIALS

Her eyes narrow sharply and she knocks my grip away. "You ask me to join your council and then ditch me on the first field trip?"

My brows shoot up my forehead, and I shake my head adamantly. "You shouldn't be here, Harper."

She tugs a dagger from the holder strapped to her thigh, curling her fingers around the hilt as she grins at me. "You wanted a hunter."

"And you decided *now* was the best time to accept the position I offered? *Here?*"

She shrugs. "I have a flair for the dramatic."

I stare at her in utter disbelief, torn between the sense of pride in my chest and the new urge to keep my human sister safe. Glancing over my shoulder, I quickly note that the guard has entered the building. Perhaps they didn't see Harper.

"How did you get here?" I demand.

She slides her hands into the pockets of her black rain jacket. "Blake told me you were leaving for the portal, so I might have gone there and waited for you."

My eyes widen. "And then what? You followed us through it?"

"Well, yeah. I didn't open it myself." She offers a little humorless laugh. "I wonder if I could, though. We share blood, right? Maybe when you killed Lucia and gained all that power, something happened to me too?"

I arch a brow, shaking my head. "Not likely."

"Eh, whatever." She glances around. "So this is hell, huh?"

"I'm taking you to the others, *now*. It's not safe for you to roam this place alone, Harper."

She tilts her head to the side, glancing past me. "Right, because I'll run into super friendly looking people like that guy?"

I turn to follow her gaze, and my body goes rigid when my eyes land on Marrick as he moves toward us, his eyes filled with darkness. "Harper, you need to—"

"I'm not going anywhere," she cuts in.

"I'm not asking," I bark back, grabbing her by the arm.

Marrick appears in front of us, and I tug Harper behind me, putting myself between them.

"Xander Kane," he says, his deep tone filled with malice. His shoulder length dark brown hair is tied back, and he's dressed in all black, appearing in his late forties despite being hundreds of years old.

"You would do well to get out of my way, Marrick."

He chuckles. "Is that so?" Instead of moving away, he begins to circle us slowly, as if he's taunting his prey.

Harper's pulse jackhammers, and she grips her dagger tighter. "I can take him," she says under her breath.

"Not happening," I hiss back. I don't care that I asked her to join my council and be my hunter, she isn't facing this bastard.

"Unfortunately, that isn't your choice." Marrick disappears from view for a split second, then slams into us with immense speed and power, knocking Harper away from me. Her dagger clatters to the ground, and she curses sharply.

I recover almost instantly, charging forward and colliding with an invisible wall as Marrick grabs Harper and hauls her upright by the throat.

Confusion and rage go to war in my chest as I slam my fists against nothing, trapped to watch Harper struggle against Marrick.

"It's quite simple, son. Give up the throne now, and I'll let her live."

My heart pounds in my chest, and I snarl, "Don't call me son. You won't live long enough to step foot anywhere near the throne."

"Is that your final answer?"

Harper's face pales and fear rolls off her in waves.

"Kill her, and you lose all your leverage." I'm resorting to calling his bluff. I don't like it, but Marrick is a coward. As Francesca said, he doesn't do his own dirty work. He's not going to kill her.

"Xander," Harper breathes, shaking her head, then mouths *please*.

"Now that's not quite true, is it?" Marrick taunts. "The hunters' daughter will die next should you continue to test me."

"You and what army?" I shoot back, trying to buy time. "Haven't found any humans to force into subjugation?"

He bares his teeth in a vicious growl, and Harper whimpers, squeezing her eyes shut.

She tries to break free, slamming her elbows back and kicking him wherever she can, but it does little more than irritate the demon.

"Perhaps I'll use this one." He smooths his free hand over Harper's hair, and she shudders, pressing her lips together as her chin quivers.

"Oh?" I cock my head, stepping to the side to test the invisible barrier. Magic has always been in play in the underworld, and it works in ways not even the oldest demons fully comprehend. "And how do you plan on doing that?" If I can use this opportunity to gain insight into Marrick's insane plan, I'm not going to pass it up.

Amusement passes over his features. "You know, I don't think Ms. Gilbert here is the ideal candidate." His grip on her throat tightens before he releases her for a moment too brief for her to get away.

She makes it two paces as he snatches her dagger off the ground, then grabs her again.

"I'm done playing games." His lips brush her ear, making her grimace as he says, "Do you have any last words for your brother?"

Tears swim in her eyes as they meet mine. "You are a *monster*. You will never be anything more than that." Marrick tightens his grip, and she cries out in pain. Gritting her teeth, tears spill down her cheeks, and her words slice into me as fatally as an obsidian blade.

A growl tears from my chest and I fight the invisible barrier keeping me from her. All the strength I came into and it does nothing when I need it the most. "Let her go," I snarl at Marrick.

Marrick laughs deeply, shooting me a cold smirk. "As you wish, boy." In the space of a second, he takes Harper's dagger and slashes her throat. Blood pours down the front of her shirt, and he drops her onto the ground with a careless *thud*.

My lungs burn as I yell, pounding my fists into the wall until it disappears, then catch my balance and stumble forward. Tightness expands in my chest, making it hard to breathe, and I collapse on the ground, rolling Harper over and clamping my hand over the wound across her throat. Her blood stains my fingers crimson as she gasps for breaths she can't take, blinking at me with equal parts terror and anger in her eyes. "This is... your fault."

I shake my head, pressing harder, but Harper's blood just spills through my fingers as the color leeches from her face and her eyes go vacant.

Pain ignites in my chest when the sound of my sister's heartbeat fades away. I lean over her, closing her eyes gently and exhaling an uneven breath. "You shouldn't have come to this place." I brush her hair away from her face. "Why did you come?" It's a useless question. It won't bring her back, but what else can I do?

My gaze lifts slowly until it connects with Marrick's. "You're dead," I vow in a voice dripping with venom.

He says nothing. Just stares at me with a blank expression.

Realization trickles in as the wind feels colder, chilling me to the bone. It feels as if it's carrying away wisps of my humanity with each breeze, and I don't fight to hang onto it. The more I let it go, the less barbed wire fills my chest with razor-sharp pain.

I inhale deeply, keeping my eyes on Marrick as a cool numbness settles over me. Pain doesn't exist and fear is nothing but sustenance.

He stalks forward, Harper's dagger in his grip, her blood dripping from the tip of the obsidian blade. Before he makes it close enough to lunge at, his form fades into dark smoke before disappearing completely.

I stare at the spot he once stood, then turn to look back at Harper. Except, she's not there. Ice slashes through my veins, but I barely feel it.

She was never here.

The royal guard files out of the stone building and approaches as a solemn unit, emulating power and darkness. Their expressions give nothing away as they regard me silently. I have half a mind to wonder if they overheard my conversation with the vision of Harper—if they know of my plan to bring the demon hunter onto my council. But it wasn't them who put her or Marrick here, it was this place and its ability to form my worst nightmares. So perhaps they don't know. Either way, that's not my most immediate problem.

Rupert bows his head, waiting for the others to follow suit before he announces, "All hail King Xander."

Those words send power crackling through me as I get to my feet. Thunder crashes deafeningly loud as the sky fills with streaks of red lightning. I've never felt this strong. Nothing can stand in the way of what I desire, and I'll take great pleasure in destroying anyone who tries.

Thirty
Camille

I barely sleep the first night Xander is gone, and when I haul myself out of bed in the morning, there's a check-in text from Harper on his phone.

> How are things? I won't be able to get there today. Rachel recruited me to teach a novice class, and if I turn that down it'll look suspicious.

Despite the pit in my stomach, I smile. Harper has always impressed the organization, and it appears they're finally acknowledging it. Of course that'll be shot to hell—quite literally—if she joins Xander's council and the hunters discover it, but I'm not about to bring that up. Knowing Harper, she's already stewing about it.

> That's great, Harper! Please don't worry. Xander and his council left for the final trial, so I'll be distracting myself until they get back. I need to call my dad, but thinking about that is really a treat for my anxiety.

> Oh babe, I'm sorry. I wish I could do that for you. I'll be there soon. Hugs!

> Thanks. Right back at you.

I pace the length of Xander's room for a while, my bare feet padding across the hardwood until I work up the nerve to call my dad. Harper sent the number last night, so all I have to do is tap on it and wait for the call to connect.

In the middle of the room, I stop moving, take a deep breath, and initiate the call.

He answers on the second ring. "Scott Morgan."

"Hey, Dad, it's me."

"Camille? Your name didn't come up."

"Um, yeah." I panic briefly then blurt, "I kinda lost my phone. It's probably somewhere at Ballard."

"Not to worry, kiddo. We can track it. Are you heading there with Noah this morning?"

I wince inwardly, biting the inside of my cheek. "No. I'm actually out of town for a while. I've really been missing Harper, and she's going through some things too, so I just need to be with her right now."

"What about your training?" he asks, his voice laced with concern.

"I'll keep up with it, don't worry."

There's a stretch of silence, then, "Is there something going on?"

"No," I lie too easily. "Everything is fine. I'll let you know when I'm back in the city and we can have dinner, okay? I love you."

"I love you too. You know where I am if you need anything."

"Thanks, Dad. I'll see you soon."

I end the call before I dig myself into a bigger hole of lies. Tossing the phone on the bed, I exhale a heavy sigh and head into the ensuite bathroom to take a shower.

After standing under the spray of water until it loses its warmth, I get out and wrap myself in a plush towel. I take my time drying off and moisturizing, enjoying the high-end products in Xander's bathroom I'd venture a guess Blake purchased.

Wrapping myself in a robe off the back of the door, I return to the room I woke in yesterday and scour the fully stocked closet for something to wear. I dress for comfort in a light gray crewneck sweater and sweatpant set, then twist my hair into two French braids before venturing downstairs to the kitchen.

"Good morning," Gio greets with a warm smile from where he sits at the kitchen island counter, sipping from a mug.

"Morning," I offer with an awkward wave.

"How are you doing? Can I make you something for breakfast?"

"I'm fine," I say automatically.

"Coffee?"

I shake my head, walking to the opposite side of the counter and leaning against it. "Not a huge fan."

"Fair enough." He finishes his coffee, setting the mug down before continuing, "Well, if you're not too busy today, you should hang out with me. I plan to get wine drunk and bake a bunch of cookies."

THE DEVIL'S TRIALS

I nearly choke on a laugh.

How is this guy a demon?

"Are you serious?"

"Very much so. I'm leaning toward a classic chocolate chip but may also try a dark chocolate and salted caramel recipe I found last night. Interested in joining me?"

"Yeah, kind of," I admit with a hint of a smile.

Gio beams. "Excellent. Now, are you a red, white, or rosé gal?"

"Hmm, usually white."

His grin widens. "Perfect. I just got a few bottles from Niagara that you're going to adore."

"You know a lot about wine?" Xander mentioned him attending culinary school, so it doesn't feel like a stretch.

"I like to think so. I worked at a hotel in Toronto for a number of years and was known in the kitchen as the wine guy."

"That's really cool," I tell him, glancing around the professional grade kitchen. "I'm ready to dive into a sugar coma whenever you are."

We spend the rest of the day sipping wine and eating cookie dough until my stomach aches. While I still worry about Xander and Harper and my parents somehow finding out where I am, the distraction of hanging out with Gio has been really nice.

I call it a night early after a delicious dinner of grilled cheese and tomato soup—all made from scratch by Gio—and head to bed with a light buzz that thankfully helps lull me to sleep faster than my thoughts can catch up.

The next morning, I wake only mildly hungover from the excessive amount of wine I consumed yesterday. After a splash of cold water on my face, I change into a workout set and wander my way to the gym.

Starting my usual warm up, I can't help but think of Noah. A quick glance at the clock tells me he's on his way to Ballard for class, and there's a pang of something in my stomach, pushing against the pit that already exists there.

I miss Noah.

As much as he annoys me and complicates things, he's also a significant source of comfort and assurance. He believed in me even when I didn't. He fought for me to retake my test, and I can still clearly see the pride shining in his eyes when I passed it.

I exhale an uneven breath, turning off the treadmill and walking over to the wall of free weights. I focus on my arms, going through several sets of workouts Noah taught me until they feel like noodles. Then I utilize the squat rack to the point my legs are shaking when I reset the bar after my last rep.

Downing my water bottle on my way to the stairs, my stomach grumbles, and I go in search of the leftover cookies from yesterday's baking marathon. Because *yum*.

It's been three days since Xander left for the final trial. I understand time passes differently in hell, but the longer he's gone, the higher my anxiety creeps.

Gio continues to cook for me and makes conversation that makes me feel almost normal, but the reason I'm here having these conversations always exists in the back of my mind, same with the nagging concern about what's going to happen if Xander doesn't pass the trial—or if he does.

I'm sitting at the dining room table across from Gio trying to convince myself to pick up my fork and eat despite the swirling unease in my stomach making me feel queasy. He put in the effort to make a perfectly fluffy quiche with a flaky, buttery crust, and I feel bad I'm just pushing bits of it around my plate.

"I'm sure they'll be back soon," he says in a gentle voice.

Glancing up, I meet his friendly gaze. "Yeah." I take a small sip of my water. "Will you know when it happens? Like how all the demons felt when the queen died?"

He considers it for a moment before shaking his head. "I don't think so. The trials are a technicality the royal guard implemented. We felt when the previous monarch died because that was the change in power. Though if for some reason Xander wasn't taking the throne, I suppose we might feel that." He offers a small smile. "This hasn't happened in quite some time. The change in power, I mean. And it's never happened like this before." He chuckles softly. "Of course Xander had to go and do something unprecedented so none of us can figure out what the hell is going to happen next." Gio's tone is fond, but I get the underlying concern in his words.

"You've known him for a while then?"

"We go way back."

THE DEVIL'S TRIALS

I chew the inside of my cheek, running my finger through the condensation on my water glass. "Do you think taking the throne will change him? I know he lost his soul when he killed Lucia, but there's still part of him that's, I don't know…"

"Human?" He offers.

My heart is still human and it remains yours.

My cheeks flush, and I give a halfhearted shrug. Gio's nice, but I'm not about to sit here and talk about my relationship with Xander with him.

Gio sighs. "Xander has always toed the line in that regard."

"What line would that be?"

"Good and evil," he says simply. "He's struggled with humanity for as long as I've known him. I thought the absence of a soul would eliminate that but it seems not."

I'm not sure what I was expecting him to say but it wasn't that. "Right," I mumble. Instead of pretending like I'm going to eat, I push my plate away and stand. "Thanks for breakfast."

His eyes flick from my plate to my face, and he smiles. "Of course. Can I make you something else?"

My stomach drops, and I rush to say, "Oh no, that's okay." I feel bad for leaving my food untouched. "Sorry, I'm just not really hungry right now." I push my chair in, picking up my plate to take it to the kitchen. "I'll, um, see you later."

I retreat to the bedroom, slipping into the en suite bathroom and turning the shower as hot as it'll go before undressing and getting under the waterfall shower head.

Steam fills the room with a hazy warmth as I use too much of the stupid expensive shampoo, conditioner, and body wash until my hair and skin smell and feel incredible.

It's only once the water gets cooler that I shut off the shower and get out. Exhaling a long breath, I wrap a towel around my hair and another around my body. I wipe the fog off the mirror and lean against the vanity, my head swimming from the heat.

I take my time dressing in comfy light gray joggers and a black crewneck sweater, combing my hair and applying body lotion, because self-care—I may be spiraling a little, but at least my skin is soft.

I pass the afternoon with an extended nap and a call to Harper, who reassures me she'll be here as soon as she can.

When my stomach grumbles around dinner time, I figure I should head downstairs and try to eat something.

I walk out to the hallway and nearly collide with someone just outside the door. Reeling back, my gaze shoots up to meet the most striking eyes I've ever seen.

"Um, hi," I stutter, taking in the rest of her otherworldly stunning appearance. She's tall and well-toned from what I can see. Her hair is long and shiny, falling in loose waves past her breasts, accentuated by the vest style top she's wearing, paired with high waisted dress pants and impressive heels.

The stranger looks me over, her gaze calculating. "You must be Xander's little human houseguest. Caitlin, right?"

I arch a brow, pulse still racing. "Camille," I correct. "And you are?"

"Francesca," she says. "Council member and Xander's oldest friend."

That sparks something in me I choose to ignore. "I thought Blake was his oldest friend."

Francesca chuckles. "Yes, well, Blake has never slept with him, so I think I still win."

Heat flares in my cheeks, and whatever response I had dies on my lips.

She props her hand on her hip. "Xander didn't tell you about me?"

I shake my head without saying anything. I'd give anything to go back in time and not leave the bedroom. Running into an ex-lover of Xander's is pretty high on my list of things I'd be thrilled to avoid—I think outnumbered only by *going to hell*.

"Ouch. I guess I wouldn't either. We were betrothed, after all."

My eyes widen as my stomach sinks. "What?"

She waves away my surprise as if it's a ridiculous reaction. "It was a long time ago."

"Why didn't you marry him?"

She purses her red stained lips. "Some things just aren't meant to be."

"Did you love him?"

Francesca laughs. "Love? It had nothing to do with love."

I frown, my brows tugging closer. "That sounds incredibly lonely."

She arches a perfectly shaped brow at me. "Do *you* love him?"

My heart pounds in my chest, as if it's attempting to break free of my rib cage. "I...um..." I sigh, and I have no idea why, but I tell her, "As much as I've tried to shake him, I just can't. He's ingrained in my soul. I know he's changed since Lucia—he didn't have a choice—but I still see flashes of the Xander I believe loves me too, which makes me want to fight for him. So I will."

Francesca rolls her eyes. "Ugh. Such fluffy human emotions." She straightens, holding my gaze. "I grew up with Xander in hell. My loyalty to him is undying."

I'm not sure how I'm supposed to respond to that. This woman scares the shit out of me, so the chance of saying the wrong thing has me keeping my mouth shut.

"You look confused," she observes. "Does Xander not share *anything* with you?"

"He does," I say in a short tone.

Her lips twitch. "Right, well, Marrick is my father. I'm sticking with Xander because I give a shit about him, but also because the man who raised me is the only creature in this world—or the underworld—that scares me." Her gaze darkens, and I'm not prepared to see the flash of fear there. "He wants to rule, to take charge of the demons by creating his own."

I blink, my stomach plummeting. Xander told me what Marrick was up to, but I had no idea his daughter was part of Xander's council—or that they were supposed to be married. Instead of seeking more information that's only going to make my head explode, I say, "Is Xander back?"

Francesca inclines her head in a subtle nod, making the butterflies in my stomach flutter at the thought of seeing him.

I swallow hard. "Is he…I mean, did he—"

"Ask him yourself," she says a moment before the hair on the back of my neck sticks up and my pulse climbs.

I know he's standing there before I move a muscle. I feel him to my very core, and being so physically aware of someone is jarring.

Inhaling slowly, I turn on my heel and face him. The air releases from my lungs in a vicious *whoosh*, and my feet become blocks of cement as I stare at his disheveled appearance. But it's the darkness in his eyes that sends a chill all the way to my bones. His posture is rigid and his all-black attire is tattered and stained.

My world narrows on him as he approaches, stopping a few feet away. Emotion clogs my throat, my muscles trembling as I stand before him. I swallow hard. "You're here," is all I can find to say.

He cocks his head to the side, his eyes roaming my face. "Appears so."

"Does that mean you passed the final trial?" My voice is low, and I can't stop my hands from shaking at my sides. I'm terrified of the answer but I have to know.

Xander nods.

A fraction of the pressure in my lungs releases. At least he won't be forced to patrol the darkest parts of hell.

But what will *he have to do?*

"Well, um, congratulations, I guess?" I offer, at a loss for anything else to come up with.

His lips twitch briefly. A ghost of a smile.

Something feels off. He's standing right in front of me, but this person seems like a stranger. Cold and detached. I've never been to hell, but I didn't think a visit to where Xander grew up would do this to him.

What happened there? What did he have to do to pass the trial?

I take a tentative step closer, searching his eyes for something, *anything* I recognize. I come up empty, and my chest tightens once more.

"You're probably exhausted," I murmur. "I'll leave you to get cleaned up and rest."

Before I make it a full step backward, Xander snags my wrist and pulls me in, quickly gripping my chin and capturing my mouth with his. Between one moment and the next, he has me pressed against the wall, his free hand wrapping around my hip as his lips devour mine.

I'm kissing him back before I even realize what's happening, but when my head catches up to my heart, everything in me screams to stop this. It's primal and possessive and devoid of any semblance of care.

This isn't the Xander I fell in love with—it's the king of hell.

I shove hard against his chest until he concedes a step. "What are you doing?" I breathe, my lips tingling.

He chuckles softly, rubbing his thumb over his bottom lip. "I thought it was clear. My mistake."

Shaking my head, I say, "I don't know what happened while you were gone but I'm here to listen if you want to talk about it." *Come back to me,* I want to say, but the words get stuck in my throat.

Xander shrugs. "There's nothing to say. The trials were a formality and now they're done."

"Okay, fine. So why are you acting like—"

THE DEVIL'S TRIALS

"Like what, Camille?" he cuts in with a jagged tone.

"Like everything I hate about you," I snap.

"Have you considered that perhaps this is who I truly am?"

My brows lift and I can feel my heart beating in my throat. "Do you hear yourself?"

"I think it's you who isn't hearing me. I'm simply showing you who I am. I haven't pretended to be anyone else in some time, and I won't start now just to make you feel better about who you're fucking."

His words are as sharp and violent as a slap to the face. I stare at him, incredulous silence hanging between us. My heartbeat thunder crashes in my chest and my lungs struggle to fill with even breaths. Because how could I be so fucking wrong about Xander, *again*?

All of a sudden, we're back where we started. The whiplash of betrayal burns, making tears prick my eyes, and I quickly blink them away. The urge to disappear from this encounter is strong, but I swallow the emotion clogging my throat and straighten my back.

"You're a coward," I say in a low voice, meeting his darkening gaze. "You can't handle a little trip to the underworld without suppressing your humanity?" I shake my head. "I thought you were stronger than that. *My mistake.*" I throw his words back at him and then I walk away, willing myself not to shed a tear until I'm behind closed doors.

Thirty-One
Xander

The rainfall shower head pelts me with hot water, washing away the dirt and blood, but it won't erase what happened, no matter how long I stand under it.

You're a coward.

Camille's words play on a loop in my head as I scrub my skin raw.

I haven't shut off my emotions completely, but they're certainly subdued. I need to keep a clear head from here on out or people—*my people*—will be in danger, and I won't allow that. Which is why I must keep distance between Camille and me, now more than ever. I can't let myself be vulnerable, and when I'm around her, that is more difficult than I care to admit.

With a sigh, I rest my forehead against the cool shower tile, letting the water hit my back as I take a few shallow breaths.

Marrick is a bigger problem now that I'm taking the throne instead of handing it to him. Dealing with that prick will be the first order of business to discuss with my council after I'm sworn in.

The ascension summit is in two weeks, during the winter solstice. There will be drinking and dancing and a very comical presentation of the crown by the royal guard. They adore any opportunity for spectacle within our world, so there's no chance I'll get out of all the ridiculous pomp and circumstance.

You wanted this, I remind myself, standing straight again and dragging a hand down my face.

So why do I feel so utterly empty?

After showering, I put on a black dress shirt and slacks, then go in search of Blake. I can't share anything about encountering Danielle in the underworld with anyone else until I get more information. There must be a reason Camille's sister is in hell, and I need to know the circumstances

THE DEVIL'S TRIALS

before I bring it up, because Camille will undoubtedly have questions. That's if she believes me at all. I'm not winning any points in the credibility department with her lately.

I find Blake in the enclosed porch off the kitchen overlooking the back of the property. The night sky is pitch black but clear and spattered with stars. Flames from the floor to ceiling fireplace crackle, and Blake swirls the drink in his glass. His eyes shift to me when I approach. "Drink?"

I wave him off, walking toward the bar cart in the corner of the room to pour myself a scotch. Drink in hand, I join him in front of the fireplace and take a sip.

He glances sideways at me. "You good?"

"I'm king," I offer in lieu of a real answer.

He chuckles, giving my shoulder a shove. "Fucking right you are, mate." Taking another drink, he asks, "Are you going to tell me what happened during the final trial?"

I shrug. "Marrick killed Harper."

His brows furrow, and he all but snarls, "What?"

"It wasn't real. They weren't actually there. But I had to face Harper hating me for choosing my throne over her life."

He blinks, and I think there's a split second of shock in his expression. "Did you know it wasn't real?"

The lie is on the tip of my tongue, but I've never been untruthful to Blake and I'm not going to start now. "No."

"So you really would've let her die?"

"No," I insist. "I would've stopped it."

He nods slowly. "Hmm. Why?"

My eyes narrow a fraction. "Because she's my hunter. My blood. *Mine*."

"How heartwarming," he mutters dryly.

I roll my eyes. "What's done is done. But I do need you to look into something else that happened while we were there."

"I'm intrigued."

"I also need you to keep it to yourself."

He scoffs. "Please. Who am I going to tell?"

I offer him a level look.

"Fine, fine. My lips are sealed. What is it?"

I down the rest of my drink, setting the glass on the wooden mantle before turning to face Blake. "Camille's sister is in hell."

"She's *what*? How do you know?"

"I saw her. Spoke to her, actually."

His eyes pop wide. "You're sure it was her?"

I nod. "She and Camille have matching tattoos among other similarities, both in appearance and personality."

"Bloody hell," he says under his breath. "How did this happen?"

"That's what I need you to find out."

"Does Camille know yet?" he asks after a moment of contemplation.

"I'm not telling her until I have more information."

"Makes sense. She's going to lose her mind…and probably accuse you of lying through your teeth."

"I know and I'll deal with that."

Blake claps me on the shoulder, finishing his drink and setting his empty glass next to mine. "Never a dull fucking moment, mate."

The following two weeks are spent preparing for my ascension summit during winter solstice. Which is essentially a giant party where demons from all over the world will come to celebrate a new dawn of our monarchy, so I get to partake in a bunch of ornamental shit like wardrobe fittings and drink and menu pairings. I wanted to do things differently than my predecessor, which means taking a more hands-on approach and attending all of the meetings I'd much rather delegate to Blake or one of the others.

Days are shorter and the weather turns dark and cold, filled with gray skies and rain. It's just as well, considering I spend most of them in meetings with Blake, Greer, Jude, Francesca, and Roman discussing next steps and where everyone will be posted. My council will stay close by in surrounding cities for the first year of my reign. Then once the growing pains have passed, they'll be given the option to relocate where they wish should they want to move.

Harper tried getting away from Seattle to join us last week, but word of my ascension flooded through the organization before she could. Everyone is on high alert, gauging how the demon population is going to react, so her getting away doesn't seem like an option at the moment, which of course isn't making things easier for Camille being here.

She's become skilled at avoiding me, and I've been giving her space. I know she's close by. Even without the connection of our souls, I feel her

THE DEVIL'S TRIALS

on a level I still don't entirely understand. But she's here and she's safe, which is what matters. Gio has been a great support for her in Harper's absence. I've seen them get closer, whether it be afternoon hikes or cooking lessons.

I'm constantly torn between keeping her at arms' length and pushing her further away. If the demons see her as someone they can use to manipulate me, that puts a significant target on her back. She didn't choose any of this, and the thought of putting her in danger so we can be together feels...selfish. I recognize that but I also know deep in the dark pit of my chest that it won't be enough to keep me from her. Because I am that selfish. I'll have Camille, consequences be damned.

Blake is still gathering information about Camille's sister, and while I've considered a trip back to hell myself, I can't disappear without inviting attention I'm not prepared to face at the moment. My actions are under a microscope now, my every move tracked and ridiculed by the royal guard and other, just as if not more, opinionated demons—most of which still aren't amenable to how I took the throne.

The tension among my kind isn't lost on me, but the only thing I can do at this point is show up and prove them wrong.

My mother ruled with a power-hungry desire for control over the masses. I've never shared that ideology. I'll punish those who deserve it—who put our kind in danger and attempt to reject my authority—but my role is to support demonkind. To help it thrive in the face of adversity, like the hunters.

The monarch's role was always supposed to be that of a leader, and it's high time we get back to that.

My confidence comes and goes in unpredictable waves. I tossed and turned all night and woke long before daylight this morning. When the sun finally rises, I roll over and grab my phone off of the nightstand. After scrolling the headlines in the Seattle press, I open my contacts and tap on Harper's name.

She answers on the first ring. "What's wrong?" Her voice is tired but filled with concern.

"Nothing," I say.

She exhales a heavy breath. "So why are you calling me so fucking early? I thought something happened to Camille."

"Camille is fine. She's still asleep."

"Why aren't you?"

I sit up, leaning against the headboard and stretching my legs out in front of me. "I don't sleep much these days."

"Boo hoo," she remarks mockingly, "Poor demon king."

I chuckle. "No sympathy for the devil, huh?"

"Nope. None. So why *are* you calling me?"

"I take it you're not going to make it here for the ascension summit later today?"

"I didn't think I had to tell you what a monumentally terrible idea that would be. A room full of demons and your human, *demon-hunting* half-sister? That's a disaster waiting to happen, Xander."

"I hear you." I thrust my hand through my hair, taming the unruly waves, messy from the aforementioned tossing and turning.

"While we're talking about it, I don't think Camille should be there either. It's not safe."

"I have no intention to have her at the summit. There's a coronation celebration happening after that she'll be attending." *If she decides to wear the dress I left for her.*

There's a small stretch of silence. "You're sure *that's* safe for her?"

"I wouldn't allow it if doing so would put her in danger. The party is for the inner circle, the people who support my reign and want to celebrate it. It'll mostly be friends and of course my council. At least, most of it."

She hums but doesn't say anything.

"I'm still waiting for—"

"I know," she cuts in.

"Are you considering it?" I'm taking it as a positive sign that she hasn't outright refused the position on my council yet.

"Considering...overthinking. Yep. Sure am."

"Anything you want to talk about?"

She laughs, but it doesn't hold an ounce of humor. "Not with you."

"Ouch. I'll try not to take offense to that."

I think I hear a smile in her voice when she murmurs, "You should go. You have a busy day ahead."

"Right. Well, I'll talk to you soon?"

"Uh, yeah. Sure."

"Okay—"

"Xander?"

THE DEVIL'S TRIALS

"Harper," I level.

Silence fills the line again. Finally, she says, "Congratulations."

My chest swells with something I can't immediately decipher, and the call disconnects.

When it's time to leave for the summit, Blake walks out to the car at my side. As much as I wish it was Camille next to me—firstly, Harper was right about it not being safe for her to be there, and secondly, I can picture the look that would fill Camille's face if I'd tried to make her—I'm glad Blake is here. I may not feel as anxious as I once was, but the immense weight of the responsibility I've signed on for is staring me right in the face.

We drive for a little more than an hour. Blake must sense that I'm not in the mood or headspace to keep a conversation, because he doesn't attempt it. Instead, we listen to music, and Blake sings along to most of the songs as he keeps his focus on the road.

As we pull into a long, winding driveway, I take a slow, deep breath, and take in the scenery out my window. Pine trees stand tall and broad in the clear, dusk sky, the air refreshingly cool. This building we drive up to appears to be an old resort property, though based on the sparsely filled parking lot, it's safe to say it no longer operates for the public.

The royal guard has control of where the summit is held but not the coronation ball, as Blake gleefully informed me when sharing his plans for the event tonight. They must own this property as they do with others scattered around North America so they have a designated place to be during their eternally ill-timed visits.

My council meets us inside the front doors, their expressions serious but hopeful. I soak it in, using their support to feed my power, and hold my head higher as I straighten my posture.

"Are you ready?" Jude asks, keeping her gaze on me as Francesca, Greer, and Roman draw closer. We stand in a modern but empty lobby area, and the buzz of too many voices to count comes from the other side of a set of double doors across the lobby.

It kicks my alertness into high gear, and I answer, "Yes," without a second of hesitation.

Blake claps me on the back, standing at my side and grinning. "Of course he's ready."

Blake moves forward and opens the door as Jude steps aside for me to walk ahead.

I lift my chin and square my shoulders as I step through the doorway. A deafening hush falls over the massive room as I move toward the front, where a raised platform with a throne-like chair awaits.

Letting my eyes roam the faces all locked on me, I make a point to meet the gazes of as many demons as I can on my way up. Men and women of differing ages fill the room; there must be at least two hundred demons here. Some appear pleased or excited, while others are more reserved and even openly suspicious

My council flanks me, and when I step onto the platform, they stand on either side of my throne. My gaze sweeps across the room, landing on mostly unfamiliar faces—until I reach the front row and my eyes connect with one of my mother's *friends*.

The sudden tightness in my chest threatens to crack the facade I've built between myself and any emotions tempted to try breaking through. Nausea rolls through me, and I clench my jaw, forcing my gaze away from the wretched woman. I haven't seen her in years—I certainly didn't expect to here—and the vivid memories of the nights we shared come rushing to the surface. To be fair, *shared* isn't exactly the right word when I wasn't given much choice in the matter. It happened all too often with the women in Lucia's inner circle, and it wasn't until I was older and moved out of the compound that I recognized how fucked up it was. How I was manipulated and used to the point it felt normal.

I shove away those remnants of my past, focusing on keeping my posture straight, regal as I stand in front of my throne.

The royal guard makes their entrance, wearing all-black pantsuits and blank expressions. They replace my council on either side of the throne, forcing Francesca, Blake, Greer, Jude, and Roman to stand behind them.

"The ascension trials are complete," Rupert announces in a deep voice that projects toward the back of the room. "Xander Kane faced internal and external conflicts to prove himself worthy and strong enough to truly take the position he is formally embracing today."

"Xander Kane," Dominic chimes in loudly as I keep my gaze trained forward. Unwavering. "Do you vow to rule our people with every ounce of strength you possess?"

I nod curtly. "I do."

THE DEVIL'S TRIALS

Lorraine steps in front of me with her back to the crowd of demons. From somewhere behind me, Malachi hands her a black crown made of wrought iron and black diamonds.

Lorraine's pitch-black eyes meet mine. "Kneel."

I follow her command, sinking to my knees before her. The pressure in my chest feels bigger now, my heart thumping faster. I school my features into a mask of cool indifference, but this is a pivotal moment. One I will carry with me for the rest of my existence.

"This crown is a symbol of your eternal power and strength," she says in a voice that carries through the room as she lowers it onto my head. A shiver races through my body, making my skin tingle as she pulls back, clasping her hands in front of her. "Rise and take your rightful place on your throne, King Xander."

I straighten, my gaze sweeping out over the crowd as I step back and sit on the plush cushion.

Lorraine moves to the side to stand next to Malachi, while Rupert steps up to my right. "Your new king has been crowned," he announces. "All hail, and long may he reign!"

The crown feels impossibly heavy on my head as I stare out at the crowd of mostly cheering and clapping demons, and a poignant weight settles over my shoulders.

Despite the flare of pride in my chest and the air of confidence I'm emanating, I can't help thinking...

What the hell have I done?

Thirty-Two
Camille

If there was ever a party I vehemently didn't want to go to, Xander's coronation celebration would take the cake.

The open bar has helped my jittery nerves and overall sense of dread, but I'd still rather not be here. Or at least have Harper to distract me. Even more so when I re-read the text she sent me this morning.

> I'll be thinking about you today and sending you all my love. Remember, you are strong, and today is just one day. Don't let it fuck with your head. You've got this. Love you!

She was supposed to come last week, and I understand why she couldn't get away, I just selfishly wish she was here.

Instead I'm left alone to drink my fourth—no, fifth—vodka soda of the evening. The haze of inebriation is a reprieve from the room full of demons celebrating Xander's ascension to the throne. He keeps close to his council as they mingle, and the royal guard creepily lingers near the walls like security, all wearing dark gray formal attire.

When I got up this morning, I found the most stunning dark purple dress hanging in the closet and, with no other appropriate clothing option, I put it on. I wish I could hate how perfectly the silk material fits, hugging my curves in all the right places with a stunning open back design. It swishes around me as I walk, just brushing the shiny marble floor. It's almost too long, but paired with the black heels that were left for me, it works.

I finish my drink, setting my glass on a high-top table as the music changes to a slow ballad. My eyes scan the room as people couple up, and I slink back toward the bar. At least, I try to. Xander comes up beside me, flashing a charming smile that makes my stomach dip despite our last encounter. *Traitorous heart.*

"Dance with me," he murmurs in my ear.

THE DEVIL'S TRIALS

I pull away, snatching a flute of champagne from a passing tray. "Leave me alone."

"This is meant to be a celebration."

I scowl, though I can't help but admire his sharp attire. No doubt Blake picked out the all-black suit and tie ensemble. His hair is tousled, and the longer style looks annoyingly good on him. Not to mention the crisp, clean scent of his cologne that threatens to mess with my head. Still, I grumble, "What exactly do you expect me to celebrate, Xander? Please enlighten me." I down half the glass, and he watches me.

He cocks his head to the side. "I thought you would be pleased I returned victorious."

"You mean *emotionless*," I shoot back, my cheeks flaring with warmth, mostly from the collection of drinks I've had.

"I'm doing what I have to," he says in a low voice, wetting his lips before he adds, "That dress looks exquisite on you, just as I knew it would."

I bite my tongue, fighting to hold his gaze as the weight of it bears down on me. "It was this or nothing," I remark dryly without thinking, then immediately regret it when something dark and suggestive flares in his gaze.

"I suddenly wish I hadn't left you the dress."

I roll my eyes, but I can't ignore the heat spreading from my chest to somewhere lower. "I—"

Xander moves before I can put space between us, trapping me in a dance with one hand on my waist, the other grasping mine.

"I hate you," I mutter under my breath, reluctantly lifting my free hand to rest it on his shoulder as we step back and forth to the music.

"Oh, come on." He dips his face closer. "You can lie better than that."

I just shake my head, keeping my jaw clenched shut as I try to ignore the weight of eyes on us.

"I also think you can dance better."

"You want a better dancing partner? Maybe you should go ask Francesca to be yours."

Surprise flickers in his gaze. "You met Francesca," he muses.

"Your betrothed," I offer, unable to keep the bitterness out of my tone and hating myself for it. "Sure did."

His brows lift, and he adjusts his hand on my waist. "She hasn't been that in a long time."

I exhale a sigh. "It really doesn't matter."

"No, but seeing you jealous is rather delightful."

My eyes narrow. "You're really just begging for me to step on your toes with these ridiculous heels you left for me to wear, huh?"

He chuckles. "Do you like them? And the dress?"

I give him a look. "I wouldn't have worn them if I didn't."

The look of amusement lingers on his stupidly handsome face. "I'll take that as a 'thank you.'"

My response is a dry, "Do whatever you want, your highness."

Xander pulls me closer, his lips brushing my ear when he murmurs, "Careful, *mo shíorghrá*. That is a very dangerous invitation."

I shiver, and my eyelids flutter almost shut before I can force them open. I look past him to the others dancing around us as the song comes to an end. As soon as it does, I step away from Xander, muttering a quick, "I need some air," before fleeing the ballroom.

The pressure in my chest doesn't lessen until I'm a good distance away. I find a bathroom and splash cold water on my face, not caring if it does anything to my makeup at this point. I'm uncomfortably hot, and my pulse is pounding like a jackhammer beneath my flushed skin.

I catch my reflection in the mirror over the vanity and let out a shallow breath as I dry my hands. Leaning against the wall, I close my eyes and focus my breathing, using an exercise I learned years ago to calm the anxiety coating my skin like a dark, sticky film.

A few minutes of breathing exercises bring my pulse to a normal pace, and I leave the bathroom, ready to get the hell out of this *celebration*.

I head for the front of the historic building, heading toward the coat check to grab my jacket and purse so I can leave. I might not be able to go home, but I don't—*can't*—stay here any longer.

"Leaving so soon?"

I stop in my tracks, curing the accented sound of Blake's voice. Begrudgingly, I turn around and face him as he approaches. "What do you want, Blake?"

"Xander needs to speak with you."

I shake my head, exhaling a low breath. "I drank too much champagne and I'm tired. I just want to go to bed."

His expression is impossible to decipher when he says, "This is important, Camille. You need to hear what he has to say."

THE DEVIL'S TRIALS

I frown, fighting the urge to cross my arms over my chest and refuse him, but something in his eyes stops me from doing that. Instead, I say, "Fine. Lead the way."

I follow Blake through the building into what appears to be a private library. It's all warm tones with dark wood and soft lighting. The faint scent of paper fills the room, reminding me of a bookstore I could roam around for hours. It would typically put me at ease, but this situation really doesn't leave any space for that.

Xander stands in front of a massive floor-to-ceiling window overlooking the property's large pond as rain falls from the dark sky. His back is to us, and he turns when the library door closes behind us. We cross the room toward him as his eyes shift from Blake to me.

"What's going on?" I demand, my pulse ticking faster. Tonight has already been a lot. I'm really not sure how much more I can handle before it triggers a panic attack. Anxiety simmers just below the surface in my chest, threatening shallow breaths and a sharp sense of doom if I can't rein it in.

"I think you should sit down," Xander offers in a level, gentle tone.

I wrinkle my nose at that. I'm sick of the back and forth, questioning if he gives a damn or feels nothing at all. "I'm fine standing."

A muscle feathers along his jaw, and he exhales a short breath, closing his eyes for a brief moment before meeting my gaze. "Your sister is in hell."

I stare at him.

He stares back at me.

And then—

Everything.

Just.

Stops.

I grit my teeth, shaking my head as tears fill my eyes. "I don't know what kind of tactic this is. I just..." My voice cracks. "Why are you doing this?" My watery gaze slides to Blake. "Is this some twisted joke?"

The regret in Blake's eyes as he shakes his head is the only thing that keeps me from fleeing the room. It cements my feet in place—I couldn't leave if I tried.

"I'm telling you the truth," Xander says in a low voice, pulling my attention back to him.

My heart pounds against my rib cage as bile rises in my throat. "This... this doesn't make any sense," I shout, and when Xander tries to reach for me, I recoil. "*No.*"

Blake slips out of the room without a sound, save for the door softly clicking shut behind him.

"I understand it's confusing. The demon who killed Danielle trapped her in hell while she was in the veil between life and death, and she's been there since. I saw her while I was there for the final trial."

I choke on a sob. "My sister is *dead.* There's been a mistake. I don't know what you think you saw—"

"I saw her tattoo, Camille. The one that matches yours. There was something so familiar about her when I saw her in hell, and I couldn't place why. When I saw her tattoo, it all made sense, and I spoke to her, confirming who she was."

I press my hands to my face as my head spins, then slide them up to grip my scalp, trying to anchor myself with the pain, but I feel the world slipping away. My ears ring and my vision blurs a little. Xander grasps my shoulders, pulling me back. I blink quickly, trying to focus on him.

"You say you saw her...and then you left her there?" Anger weaves through the confusion in my heart, and the warring emotions make me feel as if I'm losing control of myself. The longer I stand here, the less stable I feel, and the alcohol churning in my stomach isn't helping.

"I couldn't bring her back in that state."

That state?

"Is my sister a demon?" I whisper, the mounting pressure in my ribs begging me to scream. To let out everything I've kept trapped inside.

"No," he says hesitantly before adding, "but her soul is trapped in the underworld."

Barbed wire lassoes my heart, piercing it with every beat. "Trapped?" I choke out. "Can she be brought back?"

A conflicted look passes over his face, darkening his features. "It's not that simple."

"Explain it to me, then." I can't mask the desperation in my voice. Danielle is living in hell as we speak. *She has been since she died.*

Xander wets his lips. "She's been in hell for five years, but time moves differently down there. To her, it will have felt much longer. And if she returns topside, she won't be the person you remember. Being in the underworld for so long changes you—and she won't be able to return here with her soul."

Something in me snaps, and I grip the front of his shirt until my fists turn white. "I need to get her back. She shouldn't have—This never should have happened! I need you to take me there." My vision blurs with hot tears, and I clench my teeth at the utter helplessness clinging to me like a sticky film.

His forehead creases with tension, and he shakes his head adamantly. "You can't go to hell, Camille. It's far too dangerous."

"You're not going to talk me out of this. My sister needs me. She's the last person who deserves to be there. If she comes back different, that's better than her not coming back at all."

"Is it?" he presses. "Danielle died. Her human soul has been trapped in hell for half a decade in *human* years. If she returns, there's no telling who—or *what*—she'll be."

I shake my head, and a tear slips free, rolling down my cheek as I plead, "*Don't.*"

"Your sister could come back a demon without her soul. Could you and your parents handle that? Could she?"

Pressure pours into my chest, and I clamp my jaw shut to keep from screaming. I can't make sense of this. My sister—a demon. *Could I handle that?* And what about our parents? How would they, as heads of the demon hunting organization, live with having a demon for a daughter? The thought of them fighting her being brought back under those circumstances is a punch to the gut. I can't say with any certainty how they'd react, but the idea of allowing her to stay in hell after all these years now that I know where she is...

"I can't just leave her there," I say in a low, uneven voice. "Even if I can't bring her back here, there has to be something we can do to free her from hell."

His eyes scan my face, but I can't discern his expression as he says, "I want to tell you there is, but I truly don't know."

"We have to try," I insist firmly, though my voice still shakes. "I have to go after her."

"A human can't go to hell and return without consequences."

My response is immediate. "I don't care. Danielle has already lost enough. Her life, her *soul*—"

"And what of your soul?" he demands, swallowing hard, and I'm taken aback by the sudden emotion in his eyes. My heart beats like the wings of a hummingbird as I stare at him, and he stares back at me. He lowers his voice, as if he's concerned about being overheard. "I can't say what will happen down there, but there's a chance—"

"If sacrificing my soul is what I have to do to get my sister back, then so be it."

"No." He shakes his head again, blinking hard. "I can't let you do this. I won't."

I tug him closer as I'm gripped with such a profound fear my knees shake. "So you're the only one allowed to sacrifice their soul to save someone they love?"

His expression doesn't change. "This is different."

"Why?" I demand.

"Because you weren't dead. I killed Lucia to prevent you from dying." He lowers his voice once more. "Your sister is already dead, Camille."

I swallow hard, shaking my head adamantly. "If you ever want there to be a chance for us, you'll help me." My jaw clenches, and I wait for the demon before me to cackle at my weak attempt to sway him.

Except, he doesn't. Xander freezes, eyes sharp. "Are you saying there is a chance?"

My stomach dips, my brows scrunching together as more tears gather in my eyes. Everything else in my life ceases to exist in this moment. My parents, being a failure of a hunter, the awkwardness with Noah...Nothing matters but my sister, and Xander is the only one who can help me.

He grips me tighter. "*Is there a chance?*"

"Yes," I breathe, my voice cracking. I swallow. "So, *please*. Help me get my sister back."

He holds my gaze for a moment that seems to stretch on for an eternity. Finally, he speaks. It's a single word that holds so much pain it fills my veins with ice. "Okay."

Xander pulls me in without hesitation, burying his fingers in my hair as he holds me against his chest, and clinging to him is the only thing that keeps me from shattering.

Thirty-Three
Xander

"I seriously miss the days you didn't have my number," Harper muses when the call connects.

I sit on the lounge chair in front of the unlit fireplace in my bedroom, lifting my legs to rest them on the marble coffee table. "And yet, you answered my call."

"I also miss the days I had the foresight to block your number."

I chuckle, leaning back in the chair as I switch the call to speakerphone so I don't have to hold it to my ear. "You're in a delightful mood this morning."

"What do you want?" she grumbles.

Any amusement vanishes from my tone when I say, "You need to come here."

"Yeah, that's been the plan, I'm just—"

"Camille needs you here," I amend.

Harper sighs. "I know yesterday was hard for her with the whole ascension summit, but I need to put a few more things in place before I can take off without causing too much attention."

"I need you to listen to me right now. There was new information that Camille discovered last night, and she's not in a good place. I can't offer her the same comfort and support you can."

"What the fuck are you talking about?" she demands, her tone taking on a jagged edge.

"While I was in hell for the final trial, I met Camille's sister." *I also watched you die at the hands of my enemy.* I grit my teeth at the shudder that unspoken memory elicits. The weakness it taunts me with.

There's a brief silence and then, "If this is some—"

"It's not a game, Harper. I'm telling you the truth. Danielle is in hell, trapped there by the demon who stole her life five years ago."

JESSI ELLIOTT

She sucks in a sharp breath. "Fuck. *Fuck.* Camille must be losing her mind. Has she told her parents?"

"No. I think she's still too shocked for that conversation." I stand and walk into my closet to pull out dark jeans and a navy sweater. I'd much rather stay in my sweatpants and crawl back into bed—no one got much sleep around here last night—but that's not something I'm able to do. Not as king.

"I, um...Okay, let me see what I can do."

"I can have Blake book you a flight," I offer.

Harper sighs reluctantly. "Yeah, fine."

"He'll pick you up at the airport when you land."

"I'll take a cab," she insists firmly, and it sounds as if she's wrangling clothes off hangers and throwing things into a suitcase.

"Very well." I'm not going to fight with her on this. Whatever reason she has for avoiding being alone with Blake, I'm not going to push her. "We'll see you soon."

The call ends without another word.

I get dressed and find Blake in the kitchen scooping coffee grounds into a French press.

"Harper's coming. Will you book a flight and send her the details?"

He glances up, interest glimmering in his eyes. "You got it. Coffee?"

"No thanks. I told her you'd pick her up from the airport, which she immediately shot down. Is there something I should know?"

Blake smirks. "Your baby sis is obsessed with me, mate."

I arch a brow and offer a doubtful, "Really?"

"Nah, but a bloke can dream."

I exhale a short laugh. "Right. Have you seen Camille this morning?"

He shakes his head. "I went for a run with Fran and Roman, but Gio said she didn't come down for breakfast. He sent something up for her, though." Turning on the kettle, he adds, "You better keep an eye on him. Gio's gonna steal your girl."

The demon in question walks into the room, laughing deeply. "Not to worry, Xander. As lovely as Camille is, she is far from my type."

"Human?" Blake offers wryly.

"Female," Gio says, shooting him a wink.

I press a fist to my mouth, coughing to cover my laugh, then turn to walk out of the kitchen.

THE DEVIL'S TRIALS

Returning upstairs, I stand outside the bedroom Camille's staying in and listen for movement on the other side of the door. It's shortly after ten, so there's a good chance she's still asleep. The sound of her heartbeat is steady, her breathing even. When I knock softly and open the door a crack, my gaze immediately lands on where she's curled on her side facing the door. Last night's makeup streaks down her cheeks, dried in the form of tears, and her deep brown curls are splayed over the dark green silk pillows.

I hesitate before slipping into the room and softly closing the door behind me. Approaching the bed, my eyes stay locked on her face. She inhales deeply, her eyelids fluttering as she blinks them open, sucking in a soft breath when our gazes connect.

"Morning," I murmur, stopping at the side of the bed and perching on the edge as I angle myself toward her.

Camille shifts away and sits up, hugging the blankets around her. She looks exhausted and fragile, something I'm not used to, and no doubt something she resents.

I glance at the untouched bagel and fruit on the nightstand. "You should eat something."

"I'm not hungry," she says in a low, meek voice, dropping her tired gaze to her lap.

I won't push her right now. Instead, I say, "Harper is coming today. Blake is arranging her travel right now."

Her eyes lift to mine again, and I'm not sure what to do with the tears that fill them. "She is?"

I nod, fighting the urge to reach for her, worried it'll set her off. "Maybe you can talk to Gio and let him know if there's anything you and Harper would like him to cook?"

She presses her lips together, nodding absently. "Yeah."

"Do you think you're up for maybe taking a shower and getting dressed? Harper doesn't want Blake picking her up at the airport, so I thought the two of us could go."

Her brows lift at that, and she mumbles, "They're so weird."

A smile touches my lips. "On that, you and I agree."

Camille exhales a deep breath and says, "I'll go get her. You don't need to come."

I shake my head automatically. "Not going to happen."

"What if I take Gio with me?" she counters. "It doesn't have to be you, and I'm sure you're busy with royal duties or whatever."

My lips twitch. "Either we both go or I'm going alone."

She grapples with it silently, then finally mutters, "Fine. I'll get ready."

I risk placing my hand on her knee. "Take your time. There's no rush."

Her breath hitches, and she stares at my hand for a moment. "So you're emotionally available Xander today?" Her eyes lift to mine. "Or only behind closed doors? Just so I know."

I pull my hand back and stand. "I'm doing my best. We're safe here with my council. I trust them, but other demons...They can't know what you mean to me."

She pushes the blankets away and slides off the bed, coming to stand in front of me. The air gets caught in my throat when I realize she's wearing one of my T-shirts. The plain black material falls just above her knees and calls to the desire I feel for her like a siren. My hands curl into fists at my sides as I fight the urge to grab Camille and show her just what her being in my clothes does to me.

"I told you last night there was a chance for us," she murmurs.

I wait for her expression to sharpen, for her to tell me she was lying. But she doesn't.

Camille lifts onto her tiptoes and presses a soft kiss to my cheek. "I understand no part of this will be easy. We'll face adversity and danger at every turn, but nothing worth having comes easy."

I stare at her silently, completely taken by her strength and courage.

I love this woman so fucking much.

I know in my core I don't deserve Camille's love, but *I need it.*

"I don't care if you have to be the cold, emotionless demon king in public," she continues, "so long as you are the man I love when we're alone." Her lips part in a silent gasp as she realizes what she's just admitted aloud.

I close the distance between us, clasping her cheeks in my palms. "You love me?"

Her pulse races, her eyes flicking between mine as they shine with unshed tears. She licks her lips, exhaling a short breath before she says, "I do."

Thirty-Four
Camille

Xander's lips crash down on mine without warning in a kiss that's equal parts possessive and sincere. It's filled with an intense urgency that kicks my heart rate up and catches me completely off guard. One of his hands drops to grip my hip before he snakes his arm around me, tugging me against his chest as his other hand glides into my hair.

I close my eyes and loop my arms around his neck, tilting my head back to deepen the kiss as our breaths mingle, and I push my tongue into his mouth, claiming him. There will be no doubt that he is mine—I will erase any trace of it. I'm done with the back and forth, questioning my gut and how I feel about him.

I grip the back of his neck, tangling my fingers in his hair and throwing every wild emotion whipping through me into the kiss.

Xander does the same with equal fervor, and our hearts beat like drums against our chests where they're pressed together as the heat of his body radiates to warm my skin.

I decide at this very moment that nothing in this world—or the underworld—will keep us apart.

I will destroy anything or anyone that tries.

We kiss until my head spins and my lungs burn, and I lose myself in the waves of emotion flooding through me.

Xander breaks the kiss, breathing heavily. He rests his forehead against mine and says, "If we don't stop…" He trails off, but the intention of his words is clear.

"I know," I tell him, keeping my eyes shut as I catch my breath. "I need to shower and get dressed."

"Hear me out," he offers in an amused tone.

"Xander," I warn, though I can't fight the subtle upward curve of my lips as I blink my eyes open.

He chuckles, teasing the hair at my temple, then pulls away with a brief kiss to my forehead. "I'll be downstairs when you're ready." His phone chimes, and he takes it out as he steps back. "Change of plans. Harper is driving as it's faster than waiting at the airport for the next flight, so she'll be here in about three hours."

An echo of excitement blooms in my chest, but it's overshadowed by the weight of concern for Danielle.

Xander pockets his phone and brushes his knuckles against my cheek before leaving the room, the door clicking shut behind him.

With Harper arriving, I'll have another voice of support to go after my sister and bring her back from hell. It's no secret that Xander's not sold on the idea of me going, and there's still a lot to figure out—including telling my parents—but we're going to make it work.

I refuse to accept anything different.

I rush outside the second Harper pulls into the driveway shortly before dinner time. She's barely out of the car before I throw my arms around her neck, and she wraps hers around my waist, hugging me just as fiercely.

We're both sniffling, in tears when we pull back, and I wipe hers away as she does the same to mine.

"I'm so glad you're here." Part of me wants to ask how she managed to get away so abruptly, but selfishly, I don't care one bit. The only thing that matters to me right now is that she's here.

I help get her bags inside and carry them up to the room I've been staying in before we meet Xander and Blake in the main living room. A fire crackles in the massive fireplace, and the guys sit on opposite sides of the glass coffee table, Blake in one of the arm chairs and Xander on one side of the couch.

They stand as we come into the room, and Harper blows out a heavy sigh. "I need a drink," she says before either can speak.

"Nice to see you too, love," Blake remarks in an amused tone.

"Bite me," she shoots at him.

He smirks. "Nah, you'd enjoy it too much."

Her eyes narrow, and I catch her wrist when she takes a step toward him. "I think we're going to have dinner soon," I chime in, looking at Xander to step in before his half-sister and demon bestie get into a brawl in the living room.

THE DEVIL'S TRIALS

"Yes," he confirms. "Gio is almost done in the kitchen."

Once we each have a drink in our hands, we proceed to have the most awkwardly silent dinner in history.

Harper and I sit on one side of the table, while Xander and Blake sit across from us. The conversation is limited to surface-level small talk about Harper's drive and how nice the house is. Harper makes a comment about putting a Christmas tree up in the living room, and it's only then I realize we're only a few days from the holiday.

"We can," Xander offers. "I wasn't sure where we'd be for Christmas this year so I didn't buy anything, but feel free. My home is yours."

"Yeah, you don't want to tell her that," I warn, "she'll redecorate the entire place immediately."

Xander chuckles. "I'm not concerned about that."

"Yeah, it could use a splash of personality," Blake says.

"So long as it's not yours," Harper chimes in, using a sickly sweet, completely fake tone.

I glance between the two to find them locked in a death glare, though there's a spark of amusement in Blake's eyes.

When my eyes shift to Xander, I find him already looking at me. "Have you spoken to your parents yet?" he asks.

I push a little potato around my plate, shaking my head. "I think it's something I need to tell them in person."

"Your dad is scheduled to be at headquarters next week," Harper says, turning her attention to me. "So he'll probably be in Seattle for Christmas. If you ask him to come, he definitely will."

A brief frown touches my lips as I consider that Dad being in Seattle for the holidays means Noah will be spending them alone. I push the thought away. I unfortunately have more immediate things to worry about. "Right. Yeah, we can head there tomorrow."

"Uh, we can't," Blake chimes in, turning his gaze to Xander. "You have a council meeting."

"What makes you think you're invited to Christmas?" Harper asks, crossing her arms.

"Harper," I murmur, shaking my head to say, *enough*.

Of course having Xander and Blake around for the holidays would be an impossible sell on my parents, but I may need Xander there to help me explain what's going on.

"Fine," she says with a sigh, reaching over to squeeze my knee. "We'll figure it out, babe."

After we finish eating, Harper and I return to the living room while the guys clean up from dinner. We drop onto the couch, and Harper grabs the heavy throw blanket off the back and drapes it over us.

"Talk to me," she says.

"I'm not sure what Xander already told you."

"Danielle is trapped in hell. That's basically the extent of what I know."

I nod. "Right, well, I'm going to get her back."

Harper smiles. "Of course we are. We'll come up with a plan and send Xander's council there to—"

"No," I cut in, my brows knitting. "I mean, *I'm* going to hell to bring her back here."

She blinks at me, then reaches for my hands, holding them firmly in hers. "You are with the most powerful demon alive. Let him do this."

I press my lips together, unable to ignore the subtle fluttering in my stomach. "I can't. She's my sister. I...I have to do this."

Harper looks conflicted, like she understands but wants to argue with me. "You know I'm on board to help in any way that I can."

The flare of reassurance brings tears to my eyes. I'm absolutely terrified about the thought of going to hell and everything that'll come with that, which only invites more doubt to my ability to trust my instincts, but Harper's immediate willingness to get on board makes me feel like maybe I can trust my gut in this situation. "Thank you."

She squeezes my hands. "Of course. But if you're going, so am I."

My stomach sinks, my thoughts racing back to the last mission we were on together, the one where we nearly became demon food and Xander became the king of hell. After that, I vowed to never put Harper in that kind of danger again. She gets into it enough herself just by being a hunter. "No. No way. Absolutely not." I can't stand the thought of her being put in that kind of danger, and if I'm worried about her, I won't be able to focus solely on saving my sister. "You remember what happened last time, right? The monumental disaster at Lucia's compound?"

She shrugs. "So it's okay for you to risk it but not me? Besides, I can't see Xander fucking up that royally this time around."

I shake my head adamantly. "I can't take the chance of losing you too, Harper. Please." I grip her hands. "I'll need you to stay with my parents and keep them as calm as possible. That'll likely be just as difficult as what I'll be doing," I try to joke, but it doesn't land as she just stares at me.

"I don't want you going to hell period but I *especially* don't want you going alone with Xander."

I sigh despite understanding her concern and point out, "He's my best shot at bringing Danielle back."

"Are you sure there isn't another way?"

Frowning, I shake my head. "I'm not sure, but there isn't time to mess around trying to find one. She's already been trapped there for over five years, and the thought of her having to spend any more time there..." I wrap my arms around myself as my heart rate kicks up, my eyes burning as I implore my best friend, "*Please*. Do this for me."

Harper rakes her fingers through her hair, exhaling a heavy breath. She isn't trying to hide how conflicted she feels in the position I've put her in. "Fine," she finally says, her tone filled with reluctance. "Speaking of your parents. How are you going to tell them about everything?"

Her question triggers the sense of doom lingering just below the surface. I can't stop the tingling sensation at the back of my throat, as if I'm going to be sick, or the way my hands get clammy and start to shake.

"Hey," she murmurs, "deep breaths, Cami."

All I can see is the looks of shock and terror on my parents' faces as I tell them that their eldest daughter, who they believed dead for half a decade, was trapped in the underworld by the monster who killed her.

My heart pounds harder, as if it's trying to escape my chest, reverberating in my throat. I try and fail to take a deep breath, the air getting lodged in my lungs as heat crawls up my neck, making my skin flushed.

Harper squeezes my hands, but they feel numb, and she says in a gentle voice, "I'm here. You're safe. Just keep trying to breathe normally." She mimics taking slow, deep breaths, and I try to focus despite the way my vision narrows, growing dark and hazy around the edges.

The heat from the fire feels too hot as I fight the feeling that the worst possible thing is about to happen, and the walls seem to be getting closer. I'm stuck here. I can't move. Can't breathe. I'm trapped in my own body as blood rushes through my ears, drowning out Harper's attempt to pull me back from the edge of anxiety.

Control slips through my fingers like water, and I squeeze my eyes shut, gritting my teeth at the twisted knots in my stomach as bile burns my throat. Seconds feel like hours as fear claws at me, giving me nowhere to escape it.

"Come on," Harper says firmly, standing and pulling me off the couch with her. "Let's go outside for a minute. The fresh air will help."

I let her guide me out of the living room and to the front door, where she opens it, and a blast of cold air hits me in the face. Walking outside, I'm finally able to pull a proper breath into my lungs.

After several slow, deep breaths, I finally feel my pulse start to calm.

"Better?" Harper checks.

I manage a nod, glancing around the quiet patio along the side of the house that sits outside the living room windows. It's secluded by tall hedges, making me feel more secure as Harper keeps talking to me. Any patio furniture would've been stored away weeks ago, leaving the space open to pace around.

"Good. Keep breathing. We'll stand here as long as you need." She has her arms wrapped tightly around herself as our breaths fog the air. The cold air helped refocus my thoughts and disarm the anxiety charging through me, but now Harper and I are both shivering.

"I'm okay," I tell her. "We can go back inside."

She doesn't argue, and once we're on the other side of the front door with it closed, she rubs her hands up and down her arms over her sweater.

"Sorry," I say, cringing. "Try to picture yourself on a beach somewhere warm."

She freezes, cursing under her breath.

"What's the matter?"

"I totally forgot. I was going to surprise you on Christmas. I booked an all-inclusive trip for us to Puerto Vallarta next month."

My eyes pop wide, my stomach clenching with short lived excitement. "You did?"

"Yeah. I mean, we've talked about it for years, and I thought with everything that happened this year, a trip for just the two of us to kick off next year would be amazing. Of course, I couldn't foresee you taking a trip of your own. When we talked about going somewhere *hot as hell*, I didn't think you'd take it so literally."

I press my lips together. It's not funny, but I don't know how else to respond. "I'm sorry, Harper. Can we reschedule?"

She frowns, shaking her head. "Non-refundable trip."

THE DEVIL'S TRIALS

The pit in my gut doubles in size, snuffing out every ounce of excitement from a minute ago. "You should find someone else to go with."

"Nah, that doesn't sound fun."

"Would you go by yourself? It could be a good distraction while I'm...away."

"I thought you wanted me to keep an eye on your parents?"

"I do, but I'd rather you do something for yourself. I can get Noah to check in on my dad when he goes back to Seattle, and I'm sure Mom has people within the organization that'll make sure she's okay."

Her brows nudge closer. "Are you absolutely sure?"

I grab her shoulders, squeezing gently. "Yes. Go on the trip. Enjoy yourself. Maybe meet a cute guy and have a fling for the week."

Harper laughs. "Right." Pulling me into a hug, she says, "I'm going to hold you to a makeup trip, though."

"Of course," I say, hugging her back. "I love you."

"Love you more, babe." She pulls back and plants a loud kiss on my cheek. "Now if I remember correctly, Xander told me this place has a hot tub? I think we need to get some wine and have some much needed girl time before everything quite literally goes to hell."

Thirty-Five
Xander

The following day, my council gathers at the house. We meet in the dining room, and just as I'm about to close the oak double doors, Harper pushes inside.

"I hope you didn't start the meeting without me."

I blink at her. She hasn't officially accepted the council position, so her presence is a bit surprising, especially considering we discussed keeping her away from any meetings unless absolutely necessary. But here she is, dressed in hunter attire, all the way down to the obsidian dagger strapped to her thigh—which likely won't go over well with our present company.

"You couldn't have left the dagger upstairs?" I say under my breath. "While we're at it, *what are you doing*?"

"You wanted a hunter, did you not?" she throws back at me!

I arch a brow. "I thought we talked about this."

"Have you even graduated yet?" Blake taunts behind me before Harper can respond. "Maybe your skills aren't up to par."

Her eyes narrow, no longer focused on me but on the blue-haired demon at the table across the room. "Why not come here and find out?"

With a sigh, I interject, "All right, that's enough." I snare Harper's gaze. "You're sure you want to be here?"

She nods. "I decided the others should know who I am, because if shit goes sideways, I want more than just you to back me up. And I wasn't about to bring it up earlier and give you the opportunity to keep me out of the meeting."

A laugh slips out of me, and I shake my head. "Might I remind you these *demons* are loyal to *me*?"

Harper moves past me into the room, patting my chest. "We'll see about that, *brother*." The challenge in her voice is unmistakable. She thinks she can win over my council. Make them like her more than me, as if this is some kind of game.

We're more alike than she cares to admit.

I stare after her, somehow caught up in the 'brother' comment despite it sounding nothing like a term of endearment. Shaking it off, I follow Harper across the room. "Let's get started."

I take my seat at the head of the table, while Harper drops into the chair next to Greer and across from Francesca, who sits beside Blake. Rain hits the windows on the other side of the room. Despite it being midday, the sky is dark and gray, only adding to the lethargy clinging to me.

"Would you like to introduce yourself?" I ask Harper, leaving it up to her how much she wants shared with the others. I trust them with our arrangement, but I understand she likely doesn't at this point.

Harper's false bravado slips a little, and there's a faint tinge of pink in her cheeks when she says, "Uh, okay." Glancing around the table, she gives an awkward wave. "I'm Harper. If you're wondering why I'm here, don't worry, I keep asking myself the same thing. Anyway, Xander and I recently discovered that we're half-siblings, and he decided his council of demons wasn't dramatic enough—hard to believe when Blake is here, I know—so he wanted to add a hunter to the mix."

Blake rolls his eyes, while the others snicker, and I just shake my head.

"That's not exactly how I'd explain it," I point out.

Harper shrugs. "Close enough."

Francesca grins at her. "I like you already."

Jude and Roman exchange a glance before turning their gazes to me. "Problem?" I ask.

Jude wets her lips. "Not necessarily. However, you just took the throne. Is this, bringing a human—a skilled hunter, no less—onto your council, the first move you really want to make as king?"

"That's a backhanded compliment if I ever heard one," Harper mutters, crossing her arms over her chest as her heart beats faster.

Jude grants her a thin smile. "I mean no offense. I simply want to make sure our king is setting himself up for success."

"I think that ship sailed when he brought Blake on, but whatever."

I press my lips together to hide my amusement at Harper's quip. She and Blake seem to have adopted a rivalry I don't quite understand, but I can't deny its entertainment value.

Blake smirks, his eyes locked on her. "You know being mean to me gets me hot, and that's super unprofessional in this setting."

She rolls her eyes. "Bite me."

Hunger darkens his gaze. "That's twice now. Careful, little hunter. Next time you ask, I fucking will." He snaps his teeth at her.

I glance down at the table as they continue bickering, figuring Harper is comfortable enough to put Blake in his place. She doesn't need me stepping in—in fact, she'd probably put *me* in *my* place if I tried.

Instead, I focus my hearing on the level above us where I can hear Camille humming to herself and the sound of pencil strokes on paper. I wasn't sure she'd use the sketchbook I left for her, but I'm glad she is. Anything to keep her distracted from the circumstances triggering her anxiety, and there are many. I can't fix them for her immediately, as much as I wish I could, but at least I can help her manage her thoughts when they start to spiral.

"Xander," Blake's voice cuts into my focus, and I look at him, lifting my brows.

"You just completely zoned out," Greer says.

"Apologies," I say, waiting for whomever to repeat whatever I missed.

"Where's your head at?" Roman asks.

"Probably the human upstairs," Francesca says before I can respond. "Is she clouding your ability to focus on the matter at hand?"

Unless Blake and Harper quit their verbal ping pong and I missed when the real conversation started, I'm not sure my focus was truly required here.

"Not at all," I say in a level tone despite the irritation prickling along my skin at being questioned. I push my chair back and stand. "While dealing with Marrick is important, there's something else I need to attend to in the meantime." My gaze sweeps over my council members. "I trust you. I need you to prove yourselves to me now. Prove I made the right decision bringing you onto my council and giving you my trust."

"Of course," Greer says in a solemn voice, then asks, "What do you need from us?"

"By the time we return topside, I want to know exactly how Marrick is turning humans into demons. Also, where and when it has potentially been done before. Anything that will help us stop Marrick from continuing to do it now."

THE DEVIL'S TRIALS

Roman nods, though he's frowning. "What will you be doing?"

"I'm taking a trip home. Camille's sister was taken to hell by the demon who took her life years ago, and she's been trapped there since. We're going to bring her back."

Those words burn my tongue, coating my throat with acidic bile at the thought of Camille being in the wretched place I grew up. I know what it did to me, and considering just for a moment what it could do to her makes me desperate for another way to bring Danielle back. But even now, I don't have the strength to refuse Camille. The power she holds over me is irrefutable. I can't let her down—not ever again. So the thing she wants from me now puts her in the most danger she's experienced since I waltzed into her life, and the frigid, thorny vines of fear wrapping themselves around me because of it feel like a punishment I most certainly deserve for loving her as I am.

Francesca scowls, her tone unimpressed when she says, "You're leaving us to help your human plaything?"

A vicious growl rumbles in my chest and tears from my throat. "Watch yourself. Camille is my mate, soul or not. She is mine and I am hers. I will do *anything* for her, and if anyone in this room doesn't approve, you are not welcome here."

No one speaks up as I look around the table, and when my eyes land on Blake, I find him grinning. "Go help your girl, mate. The rest of us will hold down the fort here, put our detective caps on, and find something that'll help us take that bastard down when you're back."

I nod. "I was hoping you'd actually head home before we travel there. Camille won't want her sister spending another holiday alone."

Camille already took care of *my* sister's plans for the time we'll be gone, convincing Harper to go to the all-inclusive resort she'd initially booked for the two of them.

Blake drums his fingers on the table, flicking a glance toward Harper for a brief, almost non-existent moment before his gaze returns to me. "Of course."

I give him a look that expresses my gratitude without words before I walk out of the dining room, my heart beating faster in my chest as I head for the stairs. I never thought the very thing my mother loathed about me would help me rule, but it was my human heart that led me to choose my council. To fight for a relationship with my sister. To fall in love with

Camille. It seems I need to listen to it more and recognize that caring isn't a weakness as Lucia led me to believe for years.

I care more about the demons than the power ruling over them grants me, which is something the queens and kings before me would never be able to grasp.

Perhaps that is my real power.

While that might work for me topside, embracing my humanity—or what's left of it—is a dangerous gamble and something I absolutely cannot do in hell, especially not as the demon king.

Which is going to make this trip the hardest thing I've ever done.

Thirty-Six
Camille

I wasn't expecting to have dinner with a bunch of demons and my best friend, but here we are.

Gio lures us into the dining room with his incredible cooking. The aroma of grilled steak, steamed vegetables, and garlic mashed potatoes fills the room, and my stomach grumbles as Harper and I sit next to each other at the table.

The others follow, taking their seats. While Xander sits next to me in the chair at the head of the table, Blake drops into the open one on Harper's other side, much to her dismay based on the way she immediately fills her wineglass.

Francesca, Jude, Roman, and Gio sit across from us, while Greer takes the open chair on Blake's other side, leaving the opposite head across from Xander empty. My stomach dips with a pang of sadness at the evident absence of Xander's council member. I never met Declan, but I can tell how special he was to Greer by the haunted look she still carries in her eyes.

I haven't really gotten to know the demons Xander trusts, though none of them are outwardly put off by a couple of humans dining with them, so I'm doing my best to keep an open mind.

Francesca, Blake, and Gio are the only ones close to my and Harper's age, while Jude, Declan, and Greer appear in their forties—though being demons who age significantly slower, they could very well be much older.

"Dig in, everyone," Gio announces, uncovering a steaming dish with mixed vegetables.

"Thank you for preparing yet another delicious meal," Greer says to him with a fond smile.

"My pleasure." He glances my way. "There's a dark chocolate cheesecake with fresh strawberry coulis waiting in the fridge for dessert."

I smile. "You know your audience."

"*Oooh*, you might have to fight Fran for it," Blake says amusedly.

Harper snorts, leaning into Blake's space to reach the platter of steak in the middle of the table, and stabs a piece *with her dagger*.

His eyes flit between her and her weapon, blazing with intrigue as she pulls her arm back, dropping the steak onto her plate.

Francesca whistles under her breath, smirking softly at Harper. She looks...*impressed?*

"Please don't encourage her," Xander grumbles, shaking his head.

I nudge Harper under the table with my foot, arching a brow when she looks over at me. She offers me a brief smile before setting the dagger next to her plate.

"Think we can get through a meal without any violence?" Xander asks, scooping some mashed potatoes onto his plate before offering the dish to me.

"With these two sitting next to each other?" I jerk my thumb toward our best friends before taking the potatoes. "Not likely."

"Oh, come on," Francesca chimes in, sprinkling salt over her plate before wiping her hand on the napkin in her lap. "Give poor Blake a break. He's not used to being around a human that can kick his ass."

"You are so right about that one, Fran." Harper snorts at the same moment Blake scowls, though I can't help but notice his lack of argument. Or Francesca not snapping at Harper for using the nickname I've only heard Blake use.

"I think this could be the start of a beautiful friendship," Francesca says, raising her glass and clinking it against Harper's.

"More like a dangerous alliance," Blake mutters, looking at Xander. "Are you just going to let this happen?"

Xander shrugs, taking a drink of his wine. "Yeah, I think so."

I shove a spoonful of potatoes into my mouth to keep from saying anything. I don't know how thrilled I am about a potential *anything* between Harper and the she-devil who, at one time, wanted the man I love, but I recognize that while Xander is *mine*, I have no claim to my best friend. And she's smart enough to decide who she should and shouldn't allow space in her life.

"Maybe we should talk strategy so we can make the most of the time you're away?" Jude suggests, her gaze set on Xander.

THE DEVIL'S TRIALS

He nods, any trace of amusement fading from his expression. "I agree."

"Marrick is using humans, so I think we should start with them."

Heads turn toward Greer, but she doesn't notice, her eyes on her untouched plate. When the dining room falls silent, she glances up and sets her fork aside.

"Start with them?" Harper echoes, tension creasing her forehead.

Greer nods. "Marrick, as always, will cloak himself from view like the coward he is. Until he has his army, which he'll believe is enough to protect him from his enemies."

"In a perfect world, we'd stop him before the army is formed."

"Who's to say it hasn't been already?" Blake says.

"A rare good point," Francesca quips, earning a few snickers around the table, while Blake flips her off.

Roman shakes his head, wiping his mouth. "We'd hear whispers if Marrick had his army."

"The hunters would know," Harper adds. "There would be extensive reports and meetings across the North American facilities."

"Are you sure about that?" Jude chimes in.

"*Yes.* The humans would fight back," Harper insists, gripping her fork tightly. "They won't just give up their souls for nothing."

Jude swallows her mouthful. "Some will. After all, humans are simple creatures. If you allow them to feel in control, and you can manipulate them quite easily."

I open my mouth to take offense, but Harper's scowl beats me to it.

"Fuck that," she bites out.

"What I mean," Jude continues, "is that Marrick is most likely targeting vulnerable humans. Those desperate enough to feel some sense of control over their lives."

"You make it sound like there could be humans who'd willingly join him," I say in a low voice, unease swirling in my stomach.

"It's possible," Blake says.

"So, how do we stop it?" Harper cuts back into the conversation.

Greer purses her lips for a moment. "I highly doubt Marrick is going to get this right immediately. He'll be experimenting on humans. We should investigate disappearances in key locations—places with the most ley lines and high demon traffic between worlds. Cities and towns filled with chaos and suffering will be breeding grounds for this."

Blake looks at Xander. "I will ask Will and Stephen to tap into their network in New York and see what they can find out."

Xander nods. "Good. But we'll need more. I want you to send out everyone you know. Have them scour these key locations and note anything that could help us."

Everyone besides me, Harper, and Gio nod to their king. Gio has remained quiet for the majority of the meal, which makes sense with him not being an official member of Xander's council. That said, neither am I.

"We'll meet again once Camille and I return and make a plan for next steps with the information you gather." Xander finishes his wine, setting down the glass. "Marrick's plan to turn humans into demons jeopardizes the balance between our worlds, putting everyone in danger. Stopping him won't be easy, but failure isn't an option—not when the fate of both humans and demons hangs in the balance."

Xander and I rent a car and drive to Seattle the next afternoon. We check him into a boutique hotel before driving to my mom's house across the city.

"I should go in and see them first," I say when we're about ten minutes away. According to the itinerary my dad sent to our family group chat, he should already be there. "They won't be able to listen to what I'm saying with their number one enemy sitting in the same room."

Xander's lips twitch. "You think I'd make it past the front door?"

"Good point." I sigh, frowning at the thought of ruining their Christmas with the news I'm harboring. "Besides, they deserve to have a normal, enjoyable holiday before I flip their worlds upside down."

This time of year has always been my favorite, but it's difficult to enjoy the holiday season when I know my sister is suffering. And now I have to figure out how to explain that to my parents, along with how Xander is going to help me save her.

"When was the last time you had Christmas with both your parents?"

I consider it, doing some quick mental math. "Hmm, it's been over fifteen years. My dad moved to New York after he and my mom separated, and since then, we'd celebrate Christmas twice. Once in Seattle with Mom and once when we visited Dad in New York. They'd alternate years on who had the actual day, but as Dani and I got older, the schedule became more dependent on what she and I had going on."

THE DEVIL'S TRIALS

We turn onto Mom's street, where the houses on both sides are decorated with Christmas lights and giant inflatable lawn ornaments. Compared to that, the simple wreath on her front door looks a bit sad, but at least she made the effort to put something up.

Xander pulls up to the curb, shifting the car into park. "I know things are overwhelming and difficult right now, but try to enjoy your time with them before you have the conversation about Danielle. And while I can't bring her to you now, I did send Blake to be with her for Christmas, so she isn't alone and she knows we're going to bring her home."

Tightness seizes my chest as I stare at him, tears blurring my vision. "You did?"

He nods, reaching over to brush the hair away from my face, tucking it behind my ear and letting his fingers linger against my cheek.

I lean into his touch, pressing my lips against his palm. "Thank you," I murmur. Unbuckling my belt, I grab my duffel bag from the back seat, setting it in my lap as I take a deep breath, blinking back the remnants of emotion from my eyes.

"If you need anything, you call me. I'll be here."

I swallow past the lump in my throat. "Okay."

We both lean in at the same time, our lips touching in a kiss so tender I have to fight back a fresh batch of tears. And then I get out of the car, lift my bag onto my shoulder, and walk to the house without looking back. By the time I reach the door, I know Xander is gone without turning around. He wouldn't take the chance of being seen by my parents.

It feels weird knocking on the door of the house I grew up in, but I lost my key years ago and never felt the need to get a new one.

Mom opens the door with an apron tied around her waist and her hair in a messy bun, and I'm hit with the warmth from inside along with... ginger cookies?

"Hey, Mom," I say with a smile.

"Come in, come in," she says in greeting. "It's getting cold out there."

I step inside and close the door, setting my bag on the foyer bench before Mom pulls me into a hug. When we step apart, she calls out, "Scott, our daughter is here." She squeezes my shoulders. "He's getting a fire started in the living room."

"It smells amazing in here, Mom," I tell her as we walk down the hall toward the kitchen.

"Why, thank you. I've recently taken up baking," she says with a short laugh. "It's quite fun."

My brows lift. "Really?"

"You don't have to sound so surprised that your mother has a hobby."

"No, I just...No offense, but I didn't think you knew the word."

"I guess you don't want to taste any then," she teases, walking to the stove and stirring whatever she has cooking. Hawkeye is curled up on a fuzzy dog bed near his food dish, and I bend down to pet his head.

"I didn't say that," I protest with a faint grin as Dad walks into the kitchen in jeans and a knit Christmas sweater he's had since I was a baby. The fuzzy snowman slippers he's rocking, however, are definitely new, and I adore them.

"Hey, kiddo." He comes to where I'm leaning against the island.

"Hi, Dad," I say, straightening and wrapping my arms around him in a tight hug.

We hang out in the kitchen while Mom pulls a sheet of ginger molasses cookies out of the oven and replaces it with a sheet of shortbread.

"I thought we could order pizza, have some of your dad's special eggnog, and decorate the tree tonight. I know it's already Christmas Eve, but I thought it might be fun to decorate together."

"Yeah," I say, my throat suddenly thick with emotion. "That sounds really great." I didn't expect to get into the Christmas spirit this year, but I'm going to do everything in my power to make sure my parents have the best time. After struggling through my relationship with them for so long, I don't want to take these moments for granted.

An hour later, we're sitting in the living room with the fireplace warming our faces as we eat pizza and pick out a movie to watch while decorating the tree. Mom put it up by the front window, making it the focal point of the room. It's one of those pre-lit artificial ones, so all we have to do is hang the ornaments and maybe add some tinsel.

Dad sneaks Hawkeye a piece of pizza crust when Mom isn't looking, making himself a new best friend before asking, "How has your visit with Harper been?" He takes a sip of his eggnog, which is mostly whiskey, waiting for my response.

I swallow a bite of pizza that suddenly tastes like cardboard. I hate lying in any scenario, but our complicated relationship aside, lying to my parents is the worst. "Oh, um, it's been okay."

THE DEVIL'S TRIALS

Mom frowns, concern flickering across her features. "What exactly does that mean, Camille?"

My gaze drops to my lap, and I set my plate on the coffee table. "Um." I sigh, shaking my head before looking at my parents again. "I'll explain everything after the holidays, okay? Please? I really just want to enjoy this time with you guys."

Mom and Dad exchange a worried look before the latter sighs. "Okay, kiddo. We want to have a nice holiday, too, but we're concerned about you, that's all. You've completely fallen off your training program, and if you continue the way you're going, you won't graduate."

I keep it to myself that failing out of Ballard Academy is the least of my current problems.

"I promise you don't need to worry about me," I assure them. "Please trust me."

"We do," my mom says after several beats of silence, taking me by surprise. She takes a deep breath, a clear indication of the topic change, which I'm absolutely fine with. "Okay, are we watching *It's A Wonderful Life* or *A Christmas Carol*?"

I wake up in my childhood bedroom on Christmas morning to find little white flurries falling from the sky. It may not be a white Christmas, but at least it's snowing.

Soft music comes from downstairs, and I slide out of bed, grabbing the throw blanket off the end, and wrap it around myself as I head toward the source of the carols.

I find my mom and dad in the living room, chatting softly as they drink their coffee. They look up when I walk into the room, smiling and getting up. Dad takes Mom's coffee, setting both of their mugs on the small table beside the couch.

"Morning, kiddo," he says. "Merry Christmas."

"Merry Christmas." I hug him and then Mom.

"You too, honey," she says, releasing me. "Did you sleep okay?"

By some miracle, I passed out shortly after my head hit the pillow and slept through the night, which so rarely happens it didn't seem real. Maybe that was my gift from the universe. "Yeah, I did." I glance at the time on my phone, blinking in surprise to find that it's shortly after noon. "Crap, I'm sorry. I didn't realize I slept that long."

Dad chuckles. "No apology necessary. It's Christmas, and we have nothing planned outside of the house. We can take our time to do whatever we want today."

Mom smiles, looking at me. "Do you want to open your presents?"

I mirror her smile. "Absolutely." I snuck downstairs before I fell asleep last night and put their gifts under the tree, knowing they'd be up before me this morning.

The three of us sit around the living room while Dad hands out the gifts. I watch while he and Mom open my presents to them, grateful for the light expressions on their faces. Mom loves the matching black joggers and sweat set and Dad is thrilled about the cookbook and new knife set. Luckily, I was able to have things delivered to Xander's place before we left Vancouver, and I recruited Gio to pick out the knives and Harper to help wrap everything.

I open the gifts that Dad sets in front of me, excited to find a new e-reader, an emerald silk PJ set with thick black knee-high socks, and a shoebox full of my favorite sweet and salty snacks.

"Thank you both so much. I love all of this."

Mom and Dad exchange a triumphant grin, and I can't help but laugh, my chest swelling with admiration for the two of them. Not many people can say their divorced parents get along better now than they did when they were married, but Scott and Rachel Morgan are clearly better at being close friends and work partners than they were at being spouses.

"Who wants brunch?" Mom asks. "I'm making Eggs Benedict."

We sit around the dining room table, and I lose track of the conversation Mom and Dad are having about a new training facility opening in Ontario, Canada next year. I pick at my food, forcing down small bites despite my nausea making each swallow a gamble with being able to keep it down.

After breakfast, I help Mom clean up and start prepping the side dishes for Christmas dinner. She put the turkey in the oven before I even got out of bed, but I'll be damned if anyone but me makes the cranberry sauce. Growing up, that was always my job, and even with my nerves making my stomach queasy, I'm not prepared to give it up now.

We spend the afternoon cooking and listening to Christmas music, and it almost feels…normal. Almost. Except, the entire time, all I can think about is Danielle. At least she's not completely alone, and she knows

THE DEVIL'S TRIALS

we're coming for her, but this is another year she is away from her family for Christmas.

It will be the last one, I tell myself before texting Xander a quick update to let him know I'm going to tell my parents about everything today.

I'm shaking the finishing dash of cinnamon over the apple pie filling after pouring it into the dough-covered baking dish when I can't keep it in anymore.

My parents deserve to know what's going on and what I'm about to do to save my sister—their daughter—from the pits of hell.

"I, um...I need to talk to you both." I wanted to wait until tomorrow, but I can feel how close the dam is to breaking and I know once it does, I'm not going to be able to explain everything coherently.

"What is it?" Dad asks, already looking concerned.

"Is this about your training?" Mom asks.

"Not really, but I guess it's somewhat related."

"Okay, go ahead." Mom leans against the counter, folding her arms over her chest.

"I think we should sit down," I say, keeping my hands in the pockets of my hoodie so they can't see how badly they're shaking.

After exchanging a look with my dad, she nods, and we relocate to the living room. I send another text to Xander, asking him to come now, and his response is immediate. He's on his way, and this could either go badly or fatally. There is no good outcome to the situation, but it's something that needs to be done.

Mom and Dad sit on the couch while I perch on the edge of the coffee table in front of them.

"I guess I should start by explaining that I haven't been visiting with Harper for the last month. I've been in Vancouver—with Xander."

I watch as both of my parents' backs go ramrod straight.

"You what?" Mom demands in a sharp tone.

"Please hear me out," I rush to say, my chin quivering.

Dad takes Mom's hand, holding it firmly as he keeps his eyes on me. "Why would you...I don't even know what to say right now, Camille."

I blink quickly, fighting the burning in my eyes at the disappointment in his tone. "I know. It wasn't my plan. Things spiraled out of control faster than I could keep up, and all I know is that my life was in danger, threatened by a powerful demon who wants to take the throne from Xander."

"That son of a bitch is the one who put your life in danger," Mom snaps. "How could you possibly think he wants to protect you? All he's ever wanted is to use you to get close enough to the organization to infiltrate and destroy it."

My jaw clenches so tightly, my temples throb and my pulse ticks faster. "That's not true. And I know it's hard to hear and possibly even more difficult to believe, but I trust him." I look between my parents. "I love him."

"That's what you wanted to tell us? That you're in love with the king of hell?" Dad says.

I shake my head, hesitating for a moment that feels like forever before I whisper, "It's about Danielle."

Mom sucks in a sharp breath, choking on it. "What did you just say?"

I press my lips together, willing them to stop trembling so I can speak. "Xander had to complete three trials to take the throne. The final trial was in hell, and while he was there, he saw her." I swallow past the lump in my throat, unable to stop the tear that escapes and rolls down my cheek. "Danielle is in hell."

The blood drains from Dad's face while he sits in silence, head shaking.

"I'm so sorry," I cry. "I've been trying to come up with the best way to tell you, but—"

"*Enough!*" Mom yells. "I won't hear any of this." Her eyes meet mine. "Your sister is dead, Camille. Whatever that monster told you is a lie. He's trying to trick you, to manipulate you yet again, and you're falling for it once more, like a naive child."

My chest constricts as more tears spill down my face. "I wish it was a lie," I tell her through my tears. "If it wasn't true, that would mean Danielle hasn't been suffering alone for the last five years. But she has." I wipe my cheeks, sniffling. "And I'm going to bring her back."

That seems to snap Dad out of his daze. He blinks hard, swallowing and wetting his lips before he says, "No. We've lost one child. There's not a fucking chance—We can't lose you, too."

"You believe this insanity?" Mom says, turning her glare on my dad.

His jaw works and his eyes turn glassy. "You and I both know what happened to Danielle never felt right. Even after the funeral, we never felt closure. Maybe this is why, Rachel. Because she isn't truly gone."

Mom shakes her head as her eyes fill with tears at the memory of losing her daughter. "Even if...this is true. Camille, you cannot go to hell.

THE DEVIL'S TRIALS

Your father is right. We won't lose another daughter to those monsters. We just—we won't survive it."

I reach for both of their hands, squeezing them until they look at me. "I promise you won't lose me." Of course, I can't say what's going to happen in the underworld when Xander and I travel there, but my focus right now is to reassure them as much as I can. Even if it's nothing but hopeful thinking.

"This isn't happening," Mom says in a near-vacant tone, as if she's talking to herself. Her cheeks are flushed and her jaw is set tightly. I want more than anything to ease their fear, but there's nothing I can say that'll make this easier.

The pressure in my chest expands as the anxiety simmering just beneath the surface twists my stomach into even tighter knots.

"He's coming here now," I blurt, unsure how else to say it and running out of time before he arrives.

Mom's eyes snap to mine before she stands from the couch.

Dad follows suit, holding up his hands as if he's going to be able to calm her down. "Rachel—"

"Get your daggers ready," she snaps at him, reaching into the drawer of the side table next to the couch and pulling out a small but no doubt effective obsidian blade.

The sight of it gripped in her hand knocks the air out of my lungs as panic steals over me.

"Mom, *no*," I rush to say, standing to put myself between my parents and the front door just as Xander rings the bell.

Thirty-Seven
Xander

I stand at the front door with my hands in my jacket pockets after ringing the bell, light flurries falling around me as my breath fills the air with small plumes of fog each time I exhale.

My back straightens as I hear Rachel tell Scott to get a weapon and then Camille's panicked interjection.

We're not off to a great start.

The door opens while Camille and her mother continue arguing in another room, and I come face to face with her father.

It only takes a second to confirm he isn't brandishing a dagger, so I keep my hands in my pockets in an attempt to appear unthreatening.

"You are taking a very big risk coming here," Scott says in a cold tone, his sharp expression narrowed on me as he stands in the doorway, effectively blocking it.

I nod. "Yes, sir."

"Camille's mother is prepared to kill you where you stand," he continues, his hands clenched into tight fists.

"I understand that."

"Dad, please," Camille says from behind him. "Let him in so we can explain how we're going to bring Danielle back."

A muscle ticks in Scott's jaw as he keeps his eyes locked on me. "Watch yourself, demon," he says in a cold tone. "You misstep an inch, and I will not hesitate to put you down." His glare doesn't waver as he steps back and leaves the door open. He stands next to Camille as I walk inside and close the door. While I don't see a middle-aged human—hunter or not—being a match for my strength, I appreciate the sentiment enough to heed the warning.

The tension is already palpable. Getting into a verbal sparring match with Camille's parents is best avoided, for her sake.

THE DEVIL'S TRIALS

I can't say I ever expected to step foot in Camille's childhood home, but I only allow myself a few seconds to appreciate the warmth of it before turning to Scott. "Is there somewhere we can all speak?"

His gaze shifts from me to Camille, but that does nothing to lessen the tension filling the space we're in. "Where did your mother go?"

She frowns, glancing behind her momentarily before looking back at her dad. "I think she went to the kitchen. Maybe we should talk in the dining room?"

I'd be less concerned about being attacked if we weren't going to be within reach of sharp silverware...

I glance at my boots, toeing them off before I shrug off my jacket, hanging it on a hook adjacent to the front door, then follow Camille and Scott. We walk down a hallway into a dining room with an oak table and chair set and a modern chandelier hung above it. The table is set for Christmas dinner and if the situation wasn't so dire, I could perhaps appreciate how bizarre the whole thing is.

The last thing I expected was to have Christmas dinner with the most notorious demon hunters in the country.

'Tis the season, I suppose.

Rachel joins us in the dining room with a tense expression and cold stare, and I immediately notice the obsidian dagger she has sheathed against her thigh. She isn't trying to conceal it from me—no, she wants me to know it's there and that she won't hesitate to use it.

Message received.

Scott and Rachel sit across the table from Camille and me. I can feel their hatred for me like plumes of dark clouds, but I'm more concerned about the waves of anxiety rolling off their daughter.

I can tell Camille's nerves are shot by the way she can't stop her knee from bouncing under the table. I reach for her, resting my hand on her thigh, brushing my thumb back and forth in an attempt to calm her.

"You're lucky I didn't gut you the second you stepped onto my property," Rachel says, her gaze sharp and focused on me, then adds in a grave tone, "I still might."

"*Mom,*" Camille says with a deep frown, shaking her head, as if begging her mother to ease off the threats.

"No," I interject smoothly. "It's okay."

"The hell it is," Scott chimes in with a deep snarl.

"We're not going to get anywhere if you guys just sit here threatening him all night," Camille points out. "This is important. *Please.*"

Scott exhales a heavy sigh. "Fine. Say your piece, Kane, and then we'll decide if you get to walk out of here with your life."

I exchange a look with Camille, hopefully reassuring her before I focus my gaze on her parents. "Camille told you that Danielle is in my world, yes?"

They both nod without a word. A flare of concern ripples through the hatred I feel from them, though I can't decipher which hunter it comes from. Their expressions are blank. Guarded.

"When she died, the demon who took her life brought her to hell, trapping her soul there. While excruciating at the beginning, by the time I saw her not very long ago, she had adapted to the realm. It still isn't pleasant, but her being there is what's going to allow us to bring her topside again."

"And you just expect us to go along with all of this?" Rachel asks, her gaze flicking toward Camille.

"I understand why that is difficult, but I ask you to at least consider that you don't know everything about me. I have no ideas about gaining your approval, but what you need to know is that I love your daughter." I look between Camille's parents. "I wouldn't be here if I didn't."

"And yet you'd take her to hell?" Rachel offers in a sharp tone, reaching for the bottle of wine in the center of the table and pouring herself a generous glass.

"I never wanted that. I tried to talk her out of it, in fact, but she wouldn't let it go. I think you know as well as I do how stubborn she is, especially when it comes to important matters like family. If I could bring Danielle back from hell myself, please believe that I would."

"And why can't you?" Scott demands, gripping his water glass so tightly his knuckles go white. "Why do you have to put one of my daughters in danger to save the other?"

"She was taken there by the demon who killed her," I say, and Camille's mother makes a sound akin to a whimper and presses her fist to her mouth. "The rules of the underworld are fickle in that it can't be another demon who brings her back to the human world. Because I don't know who it was, the only other option is someone with a blood connection to Danielle. Someone with a pure soul."

THE DEVIL'S TRIALS

As desperately as I wanted to keep Camille from experiencing hell, making this work to bring Danielle back without her would've taken far more time to figure out. It wasn't an option Camille would accept, and this...this is her choice. I don't like it by a long shot, but I do respect it.

The sound of Camille's heartbeat quickens, and I turn my attention to her, murmuring, "You're okay. Just breathe." I'm overcome with the urge to make everything okay for Camille, no matter the cost to myself. And it's impossible to ignore as it claws at my chest.

I meet Scott's gaze. "As I sit here now, I vow to you that I will do everything in my power to keep Camille safe in hell and bring both of your daughters back to you." I turn my attention to Rachel. "You have every right to hate me. I'm not asking you to change your opinion of me, nor do I have any ideas of a truce between us, but I hope you can find it in yourselves to accept what I've told you tonight is the truth. I have nothing to gain from lying. In fact, I have everything to lose." Finally, I focus on Camille as our gazes lock. "And I can't lose you, *mo shíorghrá*."

Her throat bobs as she swallows, blinking back tears as her heart continues pounding in her chest. "You won't," she murmurs.

Rachel pulls back, her posture straightening as she glances toward her ex-husband. Something passes between them—resignation perhaps, because what other option do they have?—before she says, "When do you plan to do this?"

Camille answers before I can. "Tomorrow. I wanted to have a proper holiday with both of you before we leave."

She nods curtly. "What portal do you intend to use?"

"Why?" Camille asks hesitantly.

"So we can ensure it's not guarded by hunters."

I school my features so Rachel and Scott don't witness my shock. I hadn't expected them to help. "Olympic National Forest," I tell her.

"Fine. It will be clear tomorrow."

"We'll also ensure it's monitored by trusted hunters until you return so you don't run into any problems coming back." Scott adds.

"Thank you," Camille says in a small voice.

Scott meets my gaze. "If you don't bring both of my daughters back unharmed, I will make you wish you stayed in hell. I will torture you until you cannot stand to live a moment longer, and then I'll keep going. Do I make myself perfectly clear?"

I bristle at the threat, but nod at Camille's father. "Yes, sir."

"Good." He releases a heavy breath. "It's time to carve the turkey."

After dinner, Camille walks me to the front door. "I don't want you to leave, but I'm more than a little worried that my mom will dagger you in your sleep if you stay here."

I chuckle softly, putting on my boots and jacket. "I'd rather not push my luck." I cup her cheek, brushing my thumb back and forth. "I'll pick you up tomorrow. Try to get some rest, okay?"

She nods, catching her bottom lip between her teeth for a moment before releasing it. "You too," she murmurs, pressing a hand to my chest over my heart. "I love you, Xander."

I tilt her chin up and dip my face to press a soft kiss against her lips. "I love you."

The cold December air assaults my face as I step outside, shivering against it as I walk from the house to my car.

I slide into the driver's seat and exhale an uneven breath as I sit in the dark, gripping the cold steering wheel. The silence of the car only makes my pounding heart louder, and no matter how tightly I clench my hands into fists, they won't stop shaking.

Looking back at the house, I'm gripped with such an intense sensation. It makes my palms damp and my head dizzy as my thoughts race and scatter all over the place. Dread coils deep in my gut as realization hits me. The sensation I'm experiencing...It's *fear*.

Thirty-Eight
Camille

Once Xander is gone, I find my parents in the living room with glasses of wine. They put a movie on the TV, but I don't think either of them is paying much attention to it, not that I can blame them.

"I'm going to bed," I announce, sleep deprivation clinging to my words and making my voice deeper. "Love you guys."

They both look at me, their expressions giving away just how tired they are, too.

Today was emotionally exhausting for all of us.

Dad gets up and wraps me in a tight hug, kissing the top of my head. "I love you, Camille." He steps aside so Mom can hug me next.

It's been some time since I experienced this kind of affection from my parents, and while I recognize it's closely tied to the fear of what I'm doing tomorrow, I'm not going to take it for granted.

"Love you, honey."

I manage a small smile at her before turning to go upstairs.

"Camille?" Mom says, and I turn around. "Are you sure about this?"

My brows inch closer. "Of course, I am."

She releases a breath, nodding. "Okay." And then she goes back to the couch and picks up her wineglass again.

Dad sends me a supportive look paired with a smile, and I give him a subtle nod of acknowledgment before I walk out of the living room.

I toss and turn all night, drifting off to restless sleep for short periods every hour or so. I feel even worse the next morning than what I did going to bed the night before.

Xander arrives shortly after I get up, coming to the door. He's dressed equally formal as he was yesterday in black slacks and a dress shirt under his coat. He comes inside briefly to greet my parents, and after that awkward encounter, we're off.

I wish I could fall asleep when the car starts moving, but I'm too wired—and terrified. I know there are consequences to what I'm doing, likely bigger than I can imagine now, but my mind is made up.

I will do whatever it takes to bring my sister back.

Sacrifice whatever I must to save her from the torture she's endured far too long already.

"I can take it away," Xander murmurs.

I angle myself toward him, licking the dryness from my lips. "What are you talking about?"

"Your fear."

His words make my heart race, and I say, "You...want to feed on me?"

"In this instance, it would be mutually beneficial." He casts me a sideways glance. "I can draw the fear out of you. You wouldn't feel it anymore, and it would sustain me to make the trip."

I chew the inside of my cheek. "And if I say no?"

"Then I won't. Once we're in hell, I won't need to feed anyway—I'll absorb power from the souls there."

"Oh," I mumble.

"I was offering more for your sake. I know this is scary. And as much as I wish I could talk you out of doing this, I admire you deeply for the courage you're showing to save your sister."

I blow out a breath. "How do we, um...I mean, how do you feed? Will it hurt?"

He offers a soft smile, focusing on the road. "No, it won't hurt. You're giving yourself to me willingly, so it'll likely feel quite pleasant."

I try to mask the shock on my face as my cheeks flush. "Okay."

Xander nods. "Close your eyes."

I don't protest despite the pounding in my chest. The darkness behind my eyelids makes my head spin until Xander slowly smooths a hand over my hair.

For half an instant, I feel as if I'm being ripped from my own body. Like the sensation of each of my limbs falling asleep. My lips part in a gasp, but before I can so much as shift a muscle, a sense of calm like no other rushes in. My lips curl into a dazed smile as Xander's gentle touch makes pleasure flood through every inch of me. I've never felt anything like this.

A soft sigh escapes my lips, and then I lose track of everything.

THE DEVIL'S TRIALS

The car comes to a stop, making me stir, and I sit up, rubbing my eyes. "Are we here?"

"Yes." Xander leans over the center console and pushes the hair away from my face, tucking it behind my ear. "Are you ready?"

A jolt of panic zips through me, though more subdued than before. "I think so," I force out in a level tone.

"We can take a few minutes. If you need to—"

"No," I cut in, clearing my throat when my voice cracks. "Danielle has been trapped in hell long enough. We have to go now."

"I'll be at your side," he assures me. "You're safe with me."

All I can do is nod.

Xander gets out of the car, then helps me out, keeping his arm around me as we walk across a narrow, paved road toward the cover of trees. The air is cold and damp, and I tuck myself tighter against Xander's side as our breaths create little plumes of fog in front of us.

I follow in silence for a few minutes before we reach a small clearing. "How do you know where the portals are?" He's used this one before, but they are scattered all over the world.

He stops, pulling my dagger out of his jacket pocket. "I'm connected to them," he explains. "Each one has a beacon, like an internal tracker."

"Oh, I see." My eyes drop to the dagger, and panic coils tightly in my stomach. "What—"

He slices it across his palm before I can ask what he's doing. He grits his teeth, hissing in pain, and I frown as his blood spills onto the forest floor.

"Take my hand," Xander says in a grave voice, offering me the hand he didn't cut open. When I slide my fingers through his, he draws me into his chest. "Close your eyes and try to breathe normally. Everything is going to feel out of your control, but it will pass." He grips my chin and kisses me hard, searing my lips with his. "I've got you."

His words are lost to the sound of the ground rumbling like an earthquake. I barely manage to squeeze my eyes shut before the forest floor splits wide open under our feet, sending us plummeting into the depths of the earth.

I scream. At least, I think I do. It doesn't make a sound over the blood rushing in my ears. I lose all perception of anything as we fall.

And fall.

And fall.

JESSI ELLIOTT

I have no sense of time, but at some point, the ground is solid under me once more. My throat is raw and my eyes are sealed shut. I try to take a breath and choke on the thick, smoky air.

"You can open your eyes now." Xander's low voice in my ear sends a shiver down my spine.

I slowly pry them open, blinking until my surroundings clear, and suck in a sharp breath.

"Welcome to hell, *mo shíorghrá*."

Exclusive Hardcover Bonus Content

Spoilers for *The Devil's Trials* ahead.
Read the entire book before diving into this bonus content.
You've been warned!

Blake
Exclusive Hardcover Scene

Xander just killed his mother.

No, no, no.

Xander just killed the queen of hell.

Bloody. Fucking. Hell.

I stare at my closest friend—now my *king*—wide eyed and thoroughly confused at what just happened. A pit of discomfort unfurls in my chest, sending waves through me and making my knees shake as I grit my teeth against the sensation of weakness.

Xander's gaze is filled with darkness, stuck on his mother's lifeless body as it turns to ash at his feet.

The demons around us lower to their knees, faces stricken with pain as they experience the same gut-wrenching side effects of losing our monarch as I seem to be.

My gaze reaches Xander again, and I blink, following suit with the other demons and bowing to Xander.

It can't be more than thirty seconds later that the hunters are moving. My eyes narrow as Noah grabs Camille around the waist, hauling her out of the room as Harper steps in to help drag her away. The other hunters flee, leaving heavy silence to fill the space.

I'm the first demon to get to my feet. I move to stand next to Xander, and my voice is hoarse but firm when I say, "You trust me?"

He doesn't speak, though I catch his subtle nod.

"Good. Let's go."

I don't wait a second longer. Shock will only last so long, and we need to get out of here before it passes and what's left of the room full of demons starts demanding an explanation.

Considering Xander just committed the highest act of treason in our world to save a human, I suspect his motivation to kill our monarch won't be forgiven by the present company—or other demons, for that matter.

We move toward the back of the room, and Xander inhales sharply, as if he's just now remembering to breathe. "Blake—"

"Not yet," I nearly hiss at him as I navigate Lucia's compound to the exit where Xander's car is parked. We get in, and I glance over at Xander in the passenger seat as I slide the key into the ignition.

"Where are we going?"

I gun it, gripping the wheel hard. *Good fucking question.*

Every demon and every hunter is going to be looking for Xander. He's about to have a hell of a lot to answer for.

"Somewhere safe," I finally answer him, as we travel along the driveway at a high speed.

Thank fuck for the vacant apartment I decided to keep *just in case*. This wasn't exactly the scenario I was expecting...

"Blake—"

I can't bite back the curse that flows from my lips. "I don't think you fully understand the magnitude of what just happened, mate." Things are about to get a hell of a lot more complicated from here on out. It'll make what we've faced up to now seem like a fucking cake walk.

"I do," he says, tipping his head back against the seat and squeezing his eyes shut. Gripping the seat until his knuckles are white, he struggles for breath as his pulse continues at an unnatural speed. I've never seen Xander have a panic attack, but whatever is going on with him at this moment seems pretty damn close.

I clench my jaw as he looks my way again. "Please warn me if you're going to vomit so I can attempt to pull over." Xander keeps his car pristine. It smells clean, as if he just had it detailed.

"I'm fine," he forces out, covering his eyes with his fists, as if he's in pain. Since the ache I'm experiencing at Lucia's death is annoyingly prominent, I can only imagine what agony is tearing through him.

"Liar." I sigh. "Just hang on. I'm taking you back to Seattle. I have a place there no one knows about. We'll go there and come up with a plan to figure this shit out."

There's a beat of silence before he replies, "I killed the queen, Blake." His voice is distant, his words hollow with disbelief and exhaustion.

"I was there."

"We both know what that means. What comes next." Each sentence sounds more detached. Emotionless. He could be in shock—it would make perfect sense—but my demon senses are tingling, leading me to believe he's tuning deeper into *his* demonic side. Can't blame the bloke for it, either. This shit is insane, and if shutting off his emotions is going to help him focus on what's going to happen, I fully support it.

That said, if we could avoid it altogether, that would be best.

I tap my fingers against the steering wheel to an imaginary beat to keep myself grounded, because fuck, one of us needs to be. "Maybe not."

"There's no running from this," he says matter-of-factly. "Unless I want to face treason for killing my own mother, I don't have a choice."

Rain pours around us as we continue driving toward the city. It mixes with thunder and lightning streaks across the night sky every minute or so. I turn up the music to fill the silence and drown out the pounding of Xander's heart.

Lucia Kane was undoubtedly a monster and a tyrant who deserved what she got. Unfortunately, her death opened a door Xander never wanted or believed he'd actually have to face—taking the throne.

"What's going through your head?" I ask, breaking the silence.

Xander clears his throat. "I'm trying to process…everything."

I cut a glance toward him briefly and then turn my gaze back to the road. "Talk to me."

"I don't know where to start."

I nod, taking a moment to decide what I want to say. How I can help him. "Were you planning to kill Lucia all along?" I'd like to think he would've clued me into an ulterior play if it had been premeditated, but now I'm not entirely certain.

"No." He shoves a hand through his hair, letting out a heavy breath. "When I saw her hand wrapped around Camille's throat, something in me broke. I've never felt fear like that. I lost control of myself and acted on instinct. I couldn't let Camille die, and I was prepared to do anything to ensure her safety."

"Including sacrificing your own soul," I offer. There's no sense in avoiding it. *It* being the loss of what made him human. I used to mess with him about being a lesser demon than I am, having been born from a human and the embodiment of evil. It doesn't seem so funny anymore.

Xander nods silently.

"You notice the change, don't you?" I ask, adding, "You're a full demon now."

I'm met with more silence and then another nod.

"What's it feel like?" I've never had a soul, so I've never felt what it's like to lose it. Color me curious.

He considers it for a moment. "A space in my chest where I know something used to be but isn't anymore. It doesn't exactly hurt, but it's new and uncomfortable. And considering I've never heard of a demon getting their soul back, I'd say it's pretty much a done deal, so I need to get used to it."

"And you're okay with that?" I try to gauge his reaction, but I can't seem to tap into anything. His heart still beats at an elevated rate, but that's all I'm getting.

Xander shrugs. "I made the choice. I have to face the consequences." He never wanted to take the throne, and I must admit I'm slightly surprised his initial response to being faced with it isn't to go on the lam or into hiding.

"I'm fucking sorry, mate. I really thought we had a fighting chance." And we would have if Xander hadn't let the fear of losing Camille to his mother's wrath cloud his judgment when it mattered most. Eliminating the immediate issue only bred countless others—many we likely won't even see coming until it's too late.

"Yeah. So did I." His pulse is racing again as he stares out the windshield, his breathing shallow as if the rain falling outside is drowning him.

"Hey," I say, snagging his attention before he can spiral any further. "There's a lot happening at the moment, but you're not alone. I've got you, mate."

Again, he only nods.

I give him some time to his thoughts, needing a few myself as I go over what needs to happen going forward.

The royal guard will be all over this, and word of the queen's execution will spread like wildfire through our kind, who will feel her death like a physical loss. No doubt the news will travel through the hunter organization just as fast.

My biggest and most immediate concern is gathering support for Xander. He'll need a council, and finding a group of demons he'll be able to trust is likely going to be a challenge.

He's staring out the window when I peer over at him again after merging off the interstate, so I ask, "Were you thinking about Camille?"

The tension in his body doesn't leave even when he exhales. "You're going to tell me to forget about her."

My brows lift as I keep my eyes on the road. "Do you want to forget about her?"

"I want her," he says, not missing a beat, and his voice sounds less caring and more...possessive.

I nod, humming softly under my breath. I don't dare point out that this whole thing feels dangerously reminiscent of Romeo and Juliet.

In what world can the daughter of demon hunters survive loving the king of hell?

And if that's not deterrent enough, every hunter in the organization will have their target locked on the bloke next to me.

If Xander and Camille feared their relationship was impossible before now, I can't imagine that either grasps what they're in for after today.

How lucky for me to have a front row seat to the tragedy of a lifetime.

Gio's Dark Chocolate Salted Caramel Cookies

Prep Time: 1.5 hours
Cook Time: 12 minutes
Yield: 18 cookies

Ingredients:
1/2 cup unsalted butter
1/2 cup white sugar
1/2 cup packed brown sugar
1 large egg
1 teaspoon vanilla
1 cup flour
2/3 cup cocoa powder
1 teaspoon baking soda
1/8 teaspoon salt
2 tablespoons milk
1 1/2 cups dark chocolate chips
18 rolos
flaky salt

Directions:
    1. In a large bowl using a handheld or stand mixer, beat the butter and sugars on medium-high until fluffy and light. Add the egg and vanilla. Beat on high until combined.
    2. In a separate bowl, whisk the flour, cocoa powder, baking soda, and salt until combined.
    3. With the mixer on low, slowly pour the dry into the wet ingredients. Beat on low until combined. Switch to medium-high speed and beat in milk, then chocolate chips.

4. Cover dough and chill in fridge overnight or freezer for at least an hour.

5. Remove dough from fridge/freezer and leave out at room temperature for 10 minutes.

6. Preheat oven to 350°F (177°C) and line baking sheets with parchment paper.

7. Scoop 2 tablespoons of dough and cut in half. Roll each half into a ball. Make indent in one ball and place rolo in the center. Top with other ball of dough and seal the sides.

8. Arrange stuffed dough balls 2-3 inches apart on baking sheets.

9. Bake for 12-13 minutes or until edges look set and centers still look soft.

10. Remove from oven and sprinkle with flaky salt.

11. Cool cookies and enjoy!

Playlist

Fearless ~ UNSECRET, Ruby Amanfu
Don't Hold Me ~ Sandro Cavazza
Heal Me ~ Grace Carter
Caught in the Fire ~ Tommee Profitt, Sam Tinnesz
A Little Bit Yours ~ JP Saxe
Medicine ~ BROODS
Game of Survival ~ Ruelle
Save Your Soul ~ Lexxi Saal
Just Pretend ~ Bad Omens
With the Devil I'm Going Down ~ Steelfeather
Arcade ~ Trish Beria
Villains Aren't Born (They're Made) ~ PEGGY
Heart of Darkness ~ Steelfeather
Monsters ~ Tommee Profitt, XEAH
Down ~ Simon, Trella
The Fold ~ Wickerbird
Nothing Is As It Seems ~ Hidden Citizens, Ruelle
Far From Home ~ Five Finger Death Punch
Hurricane ~ Tommee Profitt, Fleurie
Who Do You Want ~ Ex Habit
Curtain Call ~ Chandler Leighton
I Don't Believe in Satan ~ Aron Wright
Dancing With The Devil ~ EMO
Seven Devils ~ Florence + The Machine
Sand ~ Dove Cameron
High ~ Stephen Sanchez

Breathe In Bleed Out ~ Jared Lee
Illusory Light ~ Sarah Blasko
Ivory ~ Adam French
Play With Fire (Alternate Version) ~ Sam Tinnesz, Ruelle, Violents
King Of Disappointment – Re-Imagined ~ Echos
Skin and Bones ~ David Kushner
Inevitable ~ Adam French
Beautiful Things ~ Benson Boone
Two Hearts ~ Dermot Kennedy
Why am I Falling For You ~ Josh Alexander
twisted games ~ FJØRA
Set Me Free ~ KELSON
Come Hell or High Water ~ Steelfeather
Next to You ~ Charlotte Cardin
GRAVITY ~ Matt Hansen
heartbeats duet ~ Hanniou, James TW
it is what it is ~ Abe Parker
Stay ~ Rihanna, Mikky Ekko
Do It Like A Girl ~ Morgan St. Jean
Burn ~ Astyria
Before I Ever Met You ~ BANKS
Lose Control ~ Teddy Swims
Before You Leave Me ~ Alex Warren
Army of Angels ~ KELSON
Way down We Go ~ KELSON
How Dare You ~ Rachel Grae
Right Person Right Time – Acoustic ~ Rachel Grae
Paradise ~ Anderson Rocio
lesson learned ~ Matt Hansen

worship ~ LACES
trouble ~ Camylio
SLOW DOWN ~ Jessica Baio
This is the End ~ FJØRA
Wayward Son ~ John Lensing
I'm The Sinner ~ Jared Benjamin
Hold On ~ The Rescues
Don't Try ~ Extreme Music
Just Say ~ Nine One One
A Storm Is Coming ~ Tommee Profitt, Liv Ash
Freedom ~ Lexxi Saal
Horizon ~ Aldous Harding
Sweet and Dark ~ Miles Hardt
Devil's Worst Nightmare ~ FJØRA
Burn for You ~ Nine One One
The Devil in Me (Acoustic) ~ Anthony Mossburg
It Was Real To Me ~ Caden
Cut The Rope ~ Charlotte OC
Salt in My Blood ~ SINEM
Love Is Going To Kill Us ~ David Kushner
HEAVEN ~ Isabel LaRosa
Sinner ~ Shaya Zamora
Work of Art ~ Amber Ré

Scan to listen

Acknowledgments

Another book, another opportunity to thank all of the incredible people I'm lucky to have in my corner supporting this crazy passion of mine.

To the small but mighty publishing team at Inimitable Books: thank you for helping me live out my dream of doing so many cool publishing things! Round two, let's gooooo!

To my wonderful editor, Wendy Higgins: if teenage Jessi knew that one of her favorite authors would end up editing her book, she'd squeal with delight!

To my lovely assistant, Jessica Rampersad: for keeping me organized and taking things off my plate so I can focus on writing the next book. You are an absolute rockstar—never leave me!

To my work family: your endless support in all aspects of my life warms my heart and quite honestly keeps me sane on a regular basis.

To my family, for always being there and showing up to support me. I love you, forever and always.

To Aly, Destiny, and Sam, my platonic soulmates—my feral rats. You are everything to me. Thank you for always being on the other end of the phone.

And to you, the reader: you have my eternal gratitude. There are so many books in this world, and you choosing to read mine brings me such an immense amount of joy.

About the Author

Jessi Elliott is a paranormal and fantasy romance author who lives in Ontario, Canada, with her adorable calico cat, Phoebe.

When she's not working on her next book, she likes to hang out with friends and family, get lost in a steamy romance novel, watch Friends, and drink coffee.

You can find Jessi at www.jessielliott.com and on social media under the username @authorjessielliott. Join her newsletter to stay up to date on book news!